VACANCIES

VACANCIES

Iain Houston

Spurious Books

First published in 2022 by Spurious Books

www.spuriousstories.com

ISBN 9781739263102

Typesetting and ebook creation by Laura Kincaid,
Ten Thousand | Editing + Book Design
www.tenthousand.co.uk

Cover design by Paras Ali

Printed by Amazon

To Julie, who always believed in me

1

They had been driving for an hour, and Michael was bored. The start of the school holidays was supposed to mean an end to boredom, but it seemed there were limits to his freedom. He still had to get up early in the morning, and he still had to attend memorial services.

This time it was in Dumfries, almost two hours from home. He had never been there before. Mostly, they only went to local memorial services, but this time it was a friend of Uncle Joe's. At least it was someone Uncle Joe knew. It was hard to imagine the old man having any real friends.

With almost an hour of travelling left, Michael scanned the inside of the car for any previously unexplored distraction. He had the back seat to himself, having been relegated there by Uncle Joe's driving licence and his mother's need to control the radio station. In the absence of anything else to do, he tried concentrating on the music in the car. Classical music made him feel stupid. It mocked him, taunting him with his ignorance. He felt he should know who wrote each piece, but he had no idea, and with no words to guide him, the meaning of the music was impossible for him to grasp. It grated and irritated him, not because it was ugly, but because it was probably beautiful if you were clever enough to look at it in the right way.

As boredom overcame him, he considered whether to question his mother or Uncle Joe. He decided Uncle Joe was the most likely to talk to him and least likely to turn round and tell him to be quiet. It was probably all right to talk. When Michael had attended his first memorial service five years ago, he had assumed that the proper thing was to be inconsolable with grief. He had been quiet all through that morning and, even at the age of nine, had picked at his breakfast with a melancholic distraction that few fifteen-year-olds could have managed. He continued on the journey to church and was surprised when concerned women kept asking him what was wrong. Instead of blending seamlessly into the crowd, he was a source of attention and worry. He then realised a certain level of communication was acceptable as long as he looked sad and shook hands quietly outside and inside the church.

"What's in Dumfries?"

Uncle Joe didn't turn or take his eyes off the road. To Michael, he was old, as was anyone over about forty. To be fair, he looked like his fifty-five years had all attacked him at once, then ran off, leaving him dishevelled and worn. Whenever you pictured him, it seemed like he should have a pipe and a dog, although he owned neither.

"What do you mean what's in Dumfries? The same things that are everywhere else, people, houses, memorial services."

"What is it like? Is it big?"

"Much bigger than home, about three times as big as Stranraer. Still pretty small compared to everywhere else."

Michael looked out the window. The Land Rover was higher than most cars. He could see over the fences into fields full of sheep. He wondered what it would be like to live somewhere different. There must be other boys living in cities who didn't have to travel through miles of nowhere to get to anywhere.

He had been up early this morning. That was mostly his choice. Officially, he didn't actually have a job at the hotel, but as it was the family business, he was expected to help out. He also liked to sort the mail in the mornings. Everyone had to have a hobby.

He risked another question. "Is it okay for us all to be out today?"

Again, nobody turned round. "Cathy and Janet will cope for a day. Anyway, we'll be back tonight."

"Who's the memorial for?"

He sensed his mother tense as Uncle Joe answered, "Someone I used to know a long time ago. We were at school together."

"But then he must be old?"

His mother turned this time. "Michael! Don't be so rude."

"Sorry, I thought it was someone young. I thought it would be—"

Uncle Joe saved him. "No, it's not really a memorial. It's a funeral. He was my age."

"So he wasn't…"

"No, Michael, he died in his sleep. In Dumfries. We're burying him today."

"I didn't think you could—"

"Arrangements have been made. It will be a burial."

He looked out the window. More sheep. Different sheep. He wondered what happened when animals died suddenly. Did the animals try to bury them, or did they just leave them? Maybe animals didn't die suddenly. Maybe they crawled away under something to die like they were burying themselves. Humans didn't seem to get that kind of notice very often. They had to work together to sort it out afterwards.

"Mum, have you ever been to a burial before?"

There was an intake of breath from his mother. "Not for a long time."

He thought about her answer for a few seconds. He asked the next question as soon as it came into his head. "Uncle Joe, Auntie Anne was buried, wasn't she?"

Now his mother shouted at him. "Michael! You don't ask questions like that. Just behave! Think about where we're going today!"

Again, Uncle Joe saved him. "It's okay, Mary. The boy is just curious. Yes, Michael, she was buried."

Michael couldn't remember much about Auntie Anne's funeral as he had been so young, but he sensed that more questions would be a mistake. He stared at the sheep again. He wondered why someone would want to end up as ashes. It probably wasn't a good idea to ask. It was easy to say the wrong thing. Sometimes it seemed like he always said the wrong thing. Even when he kept quiet on days like this, it seemed to be the wrong thing.

2

The funeral was difficult. He hadn't realised that you had to go to the graveside. Being outside was strange, and it made him think of the sheep. He felt sick as the coffin was lowered, scraping the sides of the grave, and he imagined the body bumping around inside. Uncle Joe didn't seem upset. Everyone had been pleased to see Uncle Joe. He had never really seen that before. Michael liked Uncle Joe, but he had noticed that people were generally happier when he left a room than when he entered it. He was that type of person.

Michael was glad to get back to the hotel. He avoided speaking to anyone on the way to his room. There was work to be done. The funeral had been a distraction, but now it was over. Waiting all day had been difficult, but now he was ready. Today was going to be special. Checking his watch as he locked the door of his room, he realised he only had one hour until he had to see Uncle Joe again. Today had been a good day. He had three things to look at. He opened the cupboard. Faces smiled at him from the inside of the door. He didn't know any of the people in the photos, but they were always pleased to see him. He took out two letters and one package. Packages were much rarer than letters. Letters arrived about once a month, packages less often. It varied, depending on what was happening out there. He knew what was in the letters, and the names were printed on the outside. The package was a mystery.

When he had first seen it that morning, he had no idea what might be in it. He had delayed picking it up for a few seconds just so he could try guessing how heavy it was first. He tried to guess what might be inside it. Maybe it was a uniform. It might be bloodstained. Or it might be something else. It was bigger than any of the packages before. It was probably still small enough to fit under his bed, although that wasn't the right place for such things. It was wrapped carefully and had been taped up more than was necessary. Someone had worried about this package. He had to sign for it, but that didn't mean anything. That was standard. Sometimes he even had to sign for the letters. When he had finally lifted it, he had been surprised at its weight. It was too heavy to be a uniform. It was something else then, but what? There were infinite possibilities, but he couldn't think of any.

He had decided to lock it in his cupboard. Getting it to his room had been easy. Usually, he didn't see many people at that time, and today hadn't been any different. Even when he did see people, nobody really wanted to talk at that time in the morning. They just said good morning. Uncle Joe told him that was usually all people said in the morning. They would talk later in the day. In the morning, they just wanted to say hello and move on. It saved the risk of getting the day off to a bad start. They said good morning instead of hello because it was nice and polite. Your identical reply reassured them everything was okay with the world and the general state of civilisation. Michael thought Uncle Joe probably thought about things too much and suspected he sometimes made things up, but he wasn't often wrong.

He had shut the package and the letters in his dark cupboard and locked the door. The smiling faces had smiled at them all day, even though it was too dark to see. They always smiled, even when terrible things happened, and it was really inappropriate. Sometimes it annoyed Michael a little, but it was hard to be angry. They were still smiling after everything they'd been through.

It wasn't just the smiling faces that kept them company, Michael's father was there as well. He was on the inside of the other door. Michael usually didn't open that one. He preferred the smiling faces. His dad looked calm and thoughtful. He looked at the package, but he didn't smile at it because he was smarter than the smiling faces. He knew the package couldn't see him.

He took out the package and his shoebox. It was full of things from other packages. From it, he selected his favourite package-gift ever. It was a six-inch knife with a name carved on the handle. He let the smiling faces watch while he used the knife to cut open the latest package before returning it, along with the shoebox, to the cupboard. He had received the knife almost a year ago. It had a story, like all the best package-gifts. The smiling faces had stories, too. They had mostly arrived in letters.

Books. There were books in this new package. They looked old. There were papers as well. It was all very disappointing. They weren't even interesting papers, like certificates. They were wrapped in bundles, some handwritten, some typed. There was also another letter like the other two. He ignored those for now. He had looked forward to opening the package all day, and now all he had found were some old books. There was nothing written on the front of them. They were dirty, with old, rough covers. He picked up one of them. As he realised what it was, his mouth fell open.

He was somewhere else, in a desert, a forest, in an aeroplane. He didn't have to imagine anything. Thoughts just filled his head. His brain grasped what this was and was so excited it forgot to tell him. Instead, images and feelings flooded his mind. His head swivelled to check the door he already knew was closed as happiness gave way to panic. Where would he keep it? What if someone found it and took it away? His heart raced. His watch said he had to be with Uncle Joe in fifty minutes, but he had time to look at his new gifts first. The smiling faces smiled back at him, satisfied with the gifts. His earlier disappointment embarrassed him, but the smiling faces didn't laugh at him. They just kept smiling. He opened the book he held. It was a diary. *One* of the diaries.

He looked for a name at the front, but there was none. He flicked through it, conversations and thoughts flashing past on the pages.

Too much to read now, too much to work out. Where would he start? *Forty-nine minutes.* He looked at the other diaries. They were similar but offered no clues. Which was first? Which was most interesting? The bundle of papers were different. They weren't part of a diary but a book. It had a title and came with a name. Jack Walker. It meant nothing. Michael didn't remember him. Had he met him? It didn't matter because he would never meet him now. These used to be Jack's diaries, but now they were Michael's diaries. Poor Jack, very sad, but waste not want not.

Michael decided he had to start somewhere and began to read the first page.

I wish they had lied to us. They could have, I know. There are some things you take for granted. The sun will come up tomorrow. Two and two make four. My government will lie to me. It was a Monday when they took my certainty away from me. I shouldn't have been out so late the night before, but it shouldn't have mattered. It was nothing difficult. I should have done it over the phone, but I thought I'd rather be out of the office. As I headed up through the unimaginative building, I avoided contact with the worker drones I passed. I knew they were just like me, trying to make a living, trying to survive.

In my job, you notice little things about people. For example, the efficient and intelligent talk quickly because they're busy and they don't want to waste time. The inefficient and annoying talk slowly. This man talked slowly. I would have hated him instantly, but I didn't have the energy. Instead, I settled for disguised contempt with an option to upgrade to a polite lack of interest. I had chosen to interview him, unnecessarily, to obtain a vacuous and predictable quote about one of his colleagues who had sensibly decided to cheat this company out of a large amount of money before disappearing and never returning. This man talked slowly because he was used to people writing down everything he said. I imagined his words being repeated back to him by his underlings after every mistake, every failed project. No doubt, he enjoyed the sound of his own words as much as he enjoyed the sound of his own voice.

I let him explain his job in unnecessary detail while I quietly marvelled at his expensive hair and cheap suit. He had barely begun when everything began to change. Something was happening outside. The drones were moving outside his office. They were talking to each other. It didn't seem right. I was polite, and I allowed him to get distracted before me. He stood up just before the knock on the door.

I waited as he talked to someone outside the door. He came back in alone and sat down.

I knew something was happening. I could have asked, but people usually tell you things more quickly if you act stupid and uninterested. "Is everything okay?"

"Something big is happening. I'm just going to see what I can find out." His fingers clattered against the keyboard. He was fast, and I remember thinking he might have worked his way up from the bottom. I wondered how many words he could type per minute.

"Where?"

"I'll just try the BBC news." He didn't look at me. Now I was a distraction.

"No, where is it happening?"

"Oh, I don't know. I think in Africa."

Africa. Something big was happening in Africa. What could be happening in Africa to interest a bunch of worker ants on a Monday morning? Something big. Pictures flashed through my mind of men in suits being assassinated and shabbily dressed people with Kalashnikovs seizing oil pipelines. I imagined planes crashing into jungles, but nothing fitted. He was wasting time. I had to speak. "Is there a television here?"

"What? No, we… The website won't load." Of course, it wouldn't. In times of crisis, his technology is useless. These people run the world but know nothing.

"A radio? Is there a radio?"

He ignored me. Why was no one calling me? Why was I not calling them? For the same reason I was not pushing him aside and finding the information I needed on the web. It would have seemed rude. I was a few seconds away from calling. My heart began to pound, and I broke. "I'll call my office." I hit the number, but there was no reply. The networks were down. Something big. Something very big. In Africa. Probably. People with no information were all trying to call each other. Desperate to confirm that they were not alone in their ignorance, they were huddling together across the networks. But the networks they had built were not strong enough. Their technology was betraying them. Millions of people who had never been alone were being cast adrift. And a storm was coming.

I tried to think. The keyboard clattered again. I was paralysed. I watched from a distance as it unfolded. Mobiles didn't work. Next, they would reach for— The phone on his desk rang. Like a crowd at a football game, the human race were all shouting the same thing at the same time. The ants were moving as one. I was not paralysed. I was mesmerised, and I realised I understood everything that was happening. I predicted everything one second before it happened. Ultimate knowledge, but utterly useless. This did not comfort me. I was more frightened than they were. Maybe this was how God felt.

It was his wife. She had no information. She was calling him for information. In an office somewhere, she was also isolated. Why didn't we leave? We couldn't. Better to be here, ignorant, afraid, and together. We didn't want to go home and have our enthusiastic televisions spill the full horror into our rooms while we were alone.

He was telling her nothing of any use, but they were huddling together against the storm. Something big. Africa. Suddenly, I saw airports filled with people panicking, screaming refugees flooding across borders. Ebola.

Something big. Africa. Ebola. Something small. Africa. A virus. They were terrified of a virus.

"I need a landline." He ignored me again.

"I know, I'm just trying to get onto the Internet, but it's not working." He looked more important now. He was the male, the protector, and he would provide stability and focus. No doubt she was smarter than him. I was interested in none of this.

I spoke loudly and deliberately, but not slowly. "I need a landline. Now." He looked up at me, annoyed. We both heard me swear, even though I did not. He saw my eyes, but he didn't see anger. He saw fear, and then he got it. The man in front of him was a journalist, someone who had probably seen wars, earthquakes, starvation, and suffering. Someone who did this for a living, and I was scared. I felt it pass between us, and his face unravelled. He was scared. The fear virus was more contagious than Ebola.

"What do you think is happening?"

"I need a landline." His arm rose slowly to point to the door, his mouth hanging open. He looked like a child. As I left, I said, "Check smaller sites, local newspapers, stuff like that. They might not be overloaded." I didn't look back. My advice would likely be useless to him. Even that small task would probably be beyond him, but I felt no guilt. He was not my problem.

Outside his office, I scanned the groups of people gossiping loudly. They looked concerned. I knew they didn't know anything. No hands were waving, no opinions being voiced, just concern. Revolution was approaching, and barriers were breaking down. Managers chatted with people who delivered things and made coffee. I needed a phone. I needed help.

The room was a large forest of partitioned cubicles. Groups were solidifying. The forest was almost empty. I needed someone unimportant and unintelligent. Important people asked questions and wanted to be involved. When they knew who I was, they would ask for information instead of helping me. My eyes rested on a dark-haired woman by the water cooler. She looked pleasant, efficient, and stupid. Her memory told her that this was where people stood to share information. She had not yet adapted to the change in circumstances. She eyed the expanding groups but was unsure where to move. I decided to give her purpose.

"Hi there, Colin said I could get an outside line here." I was a nice person, and I did not ask her to do anything. I was relying on her innate desire to please. She fulfilled her role, leading me to the nearest cubicle and showing me how to dial out. I thanked her, smiled, and dismissed her. She wandered off to the nearest group, where an important-looking woman with important hair was saying something dull.

Tony's line was busy. Emma's line was busy. Murray's line was busy. The mobile networks were down, and they were all using the landlines. I needed to call someone who wasn't important, someone no one ever needed to speak to. Someone like Mark. Perfect, he was of no interest to anyone. He wasn't invited to anything. I pulled my address book from my pocket because I didn't even know his extension. My hands trembled as I punched in the numbers, only to find the line engaged. I supposed even Mark had a mother. I couldn't believe it. How could it be? Over three minutes had passed, and still, I had no idea what was going on.

I gave up on the phone. I didn't have a car, and I was not going out on the street to wander round the city trying to find out what was going on. Then I heard it. Someone had found the radio I'd asked about earlier. They were all silent as a voice crackled from the speaker. The rhythm of the voice and the measured delivery were unmistakable. The prime minister spoke, and we were compelled to listen.

"... not only am I sure that everything that can be done is being done. I am sure that history will show that what is occurring now in Africa was the moment when humanity was able to set aside our differences and work together for a common purpose. It is incumbent upon us and our friends abroad to ensure that as our defences are prepared, normal life continues as far as is possible. I am confident that no matter the eventual outcome, we will face this challenge with the dignity, determination, and unity which our great nation has depended upon throughout the ages."

Not Ebola, something else. Something big. In Africa. Definitely. I looked round the cubicle, searching for the company directory. The drones were drowning out the radio as I headed downstairs.

Wherever I have been, whatever I have been doing, I have never underestimated the usefulness and the knowledge of the people on the bottom rung. They are the secretaries, technicians, janitors, waiters, and taxi drivers. The people who shift the scenery know more about the theatre and the play than the lead actor or the director. They could never replace the people ordering them around, but in many ways, they exceed them. They know how everything works. The people at the top are too focused. They don't live in fear of their job. They don't learn to hide, adapt, or watch.

When I knocked on the door, they let me in. Behind them, I saw the television I had been looking for. We watched it for the next hour. Within five minutes, I knew everything there was to know.

Michael thought about what he had found. This was from before it had started, before things had changed. Jack had been there. It was obvious, of course, because almost everyone had been there. Even he had been there, although he had only been five years old. People didn't usually talk about when it happened. They just talked about the difference between life now and life before. This was different. It talked about how things felt at the time and what it was like to be there. Maybe it went right through the last ten years like this. Maybe it explained everything. He thought about how much he would like to show it to his father and then about how he would never be able to.

He read more. It covered much more. It told him how it had all happened. He knew anyway, from school, but this was different. It felt like he was there. He felt so superior to the people in The Book, if that's what it was. He knew what had happened, and he saw their future. Their panicking, worrying, and mourning seemed naïve to him, even though he knew he was being unreasonable.

He read on through The Book. It described unbelievable events which everybody now accepted as everyday. The attack on Lagos and the invasion of Nigeria by… who? There had been a million dead in the first week and emergency sessions of just about everything. Armed forces mobilised across the continent, rushing towards destruction. The human race stopped arguing and throwing things across the classroom and started paying attention.

> Things weren't as confused as you might have expected. In films, it usually starts slowly. They are disguised as us and blend in, or they pretend to be our friends, then turn on us. They appear in vast, silent ships and hover for a few days while we discuss what to do. Sometimes they are invisible or skulking around fields in the middle of nowhere, mutilating cattle and abducting people in secret. That wasn't how it was. It was much more frightening. I think it was probably meant to be.
>
> They didn't wait, and They didn't make demands. They didn't appear on all the TV channels. They didn't make our leaders sign a document surrendering their planet. They just hit us hard. They didn't need to threaten us. They just did what They wanted to do.
>
> It happened quickly, and sometimes that makes the worst news stories. You don't have time to get ready, and everything happens at once, so you can't address anything.
>
> Thousands of them landed around Lagos and then moved in on the city. They didn't beam down, and they didn't carry

> amazingly advanced weapons. They carried guns and knives. Their vehicles were recognisably similar to our trucks and tanks. They didn't hover or fire lasers, and they didn't have any kind of miraculous shielding. It would have seemed strange at the time if anybody had stopped to think about it. They were fighting with the same type of technology as us.

After reading page after page of The Book, Michael looked at his watch. He had ten minutes left. He placed everything back in the package and looked at the letter. Even though he knew what it said, he wanted to read it, anyway. It opened easily. Sealed by machine, not by a human. It said what he knew it would say. The people from the government were very sorry. They regretted to inform Michael that Jack Walker was missing in action, presumed dead. He had died while doing his duty to humanity and would always be remembered.

The government wasn't specifically informing Michael. Like the rest of the letters, it thought it was informing the next of kin. Unfortunately, the bad-news machine seemed to have sent this letter to the wrong address. It was difficult to keep track of where people were from one day to another. Most of the letters probably ended up in the right place. The hotel hosted hundreds of military personnel each year. All it took was one mistake on a form, one computer error. Perhaps if you had no next of kin or no home address, you might put down your last address just to avoid embarrassment. Or if your next of kin weren't at the address anymore, maybe the bad-news machine just moved down to the next address on the list.

In these times, when entire divisions might be destroyed to the last man in a short space of time, you could imagine that paperwork might be lost or names mixed up. Presumably, most of the mistakes didn't matter, as most people would make a phone call or make an effort to forward the letter on to the right address. The first time a letter arrived, Michael read it out of curiosity. He had meant to send it on, to call someone, but he never had. Soon after, he realised he might one day receive his father's letter.

Most often, the letters arrived on their own, but not always. Occasionally there was a photograph of a family. It seemed some units made soldiers write a last letter to their family, which was sent in the event of their death. Michael had about thirty of them. He also had four letters written by commanding officers. Sometimes there were packages of personal effects, but they were very rare.

One of the packages had brought him the knife. Probably all the soldiers carried knives. He learned after some research in the school library that his was Norwegian, standard issue. It must have meant something special to someone. He imagined it might have saved someone's life or been swapped for something. The blade was dull, but he didn't want to polish it. It also had a small dent on the edge, which Michael liked to think was due to it being jammed against the bone of an enemy on some exotic battlefield. Then again, it could have been from opening a tin of something. The name *Gunnar Holstad* was embossed on the hilt. For months he had thought Gunnar was a rank, but he now knew it had been Mr Holstad's first name.

Michael considered these things gifts. He had to do without his father, and these things were compensation. He deserved them. He looked after them. The smiling faces in the photographs helped him believe that there were happy people everywhere, even these days. He gave them somewhere to stay. It wasn't like he was keeping them prisoner. If they weren't with him, someone else would have stuck them in a drawer somewhere. He appreciated them.

After everything was back in place, he looked at the smiling faces again. After everything they had lost, they were still smiling. He shut the cupboard door and let them keep smiling in the darkness. He only had six minutes left. It was time to go.

3

"You're on time." Uncle Joe was pleased to see him.

It was seven o'clock. Michael would spend an hour with Uncle Joe.

"I brought maths stuff today. Is that okay?"

"Of course."

Uncle Joe was already sitting at his desk. Michael sat beside him. Teetering piles of papers loomed over him, threatening to jump on him at any moment. Books and papers covered every surface. Uncle Joe knew everything, and each night he worked with Michael for an hour, tilting the odds in his favour.

"Do you think we still need to do this all the time, even though school is finished for the summer?"

"Of course, you're getting a head start for next year. You want to do well, don't you? How else will you become an officer?"

"I suppose."

Uncle Joe always looked at the work instead of Michael. It made it easier to ask him questions. Michael took a risk. "What if I don't want to be an officer?"

Uncle Joe didn't look up from the books. "Why wouldn't you want to become an officer? Don't you want to survive? Don't you want to help other people survive?"

"I suppose. But I was thinking maybe there are other jobs. Dad's not an officer."

Uncle Joe shifted in his seat. "He is not an officer, but he is not a regular soldier. Do these questions. Show me how you would do eight and nine."

"But maybe there are other jobs. When Dad comes back, we could ask him."

"Maybe when he comes back. You have to use the other formula for this question. Start again."

"Do you think he will come back soon?"

"I don't know. That's it. Now do number nine."

There was a pause while Michael worked and thought about what he would ask next.

"I was wondering about something we were doing in history."

"Were you? Now let's do number ten. It's differentiation."

"Do you remember anything about Lagos?"

"It was in Nigeria. Very good. Do you know how to do eleven?"

"What happened?"

"You know what happened. Everyone knows."

"Nobody ever talks about it."

"Don't they?"

Michael put down his pencil and sat back. He looked at the old man. "Uncle Joe, will you tell me about how things were before the war?"

Uncle Joe didn't look up. "The thing about differentiation is that it takes practice. You will never be able to do it if you keep getting distracted."

"Please?"

"What does it matter?"

"I don't know. I just want to talk about it."

"Why?"

"I just want to understand things."

"Is this because you are worried about your father?"

"I don't know. Maybe. Do you think he will come home?"

Uncle Joe turned and looked at Michael for the first time today. He didn't look sad, tired, or angry. He just looked. "How would I know? None of us know, Michael. Your father has one of the safest jobs in the army. He is an army padre. They are kept away from the front line, and The Enemy don't make a specific effort to kill them as they do with medical personnel. Of course, if bases are attacked, they are in as much danger as anyone else. Of course, they are. If your father is lucky, he will come home. If he is unlucky, he won't."

Michael was silent. There was nothing to say. Uncle Joe sat back and sighed.

"You know all of this, Michael. It is upsetting to talk about it. That is why people don't. They get on with their lives and try not to think about it."

"I just want to understand." He was close to tears. How had this happened? A few questions ago, he had been fine. Now he didn't know how to stop this conversation.

"Understand what? Nobody understands. Nobody can give you a reason this has happened. You are young. You think everything should be fair. Sometimes life can't be fair. Don't you think I wish your Auntie Anne was still here? Is it fair that she isn't? Is it fair that millions of people from this country have died? No. Can we do anything about it? No. Soon you will be a man, and you will have to accept these things. I cannot protect you forever."

There are several types of tears and several ways a human can cry. Mostly, people cry to show that they are upset. Usually, it is controlled at some level. When Michael started to cry, it was not. He began sobbing. It was exactly what fourteen-year-olds always thought they were not supposed to do. It was exactly what they almost always ended up doing at some point. He began crying in front of this man who was not his father. Michael realised how little he really liked him, despite his kindness and his knowledge.

"I want my dad! I want him here! I want to stop going to memorials all the time! I want everyone to stop dying! I don't want to go and fight! It's not fair! You never had to go! Why do I have to go? They won't even bring me back when I get killed! They'll send a letter, and you'll all forget about me!"

The bad-news machine would churn out another letter, and that would be it. Uncle Joe would go on being clever and running the hotel. His mother would keep on setting his place at the table every mealtime in case he came back, just like she did for his father. They would forget him, and then they would die too. Everyone would die.

Joe put his head in his hands while the boy cried. Sobs punctuated Michael's pleading, his voice a wail. Eventually, he stopped speaking. Uncle Joe let his hands fall to his lap. "Michael! Look at me, Michael. You are embarrassing me. Take your things, pull yourself together and go to your room. We will continue again tomorrow. We will never speak of this again. Go. Now."

Michael felt a terrible emptiness. He felt ashamed, but he couldn't undo what had just happened. He was surprised he could move. As he lifted the maths books and walked to the door, he wiped his eyes on his jumper and hoped nobody was in the corridor.

"Michael, there's one more thing I want to say to you," Uncle Joe said as Michael opened the door.

He looked at the old man with desperation. He wanted him to say that it was okay, that he understood, that he would talk to him tomorrow, that his dad would be back soon. Uncle Joe pointed at him. "You will never speak to your mother about this. Do you understand? You are not to upset her with these questions. Now go, and we will continue tomorrow."

There was nobody in the corridor. They were probably all downstairs getting drunk. He headed straight for his room. The only human being on the planet who couldn't cope. The only one who cried while the war created thousands of heroes every day. How could he get up tomorrow? How could Uncle Joe ever forgive him? Tomorrow he would apologise. Tonight he would practice his differentiation.

4

The next morning, there were four more letters. Just letters, no gifts. There must be something happening. A battle somewhere. Maybe everywhere. It could be just another battle, or it could be the end. The Enemy may have decided to finish it. He would watch the news today. That wouldn't be easy. Uncle Joe and Michael's mother didn't like watching the news, and he didn't have a television in his room. He didn't want to upset Uncle Joe again.

The bar opened at eleven. Cathy would be on all day. She wouldn't mind Michael helping, collecting glasses, and taking orders. Uncle Joe didn't go into the bar much, and Mum wouldn't be back from town for hours.

Michael was early, but it didn't matter how early he was. He was never the first there. He entered from behind the bar as the main door was locked. It didn't seem to be enough to stop the ghosts. Half a dozen men sat around the room. They were drinking, or at least each had a drink in front of them. They were always there. Sometimes Michael wondered if they slept there. It wasn't impossible. Maybe they walked through the locked door like real ghosts.

It was illegal, of course. No alcohol until eleven. It was now half past ten. There was no risk. The hotel sat high on a hill on the edge of the harbour. From the bar, you could see down onto the road. The police couldn't sneak up on them. Not that they would. It could have been stopped by one phone call from the police station, just as one phone call from Uncle Joe to the police had probably started it. It hadn't escaped Michael that adults found it easier to make rules than to obey them.

They didn't ignore rules because it was fun. They ignored them because it caused them less misery than obeying and enforcing them. It seemed to him that might be a fundamental difference between being a child and an adult.

Uncle Joe must have known about the ghosts in the bar just like he knew about everything else, but it must have suited him not to know. The men paid money, and the alcohol kept them happy. They had everything they needed. They had a place to do whatever it was they needed to do and alcohol to help them do it, although it wasn't clear to Michael what it was the men were doing. It was a nice day outside. They could be collecting things on the shore or walking along the harbour. He knew there were probably fishermen in the bay who would take them out on their boat for no more than the change in their pocket. Maybe they didn't know. He sensed that suggesting it to them probably wouldn't do much good.

There was never much trouble in the bar. There was no reason for violence, although there was plenty of available expertise. How could the men be angry at anyone in here? The Enemy were all out there, somewhere. Maybe that's why they didn't go out onto the shore. Maybe they were scared The Enemy would burst out of the sea and grab them. They would drag them under the waves and carry them back to the war. They might be hiding in the fishing boats or in the ice cream freezer down at the shop. It was safer in here. The door was locked, and you could see people coming.

Some of the men sat looking at their glasses. One sat staring at a drink as dark as his uniform. He talked to it in silence. As he looked at it, his face kept changing. His eyes narrowed, then widened again. He half shook his head, inhaled deeply, and let the breath out in a silent sigh. He had probably been talking to this drink all morning, going over old arguments, old stories. His lips curved in a half-smile, then he squeezed his eyes tightly shut for a few seconds to blot out some imaginary pain. When he reopened them, he wearily returned to staring at the drink.

Michael imagined he could read the memories from his face. The man had just remembered someone making a joke, then being killed seconds later. It must be boring to be the only one still around. Everyone had gone on without him. They had left him behind to remember them. One day, he would die, and all the memories in his head would rot away. Then it would be like none of them had ever existed.

How long did a memory last? Did it die at the same time as you, or did it hang on a bit longer? Did it drift out of your body and float away? If you have too many of the wrong kind of memories, they fight to get out. They can't wait until you die. They make you make a hole to let them out. Sometimes it would be Michael who found the bodies in the rooms. It was always in the head. They always put the gun there to let the memories out. He always opened a window whenever he found them. Partly because of the smell, and partly because you had to feel like you were doing something, but mainly to let the memories out. Michael didn't want them trapped in the room, in the hotel. He didn't want them getting into his head. He didn't want to have to let them out one day.

"You okay, Michael?" Cathy's cheerful voice almost made him jump.

"I'm fine. How are things here?"

"Just the usual. My boys are all doing fine." She waved her hand cheerily at the near-empty bar. Michael's eyes settled on one of the men who stared, wide-eyed, at his drink as if it might detonate.

"They're in early." Almost a question.

"Half an hour until the rush." Almost an answer.

"I thought I would come and help. Once the rush starts."

"No problem, the more, the merrier." She waved both hands this time. Michael looked at the man sitting by the window. He stared out over the harbour. His hand rested on the windowsill, his little finger stroking the glass.

Questions burned inside Michael as he looked at Cathy. *Why are you so cheerful all the time? How can you stand this? You are older than me. Don't you remember when it wasn't like this? Doesn't that make it unbearable? You must be thirty, twenty when this started? You must remember. Is it easier because you have had some good memories?* He asked the question he needed to ask. "Do you think they're okay?"

The apparently ridiculous nature of the question forced Cathy to scan the room for any subtle clues that all wasn't well with her customers. "I was just going to get Kenny a drink. You can take it over if you like."

With the help of another of Cathy's expansive gestures, Michael gathered that Kenny was a man at the back of the room with an empty glass. He occupied himself by lifting the glass to his lips, tilting it almost to the vertical, then failing to get more than a drop of liquid from it. He then returned to his thoughts before repeating the attempt.

Michael waited while she poured the drink. "Do you think they might like the television on?"

"They don't usually. You can ask if you like, but I think they're okay. They usually prefer the quiet."

Michael hoped his father didn't look like Kenny. The uniform was clean, but the body inside it was crumpled and worn. He looked about forty but could easily have been fifteen years younger. He was a ghost. They were all ghosts. Nobody would say it out loud, of course, but everyone knew that was what they were called. Michael sat the drink down. Kenny didn't look at him.

"Would you mind if I put the television on?"

Still, Kenny didn't look up. Michael switched on the nearest television and turned it to one of the 24-hour news channels. It barked the news across the room. He walked away quickly in case anyone asked him to change the channel or turn it off. Presumably, the ghosts wouldn't get up and do it themselves.

The news was halfway through a story about a demonstration. They weren't very common these days. Peace protestors had marched in the first few weeks of the war but had quickly given up as it became increasingly clear that every government on Earth agreed with them. They didn't want to fight, but after trying everything else, it soon became obvious that there was no choice. In school, Michael had been told about the tactics used in the early days of the war. There had been attempts at communication. When they'd failed, people had tried surrendering. Entire armies, entire cities, laid down their weapons and surrendered only to be slaughtered. Peace had always been unacceptable to The Enemy. Communication had always been irrelevant.

This demonstration was almost the opposite of a peace march. It was the fourth anniversary of the resignation of General Chen. The banners demanded his reinstatement to save the human race. Everyone knew who General Chen was. There was a big statue of him in Glasgow, in a place called George Square. Michael had asked to go and see it once, but Mum said it was a waste of money. At school, he had done a project on the general. General Chen was the greatest human being who had ever lived. He had led humanity's armies in the first half of the war, before the First Respite. The most brilliant military tactician in the world, the Unified Command appointed him as Commander-in-Chief of the Armed Forces soon after the start of the war. He drew together the armies of all nations and fought a pitiless war against The Enemy for five years. Perhaps a hundred million people had been killed, maybe more. He had pushed The Enemy back across Africa, fought them to a standstill, and they'd left. They'd just run away. It was a miracle. It was the greatest military campaign in history. Michael remembered his mum taking him to the victory party in Stranraer. He had been allowed to stay up all night. Everyone was crying. Nobody could believe it. Everyone prayed and gave thanks. At school, they made cards to send to the general.

It lasted a month, and then The Enemy came back worse than before. They returned in even greater numbers, and within a month, a million more people were dead. The First Respite was over. The Unified Command turned on General Chen. They said he had lost too many people, fought too aggressively, and taken too many risks. Some of them called him a murderer. There were inquiries, committees, and almost a trial. He resigned, and command was handed to a Dutch general, General Neckerman. He changed tactics and began the *Spiegeloorlog*—the *Mirror War*. It succeeded and was still succeeding, but at a terrible cost. Some people wanted General Chen back.

The room was as quiet as ever. The men had stopped looking at their drinks. They now averted their eyes, scanning their tables for something that would give them a reason to be looking there instead. They looked for some scratch or imperfection in the tabletop, anything that might suddenly be worthy of the type of focused investigation that would account for them not reacting to the television.

The television continued, unaware of its unpopularity. The newsreader talked about the latest meeting of the Unified Command. Norway had been released from its obligations for a year, although it was dependent upon how the war went, and nobody could promise anything. They had lost almost all of their young male and female population. Whole towns were empty. They were close to the dreaded DC—Demographic Collapse. Brazil was returning from release, as were New Zealand and Japan. The United Kingdom had reiterated its commitment to the war effort but warned that it too had to guard against DC and may soon have to ask for temporary release. Michael panicked for a moment. A suspension could mean no more letters, no more gifts. He then remembered that it would mean his father was coming home, and his worry turned to shame. It could also mean he would not have to go. His life could be saved.

The men were now failing to occupy themselves. A table was being tapped somewhere. Kenny was looking at the television as if he had never seen one before. Cathy cleaned glasses and avoided Michael's gaze. He just needed a few more minutes. He just needed to know where the letters were coming from.

The television continued, oblivious to the tension. Pictures from the Australian Front flashed across the screen. Most of Western and Southern Australia were now occupied. The commentators were predicting that The Enemy would drive for Sydney within the month. It wasn't where the letters were coming from. Michael wasn't even sure if Scottish soldiers were involved.

Kenny wasn't looking at the television anymore, he was looking at Michael, and Cathy was trying to catch Michael's gaze. He ignored both of them. Kenny's new drink was empty. When had he done that? It didn't matter. Michael just needed a few more minutes. He knew he was disturbing the ghosts. A few minutes ago, he was invisible. Now he was the only thing in the room. Just him and his Ouija board television.

There was always carnage in Africa, but this time it was worse than usual. The Enemy were pushing forward across Northern Africa, heading towards the Mediterranean. The Enemy were being held, but only just as usual. There were huge numbers of dead on both sides, assuming that The Enemy did die, of course. You could never be quite sure. There were some who suggested their dead might be recycled, like glass bottles. These were the battles which were feeding the bad-news machine. This was why The Enemy were sending him letters. Thousands of people were lost, and a few gifts in the post as compensation. An expensive version of the tooth fairy.

Something was about to happen. Some of the ghosts were writhing, and Kenny stared at him. He could hear mumbling from somewhere in the bar. The television flashed images of hell while it sprayed insane numbers across the room. It was always the same, and it always affected you. Totals of dead, projections for totals of dead, and estimated Enemy dead were compared as if it made any difference. Statistics so incredible that the temptation to reveal them was always too strong. They rolled from the screen, infecting the air. Territory lost in the past week, the past month, and the past four months. Biggest crisis since the last one. Projections for next year, if trends continued. Time left to turn it around, worst-case scenarios, next steps if Africa falls, plans for defence of Mediterranean, remaining manpower, remaining territory, remaining time, and remaining hope. The horror was explicit, and the unbearable was only implied. Life expectancy for the human race. Life expectancy for Africa. For Europe. For your hometown. For your family. For you.

He stared back at Kenny the Ghost. There were other names for them—spares, runners, tokens, etc. Michael preferred *ghosts*.

Everyone knew that although The Enemy never communicated directly, they placed a lot of importance on publicity and clarity of message. When soldiers or civilians were captured, they were tortured, brutalised, and butchered. All except for one. They would send one back to tell the story. The Enemy saw no point in performing without an audience. So they sent one stumbling back towards their own lines, and if they weren't accidentally shot, they would spread the word about the extraordinary cruelty of the inhuman enemy. It made everyone angry. It made them fight harder.

The ghosts were usually returned to the rear for debriefing. Michael knew, or at least was fairly sure, that the local army base handled debriefing for most of the country. Uncle Joe had some kind of arrangement with the colonel. He kept the ghosts in the hotel, and the colonel called for them whenever he was ready and paid any expenses. In return, the colonel sent Uncle Joe business. The new recruits arriving early before training was due to start, soldiers on leave, and soldiers there wasn't room for at the base all came to the hotel. They kept it functioning almost normally while the rest of the world twisted and contracted like a salted slug.

Most of the ghosts Michael saw hadn't been harmed physically. However, years ago, there had been one with a large scar down his cheek. It didn't seem to have healed properly and had stayed red and angry. Michael imagined it had been made by one of The Enemy clawing at him after he was captured. At the age of eight, Michael had been fascinated by him. His name was Henry. It didn't seem like a soldier's name, but then Henry hadn't seemed like a soldier. He was young, or at least younger than Michael's father.

At the weekend, Michael would walk along the shore collecting shells, and Henry would come out and join him. He never said much, but he smiled a lot. Michael's dad had been away for a year at the time, and his mum always seemed to alternate between busy and invisible. Henry never talked about what he had seen, and Michael never asked. Even at that age, he knew Henry had faced The Enemy and survived. He had helped stop them. One morning they must have come back because Henry decided to have a bottle of whisky for breakfast before hanging himself from the top of the stairs. Michael had found him. Henry's scar had burst open, presumably to let out the bad memories.

Uncle Joe took Michael back to his room. He explained that everything was all right and that his mother and Janet would clean everything up. Uncle Joe phoned the colonel at the army base and told him what had happened. The colonel let Uncle Joe take Michael up to the base for a visit. He sat in a truck with the soldiers, and they even took him up in a helicopter. Uncle Joe let him but made him promise not to tell his mum. He had lunch with the soldiers, and he sat in the colonel's chair.

When he came home, Henry was still gone, but everything was cleaned up. It was like Henry had never been there, and no one ever mentioned him again. They must have thought it was for the best and would help him forget. It might have worked, but when Michael had found him, he had seen the blood coming from the scar. He had touched the puddle of it on the carpet. The bad memories had got into him, and he would always have them now.

The next day, he dumped his shell collection back into the sea. A few weeks later, Henry's letter arrived.

Now, these ghosts were looking at him. He stared at Kenny, and Kenny stared back at him, trying to scare him. His dad was somewhere in North Africa. He was watching the news about North Africa, and this man was trying to stop him. This man, whose dead body his mum would probably have to clean up one day, was trying to tell him what to do. He thought he ran the hotel because he'd had a hard time once. Michael thought about the hard time he was having. Didn't that count? His dad was away, Uncle Joe was angry at him, and his future was already planned for him. Now he couldn't watch television. These men were dead anyway. Who were they to hold his family hostage?

Let them wait. The television could stay on.

Kenny lowered his eyes to the table. "Turn off the television."

Cathy looked increasingly nervous. More nightmares spilled out of the television.

Michael decided not to turn it off. To hell with them. They could live in the real world for a few minutes like everyone else. He waited for something to happen.

Kenny didn't look so big. He was a soldier or had been, but maybe Michael could catch him by surprise. If Kenny lunged forward, Michael might be able to move out of the way and knock him to the ground. He scanned Kenny for any sign of an old injury he could take advantage of.

As the soldier's head slowly lifted, Michael's heart thumped, and he began to shake with adrenaline. He tried to remember if he had anything in his pockets. He thought he might have a pen. Maybe he should go for it. Then Kenny was moving, his hand going to his pocket. It was too late. Michael shifted and braced himself, his throat going dry. *Shit.*

Kenny just looked up at him. "Please." His eyes were full of tears. They were running down his face and pooling on the table. "Please turn it off." His right arm was outstretched, his hand in a shaking fist. He held three grubby notes and some coins. Maybe enough for four more drinks. Kenny's fading voice was weak, broken. "Please, just turn it off. Take this. Please. Turn it off."

Michael was suddenly aware of the sadness in Cathy's eyes. The other ghosts looked away. Cathy had been right. Her boys had been doing fine. Now they weren't, and it was all his fault. Everything was all his fault again. He felt sick. These men were pathetic. In a war where everyone died, they were the only wounded. Nobody wanted to know these broken men. They wanted to know the heroes who died far away in some glorious, imagined battle. These men were an embarrassment because they had survived. They were spoiling the war for everyone. The hotel looked after them. Everyone here looked after them—Cathy, Janet, the colonel, Uncle Joe, and his mother. Michael was the only one who hurt them. He should try to make it right and apologise, but another thought crossed his mind. He just couldn't help it.

"If I turn it off, will you talk to me?" he asked quietly.

"Yes, okay, please, just turn it off. Please."

"Put your money away. I'll turn it off. Then we can talk."

With the television off, the ghosts retreated to their own world. Cathy stayed cleaning glasses in hers. Michael did what he felt he had to.

5

Michael asked Kenny questions for about half an hour. It was uncomfortable at first, but Kenny answered most of what he asked. Some questions he ignored, and Michael didn't ask them twice. Kenny didn't seem like a war hero. He had enlisted two years into the war and spent most of it driving supply trucks. He had no family and nowhere to go. The hotel was his address. If he killed himself, the letter would come to Michael.

His suspicions about Kenny's age had been right. He was twenty-five, but The Enemy had made him old. He must have enlisted at eighteen. Maybe slightly late, but still respectable. He didn't say how he had ended up as a ghost. He wouldn't answer that question. A whole chunk of history was missing. Kenny was driving trucks, and then he was here. He had been at the base once for debriefing but hadn't met the colonel. He would have a second interview at some point over the next week.

Michael found him disappointing. He had no deep insights or fresh philosophy and had never met General Chen or General Neckerman. He had never been on a covert mission behind enemy lines and saved the future of humanity. Kenny wasn't a perfectly trained, remorseless killing machine who was to be treated as the property of the government and considered too valuable to be allowed to leave his secret unit to seek a normal life. He was just someone who had survived. He wasn't as clever as Uncle Joe and probably knew less about the war than Michael. Even becoming a ghost hadn't made him interesting. Kenny wasn't a broken, wild-eyed loner entering a downward spiral of alcoholism and self-destruction. He was just a quiet, melancholy man who was drinking. He wasn't even the drunkest man in the bar.

It came as some relief when the soldiers burst into the bar. Their laughter contaminated the room, not even noticing the silence they were destroying. They poured in, laughing and joking, and pooled around the tables. Eventually, more than fifty filled the bar, and the ghosts became lost in the flood. The soldiers were all young men, enthusiastic and excitable. They sat down at the empty tables, rearranging chairs, and bunching in groups. The ghosts were no longer entirely safe in their isolation. The soldiers spun around so their backs left islands of ghosts marooned in the middle of the flood.

Janet joined Cathy to help with the rush of orders, and Michael had to get up and help collect glasses for the next hour. When the soldiers finally left, the bar drained as quickly as it had filled. Some of the ghosts had been swept away, but Kenny was still there, clinging to the table. Michael decided not to go back to him. Instead, he sat down at one of the windows and looked out at the sea.

Two soldiers were standing on the hill overlooking the harbour. Their green uniforms made them easy to pick out against the blue sky. They were facing each other. He watched them slowly start to circle. The first blow made him jump. The strike was high, head height. It was blocked, the crack of the impact telling him they weren't using swords but sticks. Another swing, this one was low, and another crack. Again and again it went, faster and faster. The other soldier struck back, and it was also blocked. The two hit at each other with increasing venom. You could have believed they hated each other. The speed was incredible, superhuman, and beautiful. Michael wondered if he would ever be able to fight like that. Maybe they had been able to do it before they joined up. Eventually, they stopped without ever having managed to strike each other. They paused, then started again.

Michael watched them for over half an hour. How could The Enemy win against such skill, such stamina? He imagined thousands of soldiers like them forming a line in the desert, holding a position, firing into the massed ranks of The Enemy as they swarmed towards them. Then, as The Enemy got within ten metres, the soldiers threw down their guns and drew their swords. As The Enemy crashed against the line, they hit a wall of swirling, flashing steel, shredding them by the thousand. Limbs would fly into the air, and blood would fountain until The Enemy attack was churned into a wall of blood, splashing against the human line.

The soldiers would spin and slash flawlessly, never striking a friend, never missing an enemy. The desert sun would be blocked out by the dark sheet of blood and gore being whipped into the air above their heads. Some would fight with a sword in each hand, spinning and screaming, invincible, unstoppable, more than human, pure vengeance and hatred personified. They would never tire, moving forward as one, step by step, across desert sand now turned to red mud. The soldiers could fight forever, never eating, never sleeping, swallowing the enemy's blood as it sprayed into their mouths. They would make them pay, make them sorry, and they would make us rejoice in our humanity. The only hope of The Enemy would be to throw ever more bodies forward, trying to clog the shredder and swarm over the line. Maybe they could blunt the human swords with tonne after tonne of bone and blood.

Michael knew that this was the imagery of General Chen. He had been exposed to it in films and on television, but now he saw how it was made real. Human passion and dedication could turn the individual into something magnificent.

He had noticed that one of the soldiers was female. It wasn't unusual. The Unified Command encouraged and effectively required female service in the armed forces. In Britain, female conscription had been forbidden by law, although the law had been passed so soon after the start of the war that Michael could not remember exactly how or why it had happened. It made no difference, as there was no conscription for males either. Service in the armed forces was, technically, voluntary. In reality, military service was inevitable, especially for a fit young man like Michael.

Watching the soldiers made him think that joining up might not be such a terrible thing after all. Maybe it could be the start of a new life. He could leave the hotel, improve himself, and become just like the two soldiers. Their skill inspired him and gave him hope. He left the bar without speaking to Cathy or any of the ghosts. He had found something nobody else there could understand. The war which robbed them of any purpose had just provided him with one.

6

He had been avoiding Uncle Joe all day, but knew he would have to see him at dinner. He wasn't looking forward to it. First, he would go to his room and deal with his collection.

The four letters told him nothing new. No gifts, no pictures, just names, dead names. Once, they had been alive. In the past, when people said them out loud, they would burst into life and fill people's heads with pictures and memories. Now they were just dead. They had no power anymore. People would try to make them alive. They would put them in the newspaper. Maybe they thought that the more publicly they were displayed, the more chance there was that someone would see them who still remembered them, and their power would come back.

They would be put on stone memorials for future generations of children to rush past. People who knew how much these things meant would stop and read them, trying to coax them back into life for a second, trying to imagine a picture and a story to go with them, but it wouldn't be the same. They might try harder, touching them to make them more real, to make them give out just one more jolt of meaning. Soon even that wouldn't work. They would be like skeletons. All of them would look the same. You wouldn't be able to picture a story from looking at the name, any more than you could picture a face from looking at a skull.

Michael put the letters in his shoebox with the rest of the bleached, grinning names. He wasn't finished with them yet. He might still be able to make the skeletons dance for a little while, and he started picking names. The second name was easy. He could just take that from the letter, but the first name had to be new. For most of them, he could take the whole name from the address on the letter, but they were sometimes just addressed to *Next of Kin*. Usually, it wasn't worth writing letters, but there was always a chance. There was always a chance he could squeeze something more out of the bad-news machine.

He had long ago written a standard letter he could use to ask for more information about each of the names. He used four different versions with slightly different wording and alternated them. Sometimes he also tried to make his handwriting look different from one letter to the next, with mixed results. The bad-news machine would never notice, but there was no harm in being careful.

First, he was Pamela Gray, wife of the recently deceased David. Then he was Anne Roxburgh, Gordon's mother. He had to invent Janet Campbell and Margaret Irving. Otherwise, there was no chance of the machine telling him all about Andrew and William. Yesterday's letters told him to be Thomas Gallagher and Elizabeth Anderson. He completed his task without much thought about who or where these people were. That was not really relevant. The machine only needed to know that its job had been completed properly. They were successfully grieving, and they were now anxious to know any further information regarding their loved one's/dearest son's/beloved husband's/precious daughter's final moments as this would help them come to terms with/understand/accept/endure their family's tragic sacrifice/crushing bereavement/heartbreaking loss/unexpected sorrow. The letters begged for more information in as many different ways as a cheap thesaurus would allow.

The results would not always be negative. There should be at least some limited record for every soldier in the army, although in practice, the records were often incomplete. Presumably, records were not a high priority when the human race was fighting for survival. However, there was always a chance that a file might exist somewhere. Luckily, there were always some people who felt paperwork was worth something, even when extinction might be imminent. You never knew who might survive to read it and appreciate a well-kept ledger.

The last letter was the most difficult. It shouldn't have been because it didn't really matter, but Michael felt it was important to get it right. Who should be Jack Walker's next of kin? A wife? A father? A brother? Maybe he didn't know the journalist well enough to guess. He retrieved the package from the cupboard. He looked at the diaries and the bundle of papers, turning them over in his hands, slowly examining them for… what? Why was he turning them over slowly? That's what you were meant to do. You turned things over slowly. He had seen it on plenty of television shows. The examination entirely failed to turn up anything which said: *Next of kin as follows, just after short potted biography and limited family tree…*

Maybe if he read more of The Book, he would understand more. He was going to read it anyway, but he had delayed slightly. It seemed like he should take his time. Once he had read The Book and the diaries, that would be it. It would be over. He would never again look at a page of it for the first time, never again be surprised by an ending, never again wonder what new things he would learn in the next chapter. There would never be another book like it. There would be no sequel. The man who had written it was dead. The flesh on his name was rotting away.

There was no time to read every diary as well as The Book. He picked up the bundle of papers and flicked through it, looking for names. As soon as he saw names mentioned, he began to read the chapter.

> I had been with their unit for a month. I knew all of them pretty well. Of forty original members of the unit, there were now only seven left. They had been lucky. Most of the other units in this area had been wiped out. It was a long time since I had been with English-speaking soldiers. I had spent the winter watching Indian soldiers dying by the thousand on the Northern front. When what was left of their division was withdrawn from the line, I requested a transfer to a British unit. Most of them were Scottish. It's

easier to get to know people if they think you have something in common with them. I had nothing in common with these people except their language. It was enough.

We were fighting in the jungle. Well, the unit fought in the jungle. I wrote stories and watched them die in the jungle. I think it was the jungle. I think a geography teacher once told me the only real jungles were in East Asia. You didn't get jungles in Africa. I don't remember why. Anyway, it was hot, and there were trees. We were somewhere far from the Northern Front, where The Enemy was pushing towards Asia. We fought them in the jungle. It was as nightmarish as it was ridiculous. The Enemy could have wiped us out in a few seconds, along with half the country. They could have destroyed us anytime they wanted, but I suppose that would have spoiled the game.

We had been in the jungle for weeks. We stalked The Enemy, and They stalked us. The Enemy didn't seem to be making much effort to conceal the artificial nature of the war. Small units fought small engagements. Sometimes there were large-scale confrontations, but The Enemy's heart wasn't really in it. Here the war was moving closer to becoming the sport we had always suspected it was. When They caught one of us, They always made sure we found the remains afterwards. When we caught one of them, we didn't hold back, but somehow we lacked their imagination. It was done for the sake of appearances, like graffiti without swearwords. No matter how hard we humans try and how brutal and cruel we are, we cannot become them. I think that's a good thing, but sometimes I resent it.

The jungle was the first time I really had the chance to see them up close. It was incredibly dangerous, but I had always been incredibly lucky. Besides, I was a journalist, and they didn't go out of their way to kill journalists, for which I was usually grateful.

We know so little about them. We know nothing about their society. Their language remains a mystery to us. After years of war, we still have no idea why They are here. They are infinitely more brutal and cruel than any regime or army the human race has produced. It is both horrifying and strangely comforting.

For as long as I can remember, we have felt guilt about the failures of our species. Man, the violent ape. We built machines to maim and kill, and we fought each other for territory or resources. We killed our neighbours because of arguments over religion or ideology. Wars were started over insults, breaches of protocol, or ancient grudges. We couldn't stop ourselves, and our guilt weighed heavily on us. The Enemy changed things. We were suddenly confronted with behaviour so appalling that we began to think about whether we were so bad after all.

Around a century ago, we fought a war so destructive that many people believed we would never go to war again. Of course, all our savagery had failed to approach the indiscriminate slaughter committed by an influenza virus. We killed a man a minute for four years and still failed to kill people as quickly as they were replaced. Perhaps we weren't really so good at being bad. The Enemy are very good at it.

For all their torturing and killing, I think the cruellest thing They do is ignore us. For a species like ours, endlessly curious and interested, it is unbearable. We can accept that They believe we have to be exterminated in a slow, cruel manner. Their refusal to explain the reasons behind our extermination is rude and unnecessary. They could speak to us. It would make no difference to them, but They refuse. Presumably, we are beneath them.

The first Enemy corpse I saw up close was soon after I arrived. It had fallen into a booby trap, a trench lined with spikes. It hadn't been killed immediately but seemed to have bled to death. It had put its right hand out to break its fall. One spike was through the palm of its hand, and another split its arm at the elbow. It landed on its side, impaled through what I suppose you would call its pelvis.

With its left hand, it had clawed gouges in the sides of the pit as it tried to lift itself. It might have lived for hours. Its blood was everywhere, red like ours, but maybe even more red, closer to scarlet. Its head was tilted back, its mouth open, and its sightless eyes staring past me.

I wondered how it had got here, what its name was. I wondered about its story. What had brought it here? It must have travelled an unimaginable distance just to die in agony in this pit. Had they lied to it? Did they tell it we were a threat? Did it have a family who had tried to persuade it to stay? As it bled to death and stared at a strange sky, did it think it was all worth it?

I sat down beside it, trying to imagine it as a person, and I decided to give it a name. I had no idea if it was male or female, but I called it Alexander. Was Alexander ever born? Had anything ever loved Alexander? Was Alexander ever looked after or educated? Did others worry about Alexander? Were they sad Alexander wasn't coming home? Were they proud that Alexander had died here? Was Alexander just a piece of meat grown for a single purpose in a military lab? Had Alexander been brutalised and drugged until he felt nothing but rage?

Alexander's sightless, black, expressionless eyes gave no clue. They stared past me at a tree about ten metres away. Maybe it was just the way Alexander's head had rested when he died. Then again, maybe Alexander had stared at that tree as whatever he had instead of a heart pumped out the last of his blood onto the ground. Maybe Alexander knew he was dying and had given up. Maybe that tree, one of thousands like it, held great importance for him at that moment. Maybe being able to pull himself up and reach that tree became Alexander's idea of paradise. Just the hope of being able to pull himself up off those spikes, get out of his pit, and drag himself over there helped him hold on. Maybe Alexander thought about what he had taken for granted the day before when he was able to run around, laugh, and do something other than twist in unbearable agony while his body failed him. Maybe the tree was Alexander's heaven, and his soul had settled there.

I looked at the spikes. Someone had gone to a lot of effort to hurt Alexander. They had spent a long time sharpening those spikes and positioning them, digging the hole and covering it up. Alexander was a soldier, and maybe he appreciated it. Maybe he thought all this was fair. Maybe he didn't.

A couple of Alexander's friends were nearby. One, I called it Bob, was clutching his neck with both hands. It had been almost severed by some kind of projectile, probably a sniper's bullet. Bob had fallen backwards, and his legs were caught under him, bent at the knees. It looked uncomfortable, and I had to fight the urge to straighten them. I thought Bob looked surprised, but it might have been my imagination. The second, I called it Carol, was face down. Carol's right leg was severed at the knee and her left arm at the elbow. It looked like the sniper, let's call him Dave, had taken his time. He had done this to Carol and left her bleeding. Then he'd walked up to Carol and hacked off her head. He probably walked past Alexander while he was still alive. I wondered how Alexander felt about that.

For my own amusement, I reconstructed what had happened. Alexander, Bob, and Carol walk through the forest, probably some kind of patrol. Dave watches them. Maybe his partner, let's call him Eric, acts as bait to lure them through here. Maybe Dave had watched them for days. Alexander falls into the pit. While Alexander is still falling, Dave shoots Bob in the throat. Carol has around half a second to think about it before her right knee explodes. Carol twists and falls. Dave shoots Carol in her left elbow while she's on the ground. It was probably a difficult shot, so Dave must have been close. Close enough that he walked out here to hack Carol's head off. Then Dave walked off, leaving Alexander in the pit.

Maybe I was wrong. Eric might not have existed. Maybe Dave left bait on the ground, like maps or a transmitter or something. Maybe Alexander didn't know Bob and Carol, and Alexander was the bait. Alexander might have been captured, then dropped in the pit so his screams would attract the others. Seemed like a lot of effort to go to. I was probably right the first time. It didn't really matter.

Alexander's sightless eyes kept staring at the tree, ignoring me. I couldn't compete with Alexander's idea of heaven. I thought of closing his eyes, but I didn't. Although I knew how Alexander had died, I couldn't forget one thing. Alexander was a monster. Alexander came to kill us for no reason. He killed without mercy, torturing and mutilating men, women, and children for no reason. Maybe Alexander had a family. Maybe Alexander died in agony. Good. I hope Alexander screamed as he died. Fuck Alexander. Fuck Carol and Bob.

This had been a rare win for the home team. Three of The Enemy died, and by every measure, they deserved it. Dave and Eric did a good job. Maybe no creature deserves to die in agony, alone, and such a long way from home. Maybe that's not true, and that's just something people think they're supposed to say. Maybe Alexander did deserve it. Despite all that, part of me thought it was right that Alexander hadn't died alone. All the same, before I left, I pissed on Alexander's tree. I hope he was watching.

Michael put The Book down. He wasn't sure how he felt. Would he see these things when he was sent to fight? He had assumed he would die in a battle, with thousands on either side of him. Now there were new possibilities. He could die alone, in a jungle, or in a wilderness. He could be lost, washed away in a river, buried by leaves, or eaten by wild animals. There was the chance he might be taken as a trophy, burned, or killed in a trap made by his own side.

The Enemy ate human flesh. He knew that was true. Probably people always said that about the other side when they were in a war, but in this case, it was true. It wasn't cannibalism, not really. That was when you ate your own species. They weren't human, so it wasn't cannibalism.

Michael didn't want to be eaten. They might eat him and then get killed and taken home. Then nobody would ever find him. Nobody would stumble over his body when territory was recaptured. No future archaeologist would uncover him while looking for ancient ruins and marvel at the perfectly preserved chewing gum in his dead mouth. No workman would dig him up while building a new road and get his picture in the paper. He would be gone forever. In the dead stomach of one of The Enemy, on a ship heading out into the cold darkness of deep space. He might be the furthest travelled human ever. He might get buried on their homeworld, wherever that was. Maybe it was a planet with a lilac sky and four blazing suns. Maybe they didn't have a homeworld, and they dumped their dead into space. He could end up floating around in the void forever.

He was no closer to a name for Jack's letter. He would need the newspaper for this one. Whenever a name wouldn't come, he used a newspaper. Michael had one in the cupboard for just this purpose. He opened it at the obituaries, an endless list of names. He ignored the female names, deciding Jack should have a brother, not a wife. George Walker. No. Arthur Walker. No. Richard? No. William? No. James? No. Stuart? No. Robert? No. Graham? No. Stanley. Stanley? Stanley Walker. No. Andrew, Mark, David. No. He was overthinking it. He had to just pick one. The next name. He would use the next name. Archibald Walker. Damn. No. Duncan, Charles, James again. This had gone on too long. Nothing would seem perfect now. It didn't matter. The machine wouldn't care, so just choose. Joe? No, probably not a good idea. Stephen? No. Steven? No. Hugh. Fine. Hugh Walker. Congratulations Mrs Walker, it's a boy. Oh, how wonderful! We'll call him Hugh. After his father? No, after a stranger who will be killed in an apocalyptic war thirty years from now. Fair enough, each to their own.

Finally, it was done. The letters and envelopes were written. All he needed were seven stamps. He could only find five and decided to get more the next day. It was almost dinnertime. He placed everything back in the cupboard. Tomorrow he would send the letters and trick the bad-news machine. The smiling faces shared the joke. They would watch the letters in the dark until he was ready.

7

He sat next to Uncle Joe at dinner. If the old man held a grudge, he didn't show it. Michael was uncomfortable, as he always was at mealtimes. Michael's mother faced Uncle Joe, while Michael faced his father's empty place. He had faced it for years now. It seemed rude that everyone was eating when his father wasn't. Everyone ate while his absent father waited. It had been years since they had said grace before dinner. He knew his father wouldn't eat without saying grace. He had tried for a week or so after his father had left, but it just seemed to make everyone uncomfortable. Eventually, Uncle Joe took him aside and asked him to stop because it was upsetting his mother.

The food was good. It was always good. Even though there was war, there was no rationing. The Enemy were not interested in attacking supply lines. That would have been the act of an army interested in forcing surrender or defeat. The Enemy were interested in the war continuing. They were only interested in the civilian population when their behaviour or condition interfered with that aim. In the past, there had been times when they had taken action against civilians, but slow starvation had never been used.

After a while, the silence had to be broken. It couldn't be Michael today, and Uncle Joe wouldn't feel the need. That left it to Michael's mother.

"I saw Mr Morrison today."

Not easy to work with this. On another day, Michael could have provided a much better opening move. Uncle Joe kept it simple. He didn't look up. No point wasting that move yet.

"Oh?"

The ball was returned.

"In the butcher's."

Back again. Uncle Joe wasn't going to be brought out by such a meagre offering. "Oh?"

The ball returned again. That wouldn't work a third time, but hopefully, it would force out some more information.

"Maureen wasn't there."

That was cheating. That wasn't real information. Uncle Joe looked up. He glanced at Michael but didn't meet his eye. His gaze wandered over Michael's food. What would he do against this expert gameplay?

"Maureen wasn't there?"

Clever, but it wouldn't be good enough. Michael's mother hadn't looked up yet. She looked up now.

"No. It was just Robert."

Uncle Joe was in trouble. Michael chewed and watched, fascinated. This game went on most nights. Michael was grateful not to be involved. There were so many subjects that couldn't be mentioned that there was a real skill to small talk these days. And these days, small talk was all people could bear.

Uncle Joe couldn't possibly ask where Maureen was. The news might be terrible, and he would lose the game. He couldn't mention the last time he saw either of them, as it was almost certain to have been a memorial service. Asking where they were working might lead to a conversation about reasons for changing job or reasons for moving. Uncle Joe was an expert at playing tennis in a minefield. He would find a way out.

"That reminds me, I saw Mr McGill in the street yesterday. He was with Elizabeth."

Uncle Joe had turned it all around. He deliberately gave all the trivial information, forcing a big question. Michael fought the urge to smirk. His mother was beaten, and she panicked.

"How are they?"

"They have just had news about James. They asked if we would be at the memorial when the time comes. I said we would go."

"Of course."

A forced error, and Uncle Joe won again. Uncle Joe always won. Sometimes Michael lost, sometimes his mother. He couldn't remember if his father had ever won. Maybe he didn't play. Silence fell over the table again.

When the conversation restarted, it was mundane. They talked about the numbers of guests, not soldiers, not ghosts, guests. Numbers were always a concern. The war was the source of business but also a threat to it. Soldiers were being shipped to the front in increasing numbers. That meant more soldiers coming to the hotel from the local army base, which was good for business. It also meant they were being shipped out faster. The days were gone when soldiers were idle at the base for weeks at a time. That was bad for business. The fighting was intense at the moment. That meant more ghosts, which was good for business. That also meant the country was running low on young people, and that was very bad for business.

Michael knew that Uncle Joe played the game well. He worked with the colonel to keep things running. It was in nobody's interest for the hotel to go out of business. Even Michael remembered a time when there had been half a dozen hotels along the harbour. They were all gone. Nobody came to the town for holidays anymore. They stopped over on the way to somewhere else, somewhere unimaginable. Some others—the ghosts—perhaps only ended up here because it was far enough from everywhere else to keep them out of the way, close enough for the intention not to be obvious.

There were some fishing boats. There would always be fishing boats. People always needed fish. The Enemy would probably fish here after everyone was dead and gone. They might sit at the same table, a family of them, and have uncomfortable conversations. They would go down to the shore and throw stones back into the sea. Then the sea would spend a million years washing them back onto the beach again for the next set of creatures to throw back. The sea had no loyalty.

Michael wondered if The Enemy would keep Uncle Joe. The old man would probably be useful. He imagined Uncle Joe watching out of his bedroom window as groups of The Enemy wandered into the hotel bar to get drunk. Uncle Joe would laugh as dozens of super-intelligent creatures paid him money for something that made them stupid.

Maybe Uncle Joe wouldn't work with the creatures who had tortured his relatives to death and exterminated his species. Michael knew that wasn't true. Uncle Joe would work with them if They let him. He would sell them souvenirs to take back to whatever hell They came from. He would sell them Michael's knife and his mother's ornaments. Then he would learn their language and chat on the phone with The Enemy colonel at The Enemy base. Uncle Joe would take care of The Enemy ghosts and do The Enemy favours, and every time the favours would make them need him more. At first, they would keep him around as a pet. In six months, they would not be able to imagine life without him. They wouldn't actually like him, but he would put them at ease, and sometimes that was worth more.

Uncle Joe would live forever. When The Enemy were gone, he would work with whoever or whatever replaced them, and everything would repeat. When there was nobody left to work with, he would stand on the shore, throwing stones at the sea and having it wash them back millions of years later, like a dog returning a stick. They would play in silence forever, long after the hotel had crumbled and the Land Rover had rusted to a pile of orange dust and blown away. They would continue long after the sun burned out and the sky went dark. He would be there long after the moon ground itself to dust rolling around the sky and the tides stopped. Long after the stars had all died away, he would stand there in the dark, thinking. The sea would keep coming and washing against his shoes, checking he was still there. It would grow to need him, just like everyone always did. Long after all the things that lived in it had died and left it empty, it would paw at Uncle Joe and return the pebbles he threw. They would keep each other company until the end of time.

After dinner, Michael went back to his room. He wouldn't see Uncle Joe again tonight, but he could be sure that the old man would be there tomorrow.

8

The next morning, Michael posted his letters. Two more letters had arrived, but still no gifts. Maybe there would be something tomorrow. He walked to the furthest postbox in the town. Even then, it was only a five-minute walk. He walked past the boarded-up hotels, past empty houses, past old people. When did everyone get so old? The country had been drained of young people. Now it was only children and the old. There weren't many children in the town and nobody Michael's age. There were still fourteen-year-olds. You just had to go to school in Stranraer to find them.

Michael didn't like old people very much. It was difficult to like them when they had such problems talking to him. He couldn't even buy stamps without them falling silent, trying not to look at him. It wasn't his fault if he reminded them of their sons, their grandsons, and all the people who probably weren't coming back. He suspected most of them couldn't wait until he was sent off to fight, just so they could stop looking at him.

He had only lived fourteen years. They had lived his life three, four, five times. He would have a few years, probably two or three at most, before he would have to go. The clock was ticking, and his life would be over. They begrudged him every second. The selfish old people wanted to pack him off to die just to protect their miserable little existence for a few more months. They were probably why the ghosts stayed in the hotel all the time. Even the young soldiers rarely went into town.

At school and on television, there was a lot of talk about how the war brought humanity together. The idea of fighting each other was ludicrous, even if The Enemy would allow it, which they wouldn't. Unthinkable alliances had been forged. Michael had a vague awareness that the idea of Israeli and Arab armoured divisions fighting on the same side would have seemed impossible before the war.

Michael had learned that there had also been a lot of racism before the war. The colour of someone's skin or the country they were from had been very important. Phrases like *Chinese people* or *the Chinese* would be used instead of *people from China*, and Michael knew there was a subtle difference in meaning. People had been black or white. The word human hadn't been used very much.

He couldn't remember exactly when the United Nations had become the Unified Command. Michael couldn't remember every difference between the two organisations. Still, he was fairly sure that the Unified Command was united in most things, unlike its predecessor, and he knew that the concept of nations wasn't quite as important now. Even so, despite all the changes, it still seemed that everyone was much happier when they were around people just like them. Old people liked to mix with old people. Soldiers drank with soldiers. Even ghosts seemed to prefer each other's presence to that of strangers. Maybe it was harmless, or maybe it wasn't, but that was just the way things would always be.

As Michael walked back to the hotel, he had no idea that one of his unshakeable beliefs about human behaviour was about to be turned into a childish misconception. Kenny was about to do it. He achieved this incredible feat by walking along the street towards Michael. It was not like a ghost at all. Had the roof of the bar fallen in? Was he sleepwalking? For a moment, Michael considered asking one of these questions but decided against it. It would be childish, even from a child.

Kenny was a full 400 metres from the hotel. It was quite an achievement. He was 400 metres from the bar, presumably for no reason. Michael struggled to find an analogy. It was like a tortoise being found on the moon. He walked slowly but remarkably purposefully for a man with no purpose. Michael decided to talk to him and crossed the street to intercept him.

Kenny was looking at something. Not just to avoid conversation, he was actually looking at something. He was turning something over in his hand as he walked. He seemed unaware of the inevitable conversation that would soon be inflicted on him.

Michael struck without warning. "Hello."

Kenny looked up. There was concern on his face instead of surprise.

"Hello."

"Everything okay?"

"I think I'm almost there, but I can't read this map." He continued turning the piece of paper over in his hand. It was small and grubby. Probably everything Kenny owned was small and grubby. There was a boy like Kenny in Michael's class at school. His schoolbag appeared to be some kind of machine for curling books. Jotters decayed in his hands, and paper aged instantly. For the first time, it occurred to Michael that, although the war was responsible for most of the grime and weariness you encountered, it might be unfair to blame it for everything. It may not have taken a war to turn Kenny into a worn, grubby person. He may have had a head start on the rest of the population.

The map had been drawn by hand. It looked like Janet's writing.

"Where are you going?"

"I have to go to the base. I don't know where to get the bus."

His interview. "They're not picking you up?"

"They asked if I could get there myself. They couldn't pick me up."

This was typical of Kenny. Yesterday, Michael thought he was an exciting, mysterious stranger with uncommon knowledge of distant battlefields and an unfathomable enemy. Two hours after that, he found out he was a truck driver with no stories. Now he was catching a bus to go and be interrogated. And he was lost. In Portpatrick.

"I can show you. You'll be there by eleven."

"I think that should be fine." The piece of paper disappeared. No doubt it was somewhere with a dozen other similar pieces of paper, all ageing and curling together.

They walked to the bus stop in silence. Michael had given up on talking to Kenny. He seemed to have nothing of interest to tell him. Presumably, Kenny had no interest in speaking to him. It wouldn't be long before the bus arrived. Kenny had timed it well. More likely, Janet had sent him out at the right time.

Time dragged. If the silence was uncomfortable, Kenny didn't show it. Michael was used to uncomfortable silences. It was a kind of sport back at the hotel. He would sit with his mother and Uncle Joe. All three would pretend to read or do something while the deafening silence heckled them. Michael could just about ignore it. The secret was to pick something and stare at it. You had to concentrate on whatever you were looking at. You had to make sure you weren't just listening to the silence. Most people couldn't do it. They listened to the silence and let it press down on them until it squeezed out a few words. His mother didn't find ignoring the silence quite as easy as he did, even though she churned most of it out herself. As for Uncle Joe, if he could start and win arguments in sign language, he would never need to speak again.

Michael chose a seagull sitting on a wall across the road. He stared at it. It looked grumpy and puzzled. It also looked a bit self-conscious. Michael decided there was a fair chance Kenny might still have the potential to be more interesting than a seagull. There were lots of seagulls. There weren't that many ghosts, even if they were boring. He searched for something to ask Kenny, something inoffensive. Something he didn't have to make too much effort to answer. Michael looked at Kenny standing with his hands in his coat pockets, waiting and watching the horizon for his bus. He was tired and old before his time. He was facing the wrong way. This was the man Michael had hoped would explain everything to him. This was Michael's war hero, and a bus was about to sneak up on him.

Michael decided to make the effort. Kenny deserved it. He had been through a lot. It was not very nice for him to stand there feeling like he was being ignored. Then something strange happened. Kenny spoke first. "You don't have to stay. I'll be fine."

Michael was hurt. He scanned Kenny's back for confirmation of his ingratitude. The seagull shifted from foot to foot and stared at something on the other side of the wall.

"Maybe I should stay for a while."

"You don't have to."

"I know." Michael paused while he thought of something to say. "The bus won't come from that direction. It will come from over there." He pointed, even though Kenny wasn't watching and couldn't see. They must drive on the other side of the road in Africa. Kenny was probably mixed up.

"I know."

He knew? Then why wasn't he looking in the right direction? Then Michael realised Kenny was looking the other way so he could avoid him. *Bastard.* His cheeks burned. He was doing this man a favour. He watched the seagull as it came down from the wall and landed on the pavement. Michael knew seagulls were actually highly intelligent and resourceful birds with a complex social structure. They also flew away if you threw stones at them. He scanned the ground around his feet for one that might be suitable, but he couldn't see one. He pressed on with the conversation, restarting it with his previously prepared perfect question.

"When will you be back?"

"I don't know. It depends on what they say."

"But you will be back?"

"It depends what they say."

"What do you mean?"

"It depends what they say."

Kenny just wasn't making the effort in this conversation. The seagull was trying to work up some interest in a crisp that was lying in the gutter. Alone in the whole world, Michael was making the effort. Everyone else had given up.

"You're going back." There was no answer. Probably because it wasn't a question. Michael tried again. "You're going to be a truck driver again."

"I'm going back."

The seagull gave up on the crisp and started softly shrieking. No other seagulls came to join it. They were all too busy to make the effort.

"Why?"

Why was this man going back? Nobody expected him to. He had everything he could want here. Humans were strange. Michael wondered if they were the only species on the planet that ran towards danger.

"Why not?"

There were too many answers to the question. Important answers like family, friends, and survival. Wasn't survival enough? Wasn't that a basic instinct? Even the seagull knew that. It wouldn't walk towards someone to get its head smashed in. It knew it didn't want to be killed, didn't want to be eaten.

"They'll let you stay here. You don't have to go back."

Kenny still wouldn't turn around. There was an uncomfortable pause. Pauses were usually uncomfortable. It meant a silence was about to be broken in an unpleasant way. The seagull looked up at Michael and assessed him with its horrible beady eyes set in its creepy, twitchy head. It correctly decided that he probably wasn't going to eat it. It must also have decided, correctly, but only just, that he wasn't going to throw stones at it. The bird sat down, protected by a shortage of suitable stones and the fact that it tasted horrible and was mostly feathers.

After a pause of about two seconds, which must have lasted at least a minute, Kenny said, "What would you know? You're just a boy."

Michael's brain provided a selection of possible responses. Most contained swearing and alluded to the relative benefits of youth as compared to driving trucks. Michael was young enough to be angry and embarrassed, but old enough to know that the remark wasn't as personal as it sounded.

"Maybe they won't send you back." That was unlikely. If he asked, they would probably take him and he would probably go. Not much room for sentiment these days. In truth, he was probably of more use dying on the battlefield than drinking himself to death in the hotel. Anyway, the second option would take forever, and he didn't seem very committed.

"Maybe they won't send me back."

Kenny's back seemed sad. He wanted to go, or maybe he just wanted to die. Or maybe he just wanted to be killed. Maybe he just didn't want to be here.

Soon Kenny would be off starting his complicated suicide attempt. The seagull wandered round in a circle and called out again. Its heart didn't seem in it. Other seagulls were not far away. The sea was nearby. It had a crisp. It was in seagull heaven. Still, it didn't seem very content with its relatively projectile-free existence.

For the next minute, they didn't speak. Michael wasn't comfortable. The silence squeezed him, but he couldn't speak. There wasn't enough time for any of the conversations he wanted to have.

The bus arrived. Kenny managed to get on it without looking at Michael. Michael had to speak. Kenny would soon be gone. As Kenny paid the fare, Michael called to his back, "What did you see?"

He didn't turn round. The bus driver handed him his change. Michael stepped forward and raised himself up on his toes. "What did you see, Kenny? What will I see?"

Kenny stopped and turned. Looked straight at the boy with no emotion.

"Goodbye, Michael."

Kenny walked away. Michael felt a type of panic, like something old he didn't want was being thrown away. He didn't want it, but he had the idea that somehow it was valuable or, in some way, it was useful. He would never use it, but it had been useful a long time ago. Something illogical told him it was a waste.

"You can stay. I'll speak to Uncle Joe."

Kenny walked towards the back of the bus as the door closed. "I'll speak to the colonel! You can stay."

Kenny sat down somewhere on the far side of the bus. Unsmiling faces stared through dirty windows at Michael as the bus pulled away, not interested enough to judge him. The smiling faces of the advert on the side of the bus grinned their approval at whatever Michael was doing.

He watched the back of the bus until it disappeared over the horizon. He spoke quietly, too quietly for anyone to hear, "You don't have to go."

Michael looked at the seagull. It couldn't look at him. He took a step towards it, and it flew away towards the sea. He watched it for a few seconds before glancing towards the hotel. He had to get back. Someone would have to be there when Kenny's letter arrived.

9

The hotel was still there when Michael got back. Uncle Joe was still there, upstairs, thinking. His mother was still there, upstairs, doing something, whatever it was she did. She might be watching the road from her window. Sometimes he caught her. She always pretended she had just been daydreaming. He knew she was watching and made sure he didn't catch her anymore. Maybe she had seen him walking back towards the hotel and had been disappointed. She probably saw who he was but focused on who he wasn't.

Janet was still there. She was still cleaning up everyone's mess, removing the evidence of everyone's problems, making it look like they had never even been there. Cathy was still in the bar, working. The gulls were still outside, swooping and scavenging. The fish were still in the sea, surviving until the boats came to catch them. Where should he be? What should he be doing? He couldn't see where he was meant to fit in. Michael could see a space where his father was meant to be, but he couldn't see where he should be.

The ghosts were still there in the bar, drinking and keeping out of everyone's way. All except Kenny. He was gone. Michael tried to imagine the space he had left in the bar but couldn't. There was no flesh on the bones.

A few hours later, the two soldiers were there again, standing in their spaces outside, cancelling each other out as they fought. Then, at least for an hour or so, Michael could clearly see where he was meant to be. He filled his space by the window. The ghost at the window was still there, as he had been the day before. He wasn't watching the soldiers but was looking out at the seagulls swooping in the sky.

It annoyed Michael that he wasn't watching the soldiers. Had he lost so much that he was now blind to the beauty of what the soldiers were achieving? The ghost's hand still rested on the windowsill, his little finger still stroking the glass. Maybe a tiny remnant of what he had once been could still see something beautiful in the birds and was reaching out to them. It could be he was just checking the window was still there, safely containing the world. Maybe the ghosts were being contained. Maybe an outsider would look in at them as if they were watching fish in an aquarium. A strange, quiet world, alien to their own, hoping that the glass wouldn't shatter and drench them. Was Window-ghost like a fish staring out at something he couldn't comprehend and so never considered? Maybe that was why fish became so upset when you tapped the glass. You were reminding them of the world they weren't a part of, a world they didn't understand. Maybe they knew that if the glass shattered, their whole world would empty, and they would die. It was probably better for both sides if the glass held. Everything would be fine as long as the two worlds could exist apart and you didn't tap the glass.

Outside, Michael's future spun and fought. The two soldiers swung and blocked at impossible speeds as they had the day before. A space began to appear. A Michael-shaped space. He would grow to fill it. They would feed him and stretch him until he fitted it.

Michael watched and saw that one day he would be perfected. He would grunt as his friend deflected a blow that was supposed to leave her toothless. His friend would step around him, spin, and swing. He would instinctively block the move that was meant to cave in the back of his head. They would never strike each other.

On the battlefield, thousands like them would stand together, The Enemy swarming in front of them. Nothing behind them. Only his father and, beyond him, Uncle Joe and his mother. To reach them, The Enemy would first have to overcome the perfection they had created. He would kill them all. As the last of The Enemy stood, terrified, considering its surrender, he would walk up to it, grab his sword with both hands, and ram it through its skull. He would stand over its body, bracing its head with his foot so he could yank the sword back out, scraping against bone on the way.

Window-ghost was looking at him. He jumped back into the present, into his untrained body. Window-ghost could see his fantasy and was disgusted. Suddenly, he wished the ground would open up and swallow him. But it wouldn't, probably not for at least eighteen months. He was aware of his hands. Where should they be? Where did people usually put their hands? Everything suddenly seemed unnaturally difficult. He had no drink. What was he doing here? He had to calm down. Window-ghost didn't know anything, not really. He had turned back to his window and his seagulls. Everything was fine. Everyone was in their place except Michael, but that was changing. The world would soon be ready to accept him.

The soldiers summed to zero for another half hour. Michael left, drained by ghosts and seagulls but refilled by spinning soldiers, to read The Book. He deserved it. He was worthy of it, and he was beginning to understand.

10

The first time I really talked to one of the padres was a couple of years into the war. Unlike many of my fellow humans, I hadn't taken much interest in religion since it all started. I met him in his quarters. The room was small. He was friendly and seemed calm and controlled. You don't meet many calm people these days. Even the exhausted ones, and there are plenty of them, have an urgency about them. They stumble about like zombies, but there is always an anger in their eyes. It is hard to be relaxed these days. It is hard to be relaxed when you have so little control over anything.

The padre seemed to have found something he could control, something he could make peace with and lean against. It was far less annoying than I would have expected. Maybe it was just the room. It was tidy, clean, and quiet. It also didn't have any corpses or bloodstains in it, which helped the atmosphere no end. The padre sat back in his chair, hands together, fingers interlinked. You can tell a lot about what people are thinking by the way they hold their hands. No one can control their body language all the time, not even the clergy.

"Why are you here?" He still held his hands together. I liked him. He was not judgemental, not always preaching. Most importantly, he wasn't stupid.

I stared at the ceiling. If you look at people, they try to read you, and then they jump to all kinds of conclusions. "I have to be here, as you know. Annual debriefing and informal interviews are standard requirements. It's to check

I'm not going crazy. Funnily enough, I've asked around, and no one seems to know what happens if it turns out you are crazy. I expect it gets noted somewhere."

"You don't have to be here. You could have accepted the meeting with the counsellor, but you chose to see me instead. Why?" Hands still together. Still calm.

"Maybe I want to annoy you. Maybe that's my thing. Perhaps anger at God is what gets me through. Maybe I want to talk to Him and hear Him account for his whereabouts last week when ten thousand young men and women were cut to pieces on a hill in the middle of nowhere for no good reason. Maybe I want to interview Him and get His side of the story."

Hands still together. Still relaxed. Amazing, I was beginning to think he might be on drugs. "I don't think that's why you're here. You would have asked me these things before. Why see me now?"

I was beginning to think the room wasn't as tidy as I had initially thought. The light bulb was dusty, and there was a crack in the ceiling. "The counsellors want to talk about events. They want a story that will dredge something up. They want me to deal with something. I don't need that because I don't have those kinds of problems. I'm like you. I just witness things. I don't have to deal with them. I don't take the war personally like everyone else."

"It doesn't affect you?"

"Yes, but not in the way it affects them. I don't worry like they do. I know The Enemy aren't coming to kill me. They're not coming to kill us. They're just coming to kill. Tomorrow it might be me, or I might live for years. I've accepted it."

It probably didn't sound very convincing. Hopefully, the padre wasn't listening, anyway. Amazing how people didn't seem to listen these days. They were too busy thinking about dying or staying alive another day. I was always amazed at how much time people spent repeating themselves. I thought of a young soldier the previous week. In my head, rotor blades thudded, and people screamed as he kept asking me to repeat myself.

"Are you coming?"

"What?"

"Are you coming?"

"Leave him. He's dead."

"What?"

"Leave him. He's dead."

"Get in. You're bleeding."

"What?"

"Get in. You're bleeding."

Why couldn't people listen the first time?

A while back, I'd started talking in keywords before I made an effort to stop.

"Drink. Tonight. Seven?"

"Going. Now. In. Move!"

There were good reasons for it, of course. You never knew when you might lose something important to a flying piece of something else. Even so, it seemed a shame to risk having sloppy last words.

"So, you're here because I ask less annoying questions." His fingers were steepled. He was still calm and slightly more interested. Nine fingers. Why hadn't I noticed that before? Only four fingers on his right hand. The index finger was missing. The left index finger rested on the stump.

"You've only got nine fingers." I sat forward, suddenly interested.

"I only have nine fingers." The padre's gaze didn't wander. His hands didn't move.

Suddenly, something struck me, and I had to ask. "How do you point at things? Do you use your other hand, or do you use your middle finger?"

"I try not to. It's rude to point." He didn't smile, but he didn't seem angry either.

"You must have been lucky. How did you lose it?"

"A motorcycle accident before the war."

I was stunned. It hadn't occurred to me that he hadn't been wounded in the war. Sometimes it was easy to forget that life had existed before this nightmare. It didn't seem real when you thought about it. It was like another world where nothing bad had ever happened. The news was always good, problems were always trivial, and life was always simple. For this man to have been injured in that perfect world was nonsensical. It was perverse. It was selfish.

My mind drifted to one night when I was with Egyptian forces. We were all very far from home. They let me ride with a convoy heading out to a forward position. The Enemy had been attacking for two days, and we were to bring reinforcements. It seemed like there were only two times when you could arrive anywhere. You were either just in time or too late. We arrived too late.

We were two miles away when we met the survivors. Our front line had broken, and the Egyptian armour had been annihilated. On the horizon, explosions lit up the night sky, and deep booms sounded across the desert. It was the sound of young men cooking in the metal prisons they had built to protect themselves. I imagined tank tracks churning sand as panicking drivers found reverse and hulls exploding while the crews tried to decide whether to bail out or stay put.

When I saw battle for the first time, I was slightly surprised to see how quickly explosions happened. When you watch films, everything is slowed down for your enjoyment. You get to see the fireball unfold. In real life, it happens instantly, like a balloon bursting. The flames are much more disappointing. There's a flash and a bang, but the cloud is usually dust and smoke rather than flames and fireballs. The flames come later as the wreck burns like an oily rag, charring the bodies and carrying the smell of burning flesh across the battlefield in the smoke. That's one effect the films never gave me.

The men that weren't left burning in their tanks were now streaming towards the rear. I thought the survivors would be dazed, panicking, and defeated. Instead, they raced to our vehicles. For a moment, I thought they were going to attack us. They didn't look terrified. They looked angry, racing to the drivers, screaming and pointing. The trucks shook as they emptied their men into the desert, shouting and cursing. The convoy was at a halt, and suddenly everyone was assembling and digging. They were reorganising. They were going to make a stand here.

I sat stunned, looking around at the empty desert for something I might have missed: a vast armoured division on our flanks, some miraculous geographical feature, or an impregnable historical fortress. There was nothing. They were going to dig in here and be overrun rather than be shot in the back while retreating. The soldiers fixed bayonets and set up heavy machine guns with a rage and purpose I would see many more times over the next few years. They would stand here and die out of pure spite. It was madness. I was not mad, not yet. I had to get out of there.

I looked across at my driver. He stared, unsure, at a soldier standing clutching his door. The soldier began to scream at him as my door flew open. Another dumped what looked like a body on the bonnet of our jeep. The driver threw up his hands, gestured at all around him, and pointed at the back of the jeep. Then everything happened quickly. They wanted us to take it back to the rear. The driver agreed, and they picked the body up and moved towards the back of the jeep. On the way, one of them thrust something heavy into my hands, a bundle of something. The door slammed, and I looked down at the leg in my lap. As the jeep turned, I stared at it. I couldn't believe how heavy it was. Turns out a leg can weigh about twenty kilos. You just don't feel the weight of it when it's attached to you. Something about the way muscles work, apparently. I wonder how much the padre's finger weighed when it was severed. I wonder if he was surprised.

As we drove back to our lines, we didn't speak. I wondered who was in the back of the jeep. Maybe a general, maybe someone particularly heroic, maybe another journalist like me. Maybe just someone's brother, someone's son. They might have just picked up a wounded man off the battlefield and thought they could use him as a ticket out of here. Perhaps he died on the way, and they felt guilty.

I never asked, and I never found out. I know it's my job to find little, interesting stories. But, you see, I'm not a very good journalist. I'd sometimes rather forget the question than upset myself. I'd sometimes rather stay sane than get the whole story.

As we drove back, I wondered who was crazy. They had stayed in the desert to die. They could have tried to make it back. I would survive. They would die. Where was I going? Back to what? To wait for the line to be pushed back further? Would I keep running forever? Was the aim to be the last to die? Their entire division had been wiped out in three days. Twenty thousand men had died to delay The Enemy by a few days. Maybe they just had no one to go back to. Who was I going back to?

People used to use the word casualties. Sometimes we still used it, but it was unnecessary. You could almost always replace it with the word dead. There were no prisoners, as far as we knew, and almost no wounded. The Enemy had no interest in prisoners from the battlefield. In the early days of the war, captured soldiers were butchered by the thousands. They would be tortured, mutilated, and sometimes skinned or crucified. The Enemy committed any atrocity imaginable, and a few we might never have thought of. They did everything to make us hate them, everything to induce rage in us. They made the idea of surrender impossible. Their treatment of civilians was worse, if that was possible. They massacred and mutilated men, women, and children by the thousand. They did not take hostages. They did not negotiate. They did not pause.

Almost a decade since they first appeared, there is not a single account of a meaningful communication between one of The Enemy and a human at any level. I have spoken to people who work with the Unified Command at all levels in dozens of countries, and I have never heard of any message being passed from their side to ours. I have never heard any reliable account of an Enemy soldier speaking to a human under any circumstances.

The Enemy have never respected any of our rules of warfare. They seem to target medical personnel specifically. They do this so consistently that most countries no longer provide battlefield medical support. Consequently, treating or evacuating wounded soldiers is extremely difficult, and most are euthanised on the battlefield. This fact, which once would have seemed shocking, is now readily accepted by almost every country in the Unified Command.

I talked to the padre for around an hour. He was pleasant enough, but then, he was a padre. It was probably nothing personal. I didn't manage to shake him out of his calm. He didn't provide me with the blue flash of salvation. We called it a no-score draw, and we parted company to see if we would both survive another year. I managed it, like I always do. I attended his memorial service three weeks later. Next time I saw a counsellor on the grounds that attending their memorial wouldn't upset me too much.

It was the only part of The Book so far that mentioned a padre. It wasn't Michael's father. Michael knew his father had ten fingers, or at least he had ten the last time Michael had seen him. The book didn't tell Michael anything he didn't already know, except perhaps for one thing. He grabbed his right leg and tried to lift it. It was surprisingly hard to make it go limp. It did seem heavy. He wondered what it was like to only have one leg. What would it be like to try to flex a muscle that wasn't there? Hopefully, he would never find out.

11

Michael had now watched the soldiers twice. Today would be the third. Just before they were due to begin, a ghost sat down beside him. It was the man who had been sitting at the window during the television incident a few days ago. For the first time, one of the ghosts spoke to him without asking or answering a question. Michael answered without turning around.

"You keep coming here."

"So do you."

"I like it here."

"Maybe I do too."

"You spend the whole time looking outside."

"Maybe I like it outside as well."

The ghost was annoying him. Michael was waiting to see something beautiful, something that showed that there was a point to all of this. The ghost was trying to ruin it. Just because his war hadn't gone well, he was trying to ruin it for everyone else. As if being a boring ghost wasn't enough for him.

"They could get in trouble."

Michael turned. "What do you mean?"

"They're not supposed to do it without protective equipment."

"What?"

"Even I know not to practise like that. If I had done that and got injured, I'd have been in big trouble."

Suddenly, the world had stopped making sense. The ghost could do it? He was lying. Now the ghost was looking past him, out the window. He looked young now, standing with his hands in his pockets.

"You can do that?"

"Of course, it doesn't take long to learn."

How could it not take long to learn? It looked impossible. He didn't have time for this. The soldiers had appeared. They were getting ready.

"They're really good."

"Not really. They're too slow. Probably why they're practising so much during their spare time."

Did the ghost look smug? Was he imagining it?

"They're not slow. Their reactions are really fast. Wait, and you'll see."

"It's not about reactions. It's about timing."

"We'll see what The Enemy think when they meet them."

"How will dancing worry The Enemy?"

"What are you talking about? They're not dancing. They're fighting!"

"No, fighting is when you try to hit each other. Dancing is following a sequence of steps. They don't have any music, but that's probably because they're too slow for it."

"What steps?"

"The sequence of moves. Watch. She'll swing high. He'll block. She'll swing low. He'll block. She'll spin round, clumsily if she's anything like yesterday, and strike twice from the other side. He'll hit back. She'll drop and try to sweep his feet from him. He'll jump, strike down. She'll block, and so on and so on and so on…"

"How do you know? It depends on what happens, doesn't it? I thought they—"

"Were doing it for real? God, no! It's a sequence of moves we are all taught in training. It helps you focus. Keeps you fit as well, of course."

A horrible feeling was developing in the pit of Michael's stomach. He was sweating. His cheeks were burning. The soldiers began. The female struck high. Blocked. Low. Blocked. Spun round. Now Michael noticed it wasn't as smooth as he remembered. Hit twice, blocked, dropped, swiped. He jumped. He struck. She blocked, and so on and so on and so on…

Window-ghost sneered, "You see? I told you. Nothing to it. No point in these fancy moves on the battlefield. The Enemy don't fight toe to toe. They just run straight at you. They swing up from the ground and cut you in half if they catch you right. Not much chance for fancy swordplay."

"I thought…"

"You thought it was some superhuman fight you were watching? Imagine that, lads! He's been heading down here for days to watch a couple of idiots dancing. Were you imagining that was you out there slicing up The Enemy? Are you going to be a hero?"

The room came alive with laughter. The ghosts found him so ridiculous that he was able to make them forget their misery for a few minutes. He turned to run. Window-ghost put a hand on his shoulder. "Where are you going? Not staying to learn to dance? I could teach you if you like. Then you could be a proper war hero."

He twisted away. He saw Cathy across the room. She avoided looking at him, but he could see she was smiling. He ran out of the bar and up the stairs to his room. He still imagined he could hear them laughing as he slammed his door and curled up on his bed.

12

Uncle Joe knew everything. It was difficult to keep things from him, and it was almost impossible to lie. The sound of a door slamming had attracted him. He knocked, even though he had a key. The door wasn't locked, anyway. He talked to Michael through the door for the few minutes it took him to get permission to enter a room in his own hotel. Michael told him everything. At least he told him everything he could about the soldiers outside, the bar, Window-ghost. There were things he could never tell him about, like the letters, The Book, and Kenny. Uncle Joe listened. If he was angry, he didn't show it. Michael didn't cry, but he couldn't turn and look at him.

"I can't go back into the bar."

"You will. This is our home. You will wait here for a few hours, and then you will go down to the bar. You are not staying here. I won't hear of it. I have told you before that no good comes of speaking about these things."

"I'm sorry. I really am. I don't know what to do."

"Everything will be fine. I promise you. Have I ever been wrong about these things?"

"No."

"You have to promise me you will go back down to the bar with me later. Promise me."

Michael paused. Not because a decision was being made, there was no decision to be made. The pause was because the words had to be forced together manually.

"I promise."

"I will come and get you at nine o'clock. You will be fine. As long as you are with me, you will be fine."

Uncle Joe didn't say goodbye. Michael just heard the door close.

At ten minutes past nine, they walked into the bar together. Nobody said anything to them. The hotel bar was busy, but most of the young soldiers preferred to stand at the bar, so Uncle Joe and Michael found a table easily. The ghosts were there, of course. Window-ghost was sitting by the window.

Cathy was alone behind the bar but still found the time to bring the drinks Uncle Joe had ordered across to their table. Michael had tasted alcohol before, but he certainly would not have the chance to taste it tonight.

Michael wished he could be somewhere else. It felt like everyone was looking at him. He could still feel them laughing at him. Why did he have to be there? He could avoid the bar for the next few weeks so the ghosts would gradually disappear and new ghosts would replace them. That was what always happened. But what if people talked about what had happened? They wouldn't all be replaced at once. What if the new ghosts heard about it from the older ones as soon as they arrived? What if the story stayed in the hotel forever? He would never be able to come into the bar again. He wanted to crawl under the table, to go back upstairs, but he knew Uncle Joe wouldn't let him leave. Why? Why did he want him to feel bad? He said everything would be fine. What if one of the soldiers or one of the ghosts said something? Uncle Joe was an old man. He wouldn't be able to stop them. What if he tried? What if they hurt him?

Michael tried to concentrate on the old man's voice, trying to calm down. He could see a group of soldiers near Window-ghost. What if they said something? They weren't young men, drinking and laughing, and they weren't ghosts. They were something different. These men were slightly older than the usual, slightly stronger. They looked like they could do whatever they wanted. They looked like lords or princes, discussing the day's hunting while the servants milled around them. What if they came over? Michael didn't recognise them, and that made him uneasy. He tried to focus on Uncle Joe again.

Uncle Joe wasn't in the bar very often, but he didn't look uncomfortable. He had a drink, a pint of something dark. The old man leaned back and surveyed the bar. He seemed in a good mood. They talked for a while without ever discussing anything important. The longer they talked, the more Uncle Joe tried to put Michael at ease. Michael had rarely seen him like this. He was so friendly and talkative. He might even have been enjoying himself. Eventually, he started talking about the holidays. Michael hadn't thought about what he was going to do over the holidays, and he felt guilty about it. He felt like Uncle Joe would judge him again. Later tonight, when he was going to bed, he would think about Michael and shake his head in despair while he was putting on his pyjamas. He would wonder how the boy could have turned out so wrong. Why did he always feel like this around the old man? He felt like nothing he did was ever enough.

"So, what are you planning to do with your holiday?" the old man asked.

"I don't know. I hadn't really thought about it."

"Maybe you should. The time will go past quicker than you think. That happens when you get old, like me. Not just holidays either, so make the most of this time you have."

"I thought I might just stay here." Why was Uncle Joe talking about this?

"Your mother's talking about going to Stranraer at the weekend. Maybe you could go with her."

"I don't know. I could ask her."

"You should. I think it would be good for both of you."

Something wasn't right in the bar. Tonight the ghosts weren't invisible. They were as silent as usual, but they seemed to be part of the crowd. It made Michael uncomfortable, though he wasn't sure why. A group of soldiers hovered near Windowghost. Uncle Joe didn't seem to have noticed, but then, he wasn't in the bar very much. He kept talking as if nothing had happened earlier, as if they had not had an argument a few days ago.

"What about Glasgow? You've always talked about going there, and you are old enough now. You could plan it and do it over the holidays."

"I don't think Mum would like it."

"I'm sure we could convince her. I could talk to her."

Michael thought about it, but before he could answer, something happened, just like he had felt it might. It was the kind of thing that was supposed to happen in slow motion. One of the soldiers Michael had been worrying about turned to Window-ghost. A fist slammed against the window, and Window-ghost looked up. There were at least ten of them behind him. It happened fast.

"What's your fucking problem?"

Window-ghost didn't know what to look at or what to say. There was no response.

"I said, what's your fucking problem?" The man emptied a drink over Window-ghost's head. He dropped the empty glass onto the table, where it rolled in a lazy semicircle. Window-ghost edged back but didn't stand up. His mouth gaped open, and he looked scared. He looked like a terrified child. The moment lasted forever. It was the only part that really did seem like it was in slow motion. Michael couldn't move. He couldn't stop watching as things returned to full speed.

A fist grabbed the ghost by the hair on the back of his head and smashed his face into the table. He was pulled back up, his bloody forearm hiding his face. His eyes were squeezed shut, and his face was a mess. His head was slammed down again and again, harder with each strike against the wood. Window-ghost howled, tears joining the blood. The glass jumped onto the floor and smashed. He heard a ghost beg with a broken voice for the second time in a week. "Please! No! Please, stop!"

The fist released his hair, but another slammed into his head as it dropped. The chair flew out from under him, hitting the soldier and making him angrier. The ghost hit the floor, landing on his elbows. He lifted his arms to cover his twisted, tearful, messy face.

Why was nobody doing anything? It was too fast. Everyone was still thinking. The ghost was on his own. He was still begging, bloody bubbles frothing from his mouth. Something white and hard fell out of the black and red mass, clinking as it hit the wooden floor. A boot swung into his stomach, folding him up. He howled like an animal as a soldier laughed. Another boot slammed into his back. The hollow sound was so loud and wrong, all wrong. All the sounds were wrong.

A hand clamped Window-ghost's wrist and pulled. As he reached to free himself, another soldier's huge boot cracked against his jaw. More white things flew out and skittered across the floor. He screamed, but it was all wrong. He was only screaming with his tongue. His jaw was broken. He shook and juddered like he was having a fit. Terrified, he knew he could die here, right now.

With a thump, he was thrown face down, his arms outstretched. A boot stomped down on his left hand, breaking his fingers. He screamed, no longer attempting words because nobody was listening. A boot hammered down again and again, so much weight behind it. It was like crushing a can. He would never grab another boy's shoulder with that hand. The boot crunched into his face again, more screaming, more begging, more mess.

The soldier screamed as well. "ENOUGH? MORE?"

The thing gurgled. The boot stamped on the source of the noise, and there was instant silence.

The soldier took a drink from his friend and poured it on the thing. It didn't wash it away, but the red puddle spread, losing some of its colour as it surrounded the little white islands on the floor, little stones. The soldier dropped the glass onto the silent thing. He spat on the silent thing and wiped his boot on it before they all left. On their way out, one of his friends took a napkin from a table and handed it to him. He wiped his fist and tucked the napkin into his pocket as he strode out the door.

Thirty seconds? Less? More? Why? The world restarts. Uncle Joe speaks first, his voice quiet and steady. "Cathy. Get everyone a drink. Get Janet to come down and clean this mess up."

She is stunned and not as quick as Joe but manages a word. "Malcolm."

"He's not dead. Do as I say."

"He needs an ambulance…"

"All in good time."

Her hand covered her mouth, and tears ran down her face. Michael felt sick. Real violence wasn't like television. The sounds were all wrong, crunches and squelches. He thought he might cry if he spoke.

Uncle Joe turned to one of the ghosts. "You, get him up."

Not *help him* but *get him up*.

The ghost shuffled across the room and lifted the thing, Malcolm, into a chair. Malcolm wasn't dead. Uncle Joe was right. He was always right. Malcolm was groaning.

Uncle Joe raised his voice to address the bar. He didn't bother standing up. "Everyone listen. I won't put up with this sort of thing. This is a family hotel. To avoid this in the future, if anyone sees any trouble of any kind, they are to tell me or my nephew here, Michael. I hope that's clear. I trust him to deal with anything that happens in this hotel. This troublemaker will be removed, and I hope we'll not be seeing his friends in here again either. If any of you ever think of causing trouble in my hotel, I'll make sure the colonel has you on the gallows by sunrise the next day. Spread the word. My nephew and I are running a nice family business. Now, you can all have one drink on the house to compensate for this unpleasantness. Enjoy your night."

Uncle Joe spoke to two of the ghosts, jabbing his finger in their direction to emphasise each point. "Take him outside. Make sure he's a respectable distance from the hotel. Call him an ambulance if you want. I wouldn't phone the police. I think he's had a bad enough night as it is. Make sure you sit him up, so he doesn't choke. I'll have his things taken to the hospital in the morning. Thank you for helping us out. I'll tell Cathy how helpful you've been. You won't have to pay for any drinks tomorrow. I would have done it all myself, but I'm having a drink with my nephew. I wouldn't want anything upsetting to happen to him while I was away. He's my eyes and ears in this place, and I don't know what I'd do without him. He tells me everything."

The thing was dragged away, and the soldiers turned back to their drinks. A few minutes later, Janet arrived and started cleaning up the mess. She mopped up the blood fairly quickly but had to get down on her knees to pick up each broken tooth.

Michael's stomach started to settle. Was that it? Was it over? Had everyone else forgotten it already? Maybe he had imagined it. Uncle Joe hadn't even bothered to get up.

"What just happened?"

"Used to happen all the time in the old days. Few people get drunk, a stupid argument. These things happen. Don't upset yourself and don't think about it. Everything's fine."

"They weren't drunk. I don't think there was an argument."

"Really? I wouldn't know. I wasn't watching. They probably knew each other. Probably happens all the time." Uncle Joe waved away Michael's concerns.

"What about the soldiers? Shouldn't we call the police?"

"They'll be long gone, and they won't be back. They'll probably be out of the country within a couple of days. It didn't look like they weren't here for training. They looked like regular soldiers. Probably only here for a couple of days."

"But he looked really badly hurt."

"He'll live. Everything is fine, Michael. I told you. Let's talk about something else." He would live. They just hit him everywhere that breaks, crunches, and hurts. They could have killed him, but he was meant to survive. He was meant to get a bit better, but not a lot better. He was meant to live and be sorry for a very long time.

"But someone just got hurt."

"Michael, you have seen the news. In the last few weeks, almost half a million people have been killed. There's no point in getting upset over one man being injured. Then where would we be? These things happen, Michael. That man probably just upset someone he shouldn't have. Do you understand? Tell me you understand."

Michael knew. He knew what Uncle Joe knew. He understood. Everyone in the bar understood. Malcolm understood as well.

"I understand. Sometimes things just happen. I suppose some things can't be avoided."

"That's it exactly, Michael. Some things can't be avoided."

"The colonel could find the soldiers. You could call him."

"I wouldn't get the colonel involved in this. He's far too busy. What influence do I have over him, anyway? I just run a hotel."

Michael looked Uncle Joe straight in the eye. He stared right back.

"But you have his number?"

"Yes, I have his number."

"Do you ever call him for anything?"

"Sometimes, if a problem comes up and I need a favour. But only if it's something very important to me. I wouldn't bother him otherwise."

They stared at each other. Uncle Joe didn't flinch. Michael wondered where the line was and whether he should cross it.

"Did you call him earlier?"

"I think I did speak to him earlier today. It wasn't anything important, a small problem. It's all taken care of now. He always asks about you, Michael. He remembers you."

There was a pause, and Michael knew he had found the line. He wouldn't cross it, not tonight. Instead, he stayed silent and waited for Uncle Joe to speak again. "Do you feel a bit better about being in the bar now that you've been back?"

"A little."

"Well, maybe we can leave now. Let them sort this out. I just want to speak to Cathy before we go."

He called her over. She wasn't crying anymore. He never stopped smiling as he spoke to her. It was a little unsettling.

"Cathy, I meant to tell you. I was speaking to the colonel earlier, and he mentioned a recruitment drive they are running at the moment."

The colour drained from the woman's face. "Really?"

"Yes, he was asking if I could think of anyone who was available, anyone who hadn't served yet. Asked if there was anyone I could spare. I told him I couldn't think of anyone, Cathy. I told him I needed young people around because the work is quite physical, Cathy. I told him I can't really manage on my own, Cathy. I think that's right, don't you, Cathy? That was the right thing to say, wasn't it, Cathy? I don't want him sending my best staff members off to some desert to fight, do I, Cathy?"

Cathy's hand was shaking as she picked glasses up off the table. "No. You wouldn't want that. I think that was the right thing to say. Thank you, Joe."

"Joseph," he corrected her.

"Sorry, Joseph. Thank you, Joseph."

"I mean, it's very dangerous. They might not come back. They might be dead in a month. I can't imagine what might happen to any elderly relatives of theirs who depended on them. They would probably cope for a while, but I can well imagine the little money they had wouldn't last too long. Of course, in the old days, the government would have seen to it they were put somewhere nice to see out their autumn years. I imagine that even now, the state would take it upon itself to deal with them. I don't know exactly how it works these days. There is a war on, after all. I shudder to think what heart-breaking decisions might have to be made about their care. If it was my family, I would find the thought unbearable. I know how much that would upset me if it were my nephew. I hate it when he's upset, and I always feel a responsibility to do something about it. Do you understand?"

"Yes, Joseph, I understand."

"I know you do. I know you feel as responsible for Michael as I do, and you would never let anyone upset him. I know you would never upset him, Cathy. I know that. He likes you. He's always liked you. I've always liked you."

"Thank you, Joseph. I'll try my best."

"I know you'll try. We all make mistakes sometimes, but the important thing is that we don't repeat them. I know you know that. That's why I keep you around. It is why I help to find little jobs for you to do so you have something to send back to that mother of yours. Because I can trust you, Michael told me I can trust you. He told me you are a good person. He's a good person, my nephew. He has the ability to keep things in perspective and not overreact. It's a quality I often lack."

Uncle Joe observed Cathy as you might observe a rat trying to find its way out of a maze. She shifted from foot to foot and stared at the floor. This was a girl who was scared.

"I'm sure that's not true, Joseph."

"Why don't you finish up here? I don't think there will be any more problems tonight."

"Yes, Joseph."

As they headed upstairs, Michael wondered if there was anybody else like Uncle Joe. Probably not, and he couldn't decide if that was a good thing or a bad thing. As Uncle Joe left him at the door of his room, Michael said, "Thanks for everything, Uncle Joe."

"How do you feel about going back to the bar now?"

"Fine. I think everything will be fine."

"Everything will be fine. Just make sure you get a good night's sleep. You should speak to your mother tomorrow."

"Yes, maybe I will go to Stranraer at the weekend. I think Mum would like it."

"Good lad. I think she would. I'm so glad we are all here for each other."

"So am I, Uncle Joe." And he was. He really was.

13

The bus to Stranraer only took half an hour, but it seemed longer to Michael. His mother's presence seemed to slow time down. He noticed every second. They both stared at each minute as it crawled past. It had to be checked for any potential for conversation.

The bus was almost empty. A young, unscarred soldier chewed gum near the back. An elderly couple sat near the middle. They had all nodded to each other and smiled as they got on but had not spoken since. Now the boy and his mother sat in comfortable silence, listening to the bus labouring round each corner and up each hill in a way you suspected it probably shouldn't. They sat at the front, where they could see both sides of the road.

Each day during term-time, Michael travelled this same route to school. There they had taught him how the Romans had learned to build straight roads, providing no corners for ambush and setting out the quickest route between two places. While travelling, he often wondered when people had forgotten how to build them.

It would be good to be back in Stranraer. The holidays reminded him of how isolated he was. He lived far from any other children. Uncle Joe and the hotel provided no real substitute. Stranraer was a strange place. It was usually busy, but it wasn't clear how many people actually lived there.

Michael trailed after his mother as they passed groups of soldiers. She no longer insisted that he, at fourteen, held her hand or walked right beside her. He was young enough to be grateful but old enough to feel a slight sadness that she didn't even make the futile attempt.

The soldiers wore a variety of uniforms, all similar, all cheap, and mostly clean. Their accents marked the soldiers out more than the uniforms. The Irish uniforms were a slightly different shade of green, and their voices spoke a different shade of English. He could tell North from South and city from country, not that anyone cared about such things anymore. He noted other uniforms, other voices.

On the other side of the road, a sergeant stood peering into a truck as another soldier marked things off on a clipboard and chatted in something that might have been English but probably wasn't. They all carried the same guns, all in the same casual way. They didn't expect to create or release any bad memories today.

The vehicles only differed slightly from each other. All were drab, strong, and functional with rough edges. The kind of sharp edges that wouldn't be allowed on everyday things in case you hurt yourself. It seemed that those were acceptable for soldiers. Perhaps danger focused the mind and stopped you from gashing your leg on an unfinished step. Maybe nobody really needed smooth and safe edges. Or maybe people just assumed soldiers wouldn't appreciate beautiful things.

His mother managed to ignore whatever it was the soldiers were doing despite glancing at each one, presumably to check that her husband wasn't loading trucks in Stranraer instead of working at the front line. For all their trucks and youth and lethal capability, the soldiers didn't seem to be doing very much. They seemed to be waiting, hanging around until the next ship arrived at the harbour or until the next ship left. Most of the people actually walking along the street were old, or at least as old as Michael's mother. The old people flashed past, never stopping to talk to the soldiers. The soldiers flattened against the walls, watching the world go by. They didn't seem to be going anywhere, and the old people didn't seem to be stopping anywhere.

Michael eventually followed his mother into a furniture shop. They always needed furniture. At least, his mother always said they needed furniture. Sometimes things would get broken, and sometimes they would just need replacing because they looked old. And everything looked old these days.

His mother examined a chair expertly. She grasped its wooden arm like a doctor, checking for a pulse.

"What are we looking for?"

She continued attending to the patient. "We need a chair and a wardrobe."

"Where for?"

She drifted from the clearly lifeless chair and scanned the rest of the shop. "The top floor."

The top floor. The ghosts' floor. Sometimes other guests stayed there as well, but the ghosts were never put anywhere except on the top floor. It was hard to think of anything to say in reply, not that his mother demanded it. He didn't want to know why they needed it. Or, more accurately, he didn't want her to say why. He already knew why.

A week ago, it had woken him up. He knew not to go in first and waited for Uncle Joe. It was cold. He wondered what was on the other side of the door. He knew, but he still wondered. Uncle Joe always told him he should be careful about that. Too much wondering and too much curiosity were unhealthy. When you knew paint was still wet, you shouldn't need to touch it to convince yourself. It should be enough just to know.

Michael knew what was in the room, and he knew what the noise was that had woken him up. He knew what had happened. He waited, shivered, and made sure the other ghosts went back to bed. Not that many of them got up. They no longer had any curiosity to satisfy. Most stayed in their rooms. They didn't want to open their doors and let the world in. If you didn't see it, then it wasn't really real. Just because something happened to one person a few metres away, didn't make it any more real than thousands dying a few thousand miles away. You could sleep through both. For Michael, there was still a difference, but he wasn't sure why.

Uncle Joe arrived after a couple of minutes. He didn't look tired, but then, he wasn't the type of person who let others know how he was feeling. He wasn't the type of person who let others know how he was feeling.

"I think it was this one, number sixteen," Michael whispered.

Uncle Joe used his finger to draw an invisible line a couple of metres away from the door. Michael stood behind it, and Uncle Joe produced a bunch of keys from his pocket. He selected the right key and unlocked the door. As he disappeared inside the room, the door closed silently behind him, the handle easing back into position. The silence swirled around Michael, tolerating him while they waited for Uncle Joe to re-emerge. A minute later, the door handle dipped again, and the door opened. Uncle Joe relocked the door and tested the handle to make sure. He hid something in one hand. He held the other up to Michael and spoke quietly, "Everything is fine. Nothing to worry about now. I'll call the colonel in the morning. Let Janet know. Put a note under her door. Tell her not to go into this room without checking with me first."

"I'll do it now."

"You'll manage to get back to sleep?"

"I'll be fine."

"I can get you something if you need it."

"I'll be fine."

"Right, I'll see you in the morning. Remember the note."

"I will."

Uncle Joe disappeared back down the stairs.

The next day, Michael went outside to look at room sixteen. It wasn't a warm day, but the window was open. He imagined Uncle Joe doing that first to let the bad memories drift out. He could imagine what had happened next. Towels were thrown on the floor to soak anything up that might drip through into the rooms below, the thing taken out of the ghost's hand and unloaded. Then there was nothing else to be done. The colonel would do it. Michael's father might have done something else, but he wasn't there.

The van came while everyone was at breakfast. Maybe they didn't just take the ghost but took the ruined furniture as well.

Maybe it went later, or maybe it was still there. It must have been difficult getting everything down the stairs. Even so, Uncle Joe probably thought it was better that the ghosts were on the top floor for practical reasons. After all, you could soundproof the floor in case of noise. A bullet being fired on the top floor would probably be fired upwards and so wouldn't hurt anyone else. A fire on the top floor wouldn't trap other people and stop them from getting out. Michael liked it because he always pictured the bad memories travelling upwards, seeping into the attic and escaping through gaps in the tiles on the roof before drifting harmlessly into the sky.

Michael didn't ask his mother any more questions, just let her drift through the shop, checking each of the chairs, looking for the perfect one. None of them were perfect, of course. They were all old. People didn't seem to make furniture anymore. Apparently, furniture making was one area that the Unified Command did not consider vital to the war effort.

After a minute or so, help arrived. The man seemed old to Michael, much older than Uncle Joe and his mother. Older even than the teachers at school. He looked too old to be working, too old to be smiling. Michael imagined that his tired body had given up trying to make him sit down and decay and had instead gone on strike. It had refused to make him hungry anymore, and he had become thin. This rebellion had not stopped him, and he continued to work, barely noticing.

The outside world had also turned on him. The war had tried to kill his children, bankrupt him, and scare him to death. Still, he continued. He cheerfully led Michael's mother around the shop, his hands waving in the air, drawing invisible pictures of imagined rooms where the tired furniture would burst into life again. Michael could not escape the conclusion that this furniture was only looking for somewhere to retire and pass away quietly. Still, the man tried to make his skeletons dance one last time.

After five minutes of persuasion, Michael's mother bought the furniture. More than she came for, as always. The ancient furniture man's equally ancient wife helped write the receipt with shaking hands. It would be delivered the next day, presumably by people who could carry it without snapping in half. The job was done, and there was no further reason to be in Stranraer. Even so, he persuaded his mother to stay for lunch so they wouldn't have to go back right away. They found a cafe and sat by the window. His mother scanned the street outside as an ancient waitress brought them food made by the ancient cook. His mother switched her attention from the street to the food. Michael spoke first. He decided to be cheerful. He would make her want to talk to him. "Have you ever been to Glasgow?"

"No."

"Didn't you ever go with Dad?"

"No."

"Dad has been lots of times."

The wrong subject. The worst subject. There was nowhere to go. Now she had stopped talking. He couldn't speak twice in a row. Then it happened. She spoke.

"He took me to Edinburgh once. A long time ago."

Her voice was alive again. Michael hadn't heard his mother's voice for a long time. He had heard her speak almost every day. He had heard her say things. But it had been a long time since he had heard her voice. He could have responded, but he didn't. He listened, afraid that speaking might break the spell. She didn't look at him, but it didn't matter. Her voice found him just the same.

"We went to see the castle. Your father had a couple of days off, and we decided to go. It was a long time ago, long before everything changed. I wanted to go through Glasgow, just so I could say I had been. But we only passed through it. We stayed over in Edinburgh. We saw the castle and some of the city. I was worried about taking you, but you were so young I didn't want to leave you with anyone else."

He couldn't believe it. "I've been to Edinburgh?"

"Yes. On the train."

"I didn't know."

She smiled. His mother actually smiled. "It wasn't a secret. I suppose it just never came up. We never went back. Sometimes your father had to go to Glasgow for meetings and things, but I never went with him. I stayed home to look after you."

"I remember."

She looked up, still half smiling, "We always meant to go back. We just never got around to it. You'll find out when you get older. You think you'll always have time. It's not that you put something off for a month or a year. You just think you'll do it tomorrow. Then you look at the calendar and realise it's been five years. We always meant to go back. I always meant to see Glasgow. I never wanted to see the world, just Glasgow."

"Why Glasgow?"

"Your grandfather, my father, was from Glasgow. He and your Uncle Joe grew up there."

He tried to imagine Uncle Joe when he was young. He had known Michael's grandfather. They had been brothers, little boys. How was that possible? He imagined a world of black and white. Maybe it wouldn't have been black and white. Maybe it wasn't that long ago. He had never imagined that Uncle Joe was from Glasgow. Why had nobody ever told him? "I didn't know."

"Oh yes, all your ancestors were from Glasgow. Well, on my side, at least. Uncle Joe looked it all up once, a long time ago. They lived there for hundreds of years. I always meant to go there. I just thought there would always be time. Then things changed."

"There is still time. You could go now. We could go."

"No, there's nothing there I'd want to see now. Not without your father. Maybe one day, after he gets back."

"Maybe we could all go when he comes back."

"Yes, maybe we could all go."

Neither of them believed it, but it didn't matter. They didn't ever have to go to Glasgow. They just needed him to come home. He should be here, like the soldiers outside. Michael thought about how many of them he had seen who were returning instead of getting ready to leave. There had been some. They weren't all young. They weren't all ghosts. Sometimes people came back. The more soldiers he saw coming back, the greater the chance that it would be his father's turn soon. His dad would come back. God would protect him. Hope and warmth filled him, but then panic set in. "We didn't say grace!"

"Would you like to?"

"I could do it now. It's not too late, is it?"

"No, it's not too late."

God would protect his father. You just had to ask Him. Michael would see his father again. He said grace.

They talked all through lunch, but not about anything important. They just talked, and he listened to his mother's voice. She didn't hate him. Maybe she wasn't silent because she didn't want to speak to him. Maybe it was because she wanted to speak to him so much she couldn't think of anything to say. Everything was fine now. It wasn't really fine, of course. When they stepped outside, the world would still be the same. It would never be fine again, everyone knew that, but in the cafe at that exact moment, everything was fine. It didn't matter about the war or the soldiers or the bad-news machine. Right now, a mother and son were talking. If the world had been fine, the conversation would have been just the same.

It struck Michael that maybe that was the point. That was how you survived. You had to worry and cry and mourn. You had to deal with terrible things, but sometimes you forgot about it, and it was all fine for a little while. That was what you had to hang onto. Humans could cope with anything if they talked to each other. If he had realised that a few days ago, he could have told Kenny. It probably wouldn't have done any good. Kenny's bad memories wouldn't have left him alone long enough for him to laugh in a cafe. They were screaming too loudly, desperate to be let out.

It had to end. But that was fine, just as long as you could have it again sometime. His mother would still be quiet, but he knew she was still there somewhere. He knew there was still flesh on the bones.

The world was still there when they left the cafe. It was still full of soldiers and old people. Shops were still boarded up, and houses still stood empty. His mother was silent again as they waited for the bus. He was glad they were the only people waiting. He could cope with the silence from one person. The silence from four or five might hurt his ears.

There were at least five minutes to wait, probably nearer to seven. It wouldn't be right on time. He looked around for something to think about to pass the time. A woman across the road was waiting for her bus. She was old, not ancient, just old, but older than his mother. Maybe fifty or fifty-five, and she had a tired face. She wasn't rich and was wearing old clothes, probably second-hand. Her hair was clean but looked like it wasn't.

To pass the time, Michaele tried to imagine what her life was like. She had grown up in a small village near Stranraer but had left school at sixteen. She worked in a shop, probably a supermarket, and was pregnant at eighteen, married at nineteen. They had three children together. Her husband was a… mechanic. All her children had signed up and been killed in the first few years, probably fighting under General Chen. Her husband had lost his job and was too old to serve. He worked whenever he could, but it wasn't enough. They made some money fostering children orphaned by the war. She would not be alone. The young and fit were all off being killed, but the old could look after their children. Older people, retired people, were already doing the work of the young. There was no reason for them not to raise their dead children's families. If they could not look after them, arrangements could always be made elsewhere. She would be relatively young for the role.

The war had made great demands on the older generation. Those that society had abandoned or allowed to retire had suddenly been called back into action. Previous wars had shown how women could contribute in all aspects of life. Now the elderly were in demand. The modern world found that seventy-year-olds could often work just as well as their mothers or grandmothers had when they were young during the Second

World War. Older people ran shops, made weapons, and soon they would be looking after their teenage grandchildren.

But there was a bigger problem. In the short term, losses could be replaced, at least partially, but that couldn't be sustained in the long term. Even in a small country like Britain, over half a million people turned sixteen every year, but many of them were being killed before they had the chance to replace themselves. The war was in its tenth year. There were only so many criminals you could conscript, only so many exemptions you could cancel. There was a limit on how high you could force the upper age limit. Plans had to be made for the future. Children had to be born. It was vitally important that children were born. Michael had read somewhere that some people weren't having children, even if they could, because of the war, and that was making things even worse.

As the younger generation were extinguished and the old aged and died out, the abyss would widen until society stopped functioning. Demographic Collapse. Extinction might take a lot longer than stagnation. Some young people would always survive or be exempt from service, but not enough to keep things running properly.

Of course, Michael knew that girls could have children before they went off to fight. But that only really solved one-half of the problem. Who would look after all the children when the old people were gone?

Michael wondered if one day the government could make old people have children. Would that work? Could modern medicine allow the human race to skip a generation? It would be grotesque, but there were many more horrific things happening every day. What if that was the only option other than extinction? Even then, surely, as the old got older, medical science would have to admit defeat and accept the new polarised human race consisting of the infantile and the sterile.

Society had changed, almost beyond recognition. The war had made the human race both merciless and practical. There was little bitterness towards those that could not contribute, but there was a limit to what could be done. Health care was extremely limited. Diseases could still be cured, and immunisation could still be carried out, at least in theory, but people could no longer be looked after.

People were no longer warehoused in prisons or hospitals. Prisoners were conscripted or hanged, and patients were allowed or helped to die. The mentally ill and physically disabled received a rapidly dwindling amount of assistance from the state. Those who were lucky had families to look after them or found some form of charitable support. For the others, arrangements could be made for the problem to be compassionately and finally dealt with. Humans were now judged by their usefulness to the military or to the economy. After thousands of years of civilisation, the human race had abandoned the weak. The aim was no longer perfection but survival. Someone had to survive. Something had to survive.

Michael watched the woman as she stared into the distance, waiting for her bus and surviving. He wondered if it was worth it. If humanity was to survive like this, was there any point? What were the soldiers at the front defending? Their world was already gone. They fought to prolong its tortured, deformed shadow. Why not just give in? He knew why. You couldn't because They would wipe you out. It was worth all of this just to survive another day, another week. That was bearable. What might be unbearable was the thought of winning. How could humanity be forgiven? Everyone was culpable. Who could they ask for forgiveness? God? How could they atone for everything they had done? Was there any boundary The Enemy could not force them to cross?

Humans had always killed each other, but The Enemy had managed to make them do something different. They were making humans dismantle their own societies. What else could They make humans do? Could They make the human race resort to cannibalism? Could They make humans kill each other just so they could be the last to die? Of course, there were places where people had refused to fight, refused to debase themselves.

They had been annihilated but had died with dignity. Did they die pointlessly? What was the point of all of this?

Nobody could seriously believe that the war was winnable. The future only held more nightmares, more distortion, more dead, and more sacrifice. What was the last resort? What was too far? Would children be asked to give birth before heading for the front line? Children giving birth at fifteen? Thirteen? Twelve? Would it be a new human race with a life expectancy of eighteen or nineteen? Would the maths work, and would it be enough for The Enemy? Or would They grind the human race closer to extinction? The latter seemed more likely.

Michael couldn't look at the woman anymore. He couldn't look at the soldiers preparing to travel thousands of miles to kill just to protect him. This was all wrong. It was all unfair. What was the right thing to do? Should he wait until he was old enough and sign up for the *Spiegeloorlog*? It was sick.

The worst thing was that there was nobody to be angry at. Who should he hate? The government hid nothing from him. They made impossible decisions every day. Should he hate the people who allowed people to die because they could not fight? Maybe he should hate Uncle Joe for surviving or his father for serving at the front? Should he hate the woman across the road for doing whatever she had to do to survive? Should he hate the people running things? As far as he could tell, they were honest men and women who went home at night and wept over what they had done. They were not monsters, but he wanted them to be.

I wish they had lied to us. They could have. I know. There are some things you take for granted. The sun will come up tomorrow. Two and two make four. My government will lie to me.

He understood what Jack Walker had meant when he had written that in The Book. They should have lied to him. The government should have hidden the truth. Everyone could have pretended the war was unnecessary, that it could be fought more efficiently and won. Everyone could have protested and blamed the government, the Unified Command, and General Chen.

It would have been easier to live with. Instead, they had to be honest and selfish. They were all paid to make these decisions, take the weight of all these problems onto themselves, to never be appreciated. They were selfish. Two years ago, when the prime minister's son had been killed on the front line, that was selfish. He could have kept him out of the war, and everyone could have hated him for it. It could all have been his fault. Instead, everyone had to know the truth. Why?

As the bus rumbled to a halt behind him, he was certain of one thing. If he hated the human race, he hated The Enemy more. That would keep him going and focused. That was probably what They relied on.

They were back at the hotel in around half an hour. He went straight upstairs to read The Book.

14

The book didn't care where he had been that day, or what had happened there. It didn't care what year it was, or what the future held. It only offered the truth, and that was all Michael was interested in.

> I remember the first time I was next to one of them while it was still alive. It was so close I could have spoken to it, not that it would ever have chosen to respond. It was three months after the war had started, and the world began to end. Three months since I watched the president of an African country announce his country's surrender to... who? The question quickly lost its importance. It didn't even seem very important at the time. It just had to stop.
>
> I have seen wars begin and end, leaders posing and threatening. I have seen them make peace years after thousands of other people's children died. Someone once said war is a continuation of politics by other means. I have seen it. Someone else once said war was God's way of teaching us geography, and maybe that is true. We all learned where Lagos, Ibadan, Oshogbo, and Ilorin were. In a few weeks, They taught geography to every adult and child in the world. Fear is a great teacher, and The Enemy are the greatest educators, but I still don't think I agree with whoever said it. It isn't exactly geography, but more like history. Geography is about places and people that still exist.
>
> I wonder if that president still exists. I wonder if he's cowering under a table somewhere. Maybe he's still waiting for a reply. We understand The Enemy better now, and nobody

still tries to surrender. Now they declare war on them, not that it matters. It's not like you really have any say in it. I wonder if The Enemy have a word for war. I wonder if it is the same as their word for "life" or "getting up in the morning". Do they have words for anything else?

Maybe that president understood them at the end. I wonder if he cancelled his meetings and went out into the street to fight them. Did he die on his feet or on his knees? Not that it matters, and not that They would care. They don't care how you die as long as you don't want to and you resist somehow. Even begging is a form of resistance, I suppose. I wonder if I'll resist.

Wondering. I spend a lot of time wondering. There isn't a lot of room for certainty anymore. What does the word mean? Wonder: verb, to think about but not really care either way.

Things were very different back then. Even the soldiers looked different. The uniforms had a nicer finish, and everybody still wore them. Not for identification, of course. Not much chance of mistaking one of us for one of them. Not for camouflage. They never had much problem finding us. Why? It gave you an identity. There is something strangely comforting about being in trouble and realising your best friend is right there with you, and he's also fucked.

You tell everybody that it makes it worse, that you wish they weren't involved, that you wish they'd been spared. That's a lie. It's always a lie. You don't wish you were the only one with a tax bill, and you don't wish you were the only one without a clue on the day of the exam. You certainly don't wish these things had crossed the unimaginable vastness of space just to get you. There is comfort in shared misery, and there is a surprisingly enormous amount of comfort to be found in collective doom. Imagine the peace to be found in looking around you and seeing how many people also wear the mark of Cain. Those who are also cursed with being human and have also put on a uniform to show they have some kind of plan.

It wasn't just the uniforms that were different. Everybody still looked human. They still looked like people you might meet on the street. These days I sometimes look around at the young men I see going to war. They are taller than they should be, with bigger hands than they should have. The young men with large, ugly ape-like jaws and those that are too tall and spindly. They just don't look quite right, and you can't put your finger on exactly why. It is something to do with the proportion, something wrong.

Those young men were casualties of war before they arrived at the front. Well-meaning parents, too eager to give their child an edge, were the ones to strike the first blow. They were unable to educate their children well enough to make them officers, but they had enough money in their pockets to buy the packs of growth hormones, steroids, drugs, and potions sold by people who don't care how they make their money.

You mess with nature and risk turning them into freaks in the hope that you might buy your child another day, another week, another chance. You know they'll die, of course, but maybe you can help them live just an extra day. Maybe that's what we all want. We all know we have to die. We just don't want to die today.

I often think of an American soldier I stood beside a while ago. Her unit was waiting to be ordered out of its trench to get killed by The Enemy. I didn't have to go with them, of course. Even so, it was a little closer than I like to get these days. I like suicide just fine as a spectator sport. Looking at the warped bodies and distorted faces of humans who had been specially trained not to follow their instincts and run away from danger, it was easy to imagine The Enemy has already won.

Even if we win, which we can't, we'll all be changed. Someone once said, "Choose your enemy carefully, for he is what you will become." Our enemy chose us, but the principle is the same. I was still thinking about that when something happened. As usual, the young men and women were all avoiding each other's faces, all trying not to see how scared their friends were, trying not to be the first to throw up. I looked at each of them, shuddering, mumbling, gripping their uniforms and weapons, trying to suspend thought for just long enough to obey the next order. I could hear shouting down the line of the trench, orders being passed on, and I knew it would be soon. But then music filled the air, and a voice we all recognised came from a stereo less than ten metres away.

As Johnny Cash started singing about how they were going to hang him soon, I watched the youngest soldiers put their hands to their eyes, rubbing tears away. They weren't quick enough and avoided each other's gaze.

He kept singing, counting down his last minutes. I heard something fall to the ground and watched a shaking hand pick it up. Still, the music played, and I could hear some of them begin to laugh through their tears. Hysteria, I think that's what it was. Humans are incredible things. These dead men and women were still human.

Some were laughing, some were crying, and some were still locked in their private world. The song had come too late for them, but for the others, there was a moment here among a dozen soldiers. It was a slightly less private moment and unique to them. Along a front stretching for kilometres, thousands of men and women were crying and shaking. In this small group, a few were laughing.

As the singer pleaded for help that he knew wouldn't come, the soldiers started to look at each other again. Just long enough to nod. They were together. Some had almost forgotten, but now they were ready. Straightening up, ageing by years in seconds, their grips loosened, knuckles no longer white.

The music stopped. Nobody said anything, but the silent trench around me was full of life again. This was humanity. If life were perfect, the order would have come just then.

Life is not perfect.

We waited a few more seconds. I was aware of the soldier beside me. She was young. They were all young, but she looked like she shouldn't be there. It shouldn't make any difference, but she was beautiful. She had emerged from her private world and was talking to herself. Her gaze was focused straight ahead, towards The Enemy. She squeezed her eyes shut and whispered, "Lord, have mercy on me. Have you mercy too. I never did offend you in my life. O, banish me, my Lord, but kill me not. Kill me tomorrow. Let me live tonight. But half an hour. But while I say one prayer."

I wanted to stay in the trench forever. I wanted to observe this forever. In their last moments, The Enemy squeezed beauty out of them against their will. What would die with these soldiers? The same thing that would die with any of us. But I had seen it in them. I haven't seen it in myself yet. I wanted to scream that the attack must stop, to scream that we had to wait, to scream that it wasn't fair. It would do no good. These soldiers would go, and I would see it.

I just wanted to scream. I wish I could say I wanted to go with them, but I didn't. I wanted to see tomorrow. I wanted the half hour. I wanted time for my prayer, even if I didn't use it. The moment ended the same way as the song. In the emptied trench, I watched the spot where she had been. The stereo sat a few metres away, exposed and embarrassed. I used my half hour to leave. I didn't want to see their bodies, and I didn't want to think about them again, although I often do. I left to find something else to write about.

Seeing The Enemy alive is a rare experience. They don't surrender, or at least I have never heard of such a thing. The Enemy don't like us holding prisoners. It's just the type of thing that makes them step outside the game and destroy a few thousand people with a wave of their hand. It's hard to keep anything secret from The Enemy, so it's best just to kill them rather than take them home with you. In any case, I imagine they make terrible pets and companions.

Apparently, Enemy prisoners offer no information, not that we understand their language, anyway. Their soldiers must have one. They certainly make noises, and They appear to organise and interact. They have no supernatural abilities like telepathy, as far as we know. I am told they are uncontrollable when caught, becoming even more dangerous, wild, and hateful.

If they were human, I suppose you would call them psychotic, but then that type of behaviour is generally viewed as abnormal in a human. It is probably unfair to label The Enemy as psychotic just for exhibiting behaviour that is normal for them. I don't know if there is a word for normal behaviour. Not that it matters anyway. Even if they came quietly, and even if we wanted prisoners, it might be difficult to convince our soldiers to keep them alive for long enough.

As I said, it was fairly early on in the war. I had been with some British soldiers in Benin. For the past few days, the unit I was with had been part of the defence of a ridge in front of a town somewhere in the East of the country. We were dug in, and our position was solid. They didn't use artillery, relying on charging our positions under heavy fire. Day after day, They came, and day after day, They were mown down. The Enemy must have lost thousands of soldiers while we lost a few hundred, but They didn't seem to care. They kept coming at us, again and again, charging uphill towards our positions. The Enemy casualties were horrific. We held out for as long as we could.

A river ran through the centre of the town. Some of the men thought The Enemy would stop at the river. They had heard The Enemy didn't like water. The rumour had become a lifeline and was fast becoming something like a religion. Most of the officers weren't convinced. The only thing The Enemy didn't seem to like was us. Eventually, we received word that everyone was being pulled back. If we were coping, then we were the only ones, and as The Enemy pushed forward, we could be cut off. We were running. It wouldn't be the last time.

An officer said I could go with him as he swept the town and made sure everyone knew we were leaving. It was small, maybe a few thousand people, and almost everyone had left already.

On the way there, we asked each other about The Enemy, each hoping the other would supply some information about our mysterious opponents. I had nothing much to tell but promised him I would let him know if I heard anything interesting. Actually, I knew a few things he didn't know but didn't see the point in telling him at the moment.

I had something I chose not to show him. It was a packet of paste or gel that was supposedly Enemy food. I had traded some alcohol for it with one of the soldiers a few days ago. The captain would be interested, but it wouldn't be of much use to him. I would wait until I knew a few more things and had a few more useless artefacts. Then, if the captain was still alive, I would produce them all at once. That would impress him more. I would gain more that way. I would become trusted and reliable. More importantly, I would become useful. Useful gets you into places and lets you skip queues. Useful beats qualified every time. It is only a few steps from indispensable. Useful might get you on the last helicopter out of somewhere you don't want to be.

I have always believed in saving up things and using them all at once. Back home, there was a homeless guy I used to pass on my way to work. Every day people would throw him a few coins. I guess he was grateful enough, but I never threw him a few coins. I gave him nothing. Sometimes, I'd stop and chat to him, tell him I didn't have any money, and tell him how difficult I was finding it to get by. All lies, of course. Then, every two or three weeks,

I would give him a few notes, tell him I'd had a good week or a friend had lent me some money. He thought I was the greatest guy ever. Never mind that I was giving him less than everyone else. It didn't matter. He noticed me. I was on his side. I made a difference to him. It's a tactic I have used throughout my career and has always served me well. Pretend to do the bare minimum for a few months, mention family problems, illness, whatever. Do the work but don't hand it in. Then, one Monday morning, hand in weeks' worth of work which you pretend you've done over the weekend. They think you're a miracle worker or a tortured genius. Meanwhile, all the people working harder than you don't get noticed.

We arrived at what some people might have called a hospital if they were describing it in a report. If they were threatened with admission, they would probably have called it a hall with a doctor and a few nurses. Some of our soldiers were standing outside, more were lying inside, and a large number had already been taken out the back and stacked neatly for disposal.

The captain strode in. He walked straight past the doctor, probably deliberately. He looked around at beds The Enemy had filled with some of his men. "These men will be moved. We're leaving. If any can stand, have them report to my men outside so they can be armed. I'll arrange a place for you and your staff. No need for you to wait until the wounded have left. My men will handle that if you wish."

The doctor was young, probably idealistic. He was white and British with dark, curly hair and glasses. He had probably come here to help ordinary people and ended up in this by accident. The three nurses looked like they were locals. All of them were young, maybe nineteen or twenty. One moved round the beds, behind screens, checking and doing whatever it is nurses do when the doctors don't have enough equipment or time to help anyone. Two of them hovered near the same bed, the patient hidden by screens.

"I can't allow these patients to be moved. None are fit to return to duty. I can't leave them. You'll have to leave without me."

He looked tired. Actually, everybody looked tired, but he looked completely drained. The captain turned and looked at him as if it was the first time he had really noticed he was there. "There can be no discussion. Your objections will be noted. The decision is mine. I take full responsibility."

Sometimes there are things which have to be done. You let people object and do whatever will help them sleep better that night. Once they have taken their stand, you get on with it. That's the way it's meant to go. The military understands that, and I respect them for it. They do what has to be done, and they don't complain. Those in the military kill people that have to be killed, die when they have to die, and make life or death decisions when they need to be made. They'll even let you take the moral high ground, but you have to know when to stop. Otherwise, you get problems. Some people have watched too much television and believe they are the stars of their own movie. This doctor was looking for an Oscar.

"I cannot allow these men to leave. These are no longer your soldiers. They are my patients. I will stay with them. That is final."

I was getting uneasy. There were now two soldiers behind me and more outside. I didn't want to see this young man humiliated. I didn't want to have to ride in a lorry beside him for hours afterwards. He might cry or something, and I would be expected to do something about it. I thought about leaving, but that wouldn't really have helped. Besides, I might have missed something. The captain was about to abandon diplomacy. I had seen it before. You don't tell an officer that the people he has led aren't anything to do with him anymore.

"Doctor, if you wish to check your knowledge of human anatomy, you will have ample chance to do so when The

Enemy arrive and skin these three nurses in front of you. You can have your dramatic little death scene then, but I will not leave these men to be murdered for the sake of your pride. They are leaving, and if they die, they die. Here, they are already dead."

"You are not taking them."

The soldiers moved forward to flank the captain. Two more took their place by the door. It was coming. The captain began to speak more calmly and slowly. "Doctor, you may doubt many things, your own skill, the suitability of your equipment, the chances of these men surviving the night. Take your pick, but do not doubt that these men are leaving. You can come with them or stay here. I am sorry, but events have overtaken us. The Enemy are coming. They cannot be stopped. I have no choice, and neither do you. I would rather you came with us as I have no wish to have you die a horrible death at the hands of these things. Please, let us do this in a civilised manner."

"I can't allow it."

The captain turned to address the soldiers behind him. The doctor wasn't relevant anymore. He never was, really.

"Take the men into the truck, arm any that can use a weapon. Drive as slowly as you can. Leave as soon as you can. The rest of us will withdraw soon after. We'll try to cover the rear. If any of the staff wish to go, then take them."

There were now six soldiers, and they moved forward, brushing past the doctor. I could see that the captain took no pleasure in this. He was a decent man. He had seen The Enemy do terrible things to civilians and his men. Sometimes decency is what keeps you sane. The idea that there is a proper way, a civilised way, to do things.

The captain continued talking to the doctor as the soldiers moved through the hall. He wasn't arguing or shouting, but the doctor was becoming more agitated. Something was wrong. He was asking for more time, asking for us to leave and come back. I suddenly realised that

I had allowed him to distract me. Why were those nurses standing there? They were both at the same patient, not doing anything.

I saw the future and understood, but it was too late. I was helpless. The nurses, the doctor, they were dead. They had died some time ago. I should have left, but it was too late now. My throat went dry as I realised I was going to see everything. I looked at the captain, still calm but tired. I hadn't noticed how tired. The soldiers were also tired. Four of them were very young. The other two were likely about twenty-five, still too young. One of them had a bandage on his arm, and their uniforms were dirty. They weren't heading for the front line. They had already been there and seen action. I saw what was going to happen, but I couldn't do anything. It was too late.

One of the young soldiers moved the nurses away from the cubicle. They clung to him, and I heard the clatter as a screen hit the floor. The nurses looked at the doctor, and he stared back at them. The captain continued calmly talking to the back of the doctor's head. He was having the wrong conversation. The soldier was still stumbling backwards as the captain turned to see what had happened. The doctor was heading for the cubicle. I was thinking I should have seen what was happening sooner. Maybe I could have stopped it. It was nonsense, of course. These people were already dead. That was their choice. They had made it long before I arrived.

The soldier had backed into the wall. He fumbled for something on his belt. I saw his face turn as white as the doctor's coat. One of the other soldiers had seen into the cubicle and stood looking from it to the captain and back again. The doctor threw himself across the bed, but we could all see it, and time stopped.

The doctor scrambled round to face the soldier who had paused with his hand on his belt. He held his hand up towards him, hoping to stop whatever was going to happen next. "She was wounded. It's a female. Some of the locals found her in the woods yesterday. I brought her in here."

It is hard sometimes not to marvel at the power and potency of human stupidity. An idea enters your head and then, if not dealt with quickly, spreads and strengthens until it can't be removed. The ability of people to convince themselves to do incredibly stupid things just astounds me. The different forms of this are so numerous that they have their own names: denial, delusion, obsession. There is only one name, really. Stupidity. Some people think love is the most powerful force in the universe, but I know it's actually raw stupidity. It's like a drug, and the doctor had overdosed. Sometime yesterday, the idea had flashed through his mind that this might be the right thing to do, as it might have flashed through all of our minds. He had indulged the thought. The buzz of self-righteousness it had given him had made him a junkie.

It was so badly wounded it was hard to imagine what he thought he could have done for it, anyway. I don't know how close their physiology is to ours, but if it is anywhere near similar, it was a miracle it had lasted so long. It looked like four or five bullets had almost cut it in half. The wounds were stitched now, but it must have lost a large amount of blood. The sheets of the bed were scarlet. Its breathing was laboured, and it was looking round slowly, its eyes half closed. I don't think it was really conscious. It looked slightly smaller than the ones you usually see. Maybe that was why he thought it was a female. Maybe it was. Then again, maybe he was just insane.

The captain looked shocked. The world didn't make sense anymore. "Kill it."

The doctor wasn't helping matters. He was becoming more agitated. "You can't shoot it dead. It's defenceless."

I knew he was wrong. There would be no shooting for two reasons. First, despite what you might think, probably based on what you see on television, a gunshot is one of the loudest sounds you are ever likely to hear. In an enclosed space, it is pretty deafening. The soldiers knew that wasn't necessary. The second reason is more important. Hate. There is something more personal about using a knife, something more primal. This thing was hated, and it was helpless. It would not be killed from a distance.

The soldier stepped forward, knife in hand. I felt myself relax and guiltily realised I was relieved. My body remained tensed, just in case I was wrong and there was a gunshot. I silently willed the doctor to get out of the way, but I knew he wouldn't. He put a hand on the soldier and was thrown to the floor. A nurse moved forward and was swatted away with the hand holding the knife. There was blood and screaming. Another nurse was pushed to the floor, and the third was held round the waist by another soldier.

Kill it. Kill it quickly. The knife flicked across its abdomen, opening its wounds again. It hissed, and the soldier wrapped his hand round its throat, holding the knife in its face. He wanted to make sure it understood. As the doctor stood up again, he put his hand on the soldier's arm. The soldier spun round and slammed into him. I heard the noise as the knife jammed into the wall. I heard the noise as it passed through the doctor first, pinning him there like a butterfly. There was more screaming, flailing, desperate struggling, pushing, and shouting.

I was not looking at the captain, and I knew he was not looking at me, but I knew the look that would be on his face. I saw it when we went into a village The Enemy had visited before us. The way he'd looked at the bodies of the locals, carved and mutilated.

You look at them calmly, like they're something to be endured, a dirty job that someone has to do. I look at them that way, too. Every time I see something so bad, I know I won't be able to show anyone. I see what the public doesn't. They don't need to see the worst. We don't want to show them the worst. They don't need to see the bodies of children bayoneted out of their mother's womb. I have to, but it is irrelevant to the job I have to do. I can see it properly as something that must be endured.

Some people say that time slows down when that kind of thing happens. You remember things taking longer than they should have, thinking about decisions for far longer than should have been possible. I don't think time slows down. I just think you are much more interested in events than usual. Your mind stops to take everything in, every horrible detail.

The way that nurse was holding the soldier's boot. The spit flying out of the soldier's mouth as he screamed at the doctor. All of it was stored away.

I think your mind's interest in it all verges on obsession, and that's what makes it so hard to forget. Your mind keeps going on and on about it like a child, obsessed with the most exciting parts of the film it's just seen. It's not interested in context or background, only in the depth of the horror and the violence of the deaths.

I stayed and watched it all. It wasn't easy. In addition to the obvious horror, you also have the discomfort. You might think there is some kind of dignity about people fighting for their lives, but you'd be wrong. It's loud and chaotic. There's a lot of shouting and, eventually, begging or cursing. People rarely die with quiet dignity. They squeal and cry, pushing ineffectually at people with knives who are much bigger than them. Their hands become slick with their own blood, slipping and sliding. They usually don't have thoughtful, whispered last words or witty comebacks. People scream for their mothers, or more commonly in my experience, they scream for it to stop; they scream to be spared; they scream to live for just half an hour more. They look down at their body with panic in their eyes, and you see them calculating whether they will survive if it stops now. That's what upsets me. Grown men and women broken, bleeding, and crying for mercy you know they won't get.

I knew it wouldn't be stopped. After the doctor was gone, the nurses didn't last long. It was quick, and I was grateful they only killed them. Maybe that's because I was there. Maybe I should have been flattered.

Emma once told me that the murder of female civilians in war was an assertion of male dominance and a reaction against the presence of females and their intrusion into what is perceived to be a male activity. She says things like that a lot. Maybe she's right. I should probably listen to her more but, to be fair to me, her being right doesn't make her any less annoying. Maybe I should find out if she has a diary. Then I could just flick past the long, boring lectures and read the important stuff. It's a shame you can't do that with real people.

Anyway, these women weren't civilians. They stopped being civilians when they decided to bandage up the boogeyman in cubicle three. You can't have it both ways, not anymore. You don't get to indulge your conscience and then still pretend you're on the right side. People used to be able to do it, and maybe back home, they still can. They could bore me at dinner parties, talking about the barbarity of locking up criminals while hoping none of them moved in next door. They could go on and on about all the poor people in the world and then feed me a meal that cost more than three goats and a well. Not here. Not anymore. You help The Enemy; you are The Enemy. You choose. It's like those bands of idiots that turned against their own kind and tried to join the winning side, trying to buy their own extra half hour. Much good it did them. They were killed like everyone else. I didn't really blame the nurses. I suppose I might have done the same, but if I had, I would have known what to expect.

The room was quiet afterwards. It had all been fast, although it didn't seem that way. The doctor's body was allowed to drop to the floor. I was pleased by that. It didn't look right, hanging there like that. It didn't look right at all.

There was blood everywhere. Amazing how far half a dozen pints of liquid go. I had seen it before. When you spill a pint of beer, there's always more than you expect. I had seen it but never really thought about it or noticed it. Just when it was blood, it was much more obvious.

The thing in the bed wheezed and coughed. It never spoke. It didn't beg, didn't look concerned. Maybe it was confident it was going to heaven. They made it scream.

They know how to make them scream but not how to make them talk.

As it screamed, I wondered how many people who stood in that room would ever get to heaven. I wondered if I would.

It died quickly. They moved the men out of the hospital and burned it. As I left, I passed the captain. He didn't avoid me. I stood long enough for him to speak if he wanted to but not long enough to annoy him. He stared through me while he spoke.

"My men are talking about eating them. The Enemy. Rations are short, but I don't know if I should let them. I don't know if it's cannibalism. I think it is, but can I ask them to starve? I wondered what you thought. You get so isolated here. You don't know what other people are doing."

I looked him straight in the eye and put a hand firmly on his shoulder. "From what I hear, you wouldn't be the first. I think it would be strange if you said they could do it. Why not just let it happen? Don't make a huge effort to stop it. That often doesn't achieve anything. Things are happening all over that haven't happened before. Things that would have been unforgivable anywhere else. I think people will understand."

Now he looked at me. "Do you?"

"I'm sure of it. Just keep focused on what's important."

"Of course."

I have no idea what's important, of course, but I find that if you tell people that, they usually have a pretty good idea of what they think you mean. He was calmed. I congratulated myself on my usefulness. Coincidentally, one of the useless pieces of information I had been saving up for him was that The Enemy apparently tasted a bit like beef. I was going to make him laugh with that at some point. Not much chance of that now. Never mind, I would tell him about it on the next trip, anyway. I felt confident that I would be on the next trip with him now, what with me being so useful and understanding. That's if he wasn't dead by then, of course. God knows he deserved it, the murdering bastard.

15

The hotel looked very different at night. If you concentrated, you could see it was the same quiet place where the ghosts had been hiding during the day. The same carpet. The same tables and chairs. Tomorrow it would be quiet again. Tomorrow it would be forgotten. They would be quiet, embarrassed. This same place, chaotic and hellish at night, would give them somewhere to hide during daylight if they couldn't hide in sleep. In sleep, you never knew what might find you. Everything would be bright. This would all be over. Michael had watched many times as the soldiers drank and shouted, before becoming angry and sad. The bar's calm twin would comfort them tomorrow. Then they would do it all over again at night.

Through the technicolour darkness, Michael saw them drinking. Young men, not in uniform but betrayed by their cheap and simple haircuts. They were soldiers, but Uncle Joe said they were called infantry because they were baby soldiers. It was not a description they would have recognised. Released from their towns and villages, from their families, they believed they were men. They assumed they had made it, that they were accepted. They would have been surprised to hear the colonel laughing at them with Uncle Joe. It was nothing personal. They were just younger than they thought, even the old ones. The infantry would probably have been secretly hurt if they knew what Uncle Joe and the colonel thought of them. Ironically, that was probably why they were laughed at, because it wasn't really about age. Nobody laughed at the ghosts, even the young ones.

It was almost eleven. The infantry were almost all drunk. They had been desperately swallowing glasses of happiness for the past three hours and were almost full. Soon the arguments would start, but for the moment, they had never been happier. Michael felt pity and contempt. Uncle Joe often talked about alcohol. He made it very clear that it was a drug. That wasn't necessarily a bad thing. After all, aspirin was a drug. He said alcohol was a good friend but also a liar, full of false promises. Euphoria, confusion, incompetence, Michael knew the three stages. When the euphoria passed, nothing would bring it back, and nothing good lay after the first few drinks. If you weren't careful, you would soon find that the only thing worse than the friend's tiresome company was his painful absence.

Confusion would come soon, but not quite yet. As Michael scurried across the floor between the packs of drunks, he could hear that everything was funny. Every story was worth telling. Everything was bumped into and knocked over, but apologies splashed around as freely as the alcohol. What a good idea all of this had been.

The ghosts were almost invisible. If nobody wants to see you, it's easy to be invisible. Coloured lights swept across the dark floor, but never seemed to find them. Music played, modern music, music that bound the packs together. One of Michael's jobs was to help Uncle Joe choose the music for the jukebox. They didn't have to change them too often because the infantry changed often enough.

Sometimes drunken soldiers would capture him on his way across the floor, thrust coins into his hand, and watch him pick it again with their money while they slapped his back and whooped agreement. Sometimes that was a hilarious, original idea. Often it was an original idea to give him some alcohol instead. He took it, knowing Uncle Joe wouldn't have been angry. It was necessary. Just as it was necessary that Cathy laughed and joked with the boys at the bar. It wasn't fair, and it wasn't nice, but it was necessary.

Although he helped Uncle Joe choose, his knowledge was an accident of his age. Uncle Joe's was something far more impressive, something far deeper. Michael picked music. Uncle

Joe picked songs. It was the difference between a worker and a craftsman.

Uncle Joe had explained how the infantry were like chimps at a dinner party. They weren't capable of understanding how to behave or why everyone was not throwing things and behaving badly. They assumed nobody else had thought of it and did whatever they could to show how original they were, desperately believing they were being innovative. Even when everyone else continued to behave well, refusing to look at them, they assumed it was because no one else could approach their level of creativity. Uncle Joe always said that the skill was not in seeing that everything was a game. It was in winning the game. The tragedy was that we were all the chimps at one time in our lives before we underwent our own individual, personal evolution. Some never evolved beyond, or even into, chimps. Some managed to evolve into humans. Michael imagined that some evolved further and became Uncle Joe.

At the jukebox, a chimp was about to be innovative. Maybe a clever chimp who thought he was being ironic, jumping out of the game, maybe a stupid one who just thought it was doing something funny. Whatever the reason, a coin went into the jukebox and chose a song that had already been chosen by Uncle Joe long ago. The coin wasn't worth much, but the song was intended to collect more than just one coin. It would help put many more behind the bar.

The song began as quiet confusion, which transformed into a ripple of victorious whoops and calls across the bar. Arms thrust into the air, sloshing beer out of full glasses onto the heads of other chimps who appreciated the hilarity and inevitability of getting wet in such a situation. Apologies were unnecessary, and the fun of the occasion made them impossible. The packs of animals became one for a moment, not sharing a joke, but a sentiment, which was worth far more. The song was shouted as a battle cry, a philosophy, and a call of defiance by the swaying crowd. David Bowie calmly explained about the Starman. The jukebox suddenly increased to deafening volume, even before the boys at the bar began demanding that Cathy turn the music up. Fists punched the air as voices shouted about the Starman, who was afraid to visit them in case he damaged their minds. He should have been told not to worry. Watery beer flowed into and out of the mouths of swaying boys who were clearly full already. Voices shouted guitar noises in time with the music. Michael felt a shiver, as he always did. He knew the boys would meet the Starman soon enough.

The room was alive. Uncle Joe had done this. Every week it was the same. Each week, someone would find it on the jukebox. Each week, they would congratulate themselves on their originality and accidentally worship Uncle Joe's genius by putting more money behind the bar.

There was no trouble. People didn't fight when they were singing and had their arms around each other. Michael thought they might also sleep easier when they had good memories in their heads.

The infantry caught on quickly. Michael heard "Starman" twice more that night, with diminishing effect each time, along with "Calling Occupants of Interplanetary Craft", "Spirit in the Sky", and a few more of decreasing relevance and power. "Sympathy for the Devil" was probably a little too subtle. Some of the songs from a long time ago were probably a little too contentious. Michael knew some of these songs were from an older, smaller war called the Vietnam War. Some of them seemed to confuse some of the chimps, torn between patriotism and genuine frustration, unsure whether irony was enough to bridge the gap. "War" by Edwin Starr seemed a little too anti-war and made some of the infantry uncomfortable. Michael made a mental note to tell Uncle Joe. Michael thought of finding out who Johnny Cash was and getting the song from The Book for the jukebox but decided against it. It wasn't the right idea.

By two o'clock, the infantry had made their way to bed. The ghosts had returned to the top floor long ago. Michael helped to clear up the space where the soldiers had been. His job was easy. It just involved moving glasses from one place to another. Cathy and Janet would deal with the rest. He had helped so many times. Everything was always the same. Everyone else was asleep, leaving Michael and Cathy to look after everything until they were ready to take up their places again. Michael felt like they were the only people awake in the whole world. Everything would restart in a few hours. Until then, the world was paused, and he was the only boy able to walk around in it. Except tonight, someone else was awake. The doorbell intruded into their world. The noise raced out of the hall, bursting through the empty bar. He wondered who would be calling at this time? The doorbell didn't usually ring this late. It was frightening. He was not alone in the world with Cathy. Who else was walking around tonight? Cathy didn't seem shocked. She shrugged and nodded towards the source of the noise.

Michael walked, quickly moving out of her sight. Then he paused. Who was behind the door? A vengeful soldier, still wearing the same bloody clothes as when he was carried out? A member of the infantry, drunk and lost? He imagined police behind the door. Then he imagined the real police, not jolly and friendly, but the Civil Defence. Michael didn't think they knocked on people's doors in the middle of the night anymore. He could only dimly remember a time when they had done so. Anyway, there were no bad people anymore, at least not in Portpatrick, unless he was one. Maybe they had come out of retirement for him. He flattened himself against the wall and crept out into the corridor. He imagined one of The Enemy standing on the doorstep, tapping a claw against the doorbell, snorting steam against the window. Thousands of them behind it, come to stay, come to take over. Maybe it would have Kenny by the scruff of the neck, bringing him home, complaining that they had already killed him once and that they wouldn't be palmed off with the leftovers.

He could see a shape through the frosted glass of the door. It moved slowly, and he couldn't tell anything from its shimmering outline. The doorbell screamed at him again. It wanted him. It was coming for him, and it wanted all the letters back, wanted to shout at him, ask why he had done all the things he had done. He hadn't meant to. He had meant to try his best. Maybe that was what all bad people thought. Perhaps there was no such thing as bad people, and everyone tried their best. Maybe he was a bad person. He struggled to remember when everything had gone so wrong. Still, the figure waited, shifting. He would beg for forgiveness. They would realise he was really a good person who had just made mistakes. Maybe they were coming to take him to war, even though he was only fourteen. Maybe the law had changed, and he was old enough.

The third time the doorbell shrieked, Cathy shouted to ask if he was getting the door. She used his name. Now it knew he was here. He walked towards the door and touched the glass. He spoke to the thing. "Hello?"

"I need to come in." It sounded tired. It wasn't The Enemy because They didn't speak. Not the police. They told you who they were. Now that he thought about it, probably not the Civil Defence either, if they still existed, as they probably didn't ring the doorbell. They probably smashed through the glass while swinging on a rope.

Only a ghost sounded that tired. It must have been brought during the night for some special reason. Maybe it had hitched a lift. It didn't make sense. When were ghosts ever in a hurry to get anywhere? Why was nobody with it?

"I need to come in. Please. Let me in." It wasn't angry. It was tired, sad, and desperate. Not a proper ghost. It still cared about something. It wanted inside. A real ghost wouldn't really care. Maybe it wanted a drink. Maybe. He jumped back as it put its hands on the glass. He heard it sink to the ground, falling to its knees. "Please. I need to come in."

A thought flashed through his head. Maybe he could save this one. He could let it in while it still cared and turn it back into a normal person again. Uncle Joe would be able to help him.

It rose off the ground as he unlocked the door. It might have picked up a bag.

There were only two other people in the whole world: Cathy and this stranger. The door swung open. He was unshaven, tired, and old. It seemed like it should have been raining, but it wasn't. He turned away to fetch the guest book. "There are still rooms on the top floor. Do you have your stationing-book?"

A bag dropped in the hall.

"If you don't have it, I can call the base for a new one in the morning. Have you stayed here before?"

It just looked at him, too tired to explain. It knew it didn't have to.

A glass smashed in the bar as Cathy heard the boy screaming her name. Chairs joined it on the floor as she ran past them. Only the sight of the two stopped her. It held the boy in one arm. She could hear his tears. The thing cried silently.

Its eyes closed and squeezed tears onto the boy's head. "Yes, I've stayed here before. It was a long time ago."

Somewhere at the top of the stairs, another older figure might have been standing and watching with tearless eyes. After a few seconds, it was gone, if it was ever there. Michael didn't notice it. It didn't matter if it was there because it knew it was not required. It would return when it was needed.

Upstairs, the rest of the world slept while a boy and his father held each other.

16

Usually, breakfast was not much of an event. Michael was usually sorting out the mail by the time Uncle Joe was at breakfast. It was unusual to see Uncle Joe buttering his toast, unusual to see his mother sitting beside him. Most of all, it was unusual to see the empty chair waiting, silent and indifferent, with a place set in front of it. Michael had moved his chair so that he could sit at the head of the table, closer to the empty chair.

Michael would sort out the mail later. The bad-news machine could wait. He thought it strange that he had waited for so long, and now the last few minutes were the most difficult. No one spoke. The adults tried to act as if everything was normal, which was strange as normally, people spoke to each other. The silence pressed down on him, and the effort of consciously acting out everyday activities was unbearable. Never had toast been buttered so casually or orange juice drunk so unthinkingly. Never had a part of the wall been selected so randomly so it could be stared at. Yesterday's newspaper sat on the table in front of Uncle Joe. Its edges curled up apologetically, covering up yesterday's news. Uncle Joe's hand hovered near it, defending it from the new day. It may yet be of use.

Michael stared at the glass of water in front of him. He hadn't really wanted it, and he looked enviously at the others' orange juice, which he had refused. He had chosen the water because it would tell him more. It had flowed easily out of the tap, answering a question he couldn't have asked his mother. His father was already out of the shower.

"Do I have to help in the bar today?"

The question drifted past his uncle and settled on his mother. Her eyes didn't move from the part of the wall they had no obvious reason to be looking at. "I don't think Cathy will be very busy today. We'll see."

He felt guilty for being happy, guilty that he didn't want to be quiet or behave normally. Why was nobody happy? Why did they have to play this game? He was back. It could all stop. Why hadn't they noticed? Why did he have to sit and eat toast when his father was in the next room?

Uncle Joe coughed accidentally, an admission that he existed. It left him open to questions. "Do you think it will be busy today, Uncle Joe? Do you think I'll have to help in the bar?"

The silence intensified. It grew until he could hear the orange juice squeezing between Uncle Joe's teeth as he swallowed, warping time inside the room until it crawled past twice as slowly as normal. Time squeezed into the heads of everybody in the room and clouded their brains until the simplest question required intense concentration and careful consideration. The air in the room grew thick and heavy, so even breathing required effort. The strange new environment changed you and made you adapt until you were scared to go back to normality. You were scared to break the silence, just in case you couldn't survive without it.

A second might have passed. Outside, the sea crashed against the rocks, grinding them into sand. Thousands of miles away, heroes were created, careers made and destroyed. Michael wondered if it was possible that Uncle Joe just wouldn't answer, pretend he hadn't heard the question clattering across the table. He imagined the silence increasing until the windows exploded outwards. He imagined Uncle Joe ignoring that as well, the silence booming across the sea and expanding into the sky.

Uncle Joe placed one hand on the table for support. He used the other to place his orange juice in his field of vision so he could have something to look at without moving his eyes. He steeled himself and broke the surface. "We'll see."

Michael wondered if the whole day would be like this, if it would last for months and months. Would he go to bed a tired old man, drained by the effort of staying awake for the equivalent of a whole year?

One day, he would learn not to talk to people who did not want to be talked to. One day, when he was an adult. But he was not an adult, and the day was not today.

There was a noise from outside the room. He was coming. He was back. The chair would be filled. The door opened. Uncle Joe was the only one who didn't look up. This time, Michael recognised his father. He was clean-shaven and tall. He wasn't wearing his dog collar, not to breakfast.

He sat down in the seat that had waited for him for so long. He smiled at Michael and looked around the table. "Good morning."

As Michael's mother stood up to get breakfast for her husband, Uncle Joe looked up for the first time. He spoke slowly, like it was too nice a job to rush. "Oh my goodness, it's the ghost of breakfast past." Nobody smiled, not even Uncle Joe. "James. What brings you here? Come to take our last confession?"

If there was a challenge, Michael's father did not seem to have noticed it. "No. I'm a protestant, as you know, Joseph."

"Of course, I was forgetting." Uncle Joe leaned back in his chair.

Michael saw a chance to be helpful. "Dad's staying for three days. He has leave. It took him ages to get here."

"Well, you'll be welcome here, James. If you need to know where anything is, be sure and ask."

"Thank you, Joseph. I think I'll manage."

"The boy here has missed you. Still, he knows you're busy over there. How are things? Those Christian soldiers still marching onward as to war?"

"Oh yes. And the Muslims and the Hindus… and all the rest."

"Much work to be done, I imagine, what with you only worshipping the one God. We all have to be flexible these days, of course. Maybe easier to start with a blank canvas. I suppose some of those foxholes must still have atheists in them."

"Some of them. Less than there used to be in my experience."

"Well, at least war is good for business."

"You could say that. I'm sure you say it often." There was no anger in his voice, but there was a force that was not lost on Michael.

A pause. Michael was suddenly conscious that he was sitting at his father's right hand. He seemed unconcerned by Uncle Joe. It was unusual to see anyone act like this with Uncle Joe. He decided to change the subject. "The news said there are a lot of Indian soldiers where you were. The news said there are millions of them and that they're winning."

"They are very brave," James said, the same force in his voice. He was still staring at Uncle Joe. That was accidental, and he quickly corrected himself. He turned to Michael and put his hand on his shoulder. "Yes, there are a lot of them. They are good soldiers."

Uncle Joe was not finished. "The boy follows the news, knows everything about what's going on. Well, as much as anyone. We're training him to be an officer."

"An officer?" James forced a smile, his eyes still on Michael and his hand on his shoulder.

"Oh yes, he'll have to work hard, though. It doesn't come easy to him. With my help, he'll be fine. I imagine you know plenty of officers, the circles you move in."

The hand grew tighter on Michael's shoulder. "Are you sure you want to be an officer?"

"I think so. I thought about being a journalist maybe, but I don't know much about it."

His father turned to Uncle Joe again. "A journalist? Surely that's a possibility? He doesn't have to be an officer."

"Back here, our lives are all *have to*. The boy wants to do his bit. We all have to do what we can. Isn't that what you tell them, James? I bet you tell them that when they come to you."

His father was shaken now. Michael had to change the subject again. "Neckerman is going to be on the television later.

Everyone's going to be watching. We could watch it downstairs with the men."

"Downstairs? With the young soldiers? You often do that?" The hand on his shoulder tightened so much it couldn't be left there and recoiled instead.

Across the table, Uncle Joe fixed his gaze on James and put his hand on Michael's other shoulder. "Of course. Michael knows them all. He's like a lucky charm for them. Not just the young ones, either. Some of the ones who come back have taken to him as well. You forget we get the whole before and after here. I don't know what I'd do without him. You never know. He could be running this place one day."

Michael's mother placed breakfast in front of James and sat down beside him. She edged her chair slightly closer to him, but Michael couldn't tell if it was to show support, to gain protection, or to offer sympathy. She didn't, couldn't, look at either of the men.

Michael had to say something. "General Neckerman is going to explain how the war is going. He's going to answer questions and explain what The Enemy are doing."

Uncle Joe was unstoppable. "Reminds me of that old joke about the most dangerous thing in the world being a general with a map."

"An officer. An officer with a map, Joseph! That's the joke. It's an officer with a map! The most dangerous creature in the world is an officer with a map!" His hand struck the table, making the plates and cups jump.

"I thought it was a general. Makes more sense to me that way. Generals are most important. They have the most power, don't they?"

"I don't know. There are some colonels who don't seem to do too badly." He spat the words at Uncle Joe but did not see his anger reflected in the old man.

"We'll all watch Neckerman later. It should be interesting. For now, I have work to do." The old man lifted himself up. "There's something you could help me with, actually. The

Hutchisons lost their son a few days ago. They might appreciate a visit. I know how well you used to know Robert and Sarah."

"Which son?"

"Nicholas. They lost Thomas last year. I went to see them then. I'm sure they would rather see you."

"I'll go later."

"Well, don't trouble yourself. I can always go and see them later in the week after you're gone. And don't worry about the boy. If he becomes an ordinary soldier or a journalist or whatever, he will be working as soon as he leaves school. It takes at least a year to train an officer. That's a long time these days. I'll be here to make sure nothing happens that can be avoided."

He placed the newspaper in front of Michael. "We need a new newspaper. The boy didn't drop one off this morning, and I'm too busy to go into town today. Maybe you could go and get one. Take your father when he finishes his breakfast. Maybe you should show him round the town. There have been a few changes since he was last here. It should do you both good. I find a walk along the beach to be very relaxing. I'll make sure Cathy doesn't need you in the bar later. The boy missed you, James."

"I missed him."

As the old man left, Michael thought about all of the things he would show his father. He knew the newspaper didn't really matter. While he was getting his breakfast, he had seen that day's newspaper in the bin, just where Uncle Joe had put it. Uncle Joe had probably meant for him to see it. He liked people to understand, but he hated explaining things.

17

Michael hated waiting. It seemed like most of life was waiting. Waiting for people to come home. Waiting for the bus to school. Waiting for it to arrive at school. Waiting for the bell to ring. Waiting for the day to be over, waiting for the bus home. Waiting until it arrived back in Portpatrick. Waiting for dinner. Waiting until it was time to go to bed. Waiting to grow up. Waiting for whatever happened then.

Back at the hotel, others waited. A woman waited for her husband. After waiting for so long, he had finally returned, and now she was left waiting again. Life was all waiting. In the hotel, someone else waited patiently, but for what? Whatever they were required to do next. Whatever had to be done.

Michael picked up a pebble from the beach. How many thousands of years had passed before it was its turn to wash onto the beach? How many millennia had it waited? It was worn smooth, polished by the water atom by atom for a million years. He wondered what happened to all the atoms that were chipped away. Where did they go?

He knew you didn't have to wait for a million years to polish the rocks. You could cheat and polish the rocks in a machine. One of the older boys at school had one. Michael didn't know him very well. He had given a talk on rocks once. If you weren't patient enough at the start and didn't wait properly, the rocks got scratched and never polished properly. Once Michael had seen the boy cry at a school memorial service. Probably his brother or sister had fallen. They were not polished properly, all scratched and broken, rejected by the bad-news machine.

He threw the helpless stone back into the water. Let it start again.

His father should be finished by now. The Hutchisons wouldn't keep him long. It seemed to Michael that there wasn't really much his father could do. The important thing was that he was there and making the effort. The Hutchisons had finished waiting for the moment. They had no more children left. What would they wait for now?

The trick to waiting was to think, not to watch. If you scanned the horizon all the time, it took much longer. Better to think and not notice the time passing. Over at the hotel, Michael could see some of the young soldiers sitting on the grass, talking and waiting. Behind the windows, the ghosts were waiting for the bar to open, waiting to feel better. You were only in real trouble when you didn't know how to wait anymore. When you didn't know how to let time pass or how to make it through the next minute, that was when you got problems. That was when you had to deal with things.

If you didn't accept there was a time in the future when it could be done, you had to deal with the bad memories in the present. It was better to step back and let time pass. You didn't want to step out in front of it. You didn't want a fight with time. It has been around longer than you and could turn the past into the present. It could make sure the future was just like the present. The ghosts that managed to cope turned the present into one long moment, with no future, no past. They waited in the present, treading water in order to stop themselves from sinking. If you did it long enough, you could probably live out your whole life and die peacefully without time noticing.

Seagulls circled the hotel, gliding round in circles as if beating their wings was too much effort. The soldiers didn't notice them any more than they noticed the worms and beetles in the grass around them. On the top floor, the ghosts probably heard them tap-dancing on the roof, running around, fighting over parts of something that never really belonged to them in the first place.

He often thought about the birds, wondering how much they understood, how much made sense, how much they cared. He wondered if their lives were simple or complicated, if they were happy or if their lives were "nasty, brutish, and short" as he suspected. At school, they studied a lot of philosophy, and they'd learned that this was what happened in nature when everyone did whatever they wanted. A man called Hobbes had said it, but Michael didn't remember who he was. Older people were always surprised, and probably a little impressed and intimidated, by how much children were taught to think about big questions, big responsibilities, and the way things worked.

"What are you thinking about?"

The voice came from above and behind him.

"Nothing, just waiting for you."

"I got here as soon as I could. I was longer than I thought at the Hutchisons'. They appreciated the visit. Do you know they don't even send someone round with the news anymore? They just send a letter."

Michael's father looked out across the sea as if he expected it to provide an explanation. The sea just shrugged and continued polishing the rocks.

"They've been doing that for years. It's a machine that does it. I think you can send off for more information if you want. Sometimes the machine doesn't send everything…" Michael's voice trailed off. His father seemed to be somewhere else. He'd been away for so many years, and now that he was back, he was still somewhere else.

Michael had to try to make him come back. "Neckerman will be on soon. Everyone will be watching."

"Not everyone." James's gaze fell on something between the rocks. As he picked it up, Michael saw it was red. He knew what it was. It was faded. Once, it had been a deep burgundy, but now it was a tired, washed-out scarlet.

Michael tried to move into his father's gaze as his mind wandered further away, but he couldn't compete with the object. "It's a stationing-book."

"I can't read the name."

His dad seemed worried. It was difficult to see why. It was difficult to know what to say. "Someone probably just dropped it walking across the beach." No response. "It might not even be one of the soldiers from here. Maybe someone dropped it on a ship, and it washed up here."

"Maybe."

His father didn't seem comforted. Michael tried to think of something else to say as his father continued to drift away. "They will just have asked for a replacement. You can get another one at the post office."

Michael couldn't understand where this padre was going. He was pushing him away. He felt panic and desperation. Michael had to bring him back but couldn't think of anything different to say. He wanted to shout and almost did. "It won't have mattered! You can get another one. Nobody minds!"

The man standing in front of Michael began to disappear over the horizon. He squeezed the object in his fist. A surprising amount of water ran out of it before hitting the beach and running off to rejoin the sea. His fist opened again to reveal a red ball. The man looked at it for a moment before his arm snapped out, launching the remains of the book out to sea.

It arced into the air for what seemed like an eternity, farther and farther from the beach. It spun out above the waves trudging in towards the shore, sailing over them in the wrong direction. When it finally hit them, they didn't even notice. They would bring it back when they were ready.

It was hard to know what to say. Michael was scared that if he tried to start a conversation, he would push this man further away. Maybe he could only keep him close if they didn't speak.

It was unfair, like everything was unfair. He had so little time and so many questions. He had waited so long, and now he was going to be cheated out of his time with his father. It wasn't fair. Nobody else ever told him anything. This was his only chance. He was entitled. His dad would have to come back. He would make him.

"Dad."

The man looked at him, recognition passing across the padre's face. Michael saw his father smile. Then, finally, his dad spoke.

"Sorry, I was miles away. I'm probably just tired. It's probably all a bit much, seeing your mother and Uncle Joe after all this time and then being at the Hutchisons' this morning. Maybe we should get back to the hotel."

Michael knew he should be appreciative of the smiles, small talk, and brave faces. Instead, he felt cheated.

"Dad, Uncle Joe doesn't talk to me very much about what's happening."

There was a pause. This was not how things were meant to go.

Michael spoke to the ground between them as his father settled down on the nearest rock. "I don't really have anyone to talk to."

There was another pause, both staring at the same spot.

"Mum doesn't talk much now that you're not here."

"You know I would be here if I could, Michael. It's just that we all have to—"

"I know. I understand. I understand all of that. But it's still true. She's been waiting for you."

His dad sighed and nodded. He stared without saying anything, just waiting.

"Dad, what's happening?"

"What do you mean? I'll be back for a few days. Then I have to go—"

"Home. You'll be home for a few days."

"That's what I said. I'll be home for a few days."

"What's really happening? Everywhere. What's really going on?"

James paused before saying, "What do you mean? You know what's going on."

"I know we're not meant to talk about it. There are things I've seen. Things I've read."

How could he make his father understand? How could you make someone be honest with you if you couldn't be honest with them?

"Maybe you shouldn't pay so much attention to the newspapers…"

"Not the newspapers. I read other things. I see other things, and I know what it's like—"

"I hope you don't. I hope you never do. You shouldn't have to. Not yet. There will be time enough for that. You should forget about all that just now. You don't have to think about it. Just enjoy your life for now and worry about the other things later."

"What do you think it's like here? There are soldiers everywhere. I go to memorials all the time."

"Well, Uncle Joe shouldn't take you. You're too young."

"Not just with Uncle Joe, with the school, for my friends' fathers and brothers. The war is here too. It's here every day."

"No, it's not. It's not here. Whatever you think the war is, this isn't it. You don't need to know what it's really like. That's why nobody talks about it. Not to you, not to each other. It's better to keep it over there. If you knew what went on, I don't know if you could… I don't know if you would… see why things are done the way they are… you…"

"Wouldn't understand?"

"Maybe. I don't mean it like that. You shouldn't have to understand or make those choices, those judgements. You shouldn't have to think about it. I deal with it… we deal with it, so you don't have to. We keep it over there, so everything stays normal here. To give you the time that we had."

"But I know what goes on. I know all of it. I know all about Chen and Neckerman and the *Spiegeloorlog*. I know about the letters that are sent back. I know what happened on the day everything started, and I know what's happening now. I know all the different uniforms and the different weapons and the Unified Command and the First Respite and The Enemy and how they fight and how they die and what they do to people and what we do to them. I've sat in a helicopter, rode in a truck, and seen soldiers train and drink. They've shown me their guns and everything. I know more than anyone."

His father sat with his head in his hands. He wasn't far away now. He was right beside Michael. Michael had brought him back, but he hadn't had what he was entitled to yet.

His father slowly shook his head. "You should never have been allowed to stay here. They said they'd look after you. They said this wouldn't happen."

"Why did you shout at Uncle Joe before?"

"None of this was meant to happen. We should have found another way. I shouldn't have allowed this."

"What do you mean?"

For the first time, he looked straight at Michael. "How much do you know about your Uncle Joe?"

"He looks after us, all of us, everyone."

"But he looks after you most of all, doesn't he? He'd do anything for you. You know what I mean, don't you? Has something already happened?"

Michael couldn't meet his father's gaze. He thought of a ghost lying broken on the floor. "He looks after us, makes sure all the soldiers are okay."

"I'm sure he does. Now, whatever has happened doesn't matter. That would have been him, not you, and it wouldn't have been the first time. I will tell you something about Uncle Joe. This man cares about you, probably cares about all of us more than we can understand, in a way we can't understand, and that is why you have to be careful around him. You must never ask this man for anything or tell him you want anything. Do you understand?"

"Not really."

"I think you do. He will do anything for you. I don't know exactly how deep that runs, and I don't want to. Someone who offends you, someone who bullies you, or a girl at school you like. You must be very careful what you tell him. I know you understand."

"I suppose."

"And you must never, ever betray him. Fail him, disappoint him, anger him, but never have him believe that you have turned against him."

"I know."

"I hope so. He is a good person, Michael. We have to help him as much as he helps us."

"I want to know about the war."

James was silent again before saying, "And if I don't want to tell you?"

Michael just shrugged.

"You'll ask the men in there? Those broken soldiers? You'll ask them? You'll find some other way?"

"No."

"Because they won't tell you, will they? You've already tried that. You know you won't get closer to me by getting closer to the war. It doesn't work that way."

"I know."

"Do you?"

"Yes, of course."

His father sighed and looked out to sea. "Okay, I suppose the damage has been done by now, anyway. What would you like to know?"

Another pause. The sea continued polishing the rocks, the waves marking off the seconds as he thought.

"Why are They here?"

"I have no idea. Next question."

"Will we lose?"

"No idea. Next question."

"Why don't They just destroy us? I heard They could destroy whole countries if they wanted. Why not just do that?"

"No idea. Keep going."

"Do They die? I mean, really, really die, forever."

"They seem to. Our armies make great efforts in that particular direction. They don't get back up again. Beyond that, I have no idea."

"Do They ever say anything?"

"Never, no matter how hard people try to make them, and yes, I have seen that, and no, I won't tell you about it."

"What do you do?"

"I try to make people feel better in any way I can. Life is very difficult over there."

"I heard some padres bless the missiles and the ammunition. Do you do that?"

"I do whatever makes people feel better, I told you. I don't think the specifics are important."

"Have you killed anyone?"

"Humans, no. The Enemy… that's not really any of your business, and I see no purpose in the question."

This was what he had wanted. It didn't seem like enough. His father was calm and matter-of-fact. He wanted more. Michael didn't care anymore. Everything was ruined anyway.

"Do you hate them?"

There was a pause, but it was much shorter than Michael expected. "Yes, more than anything. I have seen what They do, and I see no reason for it. I would say I only hate what They do, but that would be a lie. I hate them. Everything about them."

"Do you forgive them?"

That was unfair, but Michael didn't care. He was entitled.

"I try. Honestly… no. I can't. I should. Maybe one day."

"How can you still believe in God?"

"That is a ridiculous question. My faith is not conditional on current events. What you probably mean is how can I still believe in the kind, loving, forgiving God who I know exists? My answer is that it is not for us to know the purpose of all of this, but I have to believe that there is one."

"Do They have a God? Is He our God?"

"They don't appear to worship or acknowledge God as far as we know, but then we don't have much information, really. I often think that might be our purpose, to bring them to Him. If it took this war, if it took the death of millions, even billions of us to somehow bring them to God, then who are we to say that it would not be worth it?"

"At school, they said They might have the same God as us. Thus is the excellence of God magnified and the greatness of his kingdom made manifest; he is glorified not in one, but in countless suns; not in a single earth, a single world, but in a thousand thousand, I say in an infinity of worlds."

"They teach you that at school? Giordano Bruno?"

"Yes. They say that whatever The Enemy are, They have to be part of God's kingdom too."

"Interesting. I'm sure he would have been horrified."

"They teach us lots of philosophy at school. All about Christian war and why it is allowed. Do you think it's allowed?"

"Sometimes."

"When it's waged not for motives of aggrandizement or cruelty, but with the object of securing peace, of punishing evil-doers, and of uplifting the good?"

"Something like that."

"That was Saint Augustine."

"I know who it was, yes. Very impressive. You should have this conversation with Uncle Joe. I think I'd like to see that."

It was strange, but everything didn't seem to be ruined. Everything seemed fine, and his father was smiling again. He had one more question.

"Do you think Uncle Joe believes in God?"

"I have no idea. You should ask him that too. Can I be there?"

"Sure. I'll ask him before you go."

Michael felt an arm round him. "Maybe just before I go, at the last second as I go out the door."

"Maybe."

"Now, are we going back to the hotel? I hear there's some general being interviewed about a war or something."

"Sure. We could watch it with Mum and Uncle Joe."

"Isn't there a television in the bar?"

"Yes, but all the others will be in there."

"That's okay. Let's do that. I'm used to being around lots of people."

On the way to the hotel, Michael told his father all about the different theories he had heard about where The Enemy had come from. At school, Michael and his friends swapped theories about The Enemy all the time. Some were original, some from comic books, some from their fathers or older brothers.

His father listened politely. He had probably heard them all, but Michael didn't care. He told his father about the religious theories. How The Enemy were demons, and this was the end of the world. They were from hell, but hell in the sky instead of under the ground. He told him about another theory that The Enemy were angels sent to purify human society and bring the human race together. Then he told his father how he had read a theory that The Enemy were religious maniacs. They had arrived to wage holy war as a result of some ancient prophecy the human race accidentally fulfilled. The journalist had said that The Enemy and the war were God's way of teaching us geography, but he had probably just been joking, and Michael thought it was probably an old joke.

He told his father all about the stories he had read in comic books. Mostly those about how The Enemy had a very long history, probably because it made for better stories. His favourite was about how The Enemy were an ancient race who had seeded the planet Earth with life billions of years ago, then returned to fight their creations as sport. They had created and then slaughtered the dinosaurs. Then, They returned to do the same to the human race. One of his friends had a comic where The Enemy were supernatural. A long time ago, they had once been evil spirits, werewolves, vampires, and ghosts. In modern times, they had changed form again.

There were other comics which were similar. The stories said The Enemy had always been here. They had been the armies of the Mongols, the Nazis, and of every empire there had ever been. They had been every dictator or warmonger in history, preparing us for the final battle.

Michael told his father how once you had been able to buy action figures based on The Enemy being recruitment agents for a vast empire. The story went that the best warriors of our species were not killed. They were taken away to join a Galactic army, which was fighting other aliens who looked even cooler. They had large, expensive plastic combat vehicles, and you could buy small, expensive replicas of them if you had lots of money. If you didn't have quite so much, you could instead buy trading cards and stickers.

Some people said The Enemy were a race of xenophobes. Which, Michael explained unnecessarily, meant They detested anybody who was different. So They roamed the galaxy, exterminating any species they encountered.

Some people wanted to see The Enemy as justification for their own political opinions and recruited them enthusiastically. You could read those theories in the letter pages of the newspapers that were always in the hotel bar. Some thought it was obvious that The Enemy were environmental policemen, sent to destroy or cull us for damaging the Earth.

There were those that believed The Enemy didn't exist, and They, along with the war, were created by the Unified Command and the United Nations before them as a way to control the human race. Michael thought that seemed like an awful lot of trouble to go to. Similarly, some believed that The Enemy were a genetically engineered army built by some nation here on Earth and that the war was being fought for some political purpose. Michael found that very hard to believe, and not very many people thought it was true, but the small number who did seemed to spend all their time writing to newspapers.

A few said that The Enemy might be scientists conducting some massive behavioural experiment, others that They were renegades, outlaws, or criminals. They had been on the way to a distant prison but had rebelled, killed their guards, looked for the nearest planet, and attacked it. This theory also appeared in some of the less epic comic books that Michael had encountered.

There were stories that The Enemy had been tricked. They had been told that we were the cause of an ancient war, and They had arrived to punish us. This particular theory had been expounded in a recent film Michael hadn't been allowed to go and see at the cinema.

There was a scientist on the news one night who said he believed The Enemy were insane. That our atmosphere, or a microbe on our planet, had affected them and resulted in them becoming psychotic. He said no species so violent could ever have built a society, so their aggression must have been a recent, unnatural development. This theory appealed to a lot of people, and some dreamed of finding a cure which would end the war.

There was also the theory that The Enemy were a disease. A space-borne virus, they infected planets and multiplied. Humans were also a virus but a relatively benign one in comparison. This theory had actually formed part of a question in a philosophy exam that Michael had done very well in recently.

By the time they had arrived at the hotel, Michael was almost running out of theories. He was surprised how few of them his father had actually heard. He seemed to be getting quieter again, but at least he was paying attention and wasn't drifting away. Michael felt he had his dad back. Even if he would be gone soon, he had him back for a while.

18

The bar was already busy when they arrived. The television was on, but the sound was off. Cathy was letting the ghosts acclimatise slowly. They hid in the corners of the room. Around them, the infantry laughed at their own jokes and sneered at each other. Usually, at one o'clock in the afternoon, most of them would still be in bed or out walking off their hangovers. If they recognised Michael, they didn't show it. His father's dog collar had more power than the memory of their behaviour the previous night. The infantry nodded at him as they passed, and the swearing faded away, although never for very long.

His father existed even in the world of the ghosts. They could see him when they couldn't see Michael or the infantry. Michael guessed they might have thought about speaking to him, but his nod to each of them was enough for the moment.

Michael watched his father order a drink. Cathy was pleased to see him. Everyone was always pleased to see him. Except for Uncle Joe, he seemed to have no opinion on such things.

Michael couldn't wait to see Neckerman. It was so unusual for someone like him to give an interview. Of course, he made statements all the time, and there were recorded addresses a couple of times a year. Sometimes he even gave press conferences and answered questions, but he didn't answer all of them. You didn't really learn much you didn't already know. This time, it would be different. He was actually giving an interview. In the four years since he had taken charge, there had never been anything like it. Even the Great General Chen, who had given a lot of speeches, usually to huge crowds, had never given an interview like this one. Both of them had to think about the governments around the world that still had to run their own countries. General Neckerman, like General Chen before him, didn't want to say anything that would make it look like the Unified Command was really in charge. It was important to do things properly.

Michael realised the interview would start soon. The ghosts had all been provided with drinks to hold on to. That way, they wouldn't be swept away once the programme started. The infantry were getting quieter, slowly ending their conversations now rather than later, so it wouldn't look like they were ending them just because the program was starting. Everyone was casually beginning to look at the television instead of at each other. The jukebox was much quieter than usual, and soon it would be turned off.

Michael noticed his father was still talking to Cathy at the bar, his back to the television and everyone else.

"Shouldn't we tell Mum and Uncle Joe that we're down here?"

His father turned around. "He knows where we are, don't you worry. He's probably watching it upstairs."

"But I thought he wanted us to watch it with him."

The hand that wasn't holding a drink ruffled Michael's hair. "Don't worry. He knows where we are."

His father stared at the television, ready for the show to start.

"Dad, why is General Neckerman doing this now?"

James paused again, and Michael wondered why nobody could just answer a question.

"He must think that he has a good reason. He doesn't do much without thinking it through."

"Is it true General Chen might come back?"

"Not if Neckerman has anything to do with it." There was no pause that time.

"General Chen was a great man, wasn't he? It was a shame what happened, wasn't it?"

Michael was watching the television. He wasn't watching his father's response. There was no need. It wasn't a real question, just conversation and nothing that anyone reasonable would disagree with. Maybe one of the ghosts flickered to life for a moment. Perhaps his eyes met Michael's father's before they flicked back to his drink. Maybe. Maybe not.

"Is it always this busy?"

"Not during the day. The soldiers usually have things to do. They must have time off today. They come in at night, mostly."

As it became more crowded, Michael felt himself being lifted to sit on the bar so he could see. The infantry standing beside him all smiled. They might have been soldiers from the previous night. It was hard to tell. Soldiers all had the same haircuts.

The jukebox finally fell silent. It happened between songs, so you wouldn't have noticed if you hadn't really been paying attention. Michael thought it was interesting how much you noticed when you were the only one not drinking. You tended to notice less and less the more you drank. It was probably for the best. After all, if you didn't drink, you might notice Cathy rolling her eyes after speaking to you, your jokes getting less funny, or that the alcohol you were drinking was coming out of a different bottle and didn't taste quite as strong as it did a few hours ago. Perhaps you might even notice a surprising number of people who weren't in uniform, weren't going off to the same place as you, and were doing quite well, thank you for asking.

The silence was infectious, and soon all the conversations died. The television was the only thing in the room that was immune. It slowly increased in volume and announced that the programme, which was about to start, consisted of a live interview with General Willem Neckerman, Supreme Guardian of the Unified Command. It was hard to believe anyone in the world didn't already know. Everyone would be watching. The whole world wanted to see the interview, so it had been difficult to schedule. It was originally supposed to be conducted at noon Central European Time, the time zone of the general's birthplace of Rotterdam. It was eventually moved two hours later, probably to make things slightly easier for the Americans, who then wouldn't have to get up as early.

The interviewer was British, from the BBC. Michael knew the Dutch watched the BBC, so this wouldn't be too strange for them. The interview would also be in English, following convention. The general would have been entitled to speak in Dutch, but he was equally comfortable in English, as were almost all of his countrymen. Michael had heard him speak before. He spoke with a Dutch accent, as you might expect. His accent was from the South of The Netherlands, which meant he didn't roll his Rs and scrape his Gs as was done in a million inaccurate amateur impressions every day. Not that you saw such things on television or heard them on the radio. It wasn't actually illegal. It was just that everyone knew it wouldn't really be appropriate.

The interviewer would be firm but respectful. He probably wouldn't challenge the general directly, but he would ask difficult questions and expect answers. Everyone would.

Michael recognised the interviewer. He was old, with white hair, and very well known. Both he and Neckerman sat on large, comfortable chairs in what looked more like an old house than a television studio. The interviewer wasted no time.

"General Neckerman. You join us today as we enter the tenth year of what can only be described as a war for the survival of the human race, the fourth year under your command. It has been a difficult year. Casualties continue to climb as an increasing number of countries face Demographic Collapse. The world economy is creaking under the strain, and now there are rumours of disagreement within the Unified Command itself. People are desperately looking for hope. General, can you offer any?"

The general leaned back in his chair. His jet-black hair made him look far younger than his fifty years. He looked sharp, handsome, and as if he spent most of his time in a suit rather than the military uniform he was now wearing.

"I think we can always have hope. To my opinion, if we look hard enough, we can see ways in which the situation may improve in the future. We have had ten years of something which we were not able to avoid. Once again, I would like to take this opportunity to repeat that we do not wish for this conflict. If those who have come here are listening, I would again like to ask that They speak with us. If They want something from us, then we can discuss about it. For example, if They require land or resources, we can discuss about it and arrange this. If we have misunderstood Their culture, we would like Them to educate us, and if we have offended Them, it was not something which we wanted to do. As we do not understand why They are here, we have been forced to defend ourselves. We have no aggressive intentions toward them. I think everyone in the Unified Command, everyone in this world, can say that this is true."

The message was standard. For years, Neckerman and the Unified Command had made similar statements whenever the opportunity arose. It never led to anything. In the bar, some of the infantry were mumbling. Michael didn't bother to tune in to whatever they were saying. It was likely about the aggressive intentions that they apparently didn't have.

"You say that, General Neckerman, but is it not the case that the members of the Unified Command have different opinions on how this war should be prosecuted? For example, in your pursuit of the *Spiegeloorlog*?"

"I think that this is always true, that people will have different opinions, and this is not unusual. The Unified Command, however, has always spoken with one voice on the future of this situation. In my opinion, the *Spiegeloorlog*, as you call it, will enable us to continue this situation as long as possible."

"And that is the aim? To continue this war for as long as possible? To survive when faced with continual attacks by The Enemy?"

"What other aim can there be? I think after ten years, we have to be realistic. Survival must be our aim. This situation must be stabilised until it can be resolved."

"Can you understand, General Neckerman, that for some people what you are saying sounds like a betrayal, a betrayal of the ideals for which their sons, daughters, husbands, wives, fathers, and mothers have fought and died for?"

"Of course, we can understand this, but we must be realistic. There are those things which we can do and those things which we cannot do, and in coming years, we have to realise this. I have to tell our people that I cannot say that the day will come when we will sweep those who have come here away. Such a plan looks well when you write it, but we have to look to what can be done and what cannot be done."

"So, there are certain things that are not worth fighting for?"

The general laughed at the question, but Michael didn't feel the mood lighten. "Of course, there are many things that are not worth fighting for. Many things are worth fighting for, but perhaps we should not all rush to commit suicide to provide a good story for history books. We have to look to other ways of dealing with situations."

There was a strange silence in the bar. Everyone was concentrating, processing. If they disagreed, they knew that this was not the time to say anything. Everyone was listening. They didn't want to listen to each other's views. There would be time for that later. There would be time to shout at the television when all of this was repeated in a few hours.

"This brings us to the subject of the *Spiegeloorlog*, your *Mirror War*. As we understand it, the intention is to reduce the aggression from our side, to reduce the technology available to our soldiers, to reduce the scale, and alter the nature of our engagements with The Enemy. We do this in the belief that The Enemy will accept this and do the same. You believe that this can be done in a responsible way that will not compromise the safety of our forces."

"Yes, and this has been done. We have slowly withdrawn what remains of our air cover and armour from some areas of the battlefields. We have seen that this has been reflected in the behaviour from the other side."

"So, we can look forward to a future where we fight, not with guns and tanks, but with spears, horses, and bows and arrows?"

"This would perhaps be an outcome at some point in the future. It would certainly be one which is more sustainable than what we have done in the past."

Some of the infantry were finding it difficult to remain silent. Drinks were being moved around on tables, and feet were being shuffled. Michael looked at his father, but his father wouldn't look back. He just kept staring at the television. He lifted his drink to his lips but kept staring at the screen. Michael felt his father's hand drop onto his shoulder as the interview continued.

"You say that the Unified Command speaks with one voice, but we have had General Chen recently speaking out against the *Mirror War*."

"General Chen is not part of the Unified Command."

"No, he is not, and that is another story. However, speaking yesterday, he said, and I quote, 'The *Mirror War* is an abomination. It is an abdication of responsibility by the Unified Command. As well as risking military disaster, it risks betraying and insulting the memories of those who have fought for all that is good about humanity. It is close to an act of treason against the entire human race. If it is allowed to continue, history will record it as one of the most despicable acts in the history of warfare, diplomacy, and government. We must take the fight to The Enemy,' a term you shy away from General Neckerman, 'and cleanse this planet of their presence, whatever the cost in blood and treasure.' These are strong words, carefully chosen."

General Chen was speaking about things again? Michael looked up at his father, but again he did not return his gaze. Was he the only one in the bar who was surprised by this? General Neckerman didn't seem surprised and remained calm. The interviewer was being more aggressive than usual. Michael had never heard anyone speak to someone from the Unified Command this way. It was almost rude. Surely someone would stop him?

"General Chen is entitled to his opinion, and in coming days I am sure he will continue to express it, but if we look to the situation we are in, we must choose the course which is most likely to ensure survival. We must not return to the ways of the past, which have not delivered stabilisation and resolution."

"By that, you mean the events surrounding the First Respite and the eventual resignation of General Chen?"

"I think we are all remembering what has not succeeded in past times."

Something was shouted across the bar. Michael saw the irritation flash across people's faces, but the silence quickly reclaimed the lost ground.

"This brings us to a point that I think people would like clarified. General Chen has claimed that he resigned on the understanding that the war would continue to be fought with the utmost vigour. He now says that is not the case and that an agreement has been broken."

"I remember no such agreement. In any case, we are seeking to resolve this situation with all means at our disposal, and I think in that sense we are closer in spirit to the ideas of General Chen than he perhaps realises."

There were some snorts of disbelief in the bar. The soldier beside Michael was shaking his head. Nobody was smiling anymore, and the soldiers didn't look as friendly as before.

"I think he would disagree with your analysis, but I will leave it there for now. However, if we can look at the events of the First Respite, which have been brought back into the forefront of public attention recently, some have accused General Chen of misrepresenting those events. Others accuse him of worse, of lying to the Unified Command about the departure of Enemy forces at that time. Do you believe that? Does the Unified Command believe that?"

"I think there can often be some difficulties for commanders on the ground to know exactly what the situation is. The powerful counterattack which was launched against our forces is well documented, and we are still feeling the effects of that. I will not accuse him of lying."

"Was there a First Respite? Did The Enemy leave at any time?"

"This is not easy to say. I think different people have different opinions."

"What does the Unified Command believe? With all of your resources, all of your information. Did The Enemy leave?"

"I, we, the Unified Command… and this is from our researches in the past years, from accounts at the time… no, we do not believe that this was the case."

Nobody was surprised? Everyone was just listening, staring. How could they be listening to this? It was unheard of. General Neckerman looked unsettled for the first time. Michael could hear his English breaking up, more mistakes creeping in.

"And did General Chen know this at the time?"

"That is most difficult to say. You must ask General Chen these questions. General Chen served us well for a long time, and we have the greatest respect for him. If a man were to have made a mistake, then that… if there was a mistake made… that should not change such a thing, and I think it is not necessary that we take such an interest in these events… that we are looking to have such an importance being attached to these."

The general's hands were waving, as if he was trying to make the questions go away.

"I find that incredible, General Neckerman. Can there be a more important event in our history? Look at what happened in less than one week. Perhaps twenty million—we may never know the exact number—casualties. And let us be clear about the reality, by 'casualties', we mean deaths. We saw vast quantities of equipment lost. The Unified Command's forces were bled white. Economies around the world were stretched to breaking point. Countries were taken to the brink of Demographic Collapse. What could be more important?"

The general spoke quickly, almost tripping over his own words. "I think we must not look to results but to intentions and to the coming time and not causing stresses over past times."

"But this is not the past, is it? Only this morning, we had the Prime Minister of the United Kingdom, the man currently occupying the presidency of the European Command Council, issuing a statement in which he said, and again I quote, 'Although the resolve of the United Kingdom has remained undiminished for the past decade, our ability to contribute the required resources to the effort in Africa and elsewhere is diminishing. I would ask the Unified Command to suspend our contribution immediately. The spectre of Demographic Collapse is upon us. If our economy and our country are to continue to function in any meaningful way, we must set aside our responsibilities for the time being to refresh and rebuild so that we may better serve the collective effort in the future.' These are the words of a man who represents a country on its knees, a shadow of its former self."

Michael couldn't help himself. He whispered to his father, "Did you know about this?"

The hand on his shoulder patted him into silence as the soldiers first scowled at him, then at his father, before turning back to hear the general's answer. Michael could hear his accent becoming stronger. He was speaking quickly again, his English sounding stranger all the time, like it was drifting closer to his own language.

"Yes, and we can be sympathetic, but this is why we must have other solutions. You must be careful, and it may be that we must be putting water with the wine. We must not continue on the path which has brought us to here. We have come through water which was undeep but now is deeper, and we must ask if we can go back or if we must continue. I find that we must have a new solution. What you are calling the *Spiegeloorlog* is a way of this, and it could be that we can relieve pressure on lands like the United Kingdom and Norway while stabilising situations for the coming times, and in this way, we can get two flies with one strike. People who find that we can continue as we have been doing have this situation totally miss. We can look to the Respite, and we all know the details from our heads, but this is not a way this problem to… to… solve. If you ask me if the *Spiegeloorlog* is the right way to do things. I do not understand your question. It is the only way to do things. If we look to the outcomes we have, then can I say that… it looks well. There is a chance, a chance for the hope you asked me for earlier."

As General Neckerman became more animated, the interviewer seemed to match him by talking more quickly. Etiquette and protocol were slipping away. The truth was being stripped naked by these two men. "But can you understand why people are not prepared to accept your solution? They see it as an accommodation with The Enemy, and your reluctance to use that term is not lost on them. In General Chen, they see someone who, if he never offered them such a practical and rational programme for survival, at least offered them hope and the prospect of ultimate victory. For them, your refusal to do the same is worse than a future of catastrophic defeat and extinction. It is the world of the human race simply giving up as the world ends, of laying down to die."

"I do not find that people would prefer to die in some glorious last stand. I see the *Spiegeloorlog* as something that, instead of being immoral and strange, is perfectly natural and has happened before. We have fought many wars without using atomic weapons, for example. We did not see this as strange. We simply knew that to use our most powerful weapons would lead to our destruction, and we chose to come to some kind of unspoken understanding with our opponents. I see that we can do the same here. In fact, I would argue that the understanding has already been reached with atomic weapons. When we attempted to use them, that attempt was frustrated, and we were given a demonstration that their use would be without point. Both sides have not looked to this area since."

"You are, of course, referring to the Bioko, or Malabo, incident which occurred at a very early stage in the war."

Michael knew all about the Bioko Incident and was surprised that some of the infantry looked slightly puzzled. They were older than him. Why wouldn't they know all about it?

"Yes, when we launched a nuclear strike on their forces, it was an act of desperation, and it was an act which had no result. The interception of our missiles showed that we are dealing with a situation where many of our actions are known in advance and are either tolerated or not tolerated. I see the resultant instant destruction of the population of the island of Bioko as a direct response to that and as a demonstration of what could occur if we attempt such action in the future."

"To clarify, the Unified Command believes, as many others do, that The Enemy possesses technology which would allow them to destroy us at any time. But for some reason, they are choosing not to use it and are instead fighting a conflict which, apparently, causes them countless casualties and has so far taken ten years."

"Yes. That is our belief, and that is the reason that escalation of this war, if that is what it is, has to be very carefully considered. It is the reason that de-escalation may be a possibility."

"So The Enemy may accept a conflict which does not inevitably lead to our extinction. That would be the holy grail of the Spiegeloorlog?"

"In a sense, yes. We do not know what level would be acceptable to them."

The two men seemed to have calmed down as they relaxed back into their roles. The infantry seemed to be reacting in the opposite way. They were becoming louder as the tension eased. Some were talking quietly to each other. Others were quietly ordering drinks, although the general silence was still such that the clink of glasses was deafening.

"We are now coming back to the question of exactly what The Enemy want. It is people's general impression that They do not utilise resources such as mines or oil wells, although They will fight for them. They do not use humans as slave labour, even when it would make military sense to do so, and They do not make any obvious use of the land which they capture. Is that the case, in reality?"

"Yes, that is true as far as we are aware, although you must remember that it is difficult to know what happens in occupied areas exactly. We, for example, have no satellite surveillance and have not had any such capability for a very long time."

"So their aim is only war? War for no purpose, sacrifice for no result? You can see how ridiculous that appears."

"I can, but we have been unable to find any motivation for their actions. Although we are always prepared to listen to anything that they require if They would like to communicate this to us."

"Yet They attacked Nigeria initially, a country with vast oil resources, oil resources which they quickly seized. Why?"

"We do not know, but we can do a guess. The African continent may have been chosen because the lands which had the most developed industry and military lay outside of it and would not be directly affected by their actions."

"And presumably Nigeria was chosen as the loss of its oil resources would have increased the necessity for the rest of the world to defend it?"

"Yes, although I am sure we would have responded the same way if the country had been with no oil."

Some of the infantry laughed. Others seemed to draw themselves up straighter in agreement, as befitted their roles as guardians of all mankind.

"So The Enemy are purely using Africa as a battlefield?"

"Yes. That is our belief."

"That would, of course, introduce the possibility that the long-feared attack on the European mainland may never come."

"Perhaps, but we must consider that we have seen movement towards Asia and also into Australia. It is likely, to my opinion, that a failure to stop their forces in Africa would lead to further expansion into strategically important areas elsewhere."

"So, abandoning Africa will never be an option for the Unified Command? The *Lost Continent* approach does not inform thinking at the highest level?"

"No, I do not think so. This is a continent which once contained well over a billion people, and although the majority are thought to have fallen, we believe we will gain nothing from abandonment. In fact, it is not even clear that this would be acceptable. You will recall that all previous attempts at even limited evacuation or migration have been met with devastating and irresistible intervention. I do not think the assumptions we have made in the past about how our borders and our nationalities divide us are shared by those who have visited us. I do not think that such distinctions are of interest to them."

Michael thought of all the soldiers of different nationalities he had seen and read about, how General Chen had always spoken about how we should never say how many Americans, British, Chinese, or Indians had died, only how many humans. How we should not talk about The Enemy being in this country or that country, but instead about The Enemy being on our planet. Had there really been a time when it wasn't like this? Had people fought each other? What had they found to fight about?

As the interview continued, Michael wondered if the Unified Command would release Britain. Would his father get to stay? Maybe by the time they were ready to fight again, the war would be over, or General Neckerman would have shrunk it so much that his father wouldn't have to go. Maybe by that time, General Chen would be in charge again and would have defeated The Enemy.

What was General Chen doing? Why was he speaking out now? Why was General Neckerman giving this interview? It was like there was something going on that he couldn't tune into, something people weren't discussing with him. Michael read about the war and watched the news, but still, he was left out. He couldn't feel what others felt, the change in mood, the tension. He would be left to read about what had happened after it was all over. It wasn't fair.

The interview lasted for another ten minutes. General Chen wasn't mentioned again. The *Spiegeloorlog* wasn't mentioned very much either. The soldiers gradually lost interest, and the silence lost its power. By the time it finished, there was a queue at the bar. Michael watched it through to the end. Most of it, he knew already. It was about recent events in the war and decision-making in the Unified Command. General Neckerman finished the interview smiling as did the interviewer. The earlier tension was forgotten. Michael found it amazing how humans were able to forget unpleasantness so quickly.

As the bar restarted, his father was borrowed by the infantry. They would tell him about where they were going, where they were from, and their absent brothers and sisters. None of them ever asked him what it was like. None of them ever asked him what he had seen. Michael began to feel guilty about questioning his father earlier. As they danced around him, as his father was passed from soldier to soldier, he began to feel increasingly left out. He wondered if he should start collecting glasses, but Cathy was so busy he couldn't get near her to ask what he should do. Through everything, his father kept catching his eye, kept nodding and smiling so he would know he was still there. He tried watching the television, but he wasn't very interested in watching an hour-long discussion about a half-hour interview. In any case, it would be turned off soon.

The figure in the doorway watched the boy that nobody else was drunk enough to take an interest in. It felt his awkwardness, watched to see if it would pass, watched to see if the situation would resolve itself. It watched to see what was required.

Michael looked at the ghosts. They were still sitting with their drinks in front of them, having weathered the storm. Some of their glasses were almost empty. He tried to imagine what they were thinking about. Were they thinking about the interview? Did it matter to them? Were they thinking about what had happened to them in the war? Maybe they weren't thinking of anything. Maybe they were just waiting, watching the minutes pass. He thought of asking one of them, but he probably wouldn't say anything in reply. He might not even understand the question. Just as his feet started to move, the figure appeared over his shoulder.

"I think your mother would like some help with dinner." Uncle Joe was scanning the bar, the soldiers. Michael felt guilty. He hoped Uncle Joe hadn't noticed that he wasn't doing anything. He felt guilty for being so far from his father. Uncle Joe might think that he didn't want to spend time with him. Luckily, Uncle Joe didn't seem to be looking at anything in particular. Michael was relieved to see that he was so relaxed. He didn't seem to have any particular reason for coming downstairs.

"I'm sure she could cope without you, but I just thought you could help out."

"Maybe I should stay with Dad..." Michael's head flicked back and forth between the two men, and he nodded at his father. He may have accidentally pointed. His father was being handed a drink by one of the infantry.

"I think he'll be fine. He has other things to do at the moment. He's helping people as well."

"Okay, if you're sure."

"Sorry I didn't come down for the general. I was a bit busy upstairs."

"Did you see it?"

"I'm sure you can tell me all about it later." Uncle Joe's hand dropped onto his shoulder and guided him towards the door.

"I will. He was talking about the war, the First Respite, and General Chen. General Chen has been saying things about the Mirror War. I even heard one of the soldiers saying that he might come back. Can you imagine that?"

Uncle Joe nodded as he took the boy out of the bar. On the way out, he turned and met the gaze of the padre at the bar, who now had a drink in each hand. Uncle Joe nodded at the padre as well. He may also have pointed, but if he did, it wasn't by accident. Uncle Joe never did anything by accident.

19

Nobody mentioned anything about the seat being empty again at dinner. Michael offered to go and get his father, but Uncle Joe said he would come when he was ready. Michael kept staring at the clock. His stare focused the silence onto it until the hands could only creep round at half speed. He tried to talk, to blow away the silence, but there wasn't much to talk about. Michael told them both about the interview. Uncle Joe listened and nodded. His mother just listened. Nobody else looked at the clock. Uncle Joe talked more than usual. He asked if Michael had enjoyed his day, if he had enjoyed his dinner, if he had enjoyed his day in Stranraer. The hands of the clock sped up as Michael talked to him. For once, Uncle Joe seemed happy to talk. Usually, you accidentally said something that made him go quiet again, but not tonight. Michael even mentioned Glasgow, and Uncle Joe didn't get upset. He just said that it was something that they could think about.

It didn't seem strange that the chair was empty again. Uncle Joe didn't say anything about it, and if it had been strange, he would have said something. Michael's father was just busy helping people. It was what he was best at, and that was why they needed him so badly and why he had to be away so much. Uncle Joe did mention how happy the Hutchisons had been to see him and how helpful he had been.

After dinner, Uncle Joe asked if Michael was thinking about starting to study again. He said that the school holidays wouldn't last forever and maybe it was time he started to look at his books again. Now that he had seen his father, he would probably be able to concentrate again. Suddenly, it seemed such a reasonable idea. His mother and Uncle Joe looked at him, waiting for him to respond. Uncle Joe's shoulders shrugged, indicating that it was only a suggestion. The clock was keeping out of it, although it also looked at Michael and swirled its second hand around surprisingly quickly, as if to illustrate a point.

Maybe it wasn't such a bad idea. His father was busy downstairs, and Uncle Joe pointed out that it would make more sense to work hard and get to bed early. Then he would have the whole of the next day to spend with him. Michael decided they were right. It would be a shame to spoil the day and the evening when everyone was in such a good mood.

Uncle Joe walked him to his room and told him how pleased he was that the day had turned out so well. When the door closed, Uncle Joe could be sure Michael was happy, studying, or sleeping without worrying or being disturbed by anything. For example, he wouldn't hear his mother and Uncle Joe discussing things. If anything else happened later in the night, that wouldn't disturb him either. Not that anyone knew that anything was going to happen. That was another good reason for him not to wait up for it. If others had to wait and worry for a while, there was no need for him to concern himself about that. And later, if someone were to go downstairs, well, that also wouldn't disturb him.

20

Michael didn't want to study, not when he had something much more interesting to do. There was still lots of The Book that he hadn't read. He hadn't been reading it in order, which might have been a mistake. It was too late now. One day he would go back and read The Book from the beginning, but for now, he found it easier to just open it and start reading. At the very end, the pages weren't typed anymore. They were handwritten. He opened it near the end, at one of the first handwritten pages, and started reading.

> Sitting there in the meeting, staring at Emma and the rest of them, I couldn't help thinking about how pleased I had been when they had brought me back. Of course, I didn't get to go home. I still had to work. Meetings. I always hated meetings. I really, really hated meetings. It's tempting to say that everybody hates meetings, but I don't think that's true. Emma liked meetings. She liked sitting there with her coffee and making conversation. That's an important point. Making conversation. Not having a conversation, not taking part in a conversation… making conversation. Manufacturing conversation. What for? She thought she was conjuring it out of thin air. Wrong. She didn't know about the conservation of energy. She didn't know you can't create something from nothing.
>
> The universe is a zero-sum game. To create something, you have to take something from somewhere else. She would have known that if she hadn't spent so much time at University wearing kaftans and planning trips to faraway places where they didn't place nearly enough emphasis on

the need for indoor plumbing. She created her conversation out of my time and misery.

I remember sitting there in the first meeting after I came back, wondering why people couldn't all arrive at once. Asking myself why we had to sit and talk, waiting for the meeting to start. I knew why those people loved meetings. It's the captive audience. Nobody would even consider talking to those dullards in the real world. They had to sculpt their imaginary social life out of my time.

I was there under false pretences. I was summoned here to talk about work, and yet someone was talking about their new house. Now, you might think that as I care little about my work, I would rather hear about the damn house. However, here is the really unfair part. It was all just a trick. We were not exchanging one thing for another. This was not a positive illustration of the conservation of energy. After I hearing about the house, I would have to talk about work, anyway. Fantastic. Behold the deceitful forked tongues of the two-headed friendless dullards.

Why was I back here? Why were these people still alive? I wasn't sure if only the good died young, but I was becoming increasingly convinced that the totally useless were near immortal. Who the hell kept finding things for these people to do? Thousands of people dying every day, and we couldn't find any reason to put these people on the front line? The human race was facing extinction, and we still needed meetings? How many had to die before we couldn't get a quorum? These people were insects. You lifted a stone, and there they were, crawling around. Woodlice. Not insects. Crustaceans. Armoured, rot-inducing vermin. They were everywhere. Everywhere. They always survived. They always managed to thrive. I hated them. Why was I there? Was God desperate to find something that I despised even more than being shot at and watching other people die?

When would the meeting start? My smile was burning into my face. I tried to detach myself from my body while still leaving it nodding politely. I passed the time by trying to imagine everyone as talking corpses. In my spare time at work, I often liked to fantasise that I was some insane serial killer with a warped sense of reality. I failed miserably at manufacturing an imaginary, interesting inside that didn't match the real, boring outside.

Not for the first time, I considered that something may not be quite right. Of course, lots of things were not quite right. In fact, almost everything was entirely ruined. Only thing was that until I got back, I didn't think that included me. Something was wrong. My flesh now burned when I was around these people. I always hated meetings, but I didn't think meetings had always been unbearable.

I knew I would have to leave. I could not bear it. Not one... more... second. I tried to doodle on the paper in front of me, but I was too conscious. I suppose I did not really dislike them. Not really. I didn't really have a good reason to dislike them. They were nice enough people. They weren't evil or anything. Emma always lent me a pen. I don't think evil people do that. Well, probably not without cackling or twitching or something. Despite that, I felt such hatred for them. I thought it might be burning a hole in my stomach. It's not that I wanted to hurt them. I just wanted them to not be there, to not exist. Every word they spoke was unbearable.

My temper had been getting shorter. That morning I had kicked my kitchen bin to pieces because... because... I missed it. The piece of paper fell on the floor. It wasn't even the bin's fault. At that moment I realised something was wrong. Something was wrong with me. I wondered if anyone would care if I told them. I wonder what would happen if I picked up my glass of water and threw it over my shoulder. I wondered if it would smash. Everything was breaking. Everything was broken. I could not function. I could not go through the motions. I realised I have been staring at the same spot for a long time. Maybe minutes.

I imagined a shell around me. Their conversation swirling around me, not penetrating. I imagined it getting quieter. I tuned out. I imagined my ears filling with roaring white noise. I imagined exploding. I imagined the glass windows blowing out. I imagined pressing my hands into the plastic of the table until it melted, pressing until my hands passed through it and onto the floor, pressing into that until it melted too, us all falling into the hole, tumbling through the molten building, melting the earth beneath us, everyone screaming and tugging at my arms as I melted through the ground like the core of a nuclear reactor, squeezing my eyes shut and burning a hole deeper into the planet and bursting out of the other side. I imagined the sound of screaming in my head until I could hear nothing else. I imagined it. I concentrated until I convinced myself I could actually hear it, and I felt guilty for going crazy on purpose, but then I thought maybe you had to be crazy to send yourself crazy, so maybe it wasn't my fault. I imagined the paradox as two ghostly burning snakes crawling out of my eyes, twisting and coiling around each other in the centre of the table, and I felt so clever because I could see them and nobody else could, and I knew something was wrong. I thought something was wrong. I wondered if something was wrong, and I thought maybe I was just being melodramatic, and I had taken autopilot off on purpose because I wanted some attention. I felt empty. I felt raw. I felt like a human stripped to his core. I was an empty, shining being. I had nothing in common with those people. I did not know if I remembered how to speak. Something was wrong. Everything was wrong. I did not know how to retrain as a human being. Something was disconnected. I had disconnected it. I had learned to disconnect it. I had learned to view things passively and objectively. Now my mind couldn't find its way back. It couldn't reconnect. It was happier that way. I had to leave. Someone spoke to me. My nodding body pointed its head at them but couldn't control the eyes. I had to relearn to control my body, but it was a complicated thing. It was a puppet built for experts. When my eyes turned towards them, they were not really on. They stared through them like they were glass, through the wall behind them, through the offices and the people and the buildings and the cars. I had to leave. Something was wrong. I had to leave. I told the truth and said I was ill, and they misunderstood me in the way I intended them to. They did not believe me, and so they thought I was lying although I was telling the truth, except I was lying because I was not ill in the way they thought I was, but I was ill, but that was not really what I meant and not really what I thought they meant, and so it was a lie, really. I populated the room with imaginary snakes. The door was a thousand miles away and my guilt set my body alight and I wanted to scream but I couldn't and I got up and left and it took my body a few seconds and my mind a thousand years. The door handle was an unfathomable puzzle. I figured out how to use it in a fraction of a second. It was a trick. My disconnected mind had no concept of time and used millennia to meditate on the problem. Something was wrong.

Didn't go back to work the next day. Hard to know what to do. Thought about going home. Selfish. Bad enough me being away, never mind coming back like this. What had I done? I used to fit in there. Now I didn't. Neither one thing nor the other. Difficult, not belonging anywhere. In the end, I went back to see Dad. Told them I couldn't work in the office and would be taking a short break. Long journey. Dad was pleased to see me. Didn't say anything. Not about things. Not about the way things had turned out. No point. Everything there seemed alien. Like it was a story I had heard about someone else.

When I came back, I could have found a doctor, but I don't think it would have been easy. Maybe that's just an excuse. I suppose they knew at work. I don't know that they could have done anything. Too much to be done these days. No time. Just have to make the best of it these days. See where people fit in, see what they can do, and get them to do that. My colleagues. Not bad people. They could see I couldn't do the job there. You have to find something people can still do.

Two weeks later, they sent me back.

Michael put The Book down. He fell asleep wondering what a kaftan was. It was probably like a scarf.

21

There were often noises at night, but not like this. Something was different. Michael struggled to stay asleep. Somewhere, something needed his attention. Part of his mind was trying to get his attention. It wasn't an urgent noise, not a gunshot, not a piercing scream, not a fist hammering on his door. It was something less important, but a part of him knew it was important enough. If he would just wake up, he would understand. The knowledge of the noise was only an irritation while he was asleep. Michael struggled to ignore the noise. It seeped into his dreams, muffled but irritating and persistent. It was out of place, and it needed to be dealt with. The noise was calling him away. As the fragments of his consciousness slowly coalesced, he became aware of where he was. Whatever he had been dreaming about had made sense a second ago. Now it was quickly discarded and concealed. Bedroom. Dark. Not morning. Noise. Voices. Shouting. Close. Not upstairs. Not right. Awake.

It wasn't the ghosts. They were all on the top floor. He knew who it was. As he got dressed, he tried not to think about it. There was something horrible happening outside. Michael couldn't ignore it. He knew he would be part of it in a few minutes. He had to go anyway.

As he opened the door, the noise was much louder, much closer. The silence in the house at night was still there, amplifying any noise around. It soaked into the walls, making them thinner. At night you think you have more privacy than in the daytime, but you don't. People see you less, but they hear you more.

The people in the room probably thought they had privacy, at least at first. Now at least one of them didn't care. Of course, there had never really been any privacy, only a variable amount of clarity. Even at the beginning, their muffled conversation was audible to others. When a voice was raised, at first, it was just to a level where they could still believe in the privacy that was already gone. Now someone no longer cared. Someone was angry. If they weren't screaming loud enough to wake the dead, they were probably screaming loud enough to annoy some ghosts.

Michael was paralysed. He couldn't take another step. Another step would take him around the corner. He would be in front of their door. It sounded like the door was still closed. He couldn't go around the corner. He couldn't be there when the door opened. It would have been different if the door was already open, different if they were already outside the room. Then he would be walking into their world. That was different from them walking into his.

She was so angry. He had done it again. How could he be so cruel? How could he be so selfish? She wasn't really expecting an answer. She probably wouldn't have heard it. In any case, he wasn't trying to answer. She was the only one talking. She was the only one screaming. Maybe she was on the phone. It didn't sound like she was on the phone. Someone was moving in the room. The sound of furniture that wasn't able to move out of the way fast enough. The sound of cursing. Whoever was in there was angry at the furniture.

The screaming increased in volume. There was a brief scuffle with the furniture, probably as it tried to stop him from leaving. The door opened far wider and faster than it was supposed to. Michael heard the furniture tripping up the man as it again tried to make him stay. The door slammed shut again, and the screaming died down. There was the sound of mumbling from around where the door was. Then just the sound of breathing. It seemed very loud. Michael stood, wondering what to do. His attention was focused on what was round the corner. If there had been a figure standing far behind him, he certainly wouldn't have noticed it.

Michael had to go around the corner. He backed up a few steps so he could walk around the corner naturally, so he didn't look like he had been waiting there. He quickly realised he shouldn't have bothered. As he walked into the corridor, his dad wasn't looking at him. He wasn't really looking at anything. His father was on the floor. Almost exactly where he had fallen a few seconds ago. Instead of getting up, he had just shifted onto his side so he would be more comfortable. All of his edges were dulled, with no sharpness anymore. His head was raised just enough for Michael to know that he was awake. It drifted back and forward as if the closed eyes were watching something slow crawling around on the floor.

His father's arm was jammed into his side, propping him up. There was no reason for any of it. His body would have been as well giving up, but it didn't know that. The part of his brain which was now in charge was unaccustomed to such responsibility. Without any clear idea of what to do, it just pointed things in the right direction and hoped for the best. Subtlety wasn't an option at this stage. It would do the basics as best it could, and apologies would have to make up for the rest. Michael could smell the liquid that had soaked through the strings of the puppet until they had snapped. Dad was helpless. How could someone so helpless have done so much damage?

His mother was sobbing quietly, or at least as quietly as you could at this time of night. The silence eagerly made sure everyone knew all about it. Even through the door, Michael could hear her. He could hear her head in her hands. He could hear crying into her hands, and he could hear them overflowing. Dad must have heard it too, but it didn't seem to mean anything to him.

"Dad?"

It turned its head towards the noise, but its eyes must have had more important things to do. This response didn't seem to satisfy whatever was making the noise.

"Dad?"

The eyes half opened, and Dad breathed in and out to show his willingness to cooperate.

"Is everything all right?"

Michael imagined the journalist laughing at the question. Is everything all right? There probably wasn't anyone in the hotel who could list three things that were all right. Even if there was, it was unlikely Dad was one of them.

Dad searched for an answer. A head bobbed from side to side, searching for the right words to sum everything up. Had to be concise. Might only get one chance. No long stories, just the essence of the issue. How could it all be made clear in a few well-chosen words? His left arm didn't work very well. It was probably meant to be pointing. Instead, the hand just came up closer to his left shoulder, requiring a drastic shifting of weight to maintain balance. It stayed there as the situation was outlined, apparently to the carpet, although it had limited interest.

"Your mother's a bit upset." It wasn't enough. More was needed, something reassuring. "She'll be okay in the morning."

His head shook for longer than was necessary. The left hand headed out again, probably in a comforting gesture, but it was dangerously overconfident and panicked while it was still halfway there. It quickly headed back towards the body, where the only part of the brain which had remained at its post was desperately trying to prevent Michael's father from rolling face down. The hand finally arrived at his head and settled on his face, where it pressed hard to stop it from dripping onto the floor.

One eye opened briefly. "Are all these rooms full?"

"Yes, I think so."

"Shit." Dad sank a little further towards the floor.

It was difficult to know what to do. Michael crouched beside his father. His hand was batted away the first time but not the second. That kind of effort just couldn't be maintained. Michael looked at his watch and desperately calculated how long it had been since the last drink, how long until things would start getting better. The first answer was less than an hour. The second answer was several hours. He would have to sleep. Where? While he thought of an answer, he tried to comfort himself by thinking about how every second, things were getting better. He pictured the alcohol being destroyed in Dad's body. Too slow, but better every second. He told himself that things were getting better instead of getting worse. Even so, he knew it didn't really make any difference. It was all happening too slowly. Sleep would fix everything.

Michael tried to sound urgent and desperate. "You have to get up." There was no response.

"You have to get up now. Quick." Michael's tone was sharper but not sharp enough. There was no way of getting through. The alcohol had shut down everything. For a moment, Michael wished he was drunk. Then it might not seem so bad. They said it was always more difficult for the people left behind. He didn't think this was what they meant, but it was true anyway.

He grasped his father's clothes with both hands and tested to see if he would be able to lift him. No chance. Michael almost rolled him onto his front by accident and only steadied him by bracing his shoulder against him. He was much heavier than he looked. Michael thought of the weight of a leg. *Surprisingly heavy*, the journalist had said. All the power required was locked inside his dad. He just had to get him to help.

"Dad, please get up."

Nothing started moving except the head. It started shaking slowly. Maybe the left hand moved again. "It's okay. I'm fine here."

Michael looked at the sobbing door and considered asking for help, but he knew he couldn't. It would upset Mum. He noticed he had been whispering all the time he had been in the corridor. He must have known that his presence had to be a secret long before he had properly realised it. Maybe he could get Uncle Joe. What would he say? Would Dad be angry at him in the morning? What if he wouldn't help?

Eyes flicked open and fixed on him. The left hand gripped his arm with a force that scared him a little. As he tried to remove it, his dad spoke with unfocused eyes. "You tell Uncle Joe that he's to look after you properly. Or he'll have me to deal with."

"I will."

The hand tightened. The eyes focused. His dad was getting angry. "You tell him. You're my boy. Just because I'm not here doesn't mean anything. You're my boy, Michael."

"I know. I'll tell him. Dad, you're hurting me."

The hand loosened, and the eyes closed again. Michael rested his head on his father. He didn't know what to do. Another few minutes had passed. Another few minutes closer to everything being better. He listened to his father breathe. Everything would be different after he had slept. Maybe he could let him sleep here for an hour, and then he would be better. Then he would move. Maybe two hours. But then where? Where could he take him? Maybe to his room. Dad could have his bed, and he could sleep on the floor. For the moment, he would stay awake and let Dad sleep. He would try again in an hour. He lay and tried not to think about it.

A figure moved into his view. It spoke. "Get up, Michael."

"But he's—"

"Get up. It'll be okay."

Uncle Joe looked different. He didn't seem as cold as usual, but something else. Tired? Annoyed? Worried? No. Sad? Surely not. Why would he be sad? Probably just tired. It was the middle of the night, after all. He didn't tell Michael to go to bed, didn't explain anything, didn't give any excuses. He was just there.

Michael clung to his father. "He won't move."

Uncle Joe was calm as usual, but still, there was something different about him. He looked like he might sigh any minute. "James, you'll be moving in a minute. Come on. You can't stay there."

That was the first thing he hadn't whispered. Why wasn't it a secret that Uncle Joe was there?

He motioned for Michael to come away from his father. Uncle Joe bent over the padre and gently put his hand under the man's arm. "Come on. You'll be better off in bed, James."

The figure started to move, and Uncle Joe nodded at Michael to help. It rose under its own strength, mostly. It put its arm around Uncle Joe and found its head next to his. It seemed sadder than before.

"You're a good man, Joe. I knew everything would be fine when I came back. You'll take care of the boy. He's a good boy, Joe."

"Let's get you upstairs."

Michael wasn't sure where they were going. Uncle Joe anticipated the question and the next two.

"The top floor. It's the only place where there are free rooms. Just for tonight. It will only be for one night."

Uncle Joe didn't look at him. It wasn't the time to argue. Michael nodded and tried to pretend that if Uncle Joe hadn't answered any questions, he wouldn't have asked any.

The padre still kept moving. "What's on the top floor?"

Uncle Joe looked at him and smiled. "Bed."

The padre accepted the answer and closed his eyes. Michael was pleased that everything was all right again. At least, he was pleased things weren't so bad you couldn't pretend they were all right.

As they headed up to the top floor, Michael thought again about how things were getting better every minute. His attention stayed focused on his father as they carried him upstairs. He was blind to everything else. Michael wouldn't have seen if Uncle Joe had gestured to someone with his free hand. He wouldn't have noticed two figures far behind them. It wouldn't have mattered. Even if they had ever been there, they wouldn't be needed anymore.

Uncle Joe knew all about when people were needed and when they weren't. It was other people who needed him to tell them.

22

The seat was empty again at breakfast.

Breakfast was shorter than usual. Uncle Joe had things to do. The phone rang soon after he sat down. The rest of the world was usually asleep during breakfast, but today somebody needed him. Michael thought about whether he still needed Uncle Joe. Maybe not. Maybe everything was fixed. Maybe everything was fine again.

After breakfast, Michael went up to the top floor. It seemed like everyone was still asleep. The bar wasn't open. It was probably too early for even the ghosts to squeeze under the door. But it was not impossible that some were already down there. They might be hiding in the bar, waiting for Cathy to come in and serve them.

The doors in the corridor were all standing to attention. They eyed him warily as he passed. None of the doors opened to show him what was happening in the rooms behind them. None of them whispered or talked to him about what was happening inside. He stood in front of the door where they'd brought his father the night before. He was sure it was the right door. It remained quiet. It would still be locked.

Uncle Joe had locked it and pushed the key under the door, as Michael had seen him do many times before. It contained the situation. The door wasn't fit to imprison anyone, and Uncle Joe knew that. Somehow, he also knew that if you locked someone in a room and gave them a key to get out, they were more likely to stay inside. No easy moral victory to be had by kicking the door down, no obvious point in opening it again. Inside the room, the key reminded them they were still in control. Anyway, maybe being unable to leave wasn't enough to make a locked room a cell.

Maybe it only becomes a cell when you can't control who comes in. The key showed them the room was theirs.

The door remained loyal to Uncle Joe. They were always loyal to Uncle Joe. The key was an illusion. Uncle Joe had keys which would let him into any room. He was just too clever to use them unless he really had to. Michael didn't try the handle. The door's continued silence planted doubt in his mind. Maybe it wasn't this door. What if he had got it wrong? He was sure, but still, the door silently challenged him. How sure was he? He was sure. The door silently pointed out how similar it looked to every other door. It hinted at unspecified, unlikely events he had not witnessed. Events that he had slept through, people switching rooms in the middle of the night, and angry ghosts in the wrong beds. The door made it clear it was his choice.

If he knocked on the door, what would he say? He would be interrupting the natural course of things. While his father was asleep, time was washing away everything that had happened. The longer he waited, the better everything would be. Time was scrubbing people's memories until they weren't as sharp and painful as they had been last night. It was washing the alcohol out of his father's body. Time was repairing everything. The only problem was the small amount available. His father would have to leave in a couple of days, and time was running out. It was taking huge amounts of it to remove everything that had happened the previous night. The same time that had slowly crawled past second by second the previous night was now being used ten minutes at a time. Michael could feel it rushing past, but there was nothing he could do. It wasn't like it was being wasted. It would be worth it if his father would be back the way he was yesterday. He didn't need him to be perfect. He just needed him back the way he was yesterday.

When the war finished, he would come back for good, and there would be years of time for him to be scoured clean of everything that had happened. It might take years for him to be perfect and happy again, but that was okay. There would be time for that. For now, there wasn't much time at all. It had too many things crammed into it already. Years' worth of advice, support, and good memories. Now it would have to fit in forgiveness from people, which would usually take days or weeks. Everything had to be squeezed in. Michael imagined time like a tube of water that was being squeezed and compressed until it glowed red hot, the water rushing past even faster than before.

He had to leave his father alone for now. The door and Uncle Joe knew what was best. He went downstairs, past his room, past the bar where the ghosts might be, out the door, and walked towards the beach. Most of the world was still asleep. Even the seagulls hadn't fully resumed the previous day's argument over the best places on the roof. Looking back towards the hotel, Michael could see the window he imagined was his father's. It was closed. Bad memories wouldn't be able to get out. He imagined his father sleeping, repairing. He imagined his father's body being restored and strengthened and the bad memories drifting into the air, hanging there and slowly swirling round like brown smoke. How could he be expected to get better when he was still marinating in the previous night's poison?

Michael told himself that the bad memories would get out of the room, eventually. They would seep out through the keyhole and through gaps in the window frame. The rooms couldn't be airtight, he reasoned. Otherwise, people would suffocate. Eventually, he would get better. Eventually, he would get up and open the door or the window. Everything would be let out.

He sat on the beach for the next hour, watching the hotel and the seagulls. Eventually, the window would open. His father would get up and be just as he was yesterday. Last night wouldn't matter. They still had two days. They would still have time to talk. You could say a lot in an hour. In two days, you would probably even run out of things to say.

Even if his father hadn't been away for all those years, they probably wouldn't have spent very long talking, not properly. It might not even have been two days' worth. He would still have time to ask his father more questions. He would still be able to talk about General Neckerman's interview. Maybe he would even tell him about The Book. He could even tell him about all the other letters. He probably wouldn't need them anymore anyway, not if his father was going to answer all of his questions.

They could go to church on Sunday, on his last day. They could all go together. He would suggest it later so Uncle Joe could arrange for Cathy to take care of everything while they were away. His father might even be able to get a job at the church. Maybe he could stay. The television had said that Britain might be coming out of the war for a while, anyway. If the Unified Command agreed, there probably wouldn't be any point in his dad going back. Maybe his dad would take him to Glasgow. They could take his mum as well. He would have to wait for just the right time to ask, have to make sure he didn't go on about it and annoy anyone.

He could probably even show his dad the knife from Norway. It was his favourite thing. He probably wouldn't be able to show him his whole collection of letters and pictures. He would have to keep that hidden. Probably that would still be a bit too much. But maybe one day, if everything changed a little bit. Maybe then he would be able to show him, but probably not yet.

By the time it was nine o'clock, he had convinced himself that things weren't so bad. As long as his dad was home, things couldn't really be that bad. Everything would sort itself out as soon as he woke up, and it would all be back to normal. He might even be up already. Just because the window was shut didn't mean he wasn't up. Cathy would be up by now. She might even be in the bar getting ready for the day.

Michael lay back and watched the seagulls gliding overhead. They flew around in wide circles before returning to land on the roof again. They didn't seem very interested in going out to sea. Probably, they weren't hungry this early and were just passing the time. Some of the soldiers would probably feed them later. Even Uncle Joe had given up on trying to stop them from doing that.

Michael watched the birds. If his dad got up, someone would come and get him. No point in going back in yet. If his dad was up but wasn't ready, he would just spend the whole time waiting for him to come out of the shower, have breakfast, and so on. If he waited here, it would all happen without him being there. He imagined flying with the seagulls, sailing high over the hotel. How far did seagulls go? Could they fly to Stranraer? Could they fly to Dumfries? Maybe they could fly to Glasgow. He had always assumed it was the same seagulls walking on the roof each day. Maybe it wasn't. Maybe they lived somewhere different each day. They might spend their whole lives travelling.

He was still imagining travelling the world as a seagull when he heard someone calling his name. It was a woman's voice. He sat up and saw Cathy. She was standing outside the hotel, arms folded, shoulders hunched, shouting his name. His dad was probably awake. He started walking towards her. When she saw Michael, she slowly walked out to meet him. She looked cold, and for the first time, he noticed it was windy. She wasn't wearing a coat. As she met Michael, she immediately turned to walk back in with him.

"You have to come inside."

Michael thought about asking Cathy if she wanted to come to Glasgow with his mum and dad, but then realised that Uncle Joe might want to go. If he did, she would have to stay and look after things. He would ask her later. "Is my dad awake?"

"Yes, I think so. You have to come inside."

"Was everything all right in the bar last night?"

"Yes, it was fine. Everyone was out for twelve. I think one of the boys didn't go to bed, though. I think I heard Joseph getting up later on."

More good news. Nobody even knew about last night. As they walked towards the hotel, he was more confident than ever that everything was going to be fine. He had to remember to ask about Glasgow and church on Sunday. Apart from that, everything would take care of itself.

Cathy stopped outside the bar. "Your Uncle Joe is up on the top floor. You have just to go up."

He answered her over his shoulder as he started running up the stairs. "Okay. I'll see you later if I'm not too busy with Dad."

He could hear them well before he reached the top floor. He could hear Uncle Joe. It didn't sound like him. He was speaking much more quickly than usual. As Michael reached the top of the stairs, he saw that one of the doors had swung open to show Uncle Joe what was inside the room. He was standing in the corridor, talking to someone in the room. He looked strange, speaking quickly, gesturing with his hands. "... are being collected. You just make sure you haven't left anything here."

He turned to Michael. "Michael, you have to listen—"

"Where's Dad?" As he walked towards Uncle Joe, he could see his father in the room, bent over, picking something up.

Uncle Joe sidestepped into the doorway and pulled the door half closed, blocking Michael's view. "Michael, you have to listen. There has been a change of plan—"

"What's Dad doing?"

Uncle Joe failed to catch the boy's eye as he tried to look past him into the room. "There's been a phone call. Your father has to leave."

"No, it's a mistake. We've got two days."

"Not anymore." He turned toward the door and shouted, "Hurry up, James!"

Michael struggled to understand what was happening. Not two days, not two hours, it couldn't be, not like this.

Cathy appeared on the stairs. She talked quickly, just like Uncle Joe. She craned her neck to talk past Michael. "The car is already on its way. It should only be about two minutes. James's things are already downstairs."

Uncle Joe raised a hand in acknowledgement. "That's fine. Well done. Did you hear that, James? Two minutes!"

Michael didn't recognise the emotion. He had never seen it in Uncle Joe before, but there was no time to think about it. There were too many other things to think about. This wasn't fair. This wasn't happening. He braced himself across the corridor, one hand on each wall. "He has to stay!"

Uncle Joe looked away from the door and straight at the boy. "He has to go. If there was another way..."

"Dad could stay one more day. We have to go to church and to Glasgow. I have to show him things. Everything was busy yesterday. We only talked for a while. Dad's been away for ages. Please, Uncle Joe!"

Uncle Joe's attention was focused on the door. "You have to trust me, Michael. This is for the best. One day you will understand."

"Where's Mum?"

"She's in her room. You've not to bother her now. You can talk to her later."

He ran down the stairs, ignoring Uncle Joe as he called his name. He could hear that there were no footsteps behind him. When he reached the door, it was crying. He hammered on it, conscious that behind him, his dad could be heading down the stairs and out the front door. When there was no reply after a fraction of a second, he burst in to find his mother lying on the bed. He grabbed at her arm, but she pulled away from him. "Mum, you have to come! Dad's going! Uncle Joe's making him leave! You have to come now! You have to stop him!"

The world was coming to an end, and he was the only one who was trying to do anything. Why would nobody help him? Tears ran down his face as he realised he was helpless.

"Mum, last night was just a mistake! It's fine! Everything is fine! Make Uncle Joe give him another chance! It can still be all right! We can go to church together on Sunday! I thought we could go to Glasgow. We can go to Glasgow! Please!"

His mother wouldn't help. She took her hands from her face and put them on his. "I'm sorry, Michael."

"Don't you want to see him?"

He pushed her away as she shook her head. As she sank back onto the bed, he screamed at her, "I'll stop him then! I'll stop Uncle Joe!"

By the time he reached the top floor again, they were gone. He opened the door to an empty room. He dropped to the floor to complete his search as if his father might have been hiding. An empty vodka bottle of a brand he didn't recognise lay sleeping alone under the bed. He raced downstairs to hear Uncle Joe shouting his name.

At the door, Uncle Joe stood with Michael's father. Michael charged at Uncle Joe. The old man took a step back and caught the boy as he screamed and clawed. "Let him stay! You're not my dad! You go! I choose him! I want him!"

Uncle Joe turned the boy around and pushed him into his father. "We don't have time for this. Say goodbye to him."

Michael's father looked down at him. He looked tired. "I'm sorry, Michael. There's no other way. One day you'll understand this. None of this is your fault. Remember everything I said yesterday?"

Michael held tight onto his father's shoulders. "I want you to stay. Last night doesn't matter. I can look after you."

He pulled Michael's hands away and knelt in front of him, holding his hands. "I'm sure you could. But I have to go. There's no other way."

"I could come with you. I could come with you in the car to Stranraer."

"No, you have to stay here and look after Uncle Joe and your mother."

As he left, the padre looked at Uncle Joe. "Look after the boy for me."

The old man nodded.

The boy and the old man watched the padre get into the back of the car and drive off.

He was gone.

A hand fell on Michael's shoulder. This would be it. This would be the explanation, the apology, the instruction about how to deal with it all. He couldn't turn to look at Uncle Joe.

"Michael, I need you to go to your room. Don't come out until I tell you. Don't come out unless I come and get you. It's very important."

Michael couldn't believe it. "What?"

"Go to your room and stay there. I'll let you know when you can come downstairs. I have some things to deal with. It shouldn't be too long. Cathy will bring up your lunch if necessary, but I should be along to get you before then."

"What about Mum?"

"I'll take care of her. She'll be fine. You have to do this for me today. Stay upstairs."

Michael walked to the foot of the stairs and stopped. He turned around to look at the old man. Uncle Joe was already looking at him, expecting something.

He looked at Uncle Joe, thinking about everything that had happened. Everything he had just lost. Michael was supposed to understand one day. He didn't understand today. He looked Uncle Joe in the eye. The old man didn't flinch, didn't look away.

"Uncle Joe."

"Yes, Michael."

There was a pause.

"You shouldn't have sent him away."

There was a longer pause.

"I had to."

It seemed like a long time before Michael said anything. He spoke calmly, deliberately, almost spitting the words at Uncle Joe. "I hate you. I really, really hate you. I wish you were dead."

The old man nodded gently, but he didn't speak. They stood there for at least a minute. The silence should have made it feel like an eternity, but it seemed like no time at all to Michael. There was no silence in him. He turned slowly and went upstairs.

Nobody was there to see Uncle Joe standing, waiting. He stood until Cathy came to get him because someone was on the phone. Hard to say how much later that was. Hard to say how long he had been waiting. Maybe a minute. Maybe an hour. When she came to get him, Cathy didn't notice any tears in his eyes. There weren't any. Maybe it was because he hadn't been crying. Or maybe because he had been standing there for such a long time. It was lucky that there was an important phone call to be dealt with. Otherwise, he might just have stood there all day. As it was, he was needed. He was always needed somewhere.

23

In his room, he lay on his bed and thought about what had just happened. Not fair. Nothing was fair. He hated them, all of them, The Enemy, Uncle Joe, his mother. They were all selfish. Why couldn't he have what he wanted, just once?

He stood up, went across to the wardrobe, and opened both doors. The smiling faces smiled through everything, as usual. He tore them from the door with one hand. He looked at his father on the other door and thought about tearing that picture down as well, but decided to leave it. His father looked at him. Calm as always, he seemed to understand, but he had no answers. Michael closed his father's door again, leaving him staring into the cupboard where The Book was. He had started reading the handwritten parts at the end. Today, he would read more of them. He would read it until Uncle Joe came to get him.

The writing was messy, but he could still read it easily. He continued from the last part he had read. It was about what had happened after the journalist had been sent back to the war:

> Going back to the war felt like the right thing to do. I could have made a case for staying at home, but there wouldn't have been any point. I thought I would be happier in the company of strangers. Coming home had been like some stressful holiday. I knew going back would return me to a world that I understood. I thought at least it would be to a world full of people who weren't that interested in me.
>
> Time passes more quickly when you aren't there to observe it. Since I had been away, time had raced on at twice

its normal speed. The Mirror War was changing everything. I think that was the difference. Maybe it was Australia that was different. You would think that war is war, but there are always differences from one place to another.

I had always avoided Australia. You find it easier if you can identify with people. Most of the soldiers in Australia were Asian: Chinese, Japanese, Indian, and Thai. I didn't speak any of their languages, and learning mine wasn't much of a priority for their people anymore. Most of the 'native' Australians, and by that, I mean the people who mostly spoke the same language as me and hadn't lived there for very long at all in the grand scheme of things, weren't very obvious on the frontline. They had lost a lot of people in East Africa early in the war, then in the West of Australia, which at least was more convenient, I suppose. It gave you a greater intensity, fighting on your own doorstep. No land behind you. Any step backwards takes The Enemy that much nearer to your family and to everything you left behind.

There weren't that many Australians to begin with anyway, at least not compared to the millions upon millions of Chinese who came to die here. Even if it wasn't entirely selfless, it was still pretty inspiring. The Australians had given everything in this war. They had reached Demographic Collapse long ago. They would have been released from the war by the Unified Command years before now. Unfortunately, when The Enemy are invading your country, it doesn't really matter what the Unified Command says. There were very few Australians left at the front. There were very few Australians left.

The similarities between Australia and Africa were interesting. Both were hot. Mostly. Both had plenty of desert. Maybe The Enemy liked it hot. Maybe people in Siberia wouldn't have anything to worry about.

The skeletons were the same, bleached white, grinning, laughing. I thought about writing a piece on the end of racism. We are all the same underneath. All happy. All that seems different is transient. Maybe not a good idea. Maybe not particularly uplifting.

I had almost given up on the skeletons. Sometimes I squinted at them, trying to imagine who they were when they were alive, what colour their skin was, and whether they were male or female. It didn't really work. It was hard to connect one thing to the other. I knew the skeletons used to be people, that they were people–dead people–but it didn't seem real.

The skeletons I saw in the Australian desert smiled at me as I passed them. The modern tanks and vehicles they clung to suddenly seemed strangely antiquated, thanks to Neckerman's new war. Only a few years old, but inappropriate and outdated.

Not outdated. What is the opposite of outdated? Futuristic? Not that. Contemporary. But obsolete. Strange. Maybe they looked like a dead-end, a poor guess at what the future would be like. Like that font that looks like computer writing they used in the seventies when they wanted things to look modern. Not stupid, just incorrect in a tolerable, understandable way.

The skeletons grinned like they knew something I didn't. They likely knew plenty I didn't. Maybe they were laughing at us, but I didn't think so. Maybe it was something else. Maybe they remembered what it had been like. How much fun it was just before it ended.

It's a dirty secret, but people can enjoy war. You don't get adventure books, toys, and films about something that has no redeeming features. Men sometimes enjoy it. Women too, I imagine. It's just that these days people don't write quite so many books or make quite so many films about it. These days only the dead get to be nostalgic.

As I passed the possibly wistful skeletons, I often thought of when I studied biology at school. I saw things that looked like white stone and remembered: bone is flesh, not dead, not lifeless structure. Living tissue, the only type that stayed after death and decay. Immortal. Nearly. Wears away eventually. All back to dust. Teeth last longest. I clicked my teeth together, again and again, imagining they were alive. They were tissue like my muscle and skin.

Strange how we never think about it. We eat our food with these living parts of our body, same as if we tore it apart with our hands. Even our skin isn't what we think it is. It's not just a bag holding us together. It is an organ. It's doing things, just like our lungs and liver. Except we can touch it, but only with itself. Does that mean we aren't really touching it? The idea chased its tail for a while before I realised I was thinking too much again. I quickly switched to thinking about the ache inside my head.

Back then, my head was always sore. They had given me pills to help, but everything was still the same. People were still the same. Life was still the same. They only changed me. They did not produce a large enough change in the glass that I looked through. I felt the same. No, I thought the same but felt different. I was further away from the glass. I was even more a passive observer. My head ached. I imagined swollen, inflamed brain cells pulsing in a bath of serotonin. Corroding. Raw.

I thought the same. I felt different.

I think we are always observers. We do most things on autopilot. We have to in order to survive, but in the same way, we have to pretend we're not so we don't get freaked out.

I had tried to force myself into the moment. I was there. Right then. I was making decisions. Whatever happened in the next second was down to me right then. I used to be able to do that. If you did it properly, it paralysed you. You can't act when you're too conscious. At that moment, I couldn't do it. I was too far away.

The pills were supposed to work. Maybe it was the headache. Maybe that was what really worked. You spent so much time thinking about how much your head hurt that you stopped thinking about other things. At the same time, the pills were supposed to put down the clutch in your brain and disconnect it long enough to recover. Not for me.

Therapists might work for the same reason—for other people. They sent me to talk to someone. Don't know where they found her. I concluded that I was too intelligent. I couldn't decide if I was pleased or not. I spent the time guessing where she was going, where she was letting me go, congratulating myself when I got it right. Not very constructive. I was the patient. I didn't have to help. They had to help me. Absolved of responsibility. Nothing worked on me. Maybe I was too intelligent. Maybe I was too insane. Maybe my world was too insane.

We'd raced past the remnants of a glorious battle, which nobody really remembered. I didn't know if we had won, but I knew all the skeletons had lost. Never mind. It had been a long time ago. It was done, and they could smile about it now.

The Enemy had… retreated? No. Fallen back? It would have been nice to think so. Gone home? More important people than me had made that mistake before. Changed direction? Got bored? Wandered off? They did that a lot. They never really 'advanced' in the way you would expect.

Advance implies you are heading towards something, and They never seem to be in a great hurry. We will never be able to make a film about the war called "Doomsday". It would have to be something more like "Doomsdecade". Hopefully, even "Doomscentury". "Doomsmillennium" is probably too optimistic.

I am pretty sure I know why They do it. We all know. It is the same reason we replay a level in a computer game that is difficult. They want to do it again. To succeed, or narrowly fail, again. Except you don't die for real in a computer game. You don't watch all your friends die for real.

Maybe They don't have any friends. Maybe They only have enemies.

Anyway, whatever the reason, we had to go looking for them so they could kill us, or most of us, at least. Hopefully, my name would once again be in the right column when the survivors and the dead were counted up at the end. That was the most important thing. It was also important to win the battle.

Some people make the mistake of thinking that winning the battle is the most important thing. They are wrong, in my opinion. Just ask the skeletons, the ones that aren't too nostalgic.

There's a trick you see on TV all the time. At least, you used to see it all the time. Actually, maybe I just saw it on children's programmes when I was little. Maybe you still see it on children's programmes. It's a trick you use when you're hiding. You hide behind something, and while the bad guy looks for you, you throw a stone. It lands far away. The bad guy hears it and thinks it's you, and heads off in the wrong direction. I remember trying it a couple of times when we played hide and seek. There's only one problem with the trick. It doesn't work. A stone falling somewhere, hitting something, almost anything, sounds nothing like you walking around somewhere. Every time I tried it, I got caught. Eventually, I realised television was lying to me. It was a hard lesson. In recent years, since the television has started telling me the truth, the lessons have got much harder.

Anyway, it turned out that there was nothing new under the sun. You see the same patterns repeating everywhere. The universe is as unoriginal as it is varied. We journalists can be thankful for this because otherwise, metaphors wouldn't make much sense, and we would have to explain things properly all the time. The trick from my childhood had reappeared in a different form.

Currently, we were the good guy, and a smaller, noisier army was the stone. They would head far away from us, make a lot of noise, look like our main force, and draw The Enemy's attention. We just had to hide for the moment. As soon as The Enemy took the bait, we would hit them by surprise. Given the choice, I would rather have been with the stone, but you don't always get the choice. I only hoped the generals had employed the stone-throwing technique with more success in their childhood.

My fellow good guys provided better odds in this cosmic game of hide-and-seek than I was used to as a child. It would be easier for me to hide in their crowd than it would be for our army to hide in the desert. We didn't have to hide, really. We just had to look smaller and less important. Of course, these games should have been pointless. The Enemy should have known everything, seen everything. Except They didn't. They only knew what They wanted to know at any given time. They could forget or ignore things if it made life more interesting. An enviable ability.

Given the choice, I think I would rather pick and choose what I know from day to day.

I travelled in what once would have been an armoured column but had become something else consisting of endless trucks and no tanks. Nothing flying overhead. Trucks full of... what? Not shells. Not rocket launchers. Not mortars. Spears? Swords? Horses? Probably. The world had gone mad. No, it had always been mad. It had turned... bizarre. The whole world may always have been a stage, but it wasn't always host to some weird production of an old play with all the Roman generals on motorbikes and the Roman soldiers carrying machine guns.

Actually, it was worse than that. It was all backwards. The future imitating the past. It was pointless. That wasn't the problem. Most things had always been pointless. It was impure and inconsistent. It was ridiculous. Why were we still allowed to use trucks? Why didn't transport count? Why had it never counted? They never hit our supply lines. They never killed us while we were being shipped across the world to fight them, never sank ships carrying food, never starved us out. Never really tried to win. Doomsdecade.

I had thought about all the trucks rumbling along this road, burning fuel, spewing fumes. More trucks carrying fuel, burning fuel, more trucks to refuel the refuelling trucks, and I saw the column swallowing its own tail, twisting and smoking. I'd squeezed my eyes shut and tried to stop the thought. An impure, dirty war. Now truly like a bad dream, as it didn't make sense. Nothing more upsetting.

I couldn't get a handle on what was happening. I could see corruption everywhere, except for the pure white skeletons. Stripped of human confusion and contradiction. Contradiction. Contra-diction. I had never thought about the word before. Must have used it a thousand times. It started to split and turn in my mind. The two halves attacked each other. Contra-diction. Opposite-talking? Fascinating. Look it up in the contradictionary. I closed my eyes again. Couldn't stop thinking. Corruption. Change. Tainted. Everything tainted. Fumes in the air, bones in the desert, spears in the twenty-first century. Couldn't untangle it. Couldn't make it right. Made it worse.

The planet corrupted everything. Complicated everything, made it all a special case you mistook for the general case. Shapes altered. Assumptions skewed. Fuel in trucks taking the shape of their container, dripping out, squeezing through pipes, but that was not the way it had to be. Only on Earth. Only in that particular situation. Tank of fuel, bottle of water. Why were materials defined by their container? Mistaking corruption for truth. Up there, they didn't have to cope with gravity. Everything was pure. Up there, they were ordering perfect spheres of wine, no need for the confusion of bottles and glasses. A truck of soldiers. Defined by the truck, shaped by the truck, soldiers were men shaped by their clothes, their uniforms, pilots if coated in aircraft, drivers if holding a wheel.

The perfection altered. My mind overheated, grinding metal, boiling thoughts shining brightly in my skull, out of control. I couldn't stop thinking. I was changing, evolving. I was the only one like that. The driver looked bored. Not bored like me. Not disconnected and uninterested. His mind was paused. My mind had been ejected. I couldn't stop thinking.

How else could I make the seconds pass? They refused to pass passively anymore. I considered clawing my face off to postpone my screaming. I couldn't get out, going too fast. I shut my eyes and breathed. The air entered my lungs and raced through my body, dissolved in my blood. I breathed out invisible fumes. I polluted the world, spewing fumes like the trucks that defined us.

I tried to control my thoughts but could only observe them. My mind processed the world around it relentlessly for another half hour before the truck stopped, and I was able to find somewhere to scream.

A few days later, I was waiting. We were all waiting. I had found some Australians. Very young. Just boys and girls, really. They looked more like cadets than soldiers. A small outpost. Right by the sea. We looked after huge tanks of diesel for trucks going to and from the front that needed to refuel. The road was getting quieter. Everyone was almost in position.

They say that waiting is the worst part. I disagree. Getting shot is the worst part, or in my case, watching other people get shot. Most of the time, I didn't mind waiting. If I had to wait anywhere, I might have chosen there. At least, if I wasn't allowed to choose somewhere much further away.

Watching as the waves crashed against the beach was surprisingly relaxing. At that moment, we were waiting for The Enemy to decide what to do. I hoped they would go for the stone instead of the good guy.

It would have been nice to think that I was keen to see our strategy succeed, keen to see the home side win. Actually, I just preferred it when they were moving away from me rather than towards me. I felt bad about it, or at least I knew I should feel bad about it. It would make a better story if they came for us. I would be able to do my job better if they did. I didn't really care. Such a bad person. I suppose I was wishing those other people dead. Shouldn't feel bad about it. Most of them were probably hoping the stone would fall somewhere and sound exactly like a stone. They were hoping The Enemy would ignore it and use its trajectory to find the tree we were hiding behind.

It didn't really matter, of course. You can wish for whatever you like. It doesn't affect anything. Things fall as they do. I briefly tried wishing the waves would stop crashing against the shore. They didn't stop. I tried wishing the war wasn't happening. I realised I would have no way to tell if it had stopped. Instead, I wished it had never started. The boys were still in uniform. I became braver and wished the sun would fall out of the sky. It ignored me.

Once again, all the evidence seemed to suggest I was not God. Probably for the best. I imagined it was a great responsibility. You probably didn't get many holidays. Maybe He was having one right then. Maybe everyone was praying, but He had taken the phone off the hook. Blasphemy. Or was it heresy? Blasphemy. Slander. Only slander if it was not true. Wouldn't have been able to prove it. I'd probably have had to settle out of court. I was probably insured. Probably it was a slur on the great man. Was He still a man? Whatever He was, He was probably doing His best. How many of us could say that, either back then or now?

My head hurt. I watched the waves. What were waves? Lumps of water. Shaped water. They collapsed as they hit the beach. Disappeared. Where had the wave gone? It hadn't. It wasn't. Just thinking about the water the wrong way. Misshapen thinking. Corrupted perception. Where would I go? Ashes, dust. Disappear. I hadn't. I wasn't. Was I anything? Shaped… stuff. Dust and ashes. I was a misconception. I was a wrong assumption. Sloppy thinking. Corrupted interpretation. I tried to wish the ideas out of my head and lay back on the beach. I wished for a tidal wave that wouldn't come.

There were two suns. One in the sky, one on the windscreen of the truck further down the beach. It didn't wink at me. Didn't move. Reflection. Second-hand sunlight. Meant for the dark patch of the beach under the truck. I couldn't stop thinking.

I watched the soldiers. It had been a few days since we had arrived. No trees to hide behind. I could have applied for a forward unit, infantry, or even reconnaissance. I had decided I was interested in the life of the brave souls who drove trucks several miles away from where people were getting killed. I had decided if war was ninety-nine percent boredom and one percent sheer terror, I had more than covered the one percent sheer terror. I thought I would see what boredom was like. It turned out boredom wasn't as bad as you might think. It was just like being relaxed, except you had a feeling there was something you should be doing.

I had some vague hope that the Mirror War would make things easier. In my most hopeful moments, I pictured myself as a war tourist, like in the Crimean War over a century and a half ago, sitting on a hill high above the battle, watching everyone else die for my entertainment and education. I couldn't remember who won the Crimean War or what it was about, or who we were fighting. Russia, I decided, it had been Russia.

At that moment, it was close enough, there on that beautiful beach. Maybe a hundred of us. A few dozen tanks of fuel, one broken down truck, tents. There were, presumably, worse places to die, but there were few better places to be really, truly bored. A short rest after days of driving. Two days, maybe more. There were thousands of people in front of us. Some of the drivers called them canaries. Any trouble, and they would die first.

It was hot. The heat did strange things. It made some people short-tempered and made some people lazy. It was even supposed to send some people mad. I wasn't too worried about that, what with me being crazy already, as my aching head gently reminded me. The heat also made figures in the distance shimmer. Figures? Why were there figures in the distance? Too close. Probably fine. Probably someone bringing a message or something. Dozens of them? Probably travel in numbers for safety. Safety from what? We were safe in the rear. Probably just coming to see how we were. Dozens of them? Walking? It couldn't be Them. There were too many in front of us. Why only dozens? Didn't make sense. All would be fine. Someone was running. Why was someone running when everything was fine? One word. Plural. One word denoting many things. Endos! Shouted, long and drawn out. Interesting word. Hadn't heard it until I came to Australia. Had to ask what it meant.

Turns out that early in the war, a report was produced on The Enemy for the Australian government. The scientists gave some basic information. Not very enlightening. Pretty forgettable. One thing stuck. They said The Enemy were endotherms. All that meant was that they were warm-blooded. Don't know how they knew that. I guess they were pretty cold by the time the scientists examined them unless Australian scientists are a lot braver than I'm giving them credit for. Anyway, we're all endotherms, but someone picked up on the word, and the name stuck long enough to make the origin unimportant.

She was still shouting. I didn't know how she was doing it. I couldn't even breathe. I cursed myself for coming to a place without hills to run up and observe things from. I felt a wave of cold pass over me, which in the heat was quite interesting. I decided I would have to comment on that sometime.

I had just been thinking it was a beautiful beach. Now it was about to be famous. The Battle for Heavenly Beach. Except, neither side really wanted it. The Battle of Heavenly

Beach. Only a hundred of us. The Skirmish at Heavenly Beach. Famous? Who was I kidding? There were only a hundred of us. We could all have died there, and nobody would really have cared. Even our murderers were probably just filling in an afternoon. The whole operation we were part of could still have been a glorious victory, even if all of us died right there, right then.

My heart rate increased, and my mouth was dry. I knew if I lifted my hands from the ground, they would shake. I was afraid. I was terrified. I was going to die. I tried to comprehend it. I would die there. That day. All those years of my life, and it was going to end. I could not make it sink in. My body prepared me to fight or run. But I was not trained to fight, and I had nowhere to run. The terror helpfully continued to flood my body with adrenaline I wouldn't use. It just made me shake, unnerving me more.

Fifty of them. Not dozens. Not around fifty. Exactly fifty. We outnumbered them two to one. They knew that. It takes time to train someone to fight with swords, spears, and ride horses. The boys and girls were not yet perfectly trained killing machines. The Enemy knew that as well. That is why we outnumbered them.

Most people don't think the need for lengthy training is Neckerman's big miscalculation. Most people think it's the casualties. Full-scale battles of that type kill a lot of people. More Americans died at The Battle of Gettysburg than died in over ten years of fighting in Vietnam. Someone told me that once. Don't know if it's true. Even if it is true, I know two reasons Neckerman has not miscalculated. Firstly, we are not fighting Vietnam. We have been fighting World Wars One and Two rolled into one. Much higher casualties, anyway. Secondly, we can't afford to fight with tanks, planes, and machine guns anymore. Spears and swords, on the other hand, are cheap, as are people. In fact, there is a half-convincing argument that it's cheaper to sacrifice soldiers than it is to feed them.

The Enemy paused and slowly formed up a hundred yards away. We did not share their calm. The same adrenaline that paralysed me energised the boys and girls. It did not remind them of their mortality, only their training. In the last hour of their lives, they would switch themselves off and engage autopilot. All except the last few seconds. Then they would snap out of it and start screaming for their mothers. My training is to observe. Unfortunately, at that moment, I was not an observer. I was part of it.

I disconnected myself enough to stand up. There was nowhere to run. I was a dead man. I felt warmth spreading down my leg and realised I had wet myself. I didn't have time to think about it. I was running. I could hear what was happening. Boys and girls were getting ready to die. I was not ready. No amount of shouting would make me ready. I didn't think I cared about living or dying anymore, but right then, I realised I was lying to myself. I was strangely reassured. Maybe I was not as crazy as I thought.

I reached one of the tents. The canvas would not protect me from the killers outside, but it would stop me from seeing what was happening. I had seen enough. I sat in the corner and squeezed my eyes shut, but I could still picture everything. I heard screaming. Not shouting. Not like when people cry for help. Real screaming from the boys and girls. Squealing. With my eyes shut, the noise painted pictures for me. I forced my eyes open.

I tried to become distracted, but the white canvas of the tent was not enough. More screaming. More squealing. No begging yet. I should have been helping. I should have been doing something. I clawed at the ground and imagined digging down to hide. They would find me. I could not bear the screaming. Boys and girls. Wounded on purpose. Deliberately not killed yet. Tendons cut, bones broken, limbs hacked off. Watching and screaming. I should have been feeling sorry for them. I didn't. I wanted to, but only one thought filled my mind. Die. Stop screaming! Die.

Shut up and die! Die. Get up and kill them. Save my life! Die for me. You are paid to kill. Stop screaming!

Every moment was agony. Each second was worse than the last. My skin crawled. I would have done anything to make it stop. Except go outside. I could hear when They disengaged and left the boys and girls standing among their own screaming, begging, wounded. I heard the wounded stop screaming and would have been grateful, except I could picture why.

How had I got here? How had Mrs Walker's son ended up thousands of miles from home, dying on this beautiful beach? I was going to die. I would be dead within an hour.

When she ran in, she couldn't have really thought she would be safe. I don't think I was a great source of reassurance. She looked at me for… something. Something I couldn't give her. She was cut. Not badly, they hadn't meant to cut her badly. She was holding a knife. Probably dropped her sword. Probably just pulled out the knife. It was clean. We had lost. We? What did 'we' mean? What had I contributed? She had done it. The rest of the boys and girls and her. I was only watching. Not even that. Listening.

Her tears made me feel nothing. No emotion. I was finished. I had nothing left to say. I didn't speak to her. I was that selfish.

Two of The Enemy walked in slowly. They walked over the footprints she left when she ran in. They weren't looking at me, although They knew I was there. Their weapons looked unnecessarily elaborate. Lots of curves and grooves on their blades. They had been polished recently, but the shining steel was coated with blood. Maybe hers.

Incredible to watch them move. They were real. Beautiful, despite being dangerous. Maybe because they were dangerous. They observed her begging, crying, and screaming. If They were curious, pleased, or sympathetic, I couldn't tell. I could see their faces, but their expressions meant nothing to me.

The Enemy moved quickly, its blade flashing up from below. The girl's knife hit the floor. Maybe something else did as well. By the time she grabbed at the hand that had been holding the knife, it was back, standing next to the other one, observing again. The girl fell to her knees and stopped begging them for her life. Instead, she started begging me to help. Brown eyes. She used my name. How did she know my name? I didn't know her. One of The Enemy took a step towards me and pointed its weapon. It didn't speak. They never spoke.

The time had come for me to act. I stood up and looked straight at it. I had been doing some thinking while I had been in the tent. I realised what They were doing. I realised why They were there, behind our lines. Very rare. Small numbers. Very rare. Hitting a remote outpost. Very rare. More than that. New. I knew what They needed. I knew what to do. I reached for the camera I rarely used and showed it to them. I said the magic word. Journalist. I repeated it, although I knew They understood. She looked up at me and misunderstood completely. She was on her feet and smiling through her tears when one of them severed her right leg at the knee. It caught her and held her up as she screamed. The other one made sure I watched.

They stretched it all out for about ten minutes. I'd like to say I wished it had been me, but I'd be lying. I'd like to say I had nightmares about it, and that, at least, would be true. Except I didn't have nightmares about what I saw them do to her. I had nightmares they were doing it to me.

They just left. They just left me there. Me and the dead boys and girls. They didn't even take their own dead. I was not traumatised. At least, I was not upset. Everything had been burned away. Nothing seemed real. Inside my head, I called for myself. There was no reply. No echo. There was a time when it would all have affected me. Not anymore. When They put her head in my lap, I didn't scream. I don't think I screamed. Brown eyes. That was all I thought. How did she know my name? I think that was the first time I didn't try to get to know any of them. I just couldn't do it. It seemed they knew me, anyway.

It can be difficult to keep your distance. Their gravity draws you in. I had kept my distance, but it wasn't easy. People in their situation want to be close, want to trust you, especially when they're that young. There is always a powerful bond between the soldiers. Imagine how honest you would be with people if you thought they would never tell anyone, if they would take it to their grave. There, at war, there was a much greater chance of that. Their grave was usually only a few weeks away.

It's a strange world these days. Everything is much more frightening than it used to be in so many ways. In other ways, it's liberating. Some things you don't worry about anymore. Being scarred for life doesn't seem like such a long sentence. Never isn't such a long time. You don't have to worry about going home wounded or disabled. If you're hurt that badly, you just won't go home. All those bodies. No wounded. Nobody wants that. Nobody wants to fight Vietnam again. It destroys the will to fight. The Enemy can't allow that. We wouldn't have any choice but to patch up all the broken soldiers. The Enemy help us out by making sure it's not an issue.

What are They? How do They survive? How did They ever get this far? How do such things run a society, organise, and work together to build their ships and weapons if They are so hateful and violent? Gives you new respect for the human race. You always assume our compassion isn't selfless. You assume we exhibit the minimum possible amount of compassion necessary to avoid society collapsing. Seems it's not true. We actually look pretty good next to these things.

As I stood there on that impromptu battlefield, I hoped we were different. I hoped I was not just demonising the demons. Their bodies looked different. Their insides looked different. I could tell because their insides were now on the outside. It was upsetting, but maybe just because I knew it was wrong. It was hard to imagine all of it fitting back inside. Same for our bodies. I'd imagined how people looked inside, but it didn't look the way I'd thought. It didn't look like anything. It was dark in there. Dark inside me. I couldn't see anything. I wished it was night so I couldn't see anything.

What are we inside at night? What is outside our darkness? I closed my eyes. Not thinking straight again.

There were lots of bodies. Nobody to talk to. Didn't talk to them while they were alive, and then it was too late. Didn't care. Didn't regret it.

You see it in horror films. Everybody gets killed except a few survivors who desperately seek each other out. I always found that strange. They never bothered with each other before everyone started dying. Boring. The whole war bored me.

If I hadn't been there, nobody would know who had won that battle. Maybe I could have lied and said we did. I could have said I was a hero. I didn't care enough. Victory probably looked the same as defeat. Just numbers. If there were more of them than us, would They always win? Even if we thought we had won? What kind of victory would that be? A Pyrrhic victory? Didn't think so. Maybe a Chenic victory. I wondered what a Neckermanic victory would look like. It all had to end one day. One way or another. Surely. Long after the girl and boy soldiers had all decayed into happy, neutral skeletons. Maybe when it finally stopped, the human race would be united forever.

Years ago, before the war, I had read about someone in America who refused to give his race on his driving licence application. Just kept writing 'human'. Maybe he was just really ahead of his time. Couldn't remember what colour he was. That had probably been the point of the whole thing.

That might be their legacy. Making us all human. We'll probably have forgiven them in a few hundred years. We won't remember the details of the war. We'll just remember the results and be quietly grateful. Ends justify the means.

In that moment, it was all for nothing. One day, the war would just disappear. Disappear like the waves. Never really there. Not a substance, just the shape of something. All for nothing, unless it was about our extermination. There were easier ways to do that. Poison the water, engineer a virus, spread one of our own. It would be quicker. No need for the war. What were They trying to teach us? Whatever it was, there had to be an easier way. No need for the war. The boys and girls were all dead, and I appeared to be as mad as a fucking hatter. And my head hurt. At least I still had one. I sat back down on the beach in the same spot as before. I tried to convince myself that none of it was anything to do with me.

24

It was only two hours before Cathy came to tell Michael he could go downstairs. He chose to stay in his room. She seemed sorry, but Michael couldn't understand why. It wasn't anything to do with her. She hadn't sent his father away.

Michael lay on his bed and closed his eyes. He tried to convince himself that none of it was anything to do with him, but he didn't feel disconnected. Instead, he felt angry. He tried to imagine he was just watching all of it, floating out of his body and observing the scene from above. It didn't work. As lunchtime neared, he began to feel hungry. He used it to practice not caring. Instead of acting on his feelings of hunger, he told himself that it was just a signal from his body telling him to do something. It wasn't pain or need. It was just information. His body was telling him he was hungry. If he accepted that and ignored the repetition of the same information, the feeling should go away. He was surprised when he found that the hunger became bearable.

He wondered what else could become bearable with time. Perhaps the fault had been with him all the time. He should have been stronger. He shouldn't have let things get to him so much. How was he supposed to learn? His father wasn't here to teach him anything. He had been gone for years. His mother wouldn't teach him anything. Uncle Joe? No. Not Uncle Joe. Michael reminded himself how much he hated Uncle Joe. He would have to see him at dinner, but he wouldn't talk to him. He would never talk to him ever again. Who could tell him what to do? Who could tell him how to be a grown-up? Cathy? No. She had enough other things to do. Anyway, she'd be too scared of Uncle Joe.

The Book? The diaries? The journalist? He was dead, so he couldn't get angry. He couldn't lie, and he couldn't refuse. The only problem was the journalist was crazy, or at least had been crazy. He had been to a doctor about it, so he was properly crazy. But he hadn't always been crazy. Michael could learn things from the parts of The Book the journalist had written before he had gone crazy.

The journalist knew how to deal with people. The journalist knew how to use people. The journalist knew how to get what he wanted. That was the problem, Michael thought. He had never really tried to get what he wanted. He had just relied on his mother, Uncle Joe, and everyone else to deliver it. That was what children did. If he wanted to be an adult, he had to go out and make things happen. The Book would tell him how to do it. He had to learn from it. He had to treat it like a textbook.

He grabbed a pad of paper and a pen from his schoolbag, which he had ignored since the last time Uncle Joe had helped him study. Uncle Joe had taught him some things. He had taught him how to study. He had taught him how to summarise, how to pick out important information.

Michael needed a title for the top of the page. If he wrote the title, he would feel like he had already done something. Advice? No. Rules? No. How to be better at… stuff? No. Changes. No. Notes. That would do. He wrote it in capital letters and underlined it. He would think of a better title once he knew what exactly he was writing. For three hours, he reread The Book and made notes. At first, he didn't plan to read anything new, just the parts which he had covered already. He didn't want to read all of The Book yet. He wanted to take his time and enjoy reading what was left, as he would likely never read anything like it. However, as he read more and more, he quickly found himself reading parts of The Book he had not looked at before.

When he had finished, he looked at what he had written. Messy. He took a new sheet of paper and rewrote it neatly. Fifteen things. At the top of the page, he had written, *New Ways to Get Things Done*. The journalist had known a lot about people, how they thought, and how they could be manipulated. The things weren't all ways to get things done. Some of them were observations, some were rules, and others were obvious. Some didn't seem to make sense. Others were the opposite of what people always told you. The less you do for people, the more they do for you. Talk, but not too much, or you might disagree with someone by accident. Always look pleased to see people. Anticipate instructions. Doing things before you have to be asked is an easy way to win friends. Have small talk prepared. Remember, once you build up relationships and goodwill, it can mean you can choose to call in all your favours and achieve something really big, but maybe only once.

The list went on. Individually the things didn't seem very important, but together they looked like something. They looked like the beginning of a plan. Michael would make sure he got what he wanted, and the journalist would help him. He would try to put the plan into action as soon as possible. For now, he was hungry. The journalist hadn't said anything about not eating or ignoring what your body told you to do. At least, not in the bits where he was sane, and Michael hadn't reread the bits where he was crazy.

Things seemed a little more normal at dinner. It was almost as if his father had never been back at all. As soon as he sat down, Uncle Joe told Michael that his father had had to leave in a hurry, that there was a phone call and it couldn't have been avoided. His mother nodded in agreement. Nobody said they were sorry. They still didn't think there was anything to be sorry for. That was the last time it was mentioned, just like he had never been back. Like it had all been a dream. Like he had imagined it. There was nothing left to prove his father was ever there except maybe one thing. Later, he would check to see if it was still sleeping under the bed.

They ate dinner in silence. Towards the end, Uncle Joe spoke, just to say that he was thinking of going to church on Sunday. He had already arranged for Cathy to take care of things while they were out. They should all go, but no mention of why. As his mother nodded in agreement, Michael found himself doing the same. It had been a while since they had been to church together. They were always busy these days. Michael didn't mention a trip to Glasgow. There was no point now.

After dinner, he made his way back up to the top floor. The doors weren't expecting him this time. This time, he knew which door. He ignored their silent protests and opened the door with a master key he had taken from downstairs. Inside, there was nothing. No newly arrived ghost, no infantry having a private discussion, no Janet cleaning up, just an empty room. He hadn't expected any different, but the one thing he had hoped for was missing. He checked the space under the bed where it should have been. Actually, not should have been, might have been.

He was too late. He had known he would be. Janet was too good at her job. You can't leave things lying around after something horrible happens. Janet and Uncle Joe both knew that. You have to clean it up quickly to stop the bad memories from soaking into everything. It helps you move on quickly. There was no vodka bottle. It was important. Why was it important? It was just an empty bottle, but it was important. It was very important. Why? He didn't know. It just was.

Michael checked under the bed again. No miracle had occurred. It was still gone. Of course, it was gone. Someone had made the bed. Someone had emptied the bin in the corner. The room had been cleaned. All traces had been washed away. Not naturally, not by time, unnaturally. Janet had removed everything. People had interfered. The room was empty again, as it had been a hundred times before.

He looked at the chest of drawers in the corner. It ignored him. It had seen it all before but held its arms wide. Michael accepted the invitation and searched it quickly. It was empty. The chest of drawers shrugged, vindicated. Gone, everything was gone. One more thing he had lost. Fine, it didn't matter, anyway. He would go back downstairs. He took a last look at the room before leaving. It was nearly ready for its next occupant.

There was one more thing to be done. Before leaving, he crossed the room and opened the window.

That night, Michael worked hard. He took out the books he had not touched for weeks. Mathematics. Uncle Joe had forgotten about getting him to work during the holidays. Actually, he probably hadn't forgotten, just given up. In fact, that likely wasn't true either. He probably hadn't given up. He was just biding his time. Michael would take control of the situation. It could be used to his advantage. Anything could be used to your advantage. You just had to take charge instead of waiting for people to do things for you. He could do that. The Book had told him how to do the rest.

Michael opened the textbook. There were eighteen chapters in The Book, and they were at chapter seven, differentiation. Uncle Joe said it just took practice. There were twelve chapters to be finished. That would take a long time. That would be the stupid, childish way to do it. He had to think. What was required? What was the situation? Uncle Joe had probably planned on doing about two-thirds of The Book before the end of the summer. That would be up to chapter twelve. That would be four more chapters. Five if you counted the chapter they were already on. That was still a lot and not necessary. He had to think. Uncle Joe would be expecting nothing. If you were expecting nothing, half was a lot. Half of four chapters was two, so up to chapter nine. That could be done.

Was Uncle Joe really expecting nothing? No, chapter seven, that was what he really wanted Michael to do. That was the bare minimum. If you did the bare minimum when you were made to do it, then you were invisible. If you did it without being asked, you got noticed, even if you would have had to do it, anyway. The power of not having to be asked. Michael felt like he was learning. He was learning something far more important than differentiation. He was learning from the notes he had made earlier. The journalist was teaching him.

If he did chapter seven, he would get noticed and gain Uncle Joe's approval. If he did the other two, he would be a hero. Yes. Could he be smarter? Yes. What did people want? He looked at the list. People wanted to succeed. It was more important than money. If you gave them money, they'd just spend it on something that made them feel like they had succeeded. He could do that. What else? People had to feel needed. They often helped you because you needed them. But they helped you most when you didn't think you needed them because they liked to demonstrate their worth, liked to change your mind about whether you need them.

People usually tell you things more quickly if you act stupid and uninterested.

People are most comfortable when they know who they are. Put them in their comfort zone, put them in their box.

... stereotypes are your friend. People like stereotypes. People conform to their own stereotype. Mafia bosses only started calling each other "Godfather" after they saw the film. Let people run along the tracks that the stereotype has laid...

He had a few ideas about what to do. He jotted them down on a new page. The thinking was done. Now he had to do the easy, boring part. He had to work through the chapters. He flicked through the book. It was slightly older than the books at school, but the maths was the same. About ten exercises in each chapter. About twenty questions in each. That meant about two hundred questions in each chapter. That meant around six hundred questions to do. Too many. He would do the first two exercises in each chapter, one in the middle, and the last two. That meant about two or three hundred questions. That could probably be done in a couple of weeks with very little effort. Less than an exercise a day. Easy.

What was all this effort for? There were two reasons. To see if The Book was right and to see if he really could take control. Nobody else cared what happened to him. It was time to see if he could show himself he didn't need them. After that... well, maybe he would start to see if he could really make things happen.

It took less than thirty minutes to complete the first exercise. By the time he completed the second, he felt he had done enough. After all, it was only supposed to look like hard work.

25

Michael hadn't been to a church service since the start of the holidays. Memorial services and funerals didn't count. That would be like counting weddings or christenings. It would be even worse than that because weddings and christenings only happened a few times every year.

At school, they had assemblies and prayers daily and a proper service every week. Although he would never admit it, Michael enjoyed the school assemblies. Mainly he enjoyed the singing. Most of the boys probably enjoyed the singing. They always started with "Onward Christian Soldiers". Although Michael preferred "Stand Up, Stand Up for Jesus", which they only sang every few weeks. He didn't mind what they sang, but his heart always sank when he heard "Soldiers of Christ Arise" because it had a million verses.

The songs had changed over time. You hardly ever heard "Once Pledged by the Cross" anymore. It was a shame, but it was being used more and more at memorial services, so you still got to sing it quite often. They had probably stopped using it at assemblies because of that. Some of the boys and girls would cry during the assemblies, but nobody ever mentioned it. The girls were usually drowned out during the singing. Michael didn't think much of the girls at school. They didn't have any focus. They were either upset or they weren't interested in things. He couldn't understand it. They would have to go to fight as well, so why weren't they interested in what was happening?

He didn't speak to Uncle Joe as they walked to church. His mother didn't speak much. His mother and Uncle Joe talked about the weather and the people they saw on the way to church, but that didn't really count. Nobody said anything that meant anything. Maybe they would never really say anything again. They would do this until the next time his father came back. It was just small talk, but it was better than silence because you could pretend everything was fine. Michael would never be able to challenge their failure to discuss anything that mattered because nobody would ever admit to knowing what he was talking about. He might have to go through the next few years without speaking to anyone. He wasn't sure he had anything to say, anyway.

Uncle Joe led them into church, with Michael following. Michael was sure that he would have to sit between Uncle Joe and his mother, but Uncle Joe stopped as he reached the pew and let Michael and his mother go in first. Michael found his mother was sitting on his left, and on his right was a long space bordered by Mrs Henderson, who ran the shop where he sometimes bought stamps. She looked old. Everyone looked old, but Mrs Henderson was so old she had given up trying to look young and had instead fully embraced her little-old-ladyness. If she was younger, people might have said it was some kind of ironic statement, but cardigans and perms were rarely mistaken for the ironic statements that they really weren't. He could see the back of her little white afro as she rummaged in her bag for her glasses. He didn't like Mrs Henderson very much. She was never very friendly. Mr Henderson sat beside her, bald and solid looking. He had the kind of hairlessness that made you look like you should be sweaty, even when you weren't. Their sons lived in Glasgow. Three of their grandchildren had fallen, and the other two weren't old enough.

This could be good practice. The Hendersons didn't hate him. They just had never really shown any friendliness to him. They had never paid him much attention, never reacted to him. Well, maybe they would react if he were more like an adult. He heard the voice of the journalist. More accurately, he heard the voice he imagined the journalist had, as he had never heard him speak. The voice reminded him, *Always look pleased to see people.*

The American accent probably needed work, but that was just a detail.

He imagined the Hendersons were people he wanted to see and started smiling. Hard to smile on request. He worried that he might have crossed the line from grinning into grimacing but assumed it would sort itself out when he started speaking. He quickly glanced to check he didn't have an audience before saying, "Good morning, Mrs Henderson. Good morning, Mr Henderson."

The old lady jerked round to look at him. A large head that wasn't sweaty, but could have been, tilted out from behind her to see what was going on. "Good morning, Michael."

She was smiling. The big, unsweaty head nodded. Now for the small talk, but not a conversation. No questions, only comments were allowed. It would be just fragments, no pressure, like shaking hands. "It's a nice day. If it stays like this tomorrow, I'll be telling all the soldiers to come down to you to buy ice cream."

The old lady laughed at the fragment that didn't contain a joke and nodded as she turned back to look for her glasses. The big, unsweaty head smiled.

Success! The imaginary journalist who wasn't there didn't give a thumbs-up to show how impressed he was, but Michael imagined he might have if he had been.

Michael was smiling for real when he turned to see his mother looking at him and Uncle Joe, studying the order of service with unnecessary intensity. He ignored them and looked straight ahead. Their time would come. He just needed more practice first.

He didn't look at the order of service. He preferred to be taken by surprise. They didn't start with "Onward Christian Soldiers", which was a shame but not very surprising. Instead, it was a hymn Michael didn't know, but he was able to catch the tune halfway through the first line. Later on, they sang "Fight the Good Fight", which he had always found slow and boring. At the end, they sang "Lift Up Your Heads Ye Gates of Brass", which he had never really understood. All the songs were fairly safe. No lines in them that people couldn't get through without crying. The congregation was old, as was everyone these days. There weren't many of them, less than thirty. It was enough. Any fewer, and you would have been able to hear everybody's voices individually as they sang. As it was, there were just enough to hide, which was perfect.

When the minister led them in prayer, Michael took the opportunity, as he always did, to look up at everyone and see if anybody else didn't have their head bowed and their eyes closed. As far as he could see, it was the perfect crime. Nobody could get angry at you if they saw you because they shouldn't be looking either. As usual, he was the only one who took advantage of the loophole. At school, it was different. There was always a small, short-lived community of prairie-dog-style worshippers who rose above the rest. They were always joined by Mr Gibson, who was willing to risk eternal damnation by not praying and instead remaining alert to mouth silent threats and point at pupils like Michael. Michael felt that the boys and Mr Gibson shared something special in those brief, surreal moments. They were never mentioned afterwards. It was probably a bit of a grey area, discipline-wise.

The Lord's Prayer was different. During the Lord's Prayer, Michael employed a system he had developed from a very young age to prioritise the different requests as he saw them. He had never placed much importance in the bit about daily bread as he reasoned that they always had plenty of bread. Accordingly, he was free to open his eyes during that part and was willing to believe that doing so could even increase the power of the other bits. Of course, now he was older, he understood it wasn't really just about bread, but the habit had already formed. The part about debts or trespasses—as they sometimes called them at school—being forgiven was the most important, and he always squeezed his eyes shut in good time for that part. Even from a very early age, he had understood it wasn't actually about money. It was much more important and a matter of self-preservation. The part about temptation didn't seem very relevant, but he usually kept his eyes shut, anyway. The part about being delivered from evil was important, and he always concentrated on that. The beginning, and the end, which they didn't say at school, he didn't consider very important, and he could let his mind wander during those parts, although he didn't open his eyes.

Michael thought the minister had given a good sermon. It was all about how they should never think that God had abandoned them just because he didn't deliver everything they wanted and that they shouldn't expect God to solve all of their problems in an immediate way. How it was often difficult to understand why things happened the way they did, but that God had a reason and everything would be clear in the end.

When it came to the collection, Michael heard the journalist speaking to him. "*I have always believed in saving things and using them all at once.*" Michael was already way ahead of him. The coins which he would normally take to church for the collection were in his back pocket today. All except three of them. They were in his hip pocket and would go into the collection. The rest would go back. They would go into the collection eventually, so it wasn't wrong or anything, but that would be in a few weeks.

In the meantime, he dug in his pocket and produced a hand containing three coins, some fluff, a button of unknown provenance, a crumpled receipt for something, probably stamps, and a shell he had found on the beach a few days ago and promptly forgotten about. He picked all three of the coins out and dropped them in the collection to everyone's general approval or lack of interest. Another potential thumbs up from the journalist. By the end of the service, as the names of the recently fallen were being read out, Michael was silently congratulating himself and planning his next move. He still had homework to do. He still had more ideas to put into practice. As they left the church, he thought about all of the ways in which he could be useful and impressive.

Over the next week, Michael continued to complete the questions from the maths book. He also continued to be pleased to see people and to have short, meaningless conversations, which made people very happy and comfortable. Michael continued to do all the things he had always done around the hotel but managed to adjust things so that everyone was much happier with him. He had always collected glasses in the bar, but in the past, he had always asked beforehand or waited until he was asked. With the journalist's advice and guidance, he was able to do exactly the same thing but achieve much better results.

Instead of asking, he would just do it, preferably when nobody was watching. Then he'd casually mention it and watch Cathy become pleasantly surprised and smile at him. Instead of waiting to be asked, he'd predict when he was going to be asked and start a few minutes beforehand. If it was hard to predict when he would be asked, that was no problem. He would go into the bar, stack some glasses on a table, and wait. When he was asked to help, he would point to the table and say he had just started. In seven short days, he noticed a difference in how people treated him. They commented on how hardworking he was and always seemed pleased to see him. In fact, as his new reputation meant people were much happier to let him have time off, he was actually doing less work than ever before.

He had almost stopped then, after seven days. After all, it wasn't clear what it was all meant to achieve. However, the next time they had all been at church, things had changed. Suddenly, there was a reason to continue. There was something to aim for.

Uncle Joe had taken them all to church for the second Sunday in a row. Just as before, everything went as Michael had planned. He gave only a few coins for the collection. The rest sat in the cupboard, guarded by the smiling faces. He expected it would be around a month before it would be time to use them. The minister gave a sermon about the importance of making the right choices and not giving in to anger.

As far as Michael was concerned, everything was normal. It was only when they were leaving that he overheard a conversation that changed everything. Everyone was talking, their conversations merging into one. He wasn't interested enough to tune into one conversation and extract it from the general noise. Then he heard one word. *Chen.* The name of the greatest human who had ever lived. The name that would be remembered as long as there were humans around to remember it. You didn't hear his name very often. People didn't talk about the war very often. There wasn't very much new to say.

Michael focused on two old men standing near the door, who were taking turns shaking their heads. *Chen.* Michael concentrated on unpicking their conversation. He was listening in halfway through. He would have to reconstruct the first half of the conversation. Something was apparently unbelievable. Apparently, it wasn't clear what on Earth some people were thinking. Apparently, only God knew what might happen next. Michael suspected the men also had a fair idea of what might happen next but didn't want to suggest what it might be, perhaps out of respect. Whatever it was, it was happening in Glasgow. That was also apparently unbelievable. Apparently, one of the men had a great desire to see Neckerman's face. The other agreed but had apparently given some thought to the practicalities involved, as he wished he could be a fly on the wall when Neckerman found out. Whatever was happening, it appeared Neckerman's face was intimately involved. Whatever it was, it was just unbelievable, and no good would come of it. They couldn't understand why he had to come to Glasgow.

Chen was coming to Glasgow? Surely not. Glasgow wasn't that far away. General Chen was… he was the greatest person there had ever been. You only saw him on television and in the papers. He couldn't just walk around in Glasgow. It was ridiculous. Michael's father and Uncle Joe had been to Glasgow before. So had Michael's mother. Chen couldn't go somewhere she had been. It was ridiculous. It must be a mistake. He was bursting with questions. Uncle Joe would know. He fought the urge to ask Uncle Joe. That was what children did. He knew he should wait. A dead journalist advised him to keep quiet.

There would be time. There was always time. Michael tried to think about something else. He imagined being a fly on a wall and decided it was probably overrated. You probably had a better view from the floor or the ceiling. He wondered if flies could hear. Probably not. Given a choice, he decided he would probably be a mouse on the floor, as long as he had somewhere he could sit without being seen. He realised he was worrying about a choice he was unlikely ever to have to make.

It was a stupid idea, anyway. Why would you wish you were a fly on the wall? Why not just wish you could be at the meeting? If you were wishing anyway, you might as well wish for something a bit more sensible. Maybe people didn't really want to be at the meeting. They would rather be there and not be noticed. Michael didn't think that made much sense, as most people would notice a fly in the room. He decided to wish he was invisible. He thought that was just as likely as being turned into a fly. On the way home, he alternated between wishing he was invisible and wishing he was General Chen.

It turned out that the unbelievable was true, as usual. When he got back from church, he checked with Cathy. It would have been childish to ask her. Instead, he asked her what she thought about the news about Chen. She assumed he knew all about it already and told him everything. General Chen was coming to Glasgow in August. It would be his first public speech since he was removed from the Unified Command.

Michael knew why Chen was coming to Glasgow. If you thought about it, it was obvious. He had a lot of support in Europe and probably thought there was less chance of arrest there than in America. He had probably chosen Britain because they were asking to be released from their obligations. If he spoke in London, there might be pressure on the government to do something about it. They couldn't arrest him. That would be unthinkable, but they might have to do something, and he probably didn't want to embarrass them or put them in that position.

It was easier to choose Scotland. Edinburgh would be out for the same reason as London. It would make things difficult for the Scottish Government. Glasgow made sense. It was a large city, and it was easy to get to. Chances of arrest or disruption were reduced because of the Scottish situation. The Scottish Government wouldn't interfere as they would embarrass the British government. The British government would be unlikely to act in what they could argue was a matter for the Scottish Government. Both sides could reasonably ignore the issue until it went away.

What was complicated for everybody else was simple for Michael. He needed to get to Glasgow. He needed to get to a city he had never visited to see General Chen. Michael wasn't sure how these things worked. Did you buy a ticket? Did you just turn up? No, there would be lots of people who wanted to see General Chen. Maybe Uncle Joe would know. Except Uncle Joe wouldn't let him go. He knew he wouldn't be allowed to go. Uncle Joe wouldn't understand. His mother wouldn't go with him. If his father had still been here, he would have taken him. He realised his father had been sent back at the wrong time. The school might have taken him if it wasn't during the school holidays. At least then he could have told Uncle Joe he wanted to go because of a project he was doing at school. It wasn't fair. Nothing was ever fair. General Chen might never come to Glasgow again. He might never come to Britain again. He would be less than a hundred miles away, but it may as well be a million.

He reminded himself that there was always a chance. The problem would only arise if he asked. If he didn't ask, he could just go on his own and worry about it later. How? Even if he made it, he had no idea how to see the general. At first, he couldn't see any answer. The solution only came when he realised he had been thinking like a child. Children asked, and he reminded himself that he wasn't behaving like a child anymore. Michael reminded himself he was trying to be an adult. He had to take control and had to make sure that things went the way he wanted them to. Asking would be the wrong thing to do. He had to be cleverer than that. He had to make Uncle Joe think it was his idea. That would solve everything. There was only one problem. He had no idea how to get Uncle Joe to offer to take him to Glasgow, but at least he knew where to start. The right strategy was to get close to Uncle Joe again, and he knew how to do that. He had already started. He would get close to him first. Then the rest would hopefully resolve itself.

Eleven days after he had started and two days after he had heard about General Chen's visit to Glasgow, he was almost ready. The maths questions were almost finished. It had required some effort, but it had not been difficult. Whenever something became difficult, there was always a way around it and always a way to turn the difficulty into something he could use. Questions could be missed out or noted down so they could be used to ask for help. Despite this progress, he was aware he hadn't made a huge effort with his mother and Uncle Joe yet. Not like he had with Cathy. He had left Uncle Joe until he was sure what he was going to do. There was always the chance that nothing would work on Uncle Joe or that he would see what Michael was doing and stop him. He had to wait until he really knew what he was doing. He had to be prepared. Now he was almost ready.

Michael hadn't tried anything on his mother yet for a different reason. He hadn't tried to trick her, not because it might be too difficult, but because it might be too easy. He had noticed that all of this success had an unwelcome side effect. Although people were nicer to him and were more impressed by him, it wasn't like before. Before, when people had been pleased with him, although it had been much rarer, it made him feel happy with himself and made him like them more. Now there was something else. It still made him feel good, but there was something else as well, another feeling. It wasn't guilt. He didn't feel any guilt. Why should he? In the past, he had always tried to be nice, and everyone had just walked all over him.

If he needed proof that they hadn't kept their side of the bargain, he just had to look at how much nicer everyone was to him and how impressed they were with him, even though he was doing exactly the same thing as before. That showed that they weren't fair people. He was just taking advantage of that, and it was hard to see how that was wrong. It wasn't guilt. It was something worse. When he made Cathy smile now, he still felt good about himself, but unlike before, he didn't have nice thoughts about her. He didn't think, *Isn't Cathy a nice person? Aren't we getting on well?* Instead, he thought, *How easy is this?* With time, it was getting worse. About a week ago, he'd caught himself thinking about how stupid she was and how she was being tricked by a child. Yesterday, he had one clear thought as he turned away from her. *You stupid bitch.* He caught himself sneering. It wasn't guilt he was beginning to feel, but something else. It was contempt. He didn't want to feel contempt for his mother. He was afraid of that. More scared than he was that Uncle Joe would be angry at him.

Michael worried it was poisoning him. He found it increasingly difficult to talk to people without thinking about how stupid they were and how limited and ill-informed their opinions were. He was sneering at all of them. A lot of things were getting easier, but one thing was getting harder. It was getting harder to like people. The more he achieved, the better he felt, and the less he respected the people around them. He used to like Cathy a lot. Now, he wasn't sure. She had really disappointed him. He was very pleased, of course, because that meant things had worked, but at the same time, he was disappointed.

It was difficult being an adult. Instead of just looking up to everybody, thinking that their lives were very different from yours and were none of your business, you had to see people as they truly were. You got to test people, and you got to see where they broke down. He wasn't sure he liked it. He wasn't sure he was happy knowing Cathy might not be the clever, capable person he had always assumed she was. It was too late now, of course. Maybe that was just the price you had to pay to become an adult. He wondered what it cost to be Uncle Joe and who paid in the end.

26

At breakfast, Michael prepared to make his move. Everything depended on judging Uncle Joe properly. It was almost two weeks since Uncle Joe sent his father away, and Michael had hardly spoken to him since. He knew Uncle Joe cared about him. He guessed that Uncle Joe would take any opportunity to fix things between them. Michael didn't want things fixed, but he realised that there was nothing to be gained by Uncle Joe knowing that. He knew what Uncle Joe wanted, and he now knew that gave him power over the old man, as long as he exploited the situation correctly.

A few days after they had stopped speaking, Uncle Joe had made a mistake. He had given in to the silence at dinner and suggested he could start helping with Michael's schoolwork again if that was what he wanted. It was a mistake Michael knew he might not have noticed before when he wasn't thinking so clearly. Now he was able to see such things. It was an ugly, clumsy error. He could see all aspects of it. He saw it as an ugly black three-dimensional shape he could rotate and examine.

Uncle Joe had asked too soon. He had chosen the wrong activity. It was difficult to restart something that was such hard work. He had been fooled when there had been no objection from Michael to them all going to church. Most of all, the sentence was clumsy. The attack was half-hearted. Fearful of defeat, Uncle Joe had been overcautious. It was his caution and his failure to commit to the attack which made the defeat he was terrified of so inevitable.

He could start helping with Michael's schoolwork again if that was what Michael wanted. The second half of the statement was unnecessary. It had cleverly tricked Uncle Joe into letting it be part of the sentence. In fact, Uncle Joe did not need the escape route it promised. In any case, it was not large enough for the old man to squeeze through. Michael saw the escape route and used it. He simply told Uncle Joe that he didn't want to. Uncle Joe had been defeated, and Michael recognised that the defeat made him even weaker. He had decided to leave Uncle Joe to his misery until he was ready to exploit it. Now was the time.

His mother and Uncle Joe talked to each other, but it was still like eating breakfast in silence. Nobody was really saying anything. His mother never really said anything. He had talked to her lots of times since his father had left, but she never said anything important. He could have made her talk, but he couldn't bear to upset her. Michael waited for their pretend conversation to fade away so he could speak. He couldn't interrupt. That was what a child would do. Children didn't have any patience.

It seemed to take forever for his mother and Uncle Joe to stop talking about nothing. In time, he noticed the conversation became irritating. It had never been irritating before. He had always found this type of pointless talking better than the silence. In fact, he knew it wasn't actually pointless. It brought people together and stopped them from thinking. It was important for adults. When you didn't have anybody to ruffle your hair or hug you, then you had to have some way of feeling cared about. It was probably why adults ruffled children's hair and hugged them. They probably just couldn't think of enough small talk. Then again, maybe that worked better than small talk. Maybe they only talked to each other because they had to.

The conversation eventually paused for a few seconds. Michael waited a little longer before he spoke, making sure it was a real pause, and he wouldn't be interrupted. He made sure he wasn't looking at anybody. "It's not long until I have to go back to school."

His mother replied, just as he had expected. "You're not even halfway through the holidays yet. You still have weeks left."

"I know, but I was starting to think about school again. They said next year would be really difficult."

"Well, I'm sure it will be the same for everybody."

"I suppose. I was just thinking about it."

Now he just had to wait. He listened to Uncle Joe eating, listened to him breathing. He knew what he was thinking. Uncle Joe was deciding whether it was worth risking another defeat. Michael let him think for a few seconds. He knew Uncle Joe would ask again. He also knew there was more to be gained by not letting him. Michael knew the power of relief. He let Uncle Joe worry about what he was going to do. He waited until he heard his breathing change as he prepared to speak. Just as he was finally about to say something, Michael spoke instead. "I thought maybe Uncle Joe could help me with some things if he had time."

Again, he didn't look at anyone, but he could feel the relief in the room. When he finally did look at Uncle Joe, the old man nodded. Michael had learned from The Book that relief was a powerful thing. It was a cheap form of happiness which could be manufactured from nothing. On a normal day, things were the same when you went to bed as they were when you woke up. People stayed at a constant level of misery or happiness from morning to night. However, if you raised the possibility of something horrible happening, or if you removed something they had always taken for granted, they became worried or unhappy. When you removed the worry or restored whatever you had removed, people became happy again. Much happier than they were before you took the thing away.

If your water went off on Monday and was turned back on Wednesday, you were happy for a short time. The interesting thing was, you were happier than you were on the previous Wednesday when you had all the water you wanted but never thought about it. That could be used. Of course, to manufacture that kind of happiness, you first had to make people miserable, but that wasn't important as long as you were careful. The point was to make sure they associated the happiness with you and not the misery. If you fixed the water, you were useful, as long as they never realised you turned it off in the first place. The journalist had shown him that through such simple techniques, great deeds were carried out. Populations were kept happy. Medals were appreciated by wounded soldiers. The joy of victory was felt by those who had experienced terrible sacrifice. Old men were manipulated. Maybe. Michael would find out for sure later.

The journalist had said that the battlefield was no place for soldiers to think. There was no time. It only confused you and caused hesitation. It got you killed. The time to think was before you got anywhere near the battlefield. You had to weigh everything up before you got there and decide beforehand what you were prepared to do. On the battlefield, you ignored fresh doubts and trusted your earlier decision. You just did it and dealt with it afterwards. The only people who got to think on the battlefield were the people who weren't involved. Or those who thought they weren't involved.

Michael kept focused on the idea for hours. Even as he finally walked to Uncle Joe's room, he reminded himself that he had to trust his earlier decision. He knew what Uncle Joe was thinking and how he would act. He just had to have confidence and trust himself. You couldn't look to other people for help. Other people were a source of doubt. In the absence of confident leadership, their natural response was to challenge, doubt, and question. People were most comfortable when they had confidence in those around them. It made sense. Other people felt just the same way you felt. You had to be confident if you wanted people to believe in you. If people saw you looking to them for reassurance, they would lose confidence in you. You had to believe in yourself. Otherwise, you might just lose everything. You might just wink out of existence.

He knew this place. He knew this room. He knew this desk. Michael had sat there many times before. Today would be different. He had thought about trying to arrive first but rejected the idea. Some things should be kept the same. People were uncomfortable with change. It put them on their guard.

Michael had arrived at the usual time for this unusual experiment. Uncle Joe was already there. He was unaware he was about to be ambushed. He was unaware that Michael would have new allies with him in the room tonight. Michael let Uncle Joe speak first. "Should we just continue with differentiation? I think it was chapter seven."

It was hard to tell if Uncle Joe was pleased to be helping again. Uncle Joe never really showed what he was thinking. Michael knew he had to trust himself. He had thought for a long time about how this would work. Now wasn't the time to doubt himself or change his strategy. Michael opened his book and handed it to Uncle Joe. "I think that I've finished chapter seven."

He let Uncle Joe look at his work. Meanwhile, Michael opened the textbook and talked. With Uncle Joe distracted, it gave Michael the chance to talk without participating in a conversation. That would have meant looking for a chance to speak, maybe having to give information in the wrong order, and maybe being interrupted. This was much easier. He was free to provide background noise, which meant that the words didn't take on too much importance.

"I've been working over the past few days. I think I've finished chapters eight and nine as well. I didn't have time to do anything past that. I didn't do all the questions, but I answered some from each section, so I was sure I wasn't missing anything."

As usual, it was difficult to tell what Uncle Joe was thinking. If Michael was right, he was trying to decide whether he should be impressed. He squinted as he examined pages of answers which couldn't have made any sense at all without the questions which were in the textbook Michael was holding. Michael knew the problem Uncle Joe now faced was that he couldn't possibly say how impressed he was but also couldn't ignore so much effort. Yet if he criticised Michael or offered constructive comments, he risked sounding unreasonable or upsetting him. Michael knew the problem wasn't easily solvable in the few seconds the old man had to wrestle with it. Luckily, Michael had spent hours and hours thinking about it and found a solution days ago. He let the old man worry for a few seconds more.

"I know it's not all correct, but it was the best I could do. We can go through it all again if you think that's best. I know I shouldn't have started the other chapters without you."

The obviously crazy final statement could not be ignored.

"No, not at all, Michael. It's good that you made the effort yourself. That's very good."

Now he was talking, but the problem was still there. He didn't know what to do now. Michael produced the answer. Like the rest of the answers, it was in his exercise book.

"I couldn't do all the questions. I made a note of the ones I couldn't do at the bottom of the pages. I can't do any of the stuff about the chain rule. I had to leave that. Would you mind helping with that before we go on to the next chapter?"

Michael saw the relief on the old man's face. Things were getting more comfortable again. Everyone was back in their roles. People like to know who they are.

"No, that's fine. We can do that. You know this is very good, Michael. Making the effort yourself like this is very good. Even if there are some mistakes, it's good that you are trying so hard."

There was no problem in praising effort. The result of the effort wasn't relevant. Michael was sure Uncle Joe would have found the solution if he'd had a little longer to think. He was also sure the old man was happier that Michael had led him into it.

The rest of the hour went just as well as the first few minutes. Michael continued to fill his role. When Uncle Joe explained the chain rule for differentiation, he initially struggled. But when Uncle Joe explained it again, he suddenly experienced a flash of understanding. He saw the old man almost smile as his student successfully crossed a barrier thanks to his help. The moment, along with many others, helped to rebuild the bond between them. Michael had carefully chosen the chain rule for this moment. It was perfect for the purpose as it was part of the chapter, which he understood very well. It would have been hard to provide a sudden breakthrough in understanding if it were something he found difficult. You couldn't rely on them happening spontaneously. He accurately simulated the epiphany to the satisfaction of all concerned.

Everything went just as he had planned. Occasionally, Uncle Joe reached for something and couldn't find it. Whenever that happened, Michael immediately laid his hands on it. He found pencils in drawers and books in stacks of paper. Michael hadn't hidden anything beforehand, so it wasn't like he was deceiving anyone, but he had checked where everything was long ago. He had already spent the required minute locating each item and had just memorised their positions. Moving things would have been deception. Besides, he might have been caught. This way, the things were found just where they had been left. It didn't look suspicious. He just suddenly appeared more useful than before. To Uncle Joe, all of this might look like he was sharper than before, more interested, more switched on, less clumsy. It might look like he was maturing and becoming the adult Uncle Joe wanted him to become. Roles would be well on their way to being fulfilled. That would relax everyone.

When the hour ended, Michael thanked Uncle Joe. He was much more sincere than usual. Uncle Joe seemed much happier than before, relieved maybe. As Michael got up to leave, the time came to ask Uncle Joe to take him to Glasgow. He let it pass. It would be too obvious. It would taint everything that had just happened. Uncle Joe had to know about General Chen's visit by now, and he hadn't offered to take Michael to Glasgow. He would also know that Michael wanted to go.

When Michael had spoken to Cathy the previous day, he had made sure to mention it. He had mentioned other things as well, irrelevant things. Just enough of them to bury the important information. He would have liked to go to Glasgow to see General Chen. Buried, but not deep enough that someone of low intelligence like Cathy wouldn't be able to notice its importance. He made sure enough of it poked out of the soil to interest her. That way, she could congratulate herself on picking up on the importance of the information. She even suggested he ask Uncle Joe. She even thought it was her idea. He made sure to say that he knew Uncle Joe was too busy; it was too far away; it didn't really matter, and so on. He told her not to mention it to Uncle Joe.

It was such a mature attitude. He was confident Cathy would mention it when she relayed the information to Uncle Joe later in the day. She would be betraying Michael on purpose. It wasn't even that she thought she had something to gain. It was that people couldn't bear to keep their cleverness to themselves. Cathy thought she had worked it out herself, and so someone had to be told. She had to demonstrate her usefulness. Michael understood it all. It wasn't that you couldn't trust people. It was the opposite. You could trust them to behave like people. Uncle Joe knew Michael wanted to go. In time, he would offer to take him. Hopefully. It was always hard to tell with Uncle Joe. He didn't always behave like other people.

27

The next time they were at church, Michael was ready. He had exchanged his piles of coins for a single note the previous day. Three weeks hadn't been long enough to save enough coins to test the journalist's theory properly, so he had added some money from his savings. He made sure he was ready early and that they left the hotel in plenty of time. He didn't want them having to sit at the back where nobody would see them.

He was pleased to see everyone they met, as he always was these days. He felt a twinge of contempt each time he received a friendly response. It was getting harder to like people. Nobody was as intelligent as him. They were all so easily manipulated. Michael was beginning to realise that he had been wrong for such a long time. He had always thought he felt uncomfortable around adults because he couldn't fit in and couldn't interact with them at their level. He felt he was always the one who said something stupid or childish, and they all looked down on him.

In fact, it was now clear that they were the stupid ones. Michael was too intelligent. That had been the problem all along. He had said stupid things, but that was because he hadn't understood something very important. You didn't have to try so hard. The journalist knew that. The journalist knew that the secret was to keep quiet most of the time. You had to talk a little, but not too much. If you talked too much, you risked saying something someone might disagree with. People were simple little creatures. They just wanted to talk about things that didn't matter or their favourite subject: themselves. If you disagreed, it upset them, even when you were right. He now knew why he had been uncomfortable for so long. It wasn't that he hadn't been able to reach their level. It was that he hadn't managed to get down to it.

Sitting in church, he could feel the people around him milling around, finding their seats, and speaking to people they knew. Their irrelevance angered him. They thought they mattered. Everyone thought their conversations about their relatives and the weather actually mattered. They were just like the weather, swirling and changing at random, but if you looked hard enough, you could predict what they would do. Their consciousness was an illusion.

It occurred to him that he had no evidence to show that they felt things as he did. It was just the opposite. At school, they called it personification when you said things had feelings when they didn't, like saying storms raged because the clouds were angry. Maybe it was wrong to personify other people. They weren't like him. It was unfair that he should have to exist among them and feel like he didn't fit in. It was their fault that he didn't fit in. It was their fault that they were so stupid. Michael understood how General Chen must have felt. It must have been difficult to be rejected by people who were so inferior to you. It was worse for the general because he didn't have the option of sinking to their level. He had to keep showing them the right way to do things.

Michael shut his eyes and felt the noise of their pointless conversations run down his face. They were nothing and would never understand how people like him felt. They would never understand how General Chen felt, or the journalist, or his father. All of them simply existed, like the insects and spiders that lived underneath the floorboards. They did not understand, and they did not think. The world was ending, and they were talking about nothing. They deserved extinction. Perhaps he was on the wrong side. Maybe he should have been born as one of The Enemy. Perhaps this was why The Enemy despised humans so much.

He had been reading The Book a lot lately, maybe too much. Maybe it would have been better to understand only a little bit at a time. He had read almost all the handwritten parts. Towards the end, the journalist really seemed to understand people. He wished he could speak to him or Chen. Or his father. If he could speak to someone who understood, maybe he would feel better, or maybe not.

He exchanged friendly words with the old lady next to him. It was pointless, like two people buying each other the same Christmas present. It was a waste of time. This game bored him. He opened his mouth wide, and as he yawned, he hissed quietly. He imagined venom spurting from the back of his throat into the eyes of the old lady.

Michael's mother sat next to him. Beside her was Uncle Joe, the man who had sent his father away. He had been spending a lot of time with the old man lately. They studied almost every night. Michael was more impressive each day. He could almost have believed that Uncle Joe was happy, although it was hard to believe the word meant the same thing to Uncle Joe as it did to everyone else.

Uncle Joe hadn't mentioned Glasgow or General Chen, but hopefully, that would soon change. There was still time yet. In the meantime, the television ensured that Michael understood what was going on in Glasgow and beyond. Far away, the war continued, as it always did. Britain hadn't been released from its commitments, and the soldiers, including his father, would not be coming home yet. In Glasgow, there were plans for a rally on the day of Chen's visit. It would start at Glasgow Green and march to George Square. There it would pass the statue of the general before continuing up to the Concert Hall, where he would be speaking.

Michael knew that even if he couldn't get in to see General Chen speak, he would be able to join the march. He just had to make sure Uncle Joe offered to take him. He wasn't entirely sure how it was going to happen, but it was his only option. During the Lord's prayer, Michael ignored the parts he didn't think were important and instead prayed for the chance to see General Chen. God would be able to think of a way to make it happen. Even Uncle Joe didn't outrank God.

When the time came for the collection, Michael made sure that his note was unfolded so it would be as noticeable as possible. He had to stretch past his mother to place it on the plate. It looked out of place on the plate, next to all the coins. Uncle Joe and his mother both noticed. His mother looked surprised, maybe even slightly offended. Uncle Joe's expression didn't change at all. The old man collecting the money looked pleased and smiled at Michael. Michael smiled back and nodded. Nobody ever mentioned it again, but that didn't matter. They had noticed. He had made that happen.

Back at the hotel, after dinner, Michael went downstairs to help. It was very quiet, and Cathy was behind the bar, as usual. He waited for the ghosts to empty glasses so he could collect them. None of the ghosts had been at church, although Michael knew that some of them sometimes saw the minister during the week. Over the past few weeks, some of the ghosts had changed their faces and uniforms, but they were still the same men. They ignored him as usual. Michael sat up at the bar to read the newspaper. He spoke to Cathy but couldn't be bothered to talk to her. He had shown himself what he could do. Now it was just boring.

When one of the ghosts stood up, Michael worried he might be crazy, and there would be a scene. His uniform was dark green and looked old, as did he. Michael wondered if they threw away your uniform when you died or if they gave it to someone else. It looked like the ghost's uniform might have died more than once.

As Michael tried not to stare at the ghost, another stood up. The others continued to concentrate on their drinks. Ten men sat drinking. Two were standing at attention. They were surprisingly impressive and looked much taller than usual. After a fraction of a second, Michael turned and saw what the ghosts had seen.

The uniform of the man in the doorway had not been recycled, and it had certainly never died. It might not even have been shot at. It was dark green and fitted perfectly, unlike everyone else's. While Michael was still thinking, Cathy greeted the visitor. "Colonel Scott, back again?"

The colonel motioned with his hand, and the ghosts sat down. Michael was still thinking. *Back again?* He hadn't seen the colonel for a very long time. Cathy probably meant he was back after all this time. It was a stupid thing to say.

The colonel looked… solid. He looked like he had a purpose. Most people didn't look like they had a purpose, but military men were usually different. The infantry looked like they had a purpose they weren't going to fulfil very effectively. The ghosts looked like they might have had a purpose once but now didn't care anymore. That was the saddest of all.

The colonel always looked like he had something important to be doing. He looked like he did it well. You felt like he didn't notice you were there unless he was talking to you directly, but when he did talk to you, there was an intensity about him that made you feel you were the most important person in the world. He didn't look like Michael thought colonels were meant to look. That meant he wasn't fat and bald with a red face. Perhaps the colonel was following a more sophisticated stereotype Michael hadn't heard of. He was younger than Uncle Joe, but he was old enough that he had probably been an officer before the war had started. To Michael, he always looked like an ageing film star. Someone confident and professional. He was someone you were sure had been famous, even if it had been before your time and it meant nothing to you. Someone who was semi-retired and was now picking his roles, occasionally getting it wrong. Michael sometimes wondered if the colonel had picked the right role.

The colonel was talking to Cathy at the moment, which meant Michael was invisible. He continued thinking. The colonel was holding his hat in his hand. He usually didn't have his hat with him. There were no soldiers with him, no driver standing at the door. Michael somehow knew nobody was waiting in the car. The colonel had driven here himself. Why would the colonel drive himself? There was an answer… he just couldn't catch it, not yet.

"Good afternoon, Cathy. I need to speak with Joseph again. Is he here?"

"I think he's upstairs. I'll just call him."

Again? Speak with him again? Maybe they had spoken on the phone earlier. Actually, they always spoke on the phone. Why was the colonel here now? Michael decided it was time for the colonel to know he was there.

"Hello, Colonel Scott. I can go and get Uncle Joe if you want."

There was no surprise from the colonel. It seemed he knew Michael was there all the time. When he replied, it wasn't how Michael remembered. It was like he would rather Michael wasn't there. It seemed like he didn't want to talk to him.

"Hello, Michael. No need for that. If Cathy checks Joseph is there, I'll just go up and see him."

Cathy was already on the phone, calling upstairs. The time passed very slowly. The colonel was insisting on silence. Michael wasn't sure how he was doing it, but he definitely was.

The colonel didn't look around the bar. If he looked around, he might be distracted. He might have to engage with something else in the room. Michael couldn't help following his gaze as he watched Cathy. They both watched her as she whispered into the phone and replaced the receiver. Cathy didn't have to wait for much of a response. She wasn't asking Uncle Joe a question. She was passing on information.

"Joseph is upstairs. He'll meet you if you go up."

"That's fine."

The colonel left quickly. He didn't ask after Cathy, or the ghosts, or even Michael. He didn't say goodbye. There was a reason. Michael felt he knew what it was but couldn't name it. It was too obvious. It was too big to see clearly. He almost had it, but then Cathy spoke and derailed his train of thought. "Michael, why don't you see if any of my boys want another drink?"

He headed out towards the tables. The answer had been very close. It had passed right in front of him. It had been in the colonel's eyes when he looked at Michael and then back at Cathy. Cathy had seen it because she was meant to. It was still hanging in the air but was still invisible to Michael. He might have been able to see it in Cathy's eyes if she hadn't turned away from him to surprise some glasses by cleaning them for a second time.

Time ground to a halt in the hotel, except for Michael. For Michael, the next few minutes passed at normal speed. One of the ghosts exchanged a few words with him. Strange, they usually didn't speak. It put its hand on his arm for a second. The ghosts could see the reason. It was one thing they were accustomed to seeing.

Michael heard the reason before he saw it. The hotel must have been silent. It must have been. He hadn't noticed that, but he couldn't have heard it if it hadn't been silent. The wail came from upstairs. It came down the stairs and through the ceiling. The hotel must have been silent because he heard it clearly, even when it lost its strength and recoiled, rasping, into the back of his mother's throat. He saw the reason in Cathy's eyes, behind the tears. He saw it in the ghosts who weren't looking at him. He saw it in the way they trembled, feeling bad because they couldn't feel bad. The best they could do was not to shrug. He saw it clearly, the reason for all of it.

Someone upstairs had just killed his father.

28

Michael waited for what would happen next. Surely something had to happen next? Would everything just stop? How could it keep going?

One of the ghosts stood up and looked at Michael. Michael realised the ghost probably didn't know what to do. But, at least he had done something. They stared at each other. Michael felt his eyes begin to sting, and he felt like his legs might give way.

"Michael."

Cathy was speaking, just one word, his name. She was just checking he was still there. He wasn't sure he was. Everything was getting further away. An invisible journalist leaned against the bar. He looked at Michael and shrugged.

"Michael."

His hand raised and stopped her talking. Something was still soaking through the walls and the ceiling. Denials came tumbling down the stairs. Ugly, misshapen words. Upstairs, a wife was refusing to believe what she was hearing, over and over again. Reality was soaking through the whole building. Pure reality. It rooted Michael to the spot and cleared every mind in the hotel of any happy thought, any thought about anything other than what was happening upstairs. What was happening around the world. It dissolved everything it touched. Reality let them all see time as it passed slowly, grinding to a halt. It showed them the day that waited for all of them. Time had stopped. How would they start it again? What would they do today? What would they do in the next hour? What would they do in the next second? He would have to open the windows later and let it blow away.

He wiped his eyes on his sleeve as he left the bar. Nobody followed him. The denials became louder as he climbed the stairs. They became more real. The colonel stood on the landing. He looked down at the floor as Michael appeared in front of him. When he raised his eyes again, he said, "I'm sorry, Michael. We're all sorry. If there's anything I can do… If you want to come up and see me at the base and talk…"

Michael only had one thought. There was no post on a Sunday. The bad-news machine would have to wait until tomorrow. The colonel had heard first. He didn't look sorry. He looked like he was examining Michael, checking to make sure Michael understood how sorry he was. There was no reason for him to be sorry. It wasn't his fault, not really.

The colonel's hand fell on Michael's shoulder. His other was left holding his hat. Here it was. He would get a reason to make it all make sense. The colonel would tell him something that explained it, and then he wouldn't be allowed to feel as bad. The adults would tell him what he should be feeling. He knew it was coming. What finally came surprised him.

"Your mother needs you."

He looked up at the colonel, confused.

"She needs you. Now. Go."

The colonel stepped aside to let him pass. As Michael passed him, he walked down the stairs, his purpose fulfilled.

Before Michael was a vision of hell, he wanted to turn and run but knew he couldn't. The door to the room was open and lying on the bed was something that looked like his mother. Uncle Joe was sitting on the bed. His eyes were closed but dry. He didn't look like someone grieving. He looked like someone waiting for a storm to pass. His mother looked broken. She lay against Uncle Joe, clutching his arm and wailing. Michael wasn't sure where the noises were coming from. It sounded like it was somewhere deep inside her. He imagined all the tears had left her dry inside. The noises were dry and painful, scraping their way out of her. It was too difficult. He couldn't stay. Uncle Joe opened his eyes. "Mary, it's Michael. Michael's here."

Arms twisted, searching for him. He looked at Uncle Joe. The conversation was quick and silent.

"*You killed my father.*"

"*No, you know that isn't true.*"

"*It is true. You killed him.*"

"*This is not the time.*"

His father was gone. Uncle Joe had killed him. Tomorrow, the letter would arrive and kill him properly. He felt hatred for the old man. He heard his mother call his name. She hadn't stopped Uncle Joe. He had begged her, and she hadn't stopped him. Now she needed him. He felt something. Deep down, he felt something. What was it? His mother needed him. He felt… contempt. How pathetic. She needed him. They needed him. He looked at them both and felt nothing. As he turned and ran, he imagined an invisible journalist stepping out of his way. The journalist raised his hands and eyebrows, trying to show that it was nothing to do with him, but nobody saw because he wasn't there.

Michael passed the colonel outside. He kept running. Nobody followed, and by the time he stopped, he was on the other side of town. He had run all the way down to the beach, past the harbour and the small boats, past the small hotels which were all now boarded up, and had kept going until the pavement beneath his feet gave way to grass. All the time, the hotel was getting smaller, and the problem was getting further away. He would go back later when the reality had dispersed. He sat on the grass and wondered how long he would feel this way. Would he feel any better tomorrow morning? Would it feel this bad forever? He would always be a boy whose father was killed in the war. Whenever people talked about things like this, they always said that not a day went past without them thinking about it. Would that happen? Would there ever be a day again when he didn't think about it?

The world seemed suddenly selfish. People still walked along the beach, talked, and laughed. They all seemed so thoughtless and selfish.

It was strange that people still had things to do. It seemed like the world should stop, even just for a few minutes.

It was probably less upsetting when lots of people died at once. People would be more likely to stop if a lot of people had been killed. Why? Maybe not because they cared more, maybe not because it meant more, or because they were more likely to have noticed. It would have been less upsetting if all the soldiers had been killed all at once. Nobody would have been walking along the beach laughing and talking. All the shops would have been closed. One dead father wasn't enough. These days, it wasn't even unusual. He had some idea that this would have been enough in the past, even ten or twenty years ago. People would have cared, properly cared. It would have scarred everything. He would have been special. Instead, he was uniquely cursed. His father had died at exactly the wrong time. Too late for it to be special, too early for it to be part of the main event. He had died alone in dramatic times.

Dead. What did the word mean? He studied the surrounding area for examples. All around was life. The grass was alive. The trees were alive. Above him, the gulls called to each other. Spiders and insects busied themselves on the ground he was sitting on. Life seemed to be the natural state of things. Dead just meant *not alive*. Alive meant more than *not dead*.

Staring out across the town, he looked for death. The dead concrete of the town covered long-dead grass. Death lay in the rubbish bins behind the houses. Birds dropping into the water snatched the living fish and squeezed death into them. Dead leaves huddled in concrete corners, shrivelled and brown. They were last year's leaves, still dead. Hadn't noticed that before. The dead concrete had suspended them for all that time, far away from the life that might have consumed them.

The soldiers were alive but not as alive as the grass and the birds. The birds were oblivious to everything. Blackbirds pecking at something on the ground might die before the soldiers, but the birds still seemed more alive than them. The trees waved back and forth in the breeze, alive, growing all the time.

His father was not alive. He probably still existed, like last year's leaves, but he was not alive. His body lay somewhere, empty. It was still him, but it wouldn't move or talk anymore. Something had damaged his body, and it had stopped working. All the different parts weren't able to work together anymore. Something had broken the chain. His body had stopped working, and all the thoughts and memories in his head had just broken up and disappeared. Everything that was him wasn't there anymore.

Michael realised nobody was coming to get him. Good. They were all too busy thinking about someone who wasn't there anymore, imprisoned by guilt. If they had thought about him more when he was there, none of this would have happened. Now they felt so bad they would have to stay in their beds and cry for hours. Maybe they would never be able to leave the hotel again. Maybe nobody would ever come for him. He would have to stay away forever. It was hard to imagine ever going back to the hotel.

It took hours for night to fall, but nobody came. Nobody cared. As it became colder, Michael regretted not bringing his jacket. Nobody came, not that he wanted them to. Finally, the seagulls settled on the roofs for the night. He couldn't go back. What were you supposed to do? What was he meant to say? Uncle Joe would be angry. Everybody would be angry. What if Uncle Joe searched his room? What if he found The Book? What if he found everything? He wouldn't. Michael knew he wouldn't. He didn't know why he knew. He just knew.

When night finally came, it fell gradually but decisively. Michael could still remember when they had used the streetlights, but it was a long time ago. No point in wasting all that electricity. Soon he couldn't see the houses. Then he couldn't even see the hotel set against the sky. He could see some lights in the windows, but the outline merged with everything else. Nobody was coming. Even if he wanted to go back, he couldn't. He would never be able to find his way back, even if there was anything to go back to.

He wasn't sure what to do when he saw the lights from the torches. Moving through the town, they picked out circles on walls and on the pavement. The circles twitched over boy-sized areas in people's gardens. They were coming for him, tracing out zigzag paths along the road, merging and bouncing off each other. It would take a long time for the circles to find him. He could hide, and they would never find him. A few steps into the darkness in the right direction, and he would be invisible forever. But something made that difficult. He was still connected to something. Part of him was still connected to something.

He imagined someone else a few steps away, deep in the cold, dangerous darkness. A man he had never spoken to, standing in the shadows, disconnected, nothing to return for. He was ready to wrap the darkness around himself and walk away. A man who still had a father and had chosen to leave him. An observer who wasn't interested in observing. What would he do? He would understand everything so much better. It would all be clear to him. He would know what to do. He would know when there was no point in trying anymore, and he would know when to give up. Maybe it was a choice. Be like the journalist and cope with things or… what? Go back. Going back wasn't really a choice. But he would have to go back. He would have to. The choice was how to go back, who to be, and what to feel. He wasn't sure if he could go back to how things were. The journalist didn't have to provide the answer. That was the advantage of standing in the darkness. Michael felt guilty about thinking about a stranger when he should have been thinking of his father. Looking out onto the dark canvas where the town was usually painted, he could still see circles searching, hoping a boy wanted to be found.

Behind him, the darkness contained grass and dirt. It was dangerous. You might trip over some unseen bump and break your neck. Even so, it was the easy option. No people there. In front of him, in the town, complications searched for him. If they found him, they would make him speak to them.

What would his father do? He would do the right thing. No matter what it cost. He always did the right thing. Michael stood up and inched his way towards the town. He knew that if his father had been there, he would have been at his side. If the journalist had really been standing in the darkness, he would have stood and watched them.

It took a while to reach the circles. As he got closer, he could hear them as well as see them, lots of them. Each of the circles had two or three voices which discussed and suggested as they changed shape and crawled and twitched, sniffing the road and the pavement.

As one circle reached Michael's feet, it travelled upwards and exploded, blinding him. Other circles snapped towards him, guided by voices behind them. Eventually, they stopped blinding him and settled for illuminating his bottom half. He could hear voices quietly calling his name. They hesitated as if it might make him angry. Some of them shortened it, perhaps thinking that made it less dangerous.

White lights silhouetted dark boots and cast long shadows along the road. One figure moved a few steps forward, then hesitated. Michael was sure it was the ghost from the bar earlier but couldn't think of a good reason why. The soldiers were keeping their distance from him. Perhaps they thought grief was infectious, and it was better to wait for someone who was immune. They were silent while they waited for him. He was in no hurry. He was never in any hurry.

He wasn't hidden behind a bright circle but illuminated by the flame that burned beside him. Protected behind the glass of his lantern, it burned and brought him to life in the darkness. The torches of the men looked strangely cold and artificial by comparison. He didn't feel the same fear as the other men. When he stopped a few steps in front of Michael, it was to wait for permission, not reassurance. He followed Michael as he turned and headed back into the darkness, away from the circles which paced the ground in front of the men.

The conversation between them silently unfolded as they sat down on a nearby wall. Neither spoke. Neither looked at each other. Instead, the silence mediated between them. When it had reconciled them enough, one of them would speak. Uncle Joe looked strange in the flickering light from his lantern. The shadows and dark wrinkles on his face showed him as he really was. Michael knew he was an old man. Uncle Joe had always been an old man. As Michael aged, his perception of old moved on, but Uncle Joe had always kept pace. In the light of the flame, he looked more than old. Old meant weak and spent. He looked ancient, worn, and timeless. He didn't look like a tired version of something young. This was how he was meant to look. This was how he would always be remembered.

Uncle Joe was the first to speak. "Your mother is sleeping. She'll be fine." It might have been him making a concession. But then, perhaps he didn't really count it as speaking first. He had answered a question that would have been asked, anyway. He had just ignored the first few lines of the conversation. Whatever his reasons, it should certainly have made things easier. Michael wasn't sure if it did.

Michael realised he hadn't spoken for hours. It felt strange now. Maybe he would have forgotten how. He didn't know what to say. What do you say to the man who has killed your father? Except Uncle Joe hadn't killed him, not really. He had let someone, or something, else do it. It seemed worse for some reason. Michael imagined his father sitting beside him, silently urging him to speak. He couldn't. His father would understand.

Uncle Joe stared into the darkness towards the hotel. "The colonel came back after you left. He wanted to know if you were all right. I told him you just needed some time. I knew you would be fine."

Still, Michael had nothing to say. If his father had been there, he would have smiled and gently put his hand on his shoulder, willing his son to speak. But he wasn't there. He would never be there again. Uncle Joe would have to talk.

"He offered to come and find you. He would have had the whole army camp down here. I told him not to. He always asks about you. Remember that time we went to the base, and he had them take you up in the helicopter? He said if you wanted to go back up someday, I was just to call him. I don't think they have helicopters anymore, but he thought you might like to go, anyway."

Michael remembered. It had been payment for another death. His father wouldn't know what Uncle Joe was talking about. It had been a secret. Maybe he should have told him. Now it was too late. He looked at the lights in the distance where the soldiers were standing. They were probably not infantry. Ghosts. His father was a ghost now. He would stay a ghost until his letter arrived.

An uncomfortable memory resurfaced in Michael's mind. He had once thought about faking his father's letter to see if they would let him go and see General Chen in Glasgow. He wouldn't really have done it, but he still shouldn't have thought about using his father like that. Maybe everybody used the soldiers, the infantry, and the ghosts. Used them to do all the things that needed to be done. They used their lives to test theories and prove points. Used their deaths to manipulate people. It was easy to see when you looked for it. Easy to see when you could crack the code.

Maybe it wasn't his father that was sitting next to him. Maybe it was someone else. Someone who knew how to crack the code. He would tell Michael to talk, just like his father would, but maybe he would also help him work out what to say.

Suddenly, it came to him. He saw through it all. Now he could speak. "How much did you pay them to help you look for me?"

No reply from the old man. He must have paid them, not money, but drinks. People would do more for a drink than they would for the equivalent amount of money. Uncle Joe knew that. Buying drinks for people was good business. You could use the significance of the gesture to manipulate them.

"One drink? Two? Three?" The old man's face betrayed him. "Three drinks?" It was a lot. The silent old man had paid over the odds. "They would have done it for two."

The old man suddenly turned and said, "They would have done it for nothing. Sometimes that's not the point."

Uncle Joe was right. He was always right. It was hard to know what Uncle Joe meant exactly. Did he pay more because he wanted them to do the job well or because he wanted them to do it without complaining? Maybe he just meant that they deserved to be paid. Maybe it was just the right thing to do.

"We would like you to come home. Are you ready to come back with me?"

"I don't think so."

"But you will be back soon?"

It wasn't a fair question. Where else could he go? But he couldn't go back yet.

"Yes."

"Do you want me to stay here with you?"

"No."

It was all too easy on Uncle Joe after everything he had done. Things couldn't go back to how they were. His father would want him to forgive, but he couldn't, not now, not ever. Uncle Joe reached for something under his coat. "I brought your jacket. I thought you might be cold."

"I don't want anything from you."

"Well, you'll take a torch, at least. For when you want to come back in."

"No. I don't need anything from you."

"Then I'll ask one of the men to stay."

"No, I don't need anything."

"You have to get home safely."

"I'll get home. Even though I don't have anything to come home to."

Uncle Joe was calm but hesitated before replying, "Of course, you do. Your mother will want to see you. She will need you with her."

"There is nothing to go back to. Dad is dead."

There was a long pause. Michael knew he wasn't supposed to say these things. He was supposed to make things easier for everyone, but he couldn't help it. He was finding it harder to imagine his father sitting next to him. Uncle Joe nodded as he thought about what to say. After scanning the darkness for inspiration, he looked at Michael again. "What is it that General Chen always says when he talks about the fallen? You told me once. 'We asked them to protect us, and they were ready…' How does it go?"

General Chen had often included it in his speeches. Some people had started using it at memorial services and on monuments. Michael had heard it a hundred times. It had been in his project about General Chen at school. He didn't want to say it now. It would spoil something, stop him from doing something, but he couldn't work out what. "I don't know if I remember it."

His father would have disapproved. This was not the right thing to do. Uncle Joe didn't seem upset. He just looked off into the darkness again. "That's a shame because I think I would like to hear it. I think it fits your father well. Why don't you try to see what you remember?"

His father's memory told him it was the right thing to do. He had protested long enough. "We do it at school, sometimes at memorials. General Chen wrote it himself just after he took charge. It goes: 'We asked for their protection, and they were ready at the first call. In saving us, they could not save themselves. Death now divides us, but they wait for us where The Enemy can no longer harm them. Though gone, they still speak to us through their sacrifice on the altar of duty. Of you, they ask only that their death was not in vain and that you bring honour to their memory. We shall meet again.'"

Michael felt a shiver. He thought he might cry again. He felt sure his father would have smiled at him if he had really been sitting beside him. Uncle Joe seemed much happier. "Yes, that was it. 'We shall meet again.' I think that's just what your father believed. I think that's why he was so brave."

Michael thought that was probably true. "What happens now?"

There was a sadness in Uncle Joe's voice again. "We go home, go to bed, get up in the morning, and do what we always do. That's how it works. We have no choice."

"But everything is different. I don't know if I will be able to stand it. Not if Dad isn't there."

Uncle Joe nodded and thought for a moment. "Well, maybe it depends on how you look at it. Your father will not be home tomorrow, but he was not home today, and you coped with that. I know it is different, but maybe it can be almost the same if you don't think about it as much."

"But it can't be the same."

"Maybe."

He wasn't like Uncle Joe. He couldn't just ignore everything. That wasn't how things worked. Whoever was sitting beside him now encouraged him to ask something of Uncle Joe that would expose him. "Wasn't everything different for you after Auntie Anne died?"

Uncle Joe was surprised. On another day, he probably wouldn't have answered. He sat down beside Michael again. Even if the lantern hadn't illuminated him, Michael would still have known. He would still have heard the noises the old man made when he was forced to sit down, breathe, and think all at the same time. He answered slowly, looking off into the darkness as if he wasn't really aware he was talking. "Yes. But that was… that was a long time ago. Everything was different. Other things happened. You just have to go on. If you can cope for a minute, you can cope for an hour. If you can cope for an hour, you can cope for a day."

"Does it get easier with time? People say it does. How long will it take?"

Uncle Joe seemed to have forgotten who he was speaking to. He was somewhere else. "Maybe it does for some people. You will probably find that it gets easier with time. The world can't just stop. People have to go on. Most people manage somehow. You move on and do other things. It doesn't happen quickly."

This wasn't any help. Michael knew he couldn't just switch off like Uncle Joe. If this was all there was, he wouldn't be able to go on. Uncle Joe would never understand. Then a thought entered his head, like a suggestion from someone sitting next to him. Of course, Uncle Joe could never understand. But even if he couldn't, he could still be useful. You just had to take control of the situation and get what you wanted. He wanted to get to see General Chen. Uncle Joe might be able to do it.

Just because Michael had thought about faking the letter didn't make him responsible for what had happened, but now that it had happened, he couldn't change it. His father would have wanted him to be happy. It didn't sound like something his father would have suggested, but before he could stop himself, he said, "I don't know what to do. I have nothing to look forward to. I don't have anyone to talk to."

Uncle Joe headed in the right direction. "What is it you want to happen? What would make it easier? Would you like to go to the army base and see the colonel?"

Now it was his father's voice in his head. The last time he had been home, he had told him about Uncle Joe. *You have to be careful around him. You must never ask this man for anything or tell him you want anything.* He had another voice in his head. This one told him to get what he wanted and that he was clever enough to do so. It told him to think about exactly how to do it. Michael realised he shouldn't ask outright but should instead ask for something else that Uncle Joe couldn't give, something that would make him feel bad. Uncle Joe would provide what Michael wanted as an alternative. Michael congratulated himself. It was wrong, but he deserved it. He deserved it because of everything that had happened and because he was clever enough to make it happen. "I want my dad back. I want him to be here. That's what I always wanted."

The unspoken sentence at the end was the most powerful. It was a complaint, an accusation. Uncle Joe would fill it in himself, and it would burn into him.

Uncle Joe stood up. He looked sad. "He was always very proud of you."

Michael couldn't help himself. "Do you think we will meet him again?"

Uncle Joe looked around before letting his gaze settle on Michael again. "I think it's worth looking forward to." He picked up the lantern he had left flickering on the wall. "For now, I think it's time I was getting back. I should check on your mother."

Michael was stunned. How would he get back through the darkness? He thought of asking Uncle Joe for the torch he had offered earlier. "What about me?"

"I thought you didn't want to come back yet."

"I don't."

"Well, would you like me to stay until you're ready?"

"No. I need to think about things for a while."

"Then I'll see you back at the hotel in a little while."

"But how will I—"

"You said you would get home. I think you will. I have faith in you." He waved his hand toward the lights. "I'll tell your friends that you're fine. One of them said he would stay out and watch over you if you wanted. Would you like me to tell him to stay?"

"No, he doesn't have to. I'll be fine, I suppose."

"People don't always do things just because they have to. Why don't I tell him it's up to him? You promise you'll come back in soon?"

"I promise."

"Things will get better. You'll see."

Michael had no idea what to say. A memory provided an answer: "I suppose. I suppose you just have to keep focused on what's important."

Some of the tension seemed to leave Uncle Joe. "Exactly. I knew you would understand."

As the old man walked into the darkness, Michael thought about why he was being abandoned again. Uncle Joe had to get back. Maybe his mother wasn't sleeping. Maybe he had kept her awake. The lights drifted away, all except one. It didn't move away with the rest but kept its distance. Its owner stayed in his own darkness. He would wait until he was needed. Michael watched the remaining light. Had time made things better for the ghosts? He suspected it did not help the broken men. They had a tolerance to its effects. So did the journalist. Michael wondered if he would develop the same tolerance. Had Uncle Joe?

Long after the lights had made their way back to the hotel, Michael thought about who the ghosts really were. People who felt like he did right now, maybe even worse. His dad was gone, but he hadn't had to see it. He could choose how he remembered it. It was worse for them. They had faced The Enemy and survived when everybody else hadn't. It was probably worse than being killed. If you died, it only happened once, and the bad memories died with you. The ghosts had survived The Enemy once, but Michael knew They came back at night. They made you scream in your bed. You had to survive, and everyone else had to die all over again. At least Michael might meet his father again in dreams. The ghosts would meet something else.

Michael suddenly realised that the ghosts had left the hotel for him. He hadn't noticed before. He had also assumed they had only been helping because they were paid. That wasn't it. They had done it because they understood. He was closer to them now than he'd been yesterday. At the end of the road, a circle disappeared. A much smaller orange light replaced it. The ghost was smoking. Michael thought he could see the light shaking.

He would have to go back to the hotel. Somehow, he would have to find his way back. It was so dark, but the ghost would help him. Even so, he was surprised Uncle Joe hadn't tried harder to make him leave. He probably didn't want an argument. Probably he thought Michael needed some more time and thought it would be better if he made his own way back instead of being brought back. He probably didn't really care and had more important things to do. Michael looked up at the hotel and what he thought was his mother's window. Nobody was standing there, nobody waiting and watching. Nobody.

The journalist could have predicted all of this. His father would have shrugged it off. Which one was better? Both of them were dead. One had given up on people, and one had trusted them. One had manipulated people and been very successful. One had been nice to people, and they had cared about him. One had gone mad. One had… He stopped. A memory intruded. A man lying in a hall. One had… one had been his father.

As he cried, he was glad nobody could see him. He was glad nobody was around. It was lucky Uncle Joe had left him. As he thought about his father, he didn't notice a light going on far away in the hotel. He didn't even notice when all the lights in the hotel started to go on. The hotel stood out above the town. Not enough to find your way home, but enough so you wouldn't get lost.

Far down the road, a light went on in one of the houses. A weak light made it out onto the pavement and bled onto the street. It brightened as curtains were thrown back. The light on the road was joined by a second from the same house, which now looked at the road with two square, yellow eyes. By the time the third light joined it, a house in the next street had opened one eye.

As a young boy looked up, he saw a town waking up in the middle of the night. Some houses slept, their eyes boarded up, as their neighbours blinked into life. Yellow light spilled onto the pavement as the house next to him opened one eye, then another. The boy wiped away the tears in his eyes and saw the town lighting up. It wasn't coming to life. There was still nobody around. No doors opened, and nobody was standing at their windows. Somewhere the boy thought he could hear a phone ringing, but he might have imagined it. A ghost let his cigarette fall onto the road as he stood open-mouthed. Eventually, he switched on his torch but realised it wouldn't help him see what was happening and switched it off again.

The boy began walking through the town. He began walking home. He was already home. Maybe that was why Uncle Joe wasn't worried about him. He reached the ghost and returned his stunned look with a smile and tearful eyes. He wasn't surprised, not really. As they started walking together, the young boy knew everything wasn't fixed. He knew his father wouldn't be coming back. Uncle Joe might never be able to talk to him the way he wanted him to. He might not get to see General Chen, but for now, he was going home, and that was enough.

The boy and the ghost made their way back through the artificial twilight. When the first streetlight coughed into life, the ghost looked at it like he had never seen one. Like it was a sign from above, which in a way it was. As the rest of the streetlights flickered on, the boy started laughing. The journalist once said that if you really tried, if you called in all your favours and used all your imagination, then just once you could do something really special, something really big. Michael thought that if the journalist had known Uncle Joe, he might have felt differently. The normal rules never applied to Uncle Joe.

High above the town, an old man stood at a window. He pressed his hand against the glass. Maybe just checking it was still there, separating two worlds. It had been a cheap trick. Just a few phone calls. It didn't really change anything. They would all still have to face tomorrow, and who knew what that might bring? For tonight, it might be enough. Who could complain about a cheap trick now and then in a world like this? The colonel had asked about the memorial. He had said he would have to ask the boy if he minded the colonel coming when the time came. No reason he should. He would ask him tomorrow.

If the journalist had been there, which he wasn't, he would have stood in what was left of the darkness and watched a boy he had never met walking next to a soldier. Someone else might have walked beside them, but if you looked, you would have seen that he wasn't there either. If you really listened, you might have heard the boy laughing. If you really listened, you might have heard him laughing for miles around.

29

There was one less place set at breakfast. Nobody was waiting anymore. The table looked embarrassed, but it wasn't its fault. Michael thought his mother might have spoken to him, thought she might have come to see him. Instead, things were the way they had always been.

Uncle Joe spoke as soon as he entered the room. Technically, you're not breaking the silence if the silence hasn't started yet. However, Uncle Joe did let the silence heal over for a while afterwards.

It had been a brave choice of words. "Good Morning."

Except it wasn't. It wasn't a good morning. In a world of mornings that weren't good, this morning was exceptional. It wasn't just that it wasn't a good morning. It was that the phrase was empty. There was no point wishing someone a good morning. There was no prospect of this morning improving. There was no point wishing for the impossible. There might be no good mornings ever again.

In the silence, Michael turned the phrase over in his head. *Good morning. Good morning. Morning.* As he repeated the words in his head, they began to make less sense. They warped and unravelled. God Morning. God Mourning. Who was God mourning? Maybe not that. Maybe mourning God. He shook his head as his thoughts began to chase each other.

What would happen today? Things would go on as normal. You couldn't just stop. That was what Uncle Joe had said. The world kept turning, and you just let it take you with it. All the people whose fathers hadn't died yesterday would just keep going. You just had to play along.

Nobody had said anything since they had grunted their replies to Uncle Joe's wish that they should have a good morning. The woman whose father hadn't just died ate her breakfast. The old man whose father hadn't just died read the newspaper. Outside, the world was full of people whose father hadn't just died. Until yesterday, Michael had been one of them. He tried to remember what it had been like. It had been different, just different. He wondered if it would ever go back to the way it had been before.

The table offered him some apple juice, still embarrassed. Michael found his gaze failing to settle on his toast. They were just things. Everything had been turned into empty, naked things. Not a kitchen anymore, just a room full of things for cooking, things to eat, things to put other things on. Across from him, people lifted things from the big thing in the middle of the room and put them in their mouths.

Michael wasn't part of this world anymore. He was special. He was one of the few people in the world whose father had just died. They couldn't understand him today. Their world was irrelevant to him. Maybe tomorrow, it would be his world again. For now, everything was grey. Their food didn't taste of anything. Even if they spoke, it wouldn't mean anything to him. Maybe they were speaking, and he just couldn't hear them. The words might be tumbling through him, bouncing off him.

The older man eventually said something. Something about a place they called Dumfries. He might go there tomorrow. The woman nodded. The old man might need some help. He was asking for help from someone. Someone else in the room. Michael realised it was the body that he was inside. He couldn't make it respond. Actually, he could have forced it to respond, but… he couldn't see any reason to. He couldn't make the reason important enough. It was not irrelevant, just… insignificant. The words passed through him. The old man looked in his direction.

Uncle Joe was asking him something. Michael snapped back into the moment. Yes, he would go to Dumfries with him tomorrow. Uncle Joe went back to the newspaper, satisfied.

Michael spent the rest of breakfast watching his mother. He had to speak to her. He knew it was easy for Uncle Joe. Michael needed to know that it wasn't so easy for his mother. He had to know that his father had meant something more to her. She seemed just like Uncle Joe. She was no different than usual. She was just quieter. They didn't care. Selfish, everyone was selfish.

He began to worry that he was too upset. Maybe he wasn't really upset. Maybe he was just pretending to be as upset as he thought he should be, and he was getting it wrong. Michael shook the idea out of his head as it became too complicated. He had to speak to his mother, but he couldn't do it with Uncle Joe there. Uncle Joe would probably leave them alone. The worry that his mother would get up and leave first made the time pass slowly.

Relief washed over him as Uncle Joe finally left. He had things to do. Uncle Joe had to be Uncle Joe. He had to keep going. He probably didn't have any choice.

After the old man left the room, Michael was left alone with the woman. He felt he should say something before she escaped. What was there to say? Nothing. The woman faded away along with the rest of her world. There had to be something to say. The journalist who wasn't there couldn't think of anything to say. Neither could Michael's father, who also wasn't there. There were too many bad memories in the room, poisoning everyone. Then again, maybe there was just one really big one.

What did you do when there was nothing you could do? What were you supposed to do when everything you said would be wrong? It struck Michael that this might be why people go mad. When everything reasonable became impossible, you were only left with crazy things to do. The woman wouldn't look at him. She was very far away, probably because it all hurt less when you weren't there to feel it.

There was nothing else to do. When you can't say anything small, you can only say something big. He tried to remember what the woman was called. She might respond to her name.

"Mum."

There was no response. Why?

"Mum. Uncle Joe said Dad was very brave."

Still, the woman wouldn't look at him. "General Chen says Dad is waiting for us somewhere. He says we'll all meet again."

The woman had her head in her hands, and Michael was running out of things to say. This wasn't how it was supposed to be. She was the one who was supposed to do this, not him. He desperately tried to think of something else, anything else, to say.

"I suppose he was lucky. He... he had a good run." Apparently, you didn't always have to resort to saying crazy things. Long before that, you could say stupid things. The journalist, who wasn't there, grimaced as the woman started crying.

Michael was wrenched back into her world again. The things became a kitchen. The woman became his mother. The table sat paralysed as tears fell onto it and were quickly wiped away before they stained. Not that it would have minded.

His mother didn't look like a parent anymore or an adult. Michael started to panic as she became younger. Her tears embarrassed her. He could see that she hadn't always been his mother. She had once been just like everyone else, just like the girls at school, just like the infantry, just like everyone. Everyone except Uncle Joe? The thought briefly troubled Michael before he managed to push it away.

For the moment, he had no idea what to do. He moved towards his mother but didn't know if he should hold her. It didn't seem right. He watched her as she cried. The thought occurred to him that he should be crying, and he was surprised when he noticed that he wasn't. He had to do something.

He hovered close to her. "Mum, please don't cry."

She didn't look up. "I'm sorry, Michael, but he was my husband."

Michael felt a shiver as the bad memories multiplied. There was nothing he could do. He didn't know how to hold her. The only things left to do were crazy things. One of them didn't seem crazy, standing there. Michael walked across the kitchen to the window. He could still hear his mother crying as he released the latch on each side. As it swung open, the curtains blew inwards, knocking a cup into the sink, where it quickly began to drown. As Michael walked back across the kitchen, the curtains continued blowing against the plates and cups draining by the sink, making them chime in protest. Michael wasn't interested in them. He was more interested in the bad memories drifting out of the kitchen and into the sky. It was enough to make the woman a parent again, just for a moment. Her arm reached out to him, showing him how to hold her. As he sat beside her, he pulled her towards him. The table creaked in slow approval as her elbows lifted from it.

It took a long time to squeeze the bad memories out of her. Even then, Michael couldn't be sure that they had all left. Outside, the world was still turning, maybe because Uncle Joe was pacing around in it like a hamster in a wheel, keeping it moving. Uncle Joe and the world were distracting each other, buying Michael time. He thought the old man had been wrong. You couldn't just keep going. There was something worse than having to stop, and that was not being able to.

30

Dumfries seemed like a large place, although Michael knew that it probably shouldn't. Whenever you turned a corner, there were more houses. It was probably the same in Glasgow, although he knew Glasgow was much bigger. In Dumfries, there was still enough green for him to imagine the fields and hills underneath the tarmac and concrete. The streets were quiet, just like at home, and a lot of the houses and shops were boarded up. They were sleeping. Some were waiting for owners who might return from bigger cities and towns one day. Some were waiting for owners that would never return from places much further away.

The house they parked outside wasn't sleeping, although net curtains shielded its eyes, only letting information pass one way. Old people liked net curtains. You could watch without being seen. Michael knew that if you weren't careful, at night, they betrayed you and worked the other way, turning your house into a giant yellow fish bowl.

Michael guessed this was where Uncle Joe's friend lived. It hadn't been easy to speak to Uncle Joe on the way to Dumfries. Michael couldn't mention what had happened to his father but couldn't think of anything else to talk about. The radio meant there had been no silence to exert pressure on them. Michael was free to stare silently out of his window at the sheep for long periods. There were fewer people these days but just as many sheep. Occasionally, Uncle Joe would point out buildings and explain what they were or what they used to be used for. Michael managed to ask why they were going to Dumfries, but Uncle Joe seemed more comfortable talking about buildings than people. They were going to help a friend of his. That was all.

The friend lived in a small house. There was no upstairs, and it was attached to another sleeping house on one side, which somehow made it look even smaller. The brown sandstone walls and net curtains hid whatever was inside from Michael. There was no garden at the front, and the door opened right onto the street. Michael resisted the urge to put his face up against the window, but only because Uncle Joe was there. No one had cut the grass in the garden at the side for a long time, maybe not for the whole summer.

The door stared silently through both of them with its three eyes of frosted glass. Michael let Uncle Joe deal with the door, grabbing its brass nose and using it to knock three times. Michael saw him glance towards the garden. It seemed Uncle Joe wasn't sure if there would be an answer, but there was always the back door. Michael could see he was trying to look unconcerned, waiting for a reply far longer than he would have if he really was unconcerned. By the time he started knocking again, he wasn't showing the look of surprise or worry that a normal person would have. His lack of concern was false. He didn't look towards Michael, no reassuring glance. He was trying to stop himself from panicking, not Michael.

When the second knock went unanswered, Uncle Joe looked first at his watch, then quickly at the surrounding street. Just to show it he was keeping an eye on it, and it shouldn't think this defeat was a reason to try anything. Uncle Joe resisted the temptation to look through the spyhole in the door. Michael knew Uncle Joe was an intelligent man. He knew it would have shown him nothing. The old man's head twitched forward, showing the appeal the spyhole might have held for an ordinary mortal. Even so, his self-control was impressive.

The street stayed back from Uncle Joe as he drew himself up and planned his next move. The door continued looking through them, across the narrow street. Uncle Joe wanted to appear casual, but he also wanted an answer from the door. Michael watched as the two desires tugged the old man back and forth. He stepped back and gave the street a final look before putting his ear to the wood, listening for a heartbeat. The door held its breath and kept still.

Michael wondered if they would have to go all the way home again. Surely Uncle Joe had seen the garden?

"Maybe we can go through the garden and round to the back door?"

Uncle Joe didn't look at him and instead began inspecting the letterbox. "It's a much more modern door. Much stronger."

Michael was surprised. Surely his uncle wasn't thinking of breaking in? He glanced up and down the street himself, checking there was nobody to witness him becoming an accomplice.

"There's a key in the lock," Uncle Joe said, replying to a question he must have silently asked himself.

"Maybe he left through the back door."

"Maybe he's still inside." Uncle Joe turned the handle on the door and swung it open. "Maybe the door's open."

As Uncle Joe walked into the house, Michael could only see darkness. It didn't seem like anybody was at home. As he walked into the hall, he could see the house wasn't as dark as he had originally thought. It was just gloomy. The carpet was dark with a swirly orange pattern, and the walls were yellow, although they had probably been white at one time. Michael guessed that nobody had made swirly orange carpets for a very long time. Ahead of him, he could hear a light switch being turned on and off but could see that it was still dark. As he entered the living room, he saw Uncle Joe opening the curtains. The light revealed that it was an old person's house. Everything was brown and orange. Ornaments covered every surface. There were lots of pictures of happy young people. The latter definitely added to the old-fashioned look of the place.

"How long has the electricity been off?"

Michael looked round to see that Uncle Joe was talking to the old man in the armchair. Michael hadn't noticed him. His tartan blanket helped him blend in with the surroundings. He squinted as the light streamed into the room but he didn't look up at Uncle Joe.

"I don't know, maybe a few weeks. There are letters I still haven't read. I don't know why the phone still works. Maybe the neighbours called the electricity people when the place was empty but didn't call anyone else."

Michael realised he had been wrong. It wasn't an old man, not really old, at least. Michael guessed he was probably about the same age as his father. The same age as he had been. The thought lingered. Would his father always be the same age? Did you keep counting people's birthdays after they were gone? One day, would Michael be older than his father? He shook the idea out of his head and tried to work out what was going on. The man had been sleeping in the chair. Uncle Joe knew who he was. He must be the man they had come to help. The man looked like he hadn't shaved for days. He looked like… he looked like he might be a ghost. There was something missing. Michael wasn't sure what it was, but whatever it was, it wasn't lying around the chair because Michael's gaze was drawn there to look for it. As always, Uncle Joe provided the answer.

"Have you been drinking?"

Still, the man didn't look at him. "No, Joseph, I don't really drink. Not like that. You must be thinking of someone else."

"Have you been eating?"

"Sometimes. Sometimes there's no food around."

"Is there anything in the kitchen?"

"Sometimes the kitchen is too far away."

Uncle Joe didn't laugh, and Michael wasn't sure whether it was a joke or not. A few seconds of silence told the man his answer wasn't enough.

"There is food in the kitchen. There was food there the last time I was in there."

Uncle Joe walked across the room and opened the door to the kitchen, perhaps checking that there was such a thing. The man looked annoyed for the first time but still didn't look at anyone. "I'm not an invalid, Joe. Just because someone decides to sleep in front of the television for a few days doesn't mean… that… that there's some kind of big problem."

Michael sensed that the man had been about to say it wasn't the end of the world, but people didn't use that phrase often anymore. It probably seemed unlucky.

As Uncle Joe checked the kitchen, Michael found his attention had wandered, and he had started talking. While it wasn't being properly supervised, his mouth had gained access to his brain. "Why do you sleep in front of the television?"

The man sank further into his tartan blanket. His voice was surprisingly small now that all the annoyance was gone. "What?"

Uncle Joe looked at Michael, but to everyone's surprise, the boy continued talking. "If the electricity is off, then the television won't work. Why sit here in front of the television?"

The man looked deep in thought, staring at an ornament as if he hadn't seen it before. Finally, he sighed and shrugged. "I don't know. I think that's just what you do if you don't want to go to bed."

There was a strange moment as the three of them looked at the old television with its mock wooden finish and pondered the idea for longer than seemed necessary. Uncle Joe spoke first. "This is Michael, my nephew." Uncle Joe continued, despite the absence of any response. "He was at the funeral. We all were."

"I couldn't get back."

"I know."

"I had a good excuse."

"You certainly did."

"To be fair, he'll miss mine now, so we're kind of even."

"I suppose you could look at it like that."

"Seems so unnatural. You don't imagine you're going to outlive your parents."

It was almost a smile, and Uncle Joe reflected it back at the man.

"You're going to make me do things, aren't you, Joe?"

"Yes, I am. And we are going to help."

"I've finished the bedroom. The important things, at least. There wasn't much. The rest can all go. I've got some boxes. I got them… last week or something. I don't really remember."

"That's a good start. We can help with that."

"I think I should get up. What should I do?"

"Go and have a shower. Shave as well. Put some clothes on, and we'll make you something to eat. Then we'll get on with what is to be done."

The man nodded. He squeezed his eyes shut. "Will it take a long time?"

"Not with three of us. Go and have a shower."

And, to everyone's surprise, including his own, he did.

Uncle Joe explained some things while they made breakfast. The man wasn't a ghost. When Michael had attended the funeral in Dumfries weeks ago, it had been for the man's father and an old friend of Uncle Joe's. Now the house had to be cleared out before it was mothballed. Uncle Joe had brought Michael to help. The man hadn't been at the funeral, but Uncle Joe didn't say why.

It seemed strange to Michael that the man was so upset. It had been a long time since the funeral. Time was supposed to make things better. It should be different if your father died when he was an old man. You would expect it, so you shouldn't be so upset. It was different if you were young and cheated out of the time you were owed. The man had already had his father. He had been there when he was growing up. It was still sad but totally different from Michael's situation. He was missing out on years with his father.

After the man returned, Michael managed to work out more of the details. He looked a lot younger than before. A lot less like a ghost. He still didn't look at anyone, but as they ate together, he talked to Uncle Joe. The man worked in England. He had a very boring job and was glad to get time off from it. He had been in Dumfries for two weeks, and Uncle Joe had called him yesterday.

The man talked to Uncle Joe about his job for a while. He talked about how for years, all he had done was sit in an office and go to meetings, how he wished he had stayed in Dumfries. Michael imagined the journalist sitting at the table with them, bored by the conversation, hating every minute, trying not to explode.

Why was this to be his life? In a few years, they would send him away to fight and die. In the meantime, he had to spend his time with increasingly boring people. That was bad enough, but when the only people he wanted to talk to were being taken away, it was even more difficult. His father was gone. The journalist had been dead before he even had a chance to meet him. The ghosts wouldn't talk about anything. His mother couldn't talk to him. Now he was far from home, helping somebody who wasn't worse off than himself. It was so unfair. Uncle Joe had probably brought him here to make him appreciate what he had and to stop him from being so disappointed about not seeing General Chen.

When the adults were ready to work, he was sent to the bedroom to pack books. Uncle Joe and the man would pick out the important things from the other rooms and pack the rest up. Uncle Joe's instructions were short statements of fact. It sounded more like he was talking about events which had already happened rather than things he hoped would get done. As usual, his approach brought results. As he picked through the books in the bedroom, Michael could hear muffled conversation and the sounds of activity from the next room.

The man said Michael could keep any books he wanted. Uncle Joe encouraged Michael to find something for the car on the way back, but it was turning out to be difficult. He searched but was finding nothing of interest. Most of them were yellowing paperbacks about cowboys. To Michael, they all seemed to have much the same storyline. People living in the desert, being terrorized by outlaws and Indians, then saved or doomed by powerful strangers. He couldn't see why anyone would be interested in reading them and tossed them into the boxes two or three at a time. There were little books that seemed to be magazines and some books which were collections of other books. There were some big books that looked new. They were mostly about gardening. Michael guessed they had been Christmas or birthday presents.

The room was already almost empty by the time Michael started. Even the alarm clock had given up ticking and settled for it being seventeen minutes past three for the rest of eternity. An old, empty wardrobe had thrown its doors open to show it had nothing more to hide. The patterned orange and red carpet had resigned itself to being abandoned. The old man's acceptance of it had blinded it to a world outside where its kind was obsolete and extinct. An unmade bed and the bookcase were the only signs anybody might use the room.

The bookcase was nearly full, the books waiting patiently for whatever fate would befall them. Spaces showed where some had been rescued. The remainder leaned against each other to stop from falling over. The boy took them, handfuls at a time, and threw them into the dark boxes. As he grabbed them from the shelves, their neighbours collapsed before quickly being set upright again and thrown into the box, reunited with the others.

The house would be mothballed, and the windows boarded up. The furniture would be taken away, and anything left would be sold. Back in Portpatrick, there were several mothballed houses. You could apply for one if you wanted. It wasn't too difficult to get a house. The difficult part was having a need for one. Michael knew the job they were doing wasn't necessary. If they had left everything, it would have been cleared by someone else. He also understood that most people wanted to do it themselves. You didn't want other people looking through things unless you had looked through them first.

After he had finished filling a surprising number of boxes, he chose one of the cowboy books at random and one of the books made up of other books. It was the easiest way to make sure he didn't upset anybody, although he couldn't imagine taking the time to read either.

It sounded like Uncle Joe and the man were still busy. Michael thought the voices through the wall were louder than before, but as the words didn't make it through, he couldn't hear what they were saying. He thought about putting his ear to the wall but decided against it. Instead, he surveyed the room where someone had once lived. The walls were yellow. There was one white mark where there might once have been a picture. It looked very old, even compared to the rooms back at the hotel. When you got old, your tastes probably changed. You gradually started to like cardigans, brown things, and vegetables. He would have to watch Uncle Joe to see if he showed any signs of becoming properly old.

In the absence of anything else to do, Michael climbed up on the bed with his two books and decided to wait for someone to come and get him. He quickly decided he couldn't bring himself to read the cowboy book and opened the hardback book, which apparently contained four books. They had been condensed, whatever that meant. The first didn't look very interesting, and the second was a romance. The third was about a war, so he decided it might be bearable. He suddenly felt very grown up, although he couldn't work out why. Maybe it was just because he was reading an old man's book.

By the time he finished the first few pages and looked at the clock, it was still seventeen minutes past three. It was always seventeen minutes past three. He imagined that time might have stopped. Perhaps it was a magic room. It was always seventeen minutes past three, and it was always nineteen seventy-something. The voices in the wall continued talking.

There was no sign yet of anyone coming to get him. They probably hadn't been born yet. He returned to the book about submarines. People used to fight each other in submarines. They used to chase each other around in the dark at the bottom of the ocean. It was very complicated, difficult, dangerous, and expensive. Nobody was killed. Well, not properly, like in battles. They just chased each other to show each other how good they were at it. It had gone on for decades, and then they had stopped. Even before the war, they had stopped. One day, they didn't have to chase each other anymore.

The book was very interesting, and Michael forgot all about the voices in the wall. He became more and more tired as he read on. His eyes moved across the page, but they weren't reading properly anymore. The submarine crew found their day becoming increasingly bizarre and confusing as the boy's attention unravelled. Finally, after forty-seven pages, at exactly seventeen minutes past three, the story came to a halt as Michael fell asleep.

He broke the surface briefly. He had the feeling there was someone in the room. Maybe it was the journalist, maybe his father. There was someone behind him, but he couldn't turn around. Soon he sank back down into the silence again. Seventeen minutes past three.

He surfaced again when the door opened. There was someone behind him, someone on the submarine. No, it wasn't a submarine. The idea slipped away before he could grab it.

"I see you found a book."

This time he could turn, although he couldn't speak yet.

"Joe said you were busy." There was harmless sarcasm in the man's voice.

The man stood in front of him. Why was he here? Where was Uncle Joe? He must have thought the question too loudly because the man answered it.

"Joe is loading the car. He thinks you should be going soon. Thanks for doing the books."

"That's okay."

"Do you know what time it is?"

His brain and eyes were starting to work together, but he was still limited. His arm helped by pointing to the clock. He didn't need to look at it. "Three seventeen."

"Still? It was that time all day yesterday." Michael didn't reply, leaving the man to speak again. "Look… Joe, your Uncle Joe, asked me to speak to you. He mentioned your father. That's too bad."

There was nothing to say. There must be more coming.

"You know my father is gone, too. I know it must be difficult. I don't know much about what's going on. It must be very difficult. I don't see much of the war."

"Strange, you spend so much time in front of the television."

"Yes, but we don't speak much these days."

The man looked nervous. Maybe he wasn't nervous. Uncomfortable?

"Joe and I had an idea. You see, in my job I know some people. It might not be too easy. I would have to ask around. Call in some favours. I don't know too much about things these days. But if it could be done, we wondered… I wondered if you would like to come to Glasgow."

"Glasgow?"

"Yes. Apparently, General Chen is giving a speech. Like I said, I would have to ask around. I probably couldn't get us in. Maybe a few years ago, I could have, but even if I can't… maybe we could go, anyway. Would you like to go, anyway?"

Behind the man, an invisible journalist hovered and nodded encouragement at the boy.

"I suppose."

It had happened. Uncle Joe had made it happen. The journalist had made it happen. All his advice had made it happen.

"I can try. You never know. It's a big thing, but sometimes you can do a big thing once."

"What?"

What had he just said? The journalist raised his eyebrows. Michael's question failed to connect properly. Instead, the man interrupted himself as another thought crossed his mind. "Oh, you don't even know my name, do you?"

"No."

"You're Michael, right?"

"Yes."

"My name is John Walker."

"John Walker?" Something was very wrong. The journalist faded from view. The name was almost familiar.

"My friends call me Jack."

It was lucky Uncle Joe wasn't in the room. He had never heard Michael swear.

Time stopped as Michael stared at the man. Jack Walker. It was the name on the diary. The man who wrote The Book.

The dead man. He wasn't the journalist. He couldn't be. This man had said he didn't know anything about the war, and the journalist was dead. The journalist couldn't be from Dumfries. The journalist couldn't be this man. How could the journalist know Uncle Joe?

Soon Michael realised that time hadn't really stopped. It was just that nobody had moved or said anything for a few seconds.

"How do you know Uncle Joe?"

Jack looked surprised. He snapped back to life, choosing to ignore the boy swearing at him. Perhaps it was the fashion these days. "He knew my father for years, but I don't know where they knew each other from. He taught me English when I was at school. I think he was the reason I went down south to work."

"What do you do?"

"I work for a newspaper. Nothing very interesting. I edit the pages, set things out, sometimes write little pieces, and so on. Very boring. I'm a bit like a printer, I suppose."

"But you don't do that anymore?"

"No, I was out of it for a while. Now, I'm back here."

"Are you going back?"

"I don't have to be back for a while. You ask a lot of questions, don't you?"

"Sometimes."

The man smiled, but he didn't mean it. He looked tired, too tired to look at you properly. Like he couldn't make the effort anymore, and he didn't care. He didn't look like a printer. He looked like a ghost. Michael didn't know how he felt about the man. He was Jack Walker, and he was going to take him to see General Chen. He was one more thing. Michael wasn't sure why yet, but he was sure he was right. Jack Walker was a liar.

31

Uncle Joe explained that the man would be coming back to stay with them for a while. Actually, he didn't really explain it. He just said it. Uncle Joe sat in the front with the liar. Michael sat in the back, not reading his book about cowboys. He listened to the two men talking on the way home as his eyes moved across words he wasn't looking at, and his fingers occasionally turned pages he hadn't read. He concentrated on what he was hearing. The liar lied to the killer. He told stories about a boring job, about boring people. There were too many to just be for the benefit of the boy in the back. Uncle Joe was being lied to, as well. Why? The answer couldn't be found while Michael was there. He would hear more if he wasn't there.

Michael's head began slowly nodding as the journey didn't make him tired. For a few minutes, he fought the sleep that wasn't overcoming him. His eyes closed as he finally gave in and didn't fall asleep. Pretending to be asleep wasn't easy. Over the years, he had learned what didn't work. You didn't screw up your eyes. You just closed them. You didn't breathe at the same rate. You had to breathe more slowly. Soon Michael wasn't soundly asleep.

He waited in darkness for the voices to change, focusing on the noise from above the waves. Michael attached one sound to Uncle Joe and one to the liar. He listened silently for the noises to make a mistake. It was difficult not to fall asleep. He had to keep concentrating on the noises but be careful not to go too deep. Eventually, they became quieter, long after he had let the book close shut on his fingers. It was impossible to tell how long. A very quiet voice asked something about the boy. The other responded quietly, agreeing, mentioning something from earlier. There was a long pause as the two drifted silently. The third object was now invisible, deep below in darkness. The killer's voice reappeared first, addressing the liar.

"How long will you be staying?"

"I don't know. I might want to stay for a while after Glasgow."

"That shouldn't be a problem. They don't need you back?"

"They haven't needed me for a while. Being dead didn't help. I think they saw it as a lack of commitment, and I'm just an embarrassment now. I have some time while it all gets sorted out."

"How did it happen?"

"Long story. Like I told you when I called. The only time I've been out of the office in years. I usually avoid it, but I knew Dad was ill. I knew if I did it, I could take time off when I got back. They sent me to speak to some people in Germany. I had trouble getting back and lost my passport. Someone found it and sent it back. It got caught up in the machine along with the others, and suddenly I was dead. Nobody sent me any messages because I was dead. By the time I got back, they had sent all my things back to Dad. He was gone, and they'd bounced everything somewhere else."

"You don't know where?"

"I thought they would have forwarded it on to you, but I haven't looked into it properly yet."

"I haven't received anything. Anything important?"

"Personal stuff, diaries, work, things like that. Nothing of any interest to anyone."

"What's it like coming back from the dead?"

"Lots of paperwork. On the other hand, I don't have people phoning me all the time. Swings and roundabouts."

The lies sank down through the darkness, bursting open with gentle thuds. There was a pause as everyone absorbed the blasts. Michael realised he was sinking deeper, his thoughts unravelling. He struggled to focus, twitching as he regained control. He tried to grip onto the liar's voice. It restarted, but quieter than before.

"I was sorry to hear about James."

Only a muffled noise in reply.

"You said he came back."

Another short, muffled reply. The second voice didn't want this conversation.

"Surprising, after everything. I suppose that's an end to it all now. How's Mary?"

A more thoughtful noise.

The voices stopped as a book slipped onto the floor, and Michael sank to the bottom of the ocean. The liar probably asked something about him, and the old man probably replied, but only two people were left to hear.

32

He was a liar. Other than that, it was hard to know what to make of the man. Michael couldn't believe that Uncle Joe had listened to his story. The liar had slept late, so Michael hadn't seen him at breakfast. Soon he would surely come into the bar. There was nowhere else to go. Michael sat in the bar with the book he wasn't reading and watched Cathy doing the crossword.

The ghosts didn't look as distant as usual. Michael could see their sadness as they drank their way towards lunchtime. He didn't speak to them. He knew there was no point. The death of his father meant he was closer to them. They would probably talk to him if he asked, but he was sure they still wouldn't talk about their own experiences. Nobody was listening to the television. It remained oblivious and quietly informed everyone in great detail about issues relating to Russia's upcoming election.

When the man came in, he slowly headed for the bar. He didn't seem to notice Michael or the ghosts. Jack didn't look tired anymore, but his eyes still weren't looking at things. He still wasn't really interested, but he was making the effort. Cathy hopped off her stool and abandoned her crossword to serve him. As she reached for his drink, Michael noticed he was scanning her newspaper. After she returned to it, he waited, letting his eyes drift over the bottles on the wall. He waited just long enough so that it was clear he didn't have to have a conversation. Then he spoke just one word, casually tossing it across the bar, not even looking to see her reaction.

"Senegal."

"What?"

He only turned after she had spoken. "Eight down, West African country. Senegal."

She looked down at her crossword, accidentally talking to him. "It won't fit. There are too many letters."

The man smiled and shrugged. "Then write small."

Cathy returned his smile. "That won't work. Some of the letters are wrong."

"That's just the problem with people these days. They give up too easily."

The man had miscalculated. Cathy spoke to dozens of people every week. There was no reason she should be particularly interested in him. He was older than Cathy, and he didn't even look interested in her. Even so, Michael noticed she was paying a little more attention to him than she usually did to the infantry who tried to chat to her.

"Maybe I just like to do things properly."

The man shook his head slowly and looked down into his drink before draining it. "Fatal mistake these days. I find it more effective just to get things done."

Cathy didn't reply, and the conversation faded away. The man let it go and turned to watch the television, leaning back against the bar. It continued outlining the more obscure aspects of the Russian electoral system. He frowned at the television as Cathy continued studying the crossword.

He waited another minute before throwing another question at her. "Excuse me, do you know anything about Russian politics?"

Cathy looked disappointed and uninterested. "No, not really."

"Good. In that case, would you mind getting me another drink and talking to me for a while? The TV is boring me rigid."

Her look again changed into a smile. "Well, I am very busy with the crossword. I want to get it finished properly. Why would I leave it to speak to you?"

"Well, because I might also buy you a drink, seen as you are being so kind to a bored stranger. Plus, I don't think you know anything about West Africa, so you'll never get eight down."

"You don't know eight down either."

"Maybe, but then again, maybe I do know it, and maybe I could be persuaded to tell you if you talked to me."

"Why should I take the risk?"

"Because whatever happens, you get a free drink. I know it seems mercenary, but in my experience, that's how the world works."

"There's only one problem. I don't drink."

"Me neither. This was my first one. I'm not sure if I liked it."

"So you need another?"

"Maybe. I think I might become one of those social drinkers."

"I'm still not convinced you know anything about West Africa."

"Okay. Let's make it a bet. If I know eight down, you'll have a drink with me, non-alcoholic, of course."

"Okay. You're on, but you only get one guess."

"Fair enough. I guess... Guinea. Current population is estimated at approximately one million. The capital city is Conakry, or what's left of it. Other major cities are Kankan, Kindia, and Labe. It is bordered to the South and East by Mali, Liberia, Ivory Coast, and Sierra Leone and to the North by Senegal, which has one more letter, and Guinea Bissau, which I imagine causes no end of confusion."

Cathy's smile opened up, and she almost laughed. "How did you know that?"

"You know what it's like. Once you lose one bet about West Africa, you make sure you do your homework."

Cathy had a drink with the man. The man who knew a lot about West Africa, had a boring job, and almost never left his office. The liar.

"So, what is an expert on West Africa doing in a place like this?"

"Well, it's a long story. Basically, I'm waiting to come back to life."

"Aren't we all?"

The ghosts ignored the two as they talked. Outside, seagulls traced circles in the sky. Michael thought about where this man had been, about why he was here. It was a week before Chen would be in Glasgow. This man would take him there. For now, Michael knew he was not important to the journalist. He was invisible to him. He was a favour to be done, a sacrifice to be made. Michael would be able to stay out of sight until there was nothing else to focus on. The journalist didn't care about him.

He thought about The Book. It belonged to the journalist. Yesterday, it hadn't belonged to anyone. Now Michael was stealing it. It was in his room. The journalist was in the same building as it. Michael imagined him being able to sense it, The Book calling to him. After the lights went out, it would glow red, shining out through the wardrobe, impossible to hide. Michael couldn't give it back. He didn't want to give it back. He had given too much already. Why should he give it to this liar? This man who was ignoring him?

Michael tried to picture an invisible journalist standing beside him but couldn't, not anymore. The real journalist was sitting at the bar. Why was he a liar? Why not tell Uncle Joe the truth? A horrible thought suddenly popped into his head. What if he was telling the truth? What if The Book was the lie? What if there was no journalist? What if the man in The Book didn't exist? It was unthinkable, but it could be true.

He squinted at the man at the bar, trying to imagine him on the front line, dodging bullets, running through trenches. He wasn't sure if it suited him. Imagining him sitting at a desk was equally unsuccessful. It had to be true. The Book had to be true. There had to be something special about this man. He had to know.

Eventually, Cathy drifted away to take drinks to the ghosts. The man sat at the bar for a few minutes longer before he drifted away too. He had just been investigating. Perhaps nothing in the bar had really interested him. Perhaps there was nothing there that he felt needed his attention. Michael didn't see him again for the whole day. The man missed the ghosts drinking.

He missed Cathy reading the paper and watching television. He missed Michael working. The man missed dinner upstairs and everybody talking but not saying anything. He missed the infantry drinking at night. He missed some discussions and some drinking, but no arguments.

In the evening, the liar with all the answers walked into the town where he would surely not have found any new and interesting questions. The journalist didn't care about all the things he had missed.

Then something happened which he would never know he had missed. Michael took the opportunity to answer some of his own questions. It wasn't hard to get into the journalist's room. Nothing there would help him, of course, because things that were written down could just be more lies. You had to be cleverer than that. Michael knew unimportant people had power, and he was certainly unimportant. You had to know how to use your power. It only took a minute for Michael to use his. There was a good chance it wouldn't work, but there was no harm in trying. After he had finished, he knew he would just have to wait. He would have to stay up to see if it had worked, but that would be no problem. He had plenty to read.

33

Upstairs, deep underwater, the ghosts drifted silently, locked in their own world.

Above Michael's room, a man was in Central Africa. His friends walked alongside him. Although most were only partially drawn, like a general idea of people, the man beside him was real. He was the one who died first. The young man had seen men die before. He had seen younger men die and closer friends die. He had seen men die more suddenly, and others die more slowly, silently screaming. The young man had seen terrible things. Despite it all, it was always this man, this same man who died each night. Every night, it was the same. This man had died a thousand times beneath the waves.

As always, the man becoming a corpse was the signal to hit the ground. The two events merged into one in his memory. He could no longer really be sure which had happened first. He was still staring at the ground when They burst out of the trees for the thousandth time. Shadows raced across the ground. He knew the people screaming, but he lay there, staring at the blood. When it stopped, there would be a weight on his back. It would change him. In some important ways, it would turn him back into a child. It wouldn't kill him, but it would wake him up every night for the rest of his life.

Through the wall, in the Mediterranean, there was a troopship. A man played cards with his friends. It was from a time before everything happened. Five men laughed and joked too much. Like they had to, and something terrible would happen if they stopped. They were the five people who knew what was coming. He was happy. They shouldn't have had the alcohol, but nobody cared. He was on the same ship each night, drinking with the same people, playing the same game of cards, losing every hand.

Then something would change. There were noises on the ship, but nobody else at the table would hear them. He would start to win, over and over again. They would laugh and curse his luck. Then other things would change. His friend's hand would clutch the cards with only three fingers. He was missing fingers, but there was no blood, just two missing fingers. He would keep asking what had happened, but nobody would hear him. Everyone was laughing and joking, changing slowly.

There were noises above, something on the ship, something crawling above them. Uniforms were getting dirtier, but everyone was still happy. Then one of them would look at him, a cut across his forehead snaking down to miss his eye by an inch before stopping on its way to his ear. A wound he wouldn't have for another year. The wound he had when he was found. More things changed. Happy people with more wounds, cuts, blood, things they weren't supposed to have yet.

Nobody would let him investigate the noises. Soon he would realise that They were on the ship, everywhere, coming to take them early. Everyone at the table would die, all at once this time, all except him, the winner. As each of them slumped over the table, the rest would keep laughing and joking. Nobody would help, and nothing would stop it. Once everybody was dead, the ship would be silent except for the noises above. The noises of them coming for him. His friends would lie bleeding as always, looking at him. There would be no anger from them. They wouldn't hate him. They would feel sorry for him. He would hear The Enemy outside the room. When the door opened, he would start screaming as always. If he was lucky, he would wake up.

Nearby, in Australia, a pilot drifted in the dark, alone, chasing another, also alone. They had each become separated from their own kind, conducting their own war. The dark shape twisted in front of him, and he fought to match its every turn. Concentrating, determined, and unaware that he was only witnessing a memory. Half mad with lack of sleep, nothing else mattered, as long as the thing didn't make it home.

Hatred focused him on The Enemy, the thing inside the other aircraft. He would kill it. It would not go home. Its machine was better than his, but only slightly better. That was how it always worked. Soon, he would press a button and kill it. He hoped it didn't die instantly. He hoped the button would turn its flying machine into a lump of metal ridiculously hanging thousands of feet above the ground. Either way, it would die. Up here, down there, it didn't matter where. It would die. If it ejected, he would kill it on the way down. That was how it worked. At least that was the way They worked. Not that They ever ejected. Maybe They couldn't. He had it. It was only a matter of time. He hoped it knew it was dead. He hoped it knew nobody was coming to help.

He screamed, swore, and cursed it as it twisted and turned, matching it each time, just waiting for the chance. He shouted, demanding that the chance present itself, shouting for it to die. His aircraft swung and roared as he earned his opportunity. He was aware that from the ground things would look very different, but as they tore across the sky at high speed, nothing around them showed the danger. There were no clouds, only a featureless desert below. The air howled around them.

The pilot had cursed them when they came for him, waking him because wave after wave of The Enemy were on their way. He hadn't really been asleep, anyway. There was no time for sleep and nobody else to go. He was the dayshift and the nightshift. They gave him his injection as they carried him to the aircraft and strapped him in. The drugs woke him up, but not really. Sometimes it was hard to tell when he was awake and when he was dreaming. He knew he wasn't imagining the shape in front of him. He had to kill it. Nothing else mattered. Everything was lost anyway. This couldn't go on for much longer. They would win eventually, but not this one. This one wouldn't go home tonight. Even exhausted as he was, he couldn't help but picture the people who hadn't come home.

He threw his plane down to follow The Enemy into a dive. The shape jerked upward, roaring into the sky. Hate became panic. He pulled up, turning, but he knew he would be too late. In his head, he saw lines tracing out the paths of two objects. One arced up and back, looping round behind another one below, which had dropped and was now heading back up. He was too slow.

The pilot searched the sky for help that wasn't there. He was alone, and nobody would ever know. So stupid, he shouldn't have followed it. He shouldn't be alone, but it was too late. His plane was suddenly so slow and clumsy, betraying him, protesting, labouring. It wasn't its fault. It was his mistake. He had betrayed it. It was dead. He had killed them both.

There was a dark shape behind him. They were dead because he was stupid. He couldn't shake it. He was sweating and aware of his breathing changing. It would happen any second now. He twisted and turned but knew it wouldn't work. It had to work. Not now, he couldn't die now, not here. He had to get home.

There was a loud noise behind him, and the plane wrenched itself away from him, enraged. No, it wasn't a plane. It was just a lump of metal. Friendly electronics lit up to register their concern and fought for his attention. It was irrelevant. They were dead. The world spun, throwing him from side to side. He screamed and cried. His thoughts left, leaving only panic. He was trapped and screamed for it to stop. Screamed for his mother. He was not ashamed of his screaming desperation.

He hammered against the clear plastic above him. Something else. Something important. Warm. He was warm. Fire. Burning. He was going to burn. He thrashed in the seat, upside down, spinning, tumbling. Shrieking. The ground. He had to hit the ground before burning. Couldn't burn to death. One second of terror had lasted for an hour. Eject. Had to get out. Dark shape. Would kill him. Had to eject, couldn't burn. Not fire. He had to get out. Handle. Had to pull the handle. Not there. Impossible. Why was there no handle?

The pilot would surface before he hit the ground, as always. It was always the same distorted memory. A mind obsessed with what might have been.

The Enemy were in most of the rooms in the hotel, hiding in the darkness. The minds of the men called The Enemy back from the battlefield, back from the dead. The Enemy never tired of doing the same thing, being processed and analysed each night as the men's minds tried to make sense of what had happened. The ghosts were stuck in a loop, considering a puzzle they would never solve. Men killed and watched others be killed. The same incident repeated over and over again, different for each of them. A different snowflake for the mind to rotate and examine, the same from every angle, no reason behind the randomness, no meaning in its purposeless complexity. Nobody knew how to break the loop without turning off the machine, and most wouldn't do that. Not when there was no way to turn it back on again.

The survivors fought their own battles, alone in the dark, immortal and terrified. Most had only survived once. One had survived many times. The Enemy came for him en masse. As always, They wouldn't get him. There were too many other targets.

The front stretched for two kilometres. One hundred thousand people. Two rows in front of him, dozens behind. All were mumbling and shifting. The sword in his right hand was heavy and holding it felt unnatural. There were so many people that there was no room to swing it. The end was hooked for dragging The Enemy to the ground. It came to a point meant to pierce skull and bone. The shield strapped to his left arm was heavier. The sun stared at them from the East, adding to the heat from thousands of other soldiers. Some wore armour. Some were stripped to the waist. The ground in front of them was flat for hundreds of yards, ending in a ridge, the horizon around a kilometre away.

He could hear men talking in a language he could not understand. Men from a dozen countries stood together. The men around him had white skin, like his. Along the line, only a few metres away, he could see men who looked Asian. They had the same sword as he did. He was surprised, but then he caught himself. There was no reason they should be trained samurai warriors. They probably weren't even Japanese. All around, he could see men with darker skin than his. He wondered if any of them were African. He wondered how many Africans there were left, probably not many. Africa was a nation of ghosts. The Enemy didn't believe in refugees. They killed anyone who tried to leave. It was no good for them to have the whole human race running to one place. They wanted society to continue as normal, at least for now.

He could hear them. They were on the other side of the hill. There was silence around him. Everyone wanted to listen to them. They had seen plenty of Enemy corpses, but most wouldn't have seen one alive. Now they could hear them. The noise seemed to roll towards them across the sky like thunder. They hadn't seen the lightning yet.

They swarmed over the hill like ants. As They formed up, the man beside him dropped to his knees. He thought he recognised the man, maybe the others as well, but he couldn't think why. Around him, men dropped and prayed. Chaplains wandered among them, blessing and reassuring. Men on horses moved up and down the front line, shouting and encouraging, pulling the horses from side to side as if they wanted them to be unsettled. The men spat and raged against The Enemy, reading from tattered pieces of paper. They were to kill. There was nothing behind them. They were the last hope. They would be remembered. They would meet again. Reminders of outrages and things they had all seen. Reminders of who was responsible and what would happen if they failed.

There were thousands of The Enemy, maybe millions. They coated the hill. They started howling, screaming. He felt warmth spread down his leg. Someone was crying behind him. Why them? Why now? There was nobody else. Everybody else was dead. He felt it. There was nobody else left, nobody anywhere.

One man sat on the hill behind them, taking notes. He would survive. He would write it all down. They would all die, but not him. It wasn't fair. He couldn't see his face, but the man looked familiar. He knew he recognised him from somewhere. He knew them all but couldn't find names. Nobody recognised him. He wanted to run, run back through them all to safety. Where would he go? There was no way back, only forward. Nobody was looking at him, and nobody would offer a way out. There were so many women. They didn't look as angry as the men. He recognised them all. He knew the old woman a few feet away. The old man behind him. Who was he? It was important. He couldn't think.

The Enemy moved forward, slowly at first, then into a sprint. They were coming for them, coming for him. There was a groan from the crowd. The man on the horse held his sword high in the air. He was shouting something. It seemed to matter for some reason. He was turning the groan into a roar. The crowd surged, swords high in the air, cursing The Enemy. Suddenly, they all knew what to do. The man and the horse were gone, charging forward. Someone near him was shouting. He realised it was his own voice. He was screaming. Today would be the day it ended. They would pay for all of it. He would make them pay.

He was running, and the crowd was moving as one, sprinting towards the end. The two armies stopped as they smashed into each other. He was suddenly surrounded by dozens of small battles, pairs locked in combat. There was somebody for everyone except him. He couldn't find an Enemy soldier. Around him, swords swung, and men and Things died, but there was no place or partner for him. Each death brought a change of partner, but he couldn't find anyone. He was always too slow, always unnoticed. The man on the hill watched him do nothing. He began to recognise faces. They shouldn't be here. He thought they were dead. Relatives, young soldiers he had known, main characters, and extras. All dead people, back for an encore. All were shouting for his help.

One of The Enemy, larger than the others, strode towards him. He searched for his identification, but he knew he wouldn't find it. He screamed at it, screamed that he was a journalist, not a soldier. It didn't stop, only slowed down and looked confused. He pointed into the distance behind him. The dark figure on the hill held up identification and then turned and walked away. He stared at The Enemy soldier for a few seconds, strong, powerful, and patient. It didn't look angry. It just looked comfortable, like it knew exactly what it was doing. He backed away from it. When he started running, he knew it had also exploded into action. They sprinted back through the crowd. His sword was thrown onto the ground as he screamed for help that wouldn't come. Through it all, he could hear a voice that needed his attention. The Enemy soldier chasing him was speaking. It was his name, but it didn't sound like one of them. It sounded like a child, and it started to get louder.

He was somewhere else. He was confused. Where was he? The Enemy were after him. It was dark, and They were coming through the doorway. There was screaming again. But where was he?

The light exploded above him, shocking him into silence. His eyes struggled to stay open, blinded by the light. It was coming from everywhere, and everything was yellow. There was a boy in the doorway. Who was the boy?

"Jack, wake up."

The Enemy's voice, but it wasn't shouting. He was awake.

"Are you awake?"

"I'm awake. Where is he?" Where was who? The memory was slipping away.

"You're safe. You're here in the hotel."

Hotel? Something was after him. He was suddenly conscious of his heart beating hard. Something was after him. What was it? He was still afraid.

"You're safe. You just had a bad dream. Everything is fine."

"I couldn't find it. Someone else had it. It should have been in my pocket."

The boy knew the journalist wasn't really awake. It took a while to wake up properly. You just had to be calm, wait for everything to come together, wait for them to surface properly. It was best not to respond while they were talking nonsense. They came back quicker if you just kept reassuring them. You had to put the right idea into their head so it could defeat all the nonsense. You had to pull them out, and talking to them about it just held them under.

The boy knew to stand in the doorway to wake him up. You shouldn't approach them, should never, ever touch them, not while they were somewhere else. They might grab you and try to pull you in, killing you by mistake before they even woke up properly. They knew all sorts of ways to grab you, twist you, kill you with their bare hands, and had been trained to act quickly. You just had to call to them until they came back, then you put the light on so they could see you.

"You're safe. You're in the hotel in Portpatrick, remember?"

Hotel, yes. Joe, the boy. Michael? Michael.

"Michael?"

"Yes, I heard you screaming."

The journalist managed to sit up in bed, one hand over his eyes. Michael thought he might have seen a tattoo on his arm but couldn't see what it was.

"I had a bad dream," the journalist offered unnecessarily.

"About printing?"

There was a pause while the journalist tried to look at Michael to judge if there was anything behind the question, but it was too bright to see his face.

"I don't remember."

The journalist wasn't prepared for the offensive.

"You were shouting about The Enemy," Michael lied.

"Was I?"

"Something about being a journalist. I thought you were a printer."

"I am, I mean, I am a printer, but I sometimes do other things…"

"So you're a journalist as well?"

"Yes, no… I used to be…"

"In battles and things?"

"Sometimes, I… not really. I don't really remember just now."

"You don't remember?"

"Of course, I remember. I'm just very tired. What are you doing here, anyway?"

Michael stopped the questions. The journalist was rapidly waking up, and at any moment, he would notice that Michael was asking too many questions.

"I told you, I heard you screaming. Sometimes it's best to wake people up when they're having a bad dream, especially if it's their first night here."

"Does Uncle Joe know you do this?"

"No, I don't do it very often. Uncle Joe wouldn't like it. Were The Enemy coming after you?"

"Yes, lucky for him, you woke me up. I almost had him."

"So you've seen them, then?"

"I'm tired. I think I'll go back to sleep and finish saving the world. I'll try to sleep more quietly. Thank you for waking me up. It's just the strange surroundings. Always like this the first time somewhere new."

"It could be the heat as well. I'll open the window a little."

The journalist watched the boy walk around him and open the window. At first, the boy's lack of fear was reassuring, but then he remembered there was nothing to be afraid of. He still wasn't properly awake. His heart was beating quickly. He tried to control his breathing, hoping his heart would follow, but it ignored his optimism, preferring to trust its instinct based on experience. The boy sat down uninvited on the end of the bed, breaking his concentration.

"I had an idea for an invention once."

"Really?" The conversation seemed unavoidable. The journalist considered that he might still be dreaming.

"You see, when you have a nightmare, you can't wake up, even if you're screaming. I thought you could have a clock that detected when you were screaming and then had an alarm to wake you up."

"Shouldn't I be getting back to sleep?"

"Best to keep talking for a few minutes until you wake up properly, or you'll just fall back into the same dream or something worse. If I left now, you might fall back asleep but not realise it. You could just be lying here, and The Enemy might come out of the wardrobe or something."

The journalist's heart overheard and demanded he shoot a worried glance at the wardrobe. He hadn't noticed how tall and dark it was. He told himself it was empty. There was no Enemy in the wardrobe. His heart kept hammering, just in case. He wondered if the boy had come out of the wardrobe. Maybe he'd come out of the wallpaper.

"I think I'll be fine. What time is it?"

"Half-past two."

"I should be getting to sleep. I usually get up at three seventeen."

"If I hear you screaming again, I'll try to wake you up."

The boy closed the curtains again over the half-open window and headed for the door. On the way, he opened the wardrobe. "See? Nobody in here, you'll be fine."

The journalist was strangely relieved. Still, something wasn't right. A thought rattled around in his head. He had to ask.

"If the screaming doesn't wake someone up, how will they hear the alarm?"

"You heard *me*, didn't you? I think you can hear anything except yourself. If we could hear ourselves, everything would be fine."

The journalist didn't have any further comment. He sank back beneath the waves and took his tattoo with him.

As Michael walked back to his room, he was satisfied. He knew the journalist was lying. He had always known. Now he was sure of the truth. He was sure The Book was true. The journalist was who he wasn't saying he was. It had taken a lot of waiting. He had waited for hours for the nightmare to come. He had been relieved when the journalist finally started screaming.

Michael knew a lot about nightmares. He knew there were more of them in the summer. He knew the heat fed them. It hadn't been difficult, turning up the heating in the journalist's room. It had been necessary to boil out the bad memories. Opening the window let them out and gave him the chance to turn the heating down again. He could have just turned up the thermostat for the whole hotel, but somebody might have noticed. Besides, he didn't want the whole top floor screaming all night. That might have woken up Uncle Joe.

Soon, the waiting would be over. They would see General Chen, and the journalist would tell him everything he wanted to know. He would know what the war was really like. He would know why his father wasn't coming back, and he would probably know why. The journalist would speak to him. He had to. He had nobody else to talk to. Uncle Joe wouldn't talk to him, and there was nobody else. There hadn't been anybody else to talk to for a long time.

34

Michael didn't see the journalist the next day. He didn't join them for dinner or breakfast, and Uncle Joe didn't seem to expect him to. Jack didn't seem interested in spending time with the ghosts, either. He didn't spend the days drinking, and he didn't go into Stranraer. He just stayed in his room.

The world still turned, but things in the hotel were changing. Michael's mother was becoming even more distant. He worried she would never come back but could find nothing to say to her. His world was filled with only one thing: General Chen. The greatest human being alive would soon be in Glasgow. Michael would also be there. He might even get to see him. The journalist might be able to arrange it. His mother would have to wait. After all, she would still be there after he got back from Glasgow.

Michael spent each day turning over possibilities in his mind, trying to imagine the hall where General Chen would be speaking, trying to imagine what it would be like walking around Glasgow. He had given up on the ghosts for the moment. They would still be there when he got back, even if some of the faces changed. In any case, the journalist was more interesting. Even though he hadn't really spoken to Michael yet, he was still more interesting than the ghosts, who the journalist also hadn't spoken to. At least he had The Book. He didn't know how the journalist worked, but at least he had the manual.

Everything would be fine once he had seen General Chen. The war was changing, and things were becoming more difficult to understand. General Chen would make everything simple again. When the general came back, he would be able to defeat The Enemy, or at least keep driving them back. His father had been part of General Chen's original plan. He would be remembered forever as a hero when The Enemy were finally defeated. Wasn't it better to die like that than serve in a new war where everything was a compromise? Didn't it make it much harder to be a hero?

The day of the speech took a long time to arrive. The more he thought about it, the further it retreated into the distance. Eventually, it was time. The day before, his mother had given him money, which he didn't expect he would need. That night, he split it and shared it between the four pockets in his jacket and the four in his jeans. It seemed inevitable that he would lose some. Some things always got lost. They just disappeared from your pockets if you didn't check them often enough. It was a random, unavoidable process. If he had thought about it, the idea would have seemed ridiculous. But in the absence of this rigorous analysis, he was confident he had found a way of ensuring he couldn't possibly lose all the money at once.

They had to leave early in the morning. It was still dark, and it felt strange knowing that the rest of the world was asleep, assuming nothing was happening which was worth being awake for. It was unnaturally cold. Michael's body expected him to be asleep and had shut everything down for the night. It would warm him up again as soon as it realised he was awake.

Both of his alarms had gone off, and he had been ready by the time Uncle Joe knocked on his door to check he was awake. He would be away for a whole night, so he knew it would be hard to fit everything into just two bags. He had eventually managed, and they had been ready since the night before, waiting for him in the darkness. It took a few minutes to double-check he had everything, but soon it was all waiting in the hall, and he was free to start worrying about other things. What if the journalist had slept in? What if the road was blocked? What if the train broke down? He worried they had not left enough time, that they should all have got up earlier. What if something went wrong and robbed him of this one chance?

Jack and Uncle Joe appeared together. The journalist only had a small bag with him, and Michael felt a surge of panic as he worried he wasn't going to Glasgow after all. The journalist looked at the two bags lying gorged in the hall and said something to Uncle Joe. Uncle Joe said something about it being the boy's first time staying away anywhere.

The journalist didn't look enthusiastic about seeing General Chen. He was probably tired. He didn't look tired, even though it was early in the morning. Jack looked resigned to whatever was happening to him. He picked up one of the bags, bulging and misshapen. It swung beside his own, deflated and tired.

The car journey took a long time. They drove for two hours in the wrong direction. The trains from Stranraer left at the wrong time, so the long drive to Dumfries was as necessary as it was ridiculous. For some reason, Uncle Joe didn't want to take the car all the way to Glasgow, so there was no option. Nobody spoke much, but the silence didn't seem as uncomfortable as it should have. It wasn't as hungry as it should have been. It ignored them, sleeping in a corner somewhere. Even though nobody had said anything, there seemed to be nothing left to say. Michael got the impression that he might have missed the meal.

Outside the car, there was only darkness. It pressed against the windows, hiding everything. The headlights showed what was ahead, but everything else was invisible. There was no moon to watch them. There weren't even other cars on the road. A few army trucks passed, heading towards Stranraer, but the rest of the world was asleep. Michael felt slightly sorry for all the people who weren't going to Glasgow to see General Chen. They would just have a normal day, at least until later when they would see his speech on the news, realise how close he had been, and wonder whether they should have been there.

When Uncle Joe left them at the station, the sun was up, but it still seemed like everyone in Dumfries was asleep. Everyone except the old man at the counter in the station. The journalist paid for the tickets, although Michael wasn't sure whose money he was using.

Everything looked old and tired. It looked particularly bad to Michael, as his mother always insisted that things were done properly. Most people had given up on maintenance and appearances. There weren't enough people, enough money, or enough time, and there were better things to do with the time that was left. Nothing was cleaned anymore, and nothing was replaced until it broke down.

As the humans abandoned the fringes of their empire, others moved in. Weeds grew in the corners of the platform that were difficult to reach, safe from being trampled underfoot or scraped away by the toecaps of impatient and bored travellers. They grew, patiently watching as the humans dwindled in number and their appearance became greener, imitating their own. Smaller plants hitchhiked back and forth to Glasgow, clinging to the body of the train, barely visible, turning surfaces green as they had done for millions of years. The whole station looked like it was being abandoned. Dumfries wasn't as busy as Stranraer or as important as Glasgow. Michael wondered how long it would be before the station was unnecessary.

Michael imagined Glasgow would be different. It was larger, there were more people, and it was closer to the centre of things. It would still be cared about and maintained. The pavements would probably have been cleaned for General Chen's visit. The whole city would probably smell of paint.

Michael had never been on a train before, at least not that he remembered. He made sure he sat across from the journalist. That would mean he would have to talk to him. There were only two carriages, and both were open, with no compartments like in films. There were no other passengers. Nobody else from Dumfries wanted to hear General Chen speak. Michael suddenly felt exposed, childish. Why was nobody else doing the same thing? The journalist showed no sign that anything was wrong. He stared out the window as the station began to disappear from view. He counted the trees that passed as if they were a sign of something important, as if there was a secret message in their number that could be divined if you concentrated hard enough.

It occurred to Michael that if the journalist didn't talk, he would have to spend two days with a silent stranger. An unpleasant picture entered his head. A boy and a silent man were standing for hours in the rain, alone, outside a building where someone was giving a speech. The journalist had to talk. If he didn't, Michael would find a way to make him.

What could he say to this man? The journalist had seen so many things, but he didn't seem to want to talk about any of them. Michael had planned for this. He knew the journalist. He knew how he felt. He knew what had happened to him and had packed something in one of his bags, which he thought might help start a conversation.

"I brought some headache tablets."

The news was enough to pause the plant-based divination for a moment, but the man still didn't look away from the window.

"Oh, right."

"Just in case you wanted any. In case you have a sore head."

"Why would I have a sore head?"

Hard to answer. Stress? Medication that Michael couldn't possibly know about?

"All the travelling?"

"I'm fine."

Jack went back to counting trees. Was he irritated or maybe just puzzled? The thump on the table as Michael dumped something on it brought him back again. The journalist sighed and stopped counting. At last, he turned to look at the bottle of water on the table.

"I brought water as well."

"So I see."

"For the tablets, in case you wanted any."

"I guessed."

The spell was broken. The man leaned across the table and sighed again. "This is going to be a long journey, isn't it?"

"I brought a book. I could lend it to you if you want."

"No thanks, I don't read much these days."

"Maybe we could talk then. If you're bored."

The look said a lot. Mainly it said something about not talking much these days, either. The look had to say it because it was the kind of rude thing you shouldn't say out loud.

"I'm not bored. Besides, I'm not good with children."

It was a sentence which could only have been spoken if it really were true.

"I'm not a child."

The man looked friendly and sympathetic. Michael was annoyed but couldn't find a word to describe why. He didn't know what patronised meant, but if he had known, it would have fitted perfectly.

"I know you don't think you are, but trust me. We'll talk for a while, then I'll make a joke, you won't get it, and I'll get annoyed. It's not worth it. I'd spend my whole time explaining things."

"I'm not like that. I know lots of things."

"Of course, you do. You know all about everything. You know all about the soldiers, all about Uncle Joe, all about everything, don't you?"

"How do you mean?"

The journalist looked at him with a new intensity. "I mean, you know all about Joe being the head of the Stranraer Mafia."

The journalist kept staring straight at him. Michael's mind raced. Things started to make sense. The idea had the element of surprise on its side, took hold of him, and far too quickly, he began to speak. "Really?"

The journalist snapped back into his seat and relaxed. "No, not really. There's no such thing as the Stranraer Mafia, and that's exactly the kind of thoughtless credulity that's going to annoy me."

Michael's face burned. The idea in his head imploded and disappeared, leaving a hollow vacuum. He felt blood rushing to his face as everything regained equilibrium. Unchained hate rose in him. He thought about The Book and all the things he knew about the man. He considered the things he could show that he knew, like printers not having screaming nightmares, journalists who weren't dead, journalists who were scared to say they were journalists, and probably even scared to be journalists. Both were as bad as each other.

The man watched Michael's reaction, then tried to manage it. "What's the book?"

Anger turned to panic in the brief moment before Michael realised he wasn't talking about The Book.

"It isn't one book. It has four books in it. I found it in your... when we came to see you."

He was surprised to find he had restarted the sentence. His anger was draining away.

"Reader's Digest. A condensed book. My father had a lot of them."

"What's Reader's Digest?"

"I think it was a bit like a cult, except there weren't meetings, just magazines."

The journalist smiled to himself. Luckily, he didn't notice that Michael wasn't. It was exactly the type of thing that would have annoyed him. The trees distracted him long enough to prevent him from feeling the need to explain something not worth explaining.

"Did you ever read them?"

"No, I don't like fiction very much. The truth is always much more interesting."

"I'm sure it is."

The power of the trees again prevented the journalist from noticing Michael. This time, Michael was smiling in a way that would have been quite difficult to explain, even if he had been lucky enough for that to be necessary.

The journalist was ten miles away. That was how far the train had to travel before he spoke again. A crowd of trees sprinted past all at once and ruined the game.

"So, you looking forward to our trip?"

Michael stopped pretending to read his book. "I've never been to Glasgow before." There was never any harm in not answering questions. It made you seem more interesting. He had learned that from a book.

"Well, maybe I can show you around. You like General Chen, don't you? Joe said you did a project on him at school. There's a statue of him in George Square. We could go and see it if you like."

"Everybody likes General Chen, except General Neckerman. And there isn't a statue of General Neckerman anywhere."

"Well, they're quite alike, really. That's probably why they don't get on."

It was blasphemy. Michael was constantly amazed at how casually people insulted General Chen. What was most surprising was that it was almost always older people. People who should have known better. It wouldn't be polite to argue, so it was safer to change the subject.

"Do you think the general's speech will be good?"

"It wasn't bad. There were no great surprises. I think he's given better."

"No, I meant the speech he's giving today."

"Yes, it's not bad."

Michael was sure the journalist had heard him properly. He must have. Didn't he understand the difference between the past and the future? A teacher had once told Michael that some languages didn't have a past tense. He hadn't really believed her. Now he wondered if the journalist didn't understand the past tense.

Once Michael had stayed up all night to help when some infantry had arrived far too late and needed to be fed and processed. It had been much easier than he'd expected, but the next day, as he hadn't slept, he found time had lost some of its meaning. It wasn't as clear what yesterday meant, and the meaning of earlier wasn't as obvious as it should have been. He had concluded that sleeping might be a way of chopping up things, so people didn't get confused all the time.

Maybe the journalist hadn't slept in days. Maybe that was why he didn't come out of his room. What if he was insane?

No, Uncle Joe wouldn't have left him with him. He would have noticed. But Uncle Joe didn't really know who he was, so he might not have realised. There was nobody else on the train. He would be stuck here with a mad journalist who wouldn't admit he was a journalist. Maybe he didn't remember he used to be a journalist.

"General Chen hasn't given his speech yet."

"I know."

"So, how can you have heard it?"

The journalist looked at Michael as if he were insane.

"I haven't heard it. I've read it."

"Where? Where have you read it?"

"Actually, I called last night and had someone read it to me, so I suppose I'm lying. I did hear it, just not from General Chen."

The world had gone mad.

"How?"

The journalist finally seemed to understand the confusion. "Because Chen's people release it before the speech so journalists can read it. How else do you think people manage to write about things so quickly after they've just happened?"

"So… you can read it before it happens?"

"Of course, I thought everyone knew that."

"But… why don't other people just release it before he gives the speech?"

"Because it's embargoed. They put a date on it, and you aren't allowed to discuss it before that."

"That's ridiculous!"

The journalist shrugged. "That's how it works. That's how it must be done, or it wouldn't work."

"Someone must break the rule."

"Not really. There wouldn't be much point. It would ruin the whole system, and then we would all be in trouble."

"That's crazy!"

"No, that's common sense."

"But I thought journalists all tried to get the story first."

"Yes, sort of, within the rules, most of the time. You can't just have a big free-for-all. It would be chaos."

Michael thought about it for a moment. It was wrong. It was fake. The journalist tried to make things better by saying the wrong thing. "Would you like to read it?"

"No!"

The journalist slowly raised his hands in surrender. "Fine. I just thought I'd offer."

The journalist had travelled another twenty miles away. While he made his way back, the world was waking up. The sky brightened, allowing people to walk the streets again. The train kept stopping to allow soldiers and old men to get on and sit inside it as it hurtled towards Glasgow. Michael thought about time again. The journey seemed to take forever. He thought about how he would be in Glasgow less than an hour later. The next day, he would head home. If he thought hard enough, it was like it had already happened. A whole story, and he was stuck at one point, moving slowly through it.

As the train passed through larger towns, Michael was struck by how similar they all looked. The same boarded-up windows, the same decaying stations, and the same soldiers and old people. There were still only around half a dozen people in the carriage, but Michael no longer felt as out of place. Somewhere behind him, over his right shoulder, a soldier was talking too loudly. Even though Michael couldn't see him, he knew it was a soldier. It was so obvious he didn't even notice his assumption. It didn't make him nervous. He was used to being around the infantry. The journalist didn't seem concerned. He was still looking out the window. A few more people boarded at the next station, entering the other carriage.

The journalist reacted for no apparent reason. "Get your ticket."

Nobody had entered the carriage. Nobody else was moving except the journalist, and he was agitated. "Don't speak unless you're spoken to, Michael. Be careful."

As Michael turned to look for the ticket collector, a hand landed on his arm. "Don't turn round. Sit and read your book."

The journalist was looking at something behind Michael. Something was going to happen, something Michael wasn't going to see. There were probably only a few seconds. He made a quick decision. He dived under the table and popped up beside the journalist, grabbing his book from the other side as he resurfaced.

He glanced at the journalist, expecting him to be angry, but was surprised to find he had ignored Michael's failure to obey his instructions and was looking out the window. Perhaps he had never really expected Michael to do as he was told. Maybe he was grateful that the boy was closer to him and easier to control.

Michael watched the door to the carriage. Although the journalist was looking out the window, something was different. He wasn't looking out the window. Instead, he was looking *at* the window. He was studying the reflection. It was safer to watch the shadow of whatever was going on. He was muttering something about somebody having called them.

Michael fought the urge to ask what was going on and instead watched. Now that Michael could see the soldier, he seemed louder. He was drunk, but Michael had assumed that earlier. There was nothing unusual about that. Sometimes soldiers at the hotel came down to breakfast drunk, and nobody said anything. The soldier was talking to someone, but Michael couldn't see who it was. They were hidden by the seat facing the soldier. It all seemed friendly, just as Michael had thought before.

The journalist was doing something. He was taking his jacket and jumper off. Michael thought he might be getting ready to fight for a moment, but he quickly settled back into his seat, arms folded.

When the carriage door opened, there were two of them. The *them* the journalist said somebody must have called. They were not police or soldiers but something else. They wore black uniforms, and their hair was shaved closer than required for soldiers. Michael could see that the first had a pistol on his belt.

The police had lots of things on their belts, lots of black and shiny things. This man only had a pistol, as if he didn't need anything else. The second had a gun, a proper gun. He scanned the carriage as the first paused beside the soldier.

Michael whispered at the statue beside him, "Who are they?"

A noise hissed from the statue. "SCD. Don't stare at them."

SCD? There was no such thing anymore.

"Civil Defence? Like years ago? Real police?"

A hand muffled the noise from the statue. "Fucking militia. I don't believe it."

The soldier was being friendly towards them. They were ignoring him. The first was saying something into his radio. Numbers and random words. Michael only recognised one phrase: "Stand by." The same phrase repeated each time the radio crackled. They weren't ignoring the soldier. They were listening and nodding, not in agreement, but like they were impatient as if there was something else they should be doing, and nodding would make this go away faster. The first man lifted his hand, and the soldier protested, still being friendly. He reached to whoever was beside him and spoke to them as if to demonstrate something to the men. Michael watched events unfold.

The hand rose again, and the soldier started to rise, then sat back down. The second man did something to his gun that made it make a loud clicking noise. It was deafening, and Michael realised the carriage was silent except for the soldier. A hand rested between Michael's shoulder blades. An instinctive shudder didn't make it leave. He realised the statue was ready to push him under the table. Trees rushed past beyond the statue. The soldier stood up, edging away and protesting. Nobody needed to draw guns or threaten anything. Everyone knew it was a waste of time.

A woman edged past the soldier, who said something friendly to her. He was silenced by a finger on his chest and another click that seemed louder than the last. The hand on Michael's back didn't move. The hand prepared for the loudest sound you were ever likely to hear. Michael realised his fingers were creeping up to his ears and stopped them. The woman was upset, not crying properly but tears streaking her face. She was shaking and walking quickly as her bag struggled to keep up with her, banging off seats on the way. She was young, maybe younger than Cathy.

The soldier started to get angry and panicky. He shouted at the first of the two men next to him and doubled over instantly. The two acted as one, the second putting the butt of his gun into the back of the soldier's head. He crumpled, and the statue beside Michael jumped and shook its head, its words nearly inaudible. "Fucking outrageous."

As they dragged the soldier out of the carriage, the first man returned for his bags. The statue shook its head again. Michael watched the door close. "What will they do with him?"

"Hopefully, they'll wait and put him off at the next station."

"You mean they might not? What else could they do? Stop the train? Won't we be late?"

"No, I'm fairly sure they wouldn't stop the train."

Michael thought about the other options while the statue's hand left his back and pressed on his arm to keep him quiet.

The arm rotated until it was palm upwards. "Give me your ticket. I'll speak to them when they come over."

The second man returned and moved through the carriage. Somewhere behind Michael was the sound of a girl crying, but he seemed to be the only one who could hear her.

As he came to their table, Michael noticed the man was about the same age as his father. His uniform looked worn, as did the holster for his pistol. He looked more angry than unfriendly, but Michael thought he probably always looked angry. He didn't ask for tickets. Instead, he just stood there. His gun was impressive. The butt of it was scraped, and the metal parts were dull and scratched. It wasn't shiny but a dull, dark grey. You could buy paint that colour, gunmetal grey. You used it to paint the small plastic guns of small plastic soldiers who were meant to look like they had been on the battlefield.

"You two going into the city today?"

The journalist answered for both of them. "Yes, I just thought I'd take the boy up for a visit."

"You come far?"

"Just up from Dumfries."

"What part?"

"The centre. My father has a house there."

"But you don't?"

"No, I've been away. I'm back for a while. I'm taking the boy up today as a favour for a friend."

"Some people are expecting trouble today."

"Well, we would be staying away from anywhere there might be trouble."

Michael looked back and forth between the journalist and the man with the gun. They weren't going to get to go. They were going to be thrown off the train. The journalist had given the wrong answers, and now they would have to go home. He would have to tell Uncle Joe and Cathy that he didn't go to Glasgow after all. The government probably didn't want people going up to support General Chen. They had sent the SCD to stop all the trains!

"I'm sure. Coming all this way just to avoid trouble."

"We have tickets."

The journalist's arm, strangely uncovered, reached out towards the man, rotating as it stopped.

Silence. Michael held his breath. The man with the gun looked at the tickets, then at the journalist. He had the same angry look, but now he was wary.

"Thirty-Second?"

The journalist barely nodded. Michael looked at the black tattoo on his arm. An angry skull framed by some writing gripped a knife between its teeth.

The man was still wary. "Kaduna?"

Again, the journalist held the man's gaze and barely nodded.

The man's mood changed. He seemed to be trying to remember something. "Brother was at Kontagora. Told him you have to be careful in places you can't spell."

"Sometimes, it's not enough to be careful. Sometimes it's just about where you're meant to be. You just have to remember what's important."

The man started nodding, properly nodding. "Some people don't understand that these days."

The journalist's eyes narrowed, and he started talking quietly to the man as if he was saying something very important. "The boy just wants to be there. He just wants to be there when the general speaks."

The man copied the journalist, not whispering but talking quietly. "Steer clear of The Green. There's going to be some kind of march. Safer to stay nearer the centre."

"That's what I thought. I thought I'd take him to see the statue and the memorial. His father..."

"If anything happens, if you hear shots, hit the ground. Just lie down, don't run." He waved away the tickets. "I might get there later. Got this to deal with first."

"Bad?"

"Just drunk. Young lad from the Barlinnie Barracks, bothering some girl."

The journalist shook his head. "Boys, eh? Learned his lesson?"

The man seemed to be thinking hard again. He looked back towards the door. "He's a bit quieter now."

The journalist tutted and gave an extra big shake of his head. "Shame if he lost his chance of being where he's meant to be."

"Well... maybe it won't come to that."

"The girl is okay, isn't she?"

"I suppose."

"I expect you'll just be leaving it at that. Any more trouble would probably just upset her. You know what they're like."

The man nodded, looking towards the back of the carriage. "Yeah, that's the best. It depends on the girl, you know. But maybe that's best."

"Thanks for everything. You keep being careful. That's what I always tell the boy."

"Don't worry. Good luck today. I hope you get to hear him."

"Oh, just being there would be enough."

The man took one quick look around the rest of the carriage and headed back to the door. As he left, the statue came back to life and started putting its jumper and jacket back on. Michael was impressed. This was the journalist he had read about, the man who knew all about the war. For a moment, he had been the man from The Book. He understood the soldiers.

"Was he proper SCD?"

"Yes, you could tell because he was a total arsehole."

"What's the Thirty-Second?"

"One of the multinational divisions that fought in Nigeria before the First Respite. Everybody knows the name."

"So you were in the Thirty-Second?"

"No, I was in a place in Madrid where they do tattoos in a cheap and hygienic manner and decided getting one would be cheaper than bribing people all the time."

There was silence as the journalist continued looking out the window. He spoke again without turning round. "Don't look at me like that. It works. It's not my fault if people make assumptions and like you better if you have things drawn on you. I don't make the rules. I just work out what they are."

"But you said you were at that place. You lied."

"Not really. I didn't have to. A picture tells a thousand lies."

"But you said…"

"We're going to Glasgow, that's what you wanted, and now we've even made friends with someone from the SCD, which isn't easy, let me tell you."

There was silence again.

"Where's the Barlinnie Barracks?"

"It's to the North of Glasgow. It used to be a prison. You remember them, don't you?"

Silence.

"What did he mean when he was talking about *trouble*?"

"Ignore him. They always think there's going to be trouble. They always think there's going to be a riot or a revolution or a final reckoning. That's how they think. As far as I can see, the only final reckonings that ever occur are the ones they arrange."

Silence again. Even the woman had stopped crying, wherever she was. Michael used the silences to break up his questions. Adults didn't like being asked lots of questions at once.

"I thought there weren't any SCD anymore."

"Welcome to Glasgow. They disappeared from most places after the… you know, the…"

"Renewal."

"Not the word I would have used, but yes. They must still have a use for them when there is something big happening."

"Are they checking all the trains?"

"I don't think so. They were probably just close when the call came in. They would have needed someone quickly, and if there was nobody else available, they would have settled for a pair of thugs."

"I thought they seemed okay."

"Yes, well, you would. You're on a three-hundred-mile round trip to hear General Chen speak."

"But they solved the problem."

"Yes, they're good at that. Their methods haven't changed much."

There was silence again. Michael was going to ask another question while the journalist was in the mood to answer.

"Why didn't you help the girl?"

"What?"

"Couldn't you see what was happening?"

"Not for sure. Anyway, I'm supposed to look after you, not run around starting fights with drunks. My instructions are quite clear."

Michael had one more question. He had kept it until the end because it was the one the journalist was least likely to answer. "What happened in the Renewal?"

There was a pause.

"You know what happened. Everyone knows."

"I know, but was it like they say at school?"

"I doubt it."

"But did everyone just all agree, and then it just happened?"

"Well, not everyone agreed. The people in the prisons had some reservations, as did the people who suddenly found out they were a waste of money or weren't good enough parents. There was some disagreement there."

"But before, there was crime and everything, and people didn't care about things."

The window lost its attraction, and the journalist turned around, placing his hands on the table to draw pictures. "No, people cared, but they tolerated things. Tolerating things doesn't mean you don't care or like them. It means you put up with it because the alternative is worse. What happened was putting up with things wasn't an option anymore. We just had to accept that."

"But things are better now."

"Are they? What did you just see here? A problem solved? Are you happy that we live like this?"

"No… but people shouldn't do things like that, so they can't really complain."

"No, they can't. They really can't. You just make sure you toe the line, though. You make sure you don't make any mistakes because you're not allowed to these days."

The journalist wasn't getting angry. He should have been, but he wasn't. He was just explaining. There was a pause again while Michael thought of his next question, but before he could think of it, the journalist started speaking again. "It happened everywhere. Eventually, it happened everywhere. Everybody had to do the same thing to survive. It wasn't as bad as you might think. Once people saw what was going to happen, a lot of them made sure they were on the right side of normal. It happened in Europe as well. In Germany, it was *The Strengthening*, though I'm told the term actually translates to *The Hardening*."

Michael tried to collect his thoughts to ask another question, but the journalist started talking again. "Ten years ago, my father would have survived. There were treatments. There were people to help. That isn't there anymore, and we accept that, but you can't expect people to celebrate like it was all a great idea. Now… now my father isn't here anymore. I don't have an Uncle Joe. I don't have a mother. I don't have anybody. We're all stuck in the world as it falls to pieces, and the thought that the *bad people* are now getting what they deserve… I'm sorry, but it's not enough. It doesn't make any difference."

The journalist went back to counting trees but quickly lost interest. "You know what else gets me? The thought that the world might not be ending. The thought that these bastards might just keep us alive forever and we could've got away without doing this after all. I mean, what if the war ends? Somehow, what if it ends? I might live to see it. Twenty, thirty years from now, I might be the grumpy old man in the corner of the pub when a group of young people comes in for a quiet drink. I'll get up to leave because one of them is one of The Enemy. Except we won't call them that anymore. The landlord will agree with me, and there'll be a scene. You know the type of thing. *"I'm not serving him." "Why?" "My dad fought in the war." "Oh, come on, that was ages ago. He wasn't even born." "Don't care. Get out!"* It might form the basis of an anti-speciesism campaign. I'll be a dinosaur. Do you ever wonder what future generations will think of this if it all ends? If one day it is all over? They won't believe it, just like we don't. How will we explain all of this to them?"

The soldiers didn't come back, and the journalist didn't speak again until they reached Glasgow. When the train slowed, Michael started to stand, but the journalist waved at him to sit back down. The train seemed to continue forever. Even when the roof of the station appeared above them, it kept going. The two SCD were gone, as was the soldier. When he stepped off the train, Michael noticed the track stopped in the centre of the station. It was the end of the line. It was different from the station in Dumfries. The trains all stopped alongside each other, all coming from different parts of Scotland, all at the end of their lines. It was like the whole world was meant to come to Glasgow.

He had never seen anything like the station. A huge screen loomed over everybody, showing trains arriving and leaving. Only half of it was being used. The station wasn't as busy as he had expected. There weren't huge crowds of people. Still, it was impressive enough. The sound had a strange quality, like they were in a huge cavern, adding to the alien feeling of the place.

Michael quickly looked for his train up on the board. *Dumfries*, picked out in yellow writing. Actually, the train had come all the way from Newcastle, and Dumfries was only in small writing at the side, but it was still amazing. It was as if the place he had come from was suddenly more real because it was up on the board.

The journalist didn't seem awed and marched on, calling to him. As Michael caught up with him, he stopped and pointed at the shop by the door. "Do you want to get some sweets or chocolate?"

Michael bristled. "I'm not a child."

The journalist sighed. "Fine. Let's just go into the city centre and see if we can get some cocaine and hookers."

The huge doorway dwarfed the journalist and the boy, their conversation echoing as they left. The boy's words became lost, but an old lady walking past overheard the journalist clarifying that he was only joking and reminding the boy that he had been told not to be annoying.

She smiled to herself. It was nice to see a boy enjoying a day out with his father. These days you had to make sure you enjoyed these times while they lasted.

35

It looked bigger in real life. He had seen pictures of it lots of times, but it looked bigger in real life. No moss was growing on it, hitching a lift to the future, even high up. No hitchhikers, but it wasn't something from the past that had been abandoned. It was new. It was from a modern age, the Age of General Chen. The statue was still standing because the Age of General Chen wasn't over yet. The general wasn't in command anymore, but someone was still cleaning the statue. People still cared.

The war memorial behind it was a survivor from another age. They had updated it from time to time, but it had never gone out of fashion. Michael knew that there had been a lot of wars, but the memorial only listed three.

The journalist spoke, answering a question Michael had only thought. "It was built nearly a hundred years ago, after the First World War. It wasn't called that, of course. They didn't know there was going to be a sequel. Do you know what they called it?"

"They called it The Great War."

"Almost. That's what everyone thinks. Actually, they called it The Great War for Civilisation. Seems a bit naïve now."

Michael couldn't think of anything to say and instead let the journalist speak again. "Two hundred thousand were sent from Glasgow, and about twenty thousand were killed."

"That doesn't seem like very many."

"Not to us maybe."

There were two inscriptions. The first was obviously old:

These died in war, that we at peace might live. These gave their best, so we our best should give.

The second was modern, longer. It was the words that General Chen always used. Michael knew it by heart. The last four words made Michael think he might cry. He would meet his father again.

The journalist interrupted his thoughts. "What do you think of the statue?"

Michael looked up at it, high on a plinth, towering over the memorial. The two giant stone lions somehow seemed like pet cats behind it. "It's big."

"Yes, well, he's smaller in real life, of course. I always thought the hands on hips was a bit too much."

They both looked up at the general, standing legs akimbo, staring into the sky over the roofs of the buildings at the other end of the square.

The journalist spoke from behind Michael. "So, is that us, then?"

"I suppose."

"That's the trouble with going to see things. You spend ages travelling, and then when you get there, you just have to go back again."

"Should we just go now, then?"

"Well, why don't I go over there and take a picture of you with General Chen?"

"You could give your camera to someone else, and they could take a picture of both of us next to the statue."

The journalist looked at the camera and then at Michael. "I was forgetting. You don't get out of Portpatrick much."

Michael didn't really understand what he meant.

He would have to go some distance away to get the statue in the picture, and the journalist was almost at the other side of the square by the time he stopped. Looking across the square at him, Michael thought about how quiet the city was. He had expected there to be lots of people everywhere. On the way to the square, they had walked through some streets that were dirty. He hadn't expected that. Surely in a big city, things were done properly? If things weren't done properly in Glasgow, then where were they done properly? He had also seen the same old men and old ladies he always saw at home. Where were all the young people?

The boy hadn't noticed the soldier watching him from a few yards away. He was heavier than you might have expected for a soldier. These days there was nothing strange about such an old man being in uniform. Smart and clean-shaven, he smiled permanently. People didn't smile very much, not without a good reason, and most people in uniform didn't have one. This man seemed to have a good reason.

A picture was taken, and the man in uniform didn't move. Another picture was taken, and still, there was no movement. It was only after the third when the camera was being checked and put away, that the man started to move.

Michael was looking up at the general when a leaflet appeared in his hand. His fingers closed on it instinctively as he looked at the jolly man standing in front of him.

The man spoke quickly, with something hurrying him besides enthusiasm. "Good morning, my friend, paying the general a visit, are you?"

"Well, I was just..."

"Have you given any thought to how you could play a part yourself?"

The man nodded at the leaflet in Michael's hand. It had a picture of a very young soldier smiling with some older soldiers. At least half were female.

"I'm a bit young—"

"Never too young to think about where you should be putting your name down. Get in quick. That's my advice. Breaks my heart to see young men making a decision at the last minute, regretting it later."

"Well, it's a bit early."

The man's hand rose to backhand an idea out of the air. "Did you realise that the 4th Glasgow and Lanarkshire are offering pre-enrolment preference contracts to those fourteen and over? Let's you get your name down now for the kind of thing you want."

The man again nodded Michael's gaze down to the leaflet.

"I'm not from Glasgow."

The man's laugh was hurried. "I thought not, but that doesn't matter. We attract from all over. That's why we can be so flexible and can offer such good terms."

Michael was becoming unsettled by his attention being pulled back and forward. This time, as he looked at the leaflet, a dozen more joined it in his hand.

"Look, I can see you're the type of young man we're looking for. You've got something about you, an interest in things. Why don't you take these back home and show them to your friends? You could all join up together. All friends together, like a great adventure. You could all come up to see us sometime and spend a weekend working with the cadets. You'll have the time of your life! Fire off a few rounds, ride in a tank, see what it's like."

A tank? He had never been in a tank. "I would be allowed in a tank?"

A finger jabbed at the leaflets again as the man laughed. "Of course, the form covers you for all that. Just call us. Drop in. Come on up, or down, or whatever. You never actually said where you were from."

"Portpatrick."

"Oh, it's a lovely part of the world. I know it well. Just come and see us. No obligation."

The journalist's hand slowly dropped onto Michael's shoulder. His touch was unhurried and calm.

"Come on, Michael, we should be going," he said calmly, hardly looking at the man. "He's too young."

"Yes, Michael and I were just talking about that. No barrier these days."

"Maybe not to you. He's too young."

"Too young to get a go in a tank? Maybe we should ask Michael what he thinks about that."

The journalist finally looked straight at the man and stepped between him and Michael. "Michael thinks you should go to hell. Young people are so rude these days."

Not so jolly anymore. He was still smiling but not laughing. He drew himself up to his full height. "Well, the 4th Glasgow and Lanarkshire are just interested in helping him make the right decision."

"Well, he has your leaflet. I'm sure it's very informative."

"Maybe you should take one, a strong, fit man like you."

The journalist held Michael behind him while his other held something up in front of the man. He said, "I don't need a leaflet."

Michael couldn't see the thing the journalist was holding up, but he could tell by the look on the man's face that it clearly said, *I've been in your tanks. I've seen it. All of it. Don't remember seeing you there, though. Saw a lot of young men.* The expression on the journalist's face said *I know you're just doing your job. I understand the value of publicity, good, bad, whatever. You've done your job. Now, why don't you go away before I decide to make you and the 4th Glasgow and Lanarkshire part of mine?*

Michael could see the man was still smiling but somehow didn't look happy. "Read the leaflet, Michael. Look forward to seeing you."

Whatever the journalist held up went back in his bag as the man walked off.

"Right, Michael, we should be going now."

"The general won't be speaking for hours. We'll just be standing around for ages."

"Maybe. We should go anyway."

"What did you show him?"

"Nothing, it was... like the tattoo. Just a trick."

"Where is everybody, Jack? Is Glasgow always this quiet, or are they all at the march?"

The journalist looked uncomfortable, staring up at the statue. "They're... probably getting ready for the speech or something, or at work. It's a Thursday, remember."

"What are we going to be doing today?"

"You said you wanted to see General Chen."

"Yes, but are we going to be standing around, or are we going on the march or what? The television said you couldn't buy tickets anymore. We haven't bought tickets, have we?"

"No, we haven't bought tickets."

"Will we see him?"

"Let's just go. We'll go to the hotel first and dump your bags. I'm not helping you carry them around all day."

"What if I need them?"

The journalist smiled. "Well, you'll just have to survive for a few hours. Come on. We better get going. And for God's sake, don't sign anything while I'm not looking."

"He said I'd get a ride in a tank."

"Yes, well, you should know better than to get into tanks with strangers."

They talked all the way to the hotel. At least if everything went wrong, he could still say he had seen General Chen and had the picture to prove it.

36

After going to the hotel, they took a walk around Glasgow, and the journalist bought him something to eat. Michael wasn't sure how much of the city they had seen. There was surely much more. The centre was huge, and they passed through street after street with shops. Still, there weren't many people, and he had seen some places that were boarded up. Police and soldiers were beginning to arrive, and their identification had been checked twice already. They had searched the journalist's bag, and Michael realised why it had been best to leave his at the hotel.

The hall was at the top of a hill. There was some activity outside it, some people standing around, some of them with signs. He didn't see any television crews and was wondering if he was the only one who cared about General Chen.

"That's Bath Street."

The journalist had been pointing out things as they walked through the town, but now he stopped and was pointing up at a sign.

"There, that's Bath Street."

Michael failed to see the significance.

"Daniel MacBryden lived in Bath Street. I don't know where. I think it's quite long."

"Who was Daniel MacBryden?"

"He... was a bad guy. He killed people."

"Why?"

"I don't think he had a reason. He was just... bad. My friend Emma was going to write a book about it. She came up here, saw where he lived and everything. It was a big thing because he had been a soldier. There was some fuss about it.."

"What happened to him?"

"They caught him. He did something stupid, something to do with the postman. He… what was it? He had to sign for something, and when the door opened, the postman saw something in the hall or something. I don't remember exactly, but they caught him somehow. He had been doing it for months."

"What happened to him after that?"

"Well, there wasn't much he could do. He admitted it. Yes, I'm sure he admitted it."

"Did they hang him on Glasgow Green? A boy at school told me they hang people on Glasgow Green."

The journalist looked uncomfortable again, his train of thought interrupted. "No, they don't hang people on Glasgow Green."

The sentence didn't end properly, like there was something missing. A word had fallen off the end. Hard to tell what the word had been. Anymore? Yet? Maybe it was a whole sentence that was missing.

The journalist started walking again. "There used to be a lot of stories in a city like this. Not the same these days. People all want to read the same story. I miss the old days. Everything used to be so complicated."

The journalist was becoming less careful about lying, or he wasn't very good at it.

As they walked up towards the hall, Michael looked around to see where they could stand. At the side of the street was an armoured vehicle with two soldiers perched on top of it. Its green camouflage did little to make it invisible. The soldiers sat, guns pointed in the air, waiting. Michael had never seen one so close up before, although sometimes you saw them in Stranraer and on the road from Dumfries, being transported on trucks.

"That's a FV432!"

The journalist looked unimpressed. "Yes. I bet those tracks are useful for driving over things. Make sure you're not the one who ends up under it. Before you ask, no, you can't go and ask for a go on it. I don't care if you have got a leaflet."

The soldiers sat up on it like shipwrecked sailors sitting on a raft. There was no water around them, not yet.

Michael whispered, "There will be more of them inside."

"Yes, stored shoulder to shoulder. *In case of emergency bang on hull.* Let's not create one."

"That's a Wolf." Michael pointed at an army Land Rover parked around the corner.

"Are you going to do this all day? If you are, I might sign that form for you and leave you with them."

Michael turned to walk towards the hall and noticed the journalist didn't.

"Aren't you coming?"

"We don't have tickets, remember? We can't go in there."

Michael's heart sank. He knew they wouldn't get to go in but had hoped there would be some surprise and the journalist would produce tickets at the last minute. "Can't we stand out here, then?"

"Between the banner-wavers and the boys cleaning their rifles? I don't think so. We're going round here."

He followed the journalist as he walked farther away from the hall, further and further away from General Chen. Eventually, after turning a few corners, they reappeared beside the building again. Here there were film crews and huge lorries full of equipment. Police in yellow fluorescent jackets talked to green soldiers and black SCD. There were other people as well, big people in suits watching the road, even though it was blocked off by more police.

"Where are we now?"

"This is the back entrance."

The journalist was going to let him see General Chen, after all. They were going to watch him arrive. Michael knew the trip had been worth it. He was going to see him. Even if they didn't get any closer than this, they were only about forty metres away. Forty metres from General Chen. Forty metres from the greatest human being who had ever lived.

"Where are we going to stand?"

"Follow me, and look miserable. Here, hold my jumper and my jacket. For God's sake, try not to say anything."

Michael grabbed the two items and tried to look miserable as he followed behind the now visibly tattooed journalist.

Their identification papers let them past the first soldier. The journalist waved something else, which magically took them past a policeman. Ten yards from the door, two soldiers stood with a huge man who was wearing a suit. The journalist produced more things, coloured paper and badges. "John Walker. On the blue list, entry 343. This is the boy, Michael. Here's his letter signed by the clearance officer. If you call this number, they'll confirm the strip code."

"Where are you going?"

"Balcony two, one bag, one camera, no audio, no video. We're cleared for the evening as well. I have the green form if you need it, but that should be on the list. I had the office fax across a copy of everything yesterday, but I have it here if that makes it easier."

The soldiers looked bored. The suit looked like he thought he should do or say something. "You're a bit early."

"Wanted a few shots of the hall. Not local, couldn't do it otherwise. Plus, the boy. It was this or walk around for a few hours, and it's a cold day… well, you know."

"Thirty-Second?"

"Yes." The journalist left a long pause. "Seems like a long time ago now." He made a noise that might have been some kind of laugh but was a bit more like a snort. "Suppose I should be grateful."

The large man nodded. This was unbelievable. What was happening?

"You're only cleared for the balcony while the general is present. You'll have to stay up there throughout the speech." The man waved the form at the journalist. "If you stand here, I'll call and clear this."

"I know. Thanks."

The man took forever. The soldiers had lost interest but were still near enough to be within earshot. Jack suddenly took an interest in Michael, bringing his face down to Michael's and looking sympathetic. "Are you okay, Michael? We'll get sat down in a minute."

Michael remembered his instructions not to speak and just nodded at the madman.

"You're doing very well, Michael. The general will be here soon. You must be looking forward to that, eh?"

Michael nodded again. He worried that they wouldn't get in if the journalist didn't stop acting so strangely. He grabbed the thought as it drifted past. Get in. They were going to get in. It still didn't seem real.

The huge man came back out, talking on his radio.

As he waved them through, the soldiers stepped to the side. He walked beside them as they entered the building. "Everything is fine. Just remember to stay on the balcony once the speech has started. In the meantime, you can get something to eat inside. If you need anything, just say to someone, they'll have been informed."

They stopped, and the journalist thanked him again. As the huge man in the suit turned to leave, he stopped and crouched down, so his face was almost level with Michael. "You enjoy your day. You're a very brave boy."

Michael looked at the journalist as the man walked away. He waited until he was out of earshot, and it was okay to talk again. He whispered, just in case it wasn't. "What was that about?"

The journalist shrugged and dropped a security badge around Michael's neck. "Who knows? Some of these guys just aren't very good around children. Let's go upstairs."

37

The hall was huge, bigger than anything Michael had ever seen before. He had once been to the cinema in Dumfries, but he guessed that the hall he was now in was at least twice as big, maybe more.

The journalist sat back and waved his arm across the scene. "What do you think?"

"It's huge."

"It seats two and a half thousand, and this isn't even the only hall in the building."

Michael watched people crawling on the stage, connecting cables, pointing at things, and asking for opinions. "Are they General Chen's people?"

"No, they're TV. Just getting ready takes forever. TV always takes forever."

"We're really close. How far away do you think we are?"

"Pretty close, I'd say. Just about close enough to run up and touch him."

"Almost."

"Of course, you'd be gunned down by his highly trained bodyguard before you got within twenty yards, but the principle is still sound."

It was amazing to watch. Michael could see behind the background screens at the back of the stage. They were nothing but thin material over a temporary metal frame. On television, the background always looked so solid. He had never really thought about what it was made of. As he watched them moving the screen back and forward, a book dropped into his lap.

"I brought this. In case you were bored."

Michael wasn't sure he wanted to read about submarines. The things drifting around downstairs were much more interesting.

The journalist didn't have a book, seeming happy just to sit and wait. It would be hours until the general spoke. The balcony was empty, and again Michael worried that nobody else would appear. They would be the only people listening to him.

More people gradually came into the hall. Eventually, someone else came out onto the balcony. He was younger than the journalist. Probably too old to be a soldier. The journalist didn't turn to look at him.

"Jack! How the hell did you get in here?"

The journalist closed his eyes and mouthed something silently before turning towards the source of the voice. "Same way as you, I imagine, Murray. I just oozed under the door."

The two men obviously knew each other. Michael pulled earphones out of his pocket and put them in, leaving the men to continue their conversation in private.

"It's a small world, eh, Jack?"

"Getting smaller all the time, Murray."

Murray sat down next to the journalist and the boy, listening to his music.

"I heard you went nuts."

"Yes, well, you don't want to believe everything you hear from multiple reliable, independent sources. You should know that."

"Well, I thought it was probably just a tax thing, anyway. I said to Tony, I said it's probably just a tax thing. He probably just wants a holiday. I said if he was going to go nuts, he would have gone nuts by now. Amount of time you spent over there. You must have seen more battles than John Wayne."

"Well, I was only there for the expenses, as you know."

"What was it like being nuts?"

"Not as interesting as you might imagine. You can stop talking about it any time you like, you know."

"Is this the boy? Are you the one here with the boy?"

Murray was pointing at Michael. The journalist answered him through gritted teeth, "Yes, try to be sensitive. In fact, just leave him alone."

"He looks well."

"Yes, well, you wouldn't believe the number of apparently healthy people I've seen just die suddenly."

"He wants to see Chen speak?"

"Don't we all? Or are you just here for the buffet?"

"Well, it helps, but yes, I'm also interested in hearing what the old Nazi has to say."

"Vietnamese Nazis?"

"Worst kind."

"You know Murray, that particular criticism of the general might carry more weight if it wasn't coming from someone who thinks Paul McCartney is a fascist."

"He writes fascist songs."

"I thought we agreed to disagree about this."

"Speeches disguised as songs. You just read the lyrics to *The Frog Chorus*. That's all I'm saying. All that stuff about standing together. I know what he's up to."

"Isn't there anybody else you could be sharing all of this with?"

"George is downstairs. He was the one who heard you were here."

"My God, the people you meet when you don't have a loaded firearm."

"He's at the buffet."

"Well, the world clearly hasn't ended yet."

"It's like a seafood buffet thing. It's quite good. Better than that lukewarm breadcrumbed nonsense we got for the Neckerman interview."

"It's scandalous. I hope you wrote away to complain with a letter or something."

"Well, I'm not one to complain. I just soldier on. Not literally, of course, not with my knees."

There was laughter from Murray. Jack wasn't able to go that far but smiled, not for the first time that day.

Michael could see the hall was beginning to fill. It would still be a while before the general would arrive. A few more people appeared on the balcony, although Jack showed no sign of knowing them. Murray was using his jacket to keep a seat beside them. Around it, journalists began to scribble and read, exchanging stories and catching up with each other's lives. At last someone arrived that Murray considered important enough to displace his jacket. He was older than Jack and Murray but not as old as Uncle Joe, maybe fifty. Michael wasn't good at guessing the age of adults. He was definitely older than forty.

He sat down and immediately leaned across Murray. "Hey, Jack, shouldn't you be in a foxhole somewhere getting shot at?"

"Seafood buffet okay for you, George?"

"I've had better, but not often."

"What was it they used to say? Never have so many crustaceans died in vain?"

"I wouldn't know about that. I prefer not to dwell on all that suffering and pointlessness, unlike your good self. You still alternating between mad and dead? Which is it this week?"

"I haven't decided yet. I'll see what's on tonight."

"Well, just so long as you don't start thinking you're Napoleon or anything during the speech. I saw some of Chen's men outside. They were looking a bit twitchy if you ask me. You start making chicken noises or anything during the general's big moment. They're likely to start blazing away. Probably no skin off your nose given your background, but I'm more used to sex, drugs, and sausage rolls these days."

"I'll try to keep it under control."

"Must have been great getting out in all that fresh air. God, I wish I could have been there with you, notebook in hand, facing an angry foe, the camaraderie, the singsongs, the poetry. I only wish they would have let me go."

"Yes, I remember thinking it was a shame you weren't there instead of me."

The hall filled as the men talked, never saying anything. The general was coming. His men entered first. There were already two on the balcony, unsmiling, vigilant, twitchy.

There were another two on the balcony and more downstairs. The audience became quieter, sensing the change of mood. Michael could see men appearing behind the screen on the stage, men taking the seats which had been left empty at the end of each row. Murray nudged Jack. "He likes to make an entrance, doesn't he?"

Michael knew they were all armed. He knew there would be more he couldn't see. He began to wonder if he was the only real person in the building. Maybe everyone else was security, police, army, bodyguard, SCD. The doors were locked and guarded, and there were eyes everywhere.

A figure walked out onto the stage, and Jack's hand stopped Michael from standing up. It wasn't General Chen. The man was introducing him. It was a long introduction, building slowly, reciting all the general's former titles. Out of sight, General Chen grew in stature. General Chen of the Unified Command, preparing to speak. General Chen, former Supreme Leader of the Unified Command. Chief of this, Grand Marshal of that, Protector of the other. He was becoming so large the stage couldn't possibly accommodate him. Not a man, but an idea. George whispered, "Does he think this is a boxing match?"

Jack just nodded, watching the stage.

Finally, the man stopped. The idea hung over all of them, this man, this figure, this ideal. It filled the hall, the great space above them, entered everyone, absorbed through their skin, drew their eyes to the same point, stopped their breathing, and let them hear their own hearts beating. The man had to focus the idea and bring it back to a point. With five words, the idea imploded, collapsing to one point. "I give you… General Chen!"

General Chen. Not a figurehead, not a politician, but more than that. The general. He was everyone's friend. The music was loud, and the lights flashed on. The crowd rose, and there was no hand to stop Michael this time. A standing ovation before the general even started. George smiled and whispered incredulously, "Is that Black Sabbath?"

As he entered from the side of the stage, waving to the crowd, Michael was surprised. He looked at Jack, who smiled at him and leaned closer to whisper, "Told you he was shorter in real life."

General Chen was short, not very, very short, but he wasn't tall. It must not have been obvious on television or when he had seen the statue. He was in full black dress uniform with a pistol on his belt.

Eventually, the applause died down with the music. The general pushed the audience back into their seats with a glance. He stood to the side of the podium they had provided for him with his hands on hips, just like the statue. He stood there, showing he didn't need the podium to hide behind. Even after the crowd was quiet, he remained silent, standing there for an age. The hall filled with increasing and amplifying silence. He scanned the audience and waited… for what?

Jack whispered an answer to the question Michael was sure he had only thought. "He's gauging the audience."

At last, the general took two loud steps across to the podium. He gripped it with both hands, staring at the audience, the intensity in his eyes holding them silent.

"Good afternoon."

The release of tension made Michael want to start applauding again.

"I stand before you at a time of great darkness. For ten long years, your brothers and sisters have sacrificed all for our species. The war which we did not ask for has all but destroyed one of our continents. It has laid waste to countless lands and taken hundreds of millions of lives. The Enemy is strong. He fights with great intelligence. His armies are agile, and his warriors are countless. His war is merciless. He kills without pity, and he fights without honour. Even as I speak, he advances, driven by barbarous instinct or malicious design, moving closer to our towns, our homes, our families. He outnumbers us on every field. He pursues us when we retreat and murders us when we surrender."

The quiet, calm voice of the general patiently continued listing and summarising. As he outlined that which was already known, his words burned into his audience. They drew the knowledge to the surface, the memories and fears of each of them illustrating his words. The audience squirmed in their seats as despair drove the silence out of the hall. Doom, destruction, and the end of the world. The space pulsed with unsolvable problems, inescapable facts, and inevitable decline. Six slow, calm words ended it. "That is where we stand today."

There was silence again, but he was not finished, and nobody dared speak. The general's hands left the podium and headed away from him on outstretched arms as his voice lost its calm, becoming livelier, engaging them. "So, what is being done to tackle this situation? What is being done to prevent The Enemy from advancing towards your town, your home, your family? Is your government mobilising every man, woman, and child to aid in the defence of our way of life? Are they employing every means at their disposal, every weapon in their armoury? Are they guiding you? Telling you what sacrifices are to be made? Are they helping you do all you can?"

Questions, there were endless questions without answers. The despair they had all absorbed was becoming frustration, each question landing heavily on their chest, shaking them into asking the questions they had tried to ignore. Each question also contained the shadow of a solution, something which could be done, something which was not being done. It was all so important, and nothing was being done.

He paused, the silence building again. General Chen's left hand dropped back onto the podium. His right pointed at his audience, and his voice dropped again, confiding in them, becoming quieter but with anger behind it. "I will tell you what is being done. Your leaders have grown bored of the sacrifices you have made. They have grown tired of the burden you have shouldered. They will no longer suffer as you suffer. They say it is too much. They say you can take no more. They speak for you, and this is what they say. They say you wish to live as slaves. They say you wish only to survive, whatever *survival* may mean. They plan to move away from a fight for the existence of what we are. Instead, they will play some game with rules. A game they expect and intend to lose, but not too badly. They ask you not to bear the unbearable, not to sacrifice, not to suffer, but to survive. That is all they require of you. That is the extent of their imagination. Do not sacrifice all. Do not suffer. Sacrifice only your dignity, for it is not worth dying for. Our leaders would have a *mirror war* with each side doing as the other does. Well, I would rather strike at the devil than dance as his whore! A mirror war? I will not imitate The Enemy's behaviour, their culture, or their morality. I say what our leaders dare not to! I say The Enemy are a repugnant and abhorrent abomination. I find them unworthy of the study and attention of the magnificent and exalted human race! I mirror only their hate, their resolution, and their desire to kill!"

Frustration became rage, listing actions, betrayals, atrocities, and leaders unfit to govern. The general was not afraid to call them by name. The crowd hung on his every word, drunk with his rage. Each jab of his finger, each snarl, each shout was like an injection of adrenaline. The world was rotten, everything lost, no solution, no hope. There was only rage. His hands balled into fists, pressed against the podium. The general's voice rose and fell with each sentence.

"So, this is the path we all choose? I will not. I refuse. I choose to remain human. I choose not to crawl back into the oceans, leaving our land for a more determined race. I choose not to deny and abandon our achievements. I choose not to betray our ancestors, who forged this world in blood and steel. There is another path. We must mobilise. We need more men, women, and children than ever before. We must be prepared to sacrifice all. No longer is it enough to sacrifice ourselves for the good of our families. No longer is it enough to hope that they will survive us. We must accept our purpose in this conflict. It can be nothing less than the survival of our species, not just in any form, but as a species preserving the vigour and determination of its ancestors. There will be no accommodation with a savage and bestial enemy. There will be destruction. Only the strong will or should survive. Your governments will tell you that The Enemy are invincible, infinite, and unstoppable. However, I choose not to worship our enemy as gods, but to exorcise them as demons. Invincible? If our dead are counted in the hundreds of millions, I say theirs have been tenfold, a hundredfold! Infinite? Perhaps. Let us kill more and see. Perhaps we will find that one day we will have killed enough! Unstoppable? Lies! They have been stopped before, and they shall be stopped again! We have the armies to push this verminous enemy into the sea, and it must be done, no matter the cost. What is my solution? Not one step backward! Not one battle left unfought. Not one curse left unuttered! Kill The Enemy! Purify your thoughts and your societies with that one aim in mind! Kill! Aid others to kill! Reward those who kill! Curse those who will not!"

General Chen's voice dropped almost to a whisper again, confiding in the crowd. "There are those who say that I would see our race wiped out. That I would sacrifice us all for an ideal. That I ask only to be the last to die. To those people, I say only this…"

The general's voice suddenly rose into a shout, screaming, hammering the podium with his fists, welding the crowd together until they thought as one.

"I say I would see our race wiped out! I would sacrifice all at the altar of our culture and our morality rather than have them enslaved or their vigour diluted by some faceless evil! If that is to be the only outcome of our struggle, I ask merely to be the last to die so that I may curse our murderers with my dying breath. To tell them that when they return to whatever hell gave them flesh, they should tell others that the human race chose extermination rather than survival as a changed race, moulded by their twisted hand! They should tell them that the human race still endures! It lives on in the blood-soaked soil of this world, ground into the living rock on which it stood in its final struggle, standing against the savage power that was sent to enslave it! I ask you, my people, will you not join me?! Are we not as one?! Our ancestors, our glorious dead, and those yet unborn, are we not as one?! Will you not be ready at the first call?! Will you not follow those who have already passed into eternity?! Fear nothing but the shame and scorn of those who have gone before you! Crave nothing but their brotherhood! We shall endure! The story of our sacrifice shall nourish and strengthen a thousand generations who shall follow us! When you are struck down, look around at your murdered brothers and scream at your killers! We are humanity! WE SHALL MEET AGAIN!"

Two and a half thousand voices howled in worship, the hall shaking, the floor hammered by thousands of feet. They stood, hands raised towards this man, this god. Michael was only dimly aware of George's voice somewhere to his right. "My God, he's insane! He's actually insane! The speech! That wasn't the speech!"

The general reached out to his people. Michael's hands reached to him, thirty yards away, delirious. General Chen saw him just for a second before he turned away. His eyes burned and narrowed briefly to acknowledge the boy. They said he would see his father again. There had been no sacrifice. The sacrifice was yet to come. It would be glorious. The Enemy would be defeated. The day was coming.

Jack's panicked voice came from beside him. "They're going to arrest him. They'll have to." Downstairs, police and soldiers looked at each other, unsure what to do. The general's men were too many. They were standing everywhere, not looking at the crowd anymore, looking at the police, the soldiers. A few guns clicked, just clarifying things. The crowd screamed and cheered louder than ever. A book disappeared from beside Michael and went into Jack's bag. "We can't stay! Michael, get ready to go."

An arm grabbed Jack as he looked at the door. Murray said, "Wait, the doors are locked, anyway. We're fine. It's fine. Wait. It'll pass. They won't make a move here."

Michael ignored them. They didn't matter anymore. They didn't understand, couldn't understand. He could hear George's voice. "Jesus Christ, what do you think's happening outside?"

Michael pictured two panicking soldiers rocking on top of their armoured personnel carrier, a raft amid a sea of people.

"Nothing will be happening. It's fine. Wait it out. Just sit down," Murray reassured again.

Nobody moved on the general. He stood surrounded by his men. Michael knew his day was coming. He was back. It was minutes before he left the stage, but Michael no longer had any sense of time. It could have been hours. After he left, the crowd stayed, cheering and shouting for him. Eventually, they started to sit down as the general's men began to disappear. There was a loud noise as a dozen doors were unlocked simultaneously.

The three journalists beside Michael sat staring at the empty stage. Murray spoke first. "Maybe the world is ending. Maybe this is what it's like."

Jack replied, "Maybe not. Maybe it's still just slowing down like it was yesterday. I wonder what's happening outside."

Nobody answered him. Maybe they were all wondering.

Jack looked around the hall. "Do you ever wonder if this is all a dream? Maybe none of it's real. Maybe one of us is dreaming this."

Murray offered his thoughts first. "I don't think it's me. I don't really dream about things like this."

Nobody asked him to expand on his answer.

George smiled. "I've got to be honest. I don't think I have this much imagination. If it was a big snake chasing us or something, I could see it being me, but… not this."

Jack thought for another moment. "Maybe one of us is dead. Maybe this is hell."

Murray said, "Well, that could have been me. I was never that careful around machinery. And I cheated on my swimming certificate at school. Touched my feet on the bottom when I was halfway round. Do you get sent to hell for that?"

They all looked at George. "I don't think I'm dead. It's probably you, Jack."

"Well, I'm only dead officially. Surely I can't be officially dead but actually alive, but actually dead, really. The paperwork would be hell. Can you imagine explaining that at the post office?"

There was silence for a moment.

George nodded at the stage. "He should have finished on a song. Then it would have been perfect."

The rest of the journalists moved towards the exit. A head appeared at the door. "Reports say the first minister is speaking with the prime minister. General Chen could be arrested within the hour. The streets are quiet outside. Police are putting down protests in London and Paris."

Murray stood up. "Time to go, work to be done. Will we see you tonight, Jack?"

"I'll see, you know."

"Of course. I hope the boy enjoyed the day. Come along, George. The people have a right to know what happened here."

"What did happen here?"

"I'm not sure. We'll work it out on the way down the stairs."

The journalists all filed out, leaving Michael sitting alone with Jack.

"Will they really arrest General Chen?"

"No, no chance. He's on his way to the airport with an army in tow. He'll be gone by the time they get their act together. That way, everyone is happy. Nobody will want any trouble. The battle won't be today."

"Is General Chen coming back?"

"Who knows? Stranger things have happened."

"Don't you need to work?"

"No."

"But you're a journalist."

"No, I'm not. I've told you."

"But you've seen more battles than John Wayne."

"You heard that?"

Michael slowly pulled the wire attached to his earphones until it came out of his pocket, the connector at the end dangling from his hand.

Jack sighed. "Not attached to anything. You weren't listening to music."

"No."

Another sigh. "A clever child. Whatever next?"

Michael smiled. "A printer that gets declared dead by accident?"

Jack smiled back at him. "It could have happened. You don't know."

"Why doesn't Uncle Joe know?"

"He's too close. Sometimes people don't see things properly if they're too close to them. Just like sometimes, you can hear everyone else's voice, but not your own."

Michael watched the hall downstairs as the cleaners picked the seats clean, and the TV people started to disconnect cables. "Why have people been talking about me today?"

"You know why. You're just too close to see it. Step away and think about it."

The soldiers and policemen were almost all gone. It was hard to believe it was the same hall. "They think I might be ill."

"Yes. See? That was obvious. What else has happened today?"

"We got in here. That's connected."

"Yes. That was obvious. You should have seen that."

Michael's attention was finally drawn away from downstairs. "I got in here because you told them I was ill!"

"Yes."

It was unbelievable. That was why the man outside had said he was a brave boy. "How ill am I?"

The journalist laughed, "Well, we don't like to discuss it with you. You're so young."

One of the other journalists had said he was looking well. He was surprised. "Am I dying?"

"We're all dying. The rest is just a matter of timescale. I may have shortened yours a little."

It was all fitting into place. Jack had told the other journalist to be sensitive. "By how much?"

"Well, don't go reading any long books in front of people. They'll get suspicious."

How could people do such things? "But that's lying!"

"How can it be lying? I've got a letter from a doctor and everything."

"What if they found out?"

"Why would they find out? You're not going to tell them, are you?"

"No, but why didn't you tell me? What if I'd said something when we were getting in?"

"People make better liars when they don't know they're lying. Children aren't very good actors in my experience."

He thought about the other two journalists. Jack had lied to them as well. "What if George and Murray found out?"

"I'd never hear the end of it. They'd go on about it forever."

"But they might be angry because it's wrong."

The journalist laughed again. "You're joking, aren't you? Murray would have shaved your head."

"It's wrong. It's sick."

"Well, you wanted in here, didn't you? I was the one who did it. I'm the one who's going to hell. You have nothing to feel bad about, except your impending painful death, of course. Come on, let's get downstairs before there's no food left."

Jack headed for the door, and Michael looked at the stage one last time before following.

"What's it like to drive a tank?"

"How would I know? I'm a printer."

"You can't do that anymore. You have to tell me things."

"Oh no, all I had to do was bring you here. In fact, technically, I've now done that, so I could just leave you here, and you'd never find your way home or to the buffet."

The boy followed the journalist down the stairs. It was strange. Things were always so difficult, but they always seemed to work out in the end.

38

The speech was over, but the building was still busy. There was far less security, and the main hall was empty, but several smaller halls were full of people who showed no signs of going home. Michael had been surprised to learn that the food was only for important people and the boy who was supposed to be dying. He had left the journalists, now finished whatever it was they had to do, so he could wander around and see what was going on. He thought it was a terrible waste to come such a long distance and then sit at a table talking and eating.

Even the small halls were impressive. The one Michael found himself in was full of stalls. They were piled high with leaflets and manned by cheerful people who were happy to talk. At least two people sat at each booth and were surrounded by a small crowd. The only problem was that nobody really seemed to want to talk to Michael.

Walking around the room was uncomfortable. Everyone else seemed to have someone to talk to and knew where they should be standing and what they should be doing. He kept walking, passing lots of stalls recruiting for different branches of the military. These, if their leaflets and posters were to be believed, were apparently all staffed exclusively by smiling females and friendly older brother types who all liked nothing better than helping out new recruits. Other stalls offered books and leaflets for sale. Some, like *The Wisdom of The General*, were simply collections of speeches and sayings. Others looked more argumentative and had titles like *The Coming War, How Victory Was Lost, The Death of Sacrifice,* and *Lions and Chickens*. He was sure his emergency money would buy him at least one, but he thought he'd better not. There was still plenty of time for there to be an emergency.

Everyone else knew where they should be and what they should be doing. What should he do? Time was passing far too slowly to do nothing. He walked up and down the hall, past the stalls all selling or saying the same things. He dreaded bumping into the cheerful man from George Square but relaxed after seeing that the stall for the 4th Glasgow and Lanarkshire had chosen a pair of smiling female soldiers to represent them. Michael wondered if the old man in George Square had been replaced by them, reduced to standing out in the cold, annoying strangers. He was probably just doing as he was told. Michael thought his father would probably have done the same if he was told to and tried to picture him handing out leaflets to people who didn't want to stop and talk. The thought was upsetting, and he shook it out of his head rather than consider it further.

Most of the people in the hall would be of no use as recruits. They were too old and only interested in telling stories, not being a part of new ones. At the very end of the hall, past the recruiters, salespeople, and petitions, there was a stall nobody else was interested in. A young girl sat behind it, and a slightly older boy sat further back, piling up small pieces of paper. The girl looked even younger than Michael and was dwarfed by a large black cardboard box sitting on the table beside her. Michael could see it hadn't always been black. Someone had spent some time painting it and making a lid for it. The slit at the top suggested something was supposed to go in it. Michael guessed it was the small pieces of paper.

The two were so young that they were scaring away most of the people in the hall. Their age suggested they had no stories to tell and that they were unlikely to listen to anyone else's without asking annoying questions. Despite there being nobody else around, the girl didn't speak to Michael until he was standing right in front of her. Even then, she wasn't very welcoming. She was businesslike, as if she knew what she was doing was right but was expecting to be challenged on it. Michael couldn't remember the last time he had seen a girl who wasn't in a school uniform. There weren't any girls in Portpatrick that were anywhere near his own age. This girl was in some kind of uniform, probably. She was entirely in black, and so was the boy. They wore black trousers and jumpers. It was hard to tell if it was a proper uniform or if it was something they had put together themselves. The girl's blonde hair didn't touch her collar. It looked like it had been cut to prove a point rather than for aesthetic reasons, as not much care had been taken over it. Michael wondered if she had done it herself.

She looked up at him, remaining seated. "Would you like to vote on our question?"

"Okay."

There was a small pile of magazines on the table beside her. His eyes were drawn to the front cover of the one on the top. It was a picture of General Neckerman kneeling at the feet of General Chen's statue. It wasn't very professionally done, and Michael could see that someone had just cut out pictures from a newspaper and stuck them together to make the image. The pictures had sharp edges and corners from the scissors. It made him think of her hair again.

"Is that your magazine?"

"The Patriot is published by us every two months. Would you like one?"

He wasn't entirely sure why he said yes, but he realised that this would have to count as an emergency. It wasn't a very big one, anyway. It wouldn't make much of a dent in the money. In any case, the money had to be meant for something, and after he had read the magazine, it would be something he could show to his mother and Uncle Joe.

As the girl handed it over and took his money, she nodded at the front cover. "Craig did the picture. Lewis Gray bought two just because of the cover."

"Who's Lewis Gray?"

The boy behind her laughed, and the girl's own disbelief meant she had to repeat his question. "Who's Lewis Gray? Who doesn't know who Lewis Gray is?"

"I'm from Dumfries." He tried not to make it sound like an apology but was mostly concerned that it didn't sound like a correction. He said Dumfries instead of Portpatrick because he thought she might have heard of Dumfries, but he immediately thought Stranraer might have been better.

The boy behind her handed a small piece of paper to Michael along with an unnecessary explanation. "Here's your ballot paper."

It asked whether General Neckerman should be put on trial for his crimes instead of just dismissed. It wasn't too controversial, and so Michael immediately put it on the table in front of the girl and ticked *Yes* with a casual gesture that he hoped made it look like he didn't even have to think about the question. She couldn't have missed him ticking the correct answer. As well as passing the test, he had shown that he didn't care who knew it. He didn't care because he had already checked there was nobody else around to see.

The girl immediately became less guarded. "Lewis is probably going to be at the talk tonight. Are you going?"

Michael thought about the journalist. Was he allowed to go to things? He would check later. "I don't know. I wasn't planning to."

"It's in one of the rooms upstairs. Seven o'clock. I'm Lisa. Just mention my name at the door."

"Oh, okay."

Lisa. He would have to remember the name. She turned back to the boy sitting behind her, and Michael realised that the conversation was over. He felt the need to speak again before he walked away. "See you later, then."

There was no reply. As Michael left, he looked at the magazine in his hand. It was printed on cheap paper and didn't have very many pages. He would ask the journalist about it. He had decided not to ask Lisa if the journalist could come to the talk as well. As he left, none of the recruiters bothered him. It was all going well so far. Maybe the journalist wouldn't want to go, so all Michael would have to do was check he was allowed to go alone.

When he found Jack, he was sitting with George and Murray at one end of a long table. There were others as well that Michael didn't recognise. The table was big enough to seat ten people, and there were still three or four empty seats. He sat down between George and Jack and waited for a gap in their conversation. Murray sat eating, listening to their conversation and that of the group at the other end of the table.

"Well, Jack, as Burns said, 'Facts are chiels that winna ding'"

Jack laughed. "What does that mean?"

"It means facts are facts. You can't argue with facts."

"I know that, but… why? What's a chiel?"

George thought for a moment before laughing. "I don't know. You know, I've just realised… I think I've always pictured it as a type of pot that you hit with something to make a noise. That can't be right, can it?"

"I doubt it."

Michael saw his chance and barged into the conversation. "It's a young man. Ding means to defeat. It means they're the young men who won't be defeated."

They both looked at him. George eventually asked, "Is he right?"

"How would I know? I'm just some dead guy."

"So is Burns."

"That's true."

"I got a magazine," said Michael, taking charge while he had the chance. He didn't want to admit to buying it until he saw their reaction. He slid it across the table to Jack.

"What have I told you about accepting things from strangers? You didn't sign anything, did you?"

"A girl in the hall gave me it."

George's brow furrowed in mock concern. Jack studied the magazine, his voice thoughtful as he said, "A girl? There's a girl involved? I suppose I should be grateful you didn't come back in a tank, waving a piece of paper."

Murray pulled the magazine out of Jack's hand as he chewed on a sandwich. He glanced at it and threw it to George. "Uh-oh, George, he's found a Chen-friend."

George shook his head. "A Chen-friend? What is it you do if you're approached by one? Do you try to make yourself look bigger, or do you just stand still? I can never remember."

Murray's concern didn't look as feigned. "It's not that young blonde one, is it?"

George laughed. "The one from the buffet?"

Jack's expression brought an explanation from Murray. "Yes, little cow swanned in handing out leaflets, saying she hoped we'd all be fair to General Chen for a change. Bloody cheek. Lucky she got thrown out before I backhanded her."

George passed the magazine back to Michael. "I think he'll be safe enough. I don't think they mate like normal people. I always assumed they were bred in some military research facility."

"I think I know how it happened, George. She asked him what his star sign was—"

George almost jumped out of his chair. "And he said, cancer!"

As the two laughed, Michael looked at Jack, who looked up at the ceiling guiltily. "Sorry. Don't worry. They won't tell anyone."

George pointed at Michael. "And he's right. Murray would have shaved your head."

Michael ignored them. "Who's Lewis Gray?"

Jack turned to Murray, who again had a mouth full of something. "Lewis Gray. Murray?"

"Big Chen type, he's the assistant to the secretary of the Scottish minister for… procurement? Recruitment? Youngest something or other to ever achieve something or other. Worshipped as a god in some primitive cultures, especially those inclined to produce cheap, badly written magazines with a circulation smaller than their staff."

Jack looked at Michael and pointed at Murray. "There you go."

"The girl said they've got a thing on here tonight, a talk."

Jack shook his head. "You're not going. Or, more accurately, I'm not going, and you're not going without me." He looked at Murray again. "Talk tonight, Murray?"

"Recruitment. Talk from a war hero, inspiring speeches, then lock the doors and sign up anybody who can hold a pen. New Volunteer Act states anybody of mature disposition can sign a pre-registration contract which is legally binding when they come of age. Probably."

"You're not going."

George leaned across Michael and put a hand on Jack's arm. "Come on, Jack, let's not be too hasty. If he goes there for a couple of hours, you can come back with us and have a drink. As long as he promises not to take the cross, it should be fine.

"You're joking. You saw him during Chen's speech. He'd have signed all of us up. Between the blonde, the war hero, and the promise of getting a go at beeping the horn on a tank, he won't stand a chance. He'll be charging machine-gun nests by teatime tomorrow."

Michael watched them argue. He knew he should have been offended or angry. He knew he should have been shouting or arguing. The truth was, he was paralysed. He wanted to go so badly he could only watch them decide for him. Jack was probably right, but that didn't mean he would win the argument. There was alcohol involved, and Michael knew alcohol didn't fight fair.

Jack delivered what should have been the killer blow. "Besides, George, I don't really drink."

Murray interrupted, "Why is that, Jack? Why don't you drink?"

"Because I like the world to be realistically annoying."

Murray looked disgusted. "Not me. I like my edges blurred and my news sugar-coated. You can watch us drink, and we'll tell you what everybody said about you after you were dead. Let the boy go. He's dying, anyway."

"That's true. He is." Jack was clearly thinking. "Okay, he can go… but I'm delivering and collecting him."

George clapped his hands together. "Excellent. See, Michael, everything always works out all right in the end. You'll have a great time. Just stay away from people with pens."

39

"Now, what you are going to is known as a fringe meeting. Or, in this case, a lunatic fringe meeting."

Jack didn't laugh at his own joke, and Michael didn't get it.

"You will sign nothing, and you will agree to nothing. You will go to the meeting, and you will listen, filled with patriotic fervour. But you will not sign anything, even if they offer you the keys to a large, tracked armoured vehicle."

"Okay."

"You will not drink alcohol. You will not leave this building. I will be back to get you in a couple of hours."

"I know."

"Remember, you're dying. Don't go on about it or anything. Don't even mention it to anyone. If anyone mentions it to you, be friendly, but say you don't want to talk about it."

They were twenty yards from the door. It had seemed like a good idea earlier, but now Michael wasn't sure. He didn't know anyone. What if he didn't have anyone to talk to? What if the girl wasn't there? What if there was nobody there?

"We're very early."

"You're very early. I'm not going, remember? It's better to be early. Get sat down, claim your territory. You don't want to walk in late and have everyone looking at you when you go in."

"Are you sure it's here?"

"Yes, this is it. I checked everything."

There were ten yards to the door. What was in the room?

"Do you think I'll need money?"

"I've given you money. Everything you need is in the envelope. Come on now, or you'll miss your chance to meet Lewis Gray."

Two more yards to the door.

"I'll be back at nine. Call me at the hotel if you finish earlier. The number is in the envelope. Don't spend your money all at once, and don't come back with any more magazines."

The room was almost empty. It was large, maybe the same size as the bar back at the hotel in Portpatrick. Michael was relieved to see Craig on the door. He showed no sign that he recognised Michael but allowed him to walk straight through.

There was a bar at one end of the room, staffed by a single barmaid older than Cathy. There were two men in suits, only just young enough to be in the army, their hair only just long enough to show that they weren't. The seats were arranged in a semicircle, more or less. There was nothing at the centre for now.

Michael sat down near the back. There was no sign of Lisa, but there was more than half an hour to go yet. Just as he sat down, Jack's head appeared at the door, scanned the room, and disappeared again. He didn't speak to Michael, although he must have seen him. Probably just checking he was settled. While everybody ignored him, Michael fished around in his pocket for the envelope. In it, he found two pieces of paper, which he opened out. The money stayed in the envelope, which went back into his pocket. One piece of paper gave the phone number for the hotel they were staying in. The second was larger, and when he opened it out, he found it was a list of names with short descriptions. Next to each name was a drawing. Murray clearly wasn't much of an artist. Most people apparently had perfectly round faces and differed only in their hairstyles and whether they wore glasses. Lewis Gray's name was at the top next to a circle, with a side parting and glasses. His description said:

Lewis Gray: Big fish, little pond. Loves Chen, loves himself more. Suggestion: Ask if he still works for Sandra Jennings–minister for something.

Next to a circle with spiky hair and an earring it said:

Patrick Armstrong: Head of Youth Wing. Probably organised talk. Big on Chen but also big on General Dragan, probably because he thinks nobody else will have heard of him. Suggestion: Mention that you think Dragan is the only sensible voice left in the Unified Command.

The list went on. There were eight pictures in all. At the bottom was a blank circle:

Recruiter/War hero: Don't ask the recruiter what's the best regiment to join. Ask where you can do most good. Standard question they always plant in the audience, anyway. Ask him what unit he was with, NOT the regiment–they love to talk about their unit. DO NOT ask for a gory story!

He thought about what Murray had told him earlier about the "minions" he would meet. He said if they tried to make Michael feel small, he should tell them huge lies about what his local group had achieved for the cause, and that would make them back off. Murray had suggested some lies to tell, some more outrageous than others. He said if they were friendly, Michael should ask where they meet and hint that he might come to a meeting. Murray said they were always desperate for members, especially members who actually did things. He said not to talk about politics too much. He said people in politics didn't actually talk about it very much when they were together.

Michael was just thinking how ridiculous that statement and the list were when a young man walked in. Patrick was wearing a black t-shirt with red lettering. There was a picture of an old man's face, and below it, the words *Not slain yet!* Behind him, Michael recognised Theresa Osborne, even though he had never seen her before. She had apparently edited the magazine Michael had bought earlier. Her dark hair was exactly the same as her picture, and Michael couldn't suppress a smile.

Patrick wandered over to the two suits who had arrived before Michael. He talked briefly before walking towards Michael on his way to the bar.

Michael took a risk. Maybe it was the list that had filled him with confidence, or maybe it was the feeling that he had nothing to lose.

"Hello."

Patrick smiled automatically and adjusted his stride to head right for Michael. "Hi there."

"I'm Michael." He knew that if you said your name, people almost always said their name in reply.

"Patrick. Nice to meet you. I'm—"

"Head of the youth wing, I know. Is Lisa coming tonight?"

The mention of Lisa's name put Patrick at ease. "Lisa? Yes, I just saw her in the corridor. She's speaking to Lewis."

"Oh. Is he still working for Sandra?"

Michael felt he was pushing his luck now, but Patrick didn't seem to notice. "Yes, she won't be here, of course, but he's still there."

Patrick was now completely comfortable. Michael nodded at his t-shirt. He didn't think it would be right to just come out and say he liked it. "I think he's about the only hope on the Unified Command these days. They always go on about General Chen being gone, but they always forget General Dragan is still there."

Patrick's eyes lit up. "I know. Do you know he still hasn't signed this year's declaration? Every time they ask him, he says the translation isn't right, and they can't change it without reconvening the General Council. That's why General Chen still has his official bodyguard!"

Michael had no idea what Patrick was talking about but smiled and laughed with him. He sensed the game was getting a little dangerous and that it was time for a change of subject. Luckily, Lisa appeared at the door along with Lewis. His picture didn't do him justice. His hair was much better drawn in real life. He shook Theresa's hand while simultaneously using his other hand to pat Lisa on the back. The pat on the back didn't look like the push it really was. It sent Lisa off, walking on her own across the room.

As Patrick continued talking, mistaking random noises from Michael for the other half of his conversation, Lisa headed towards them, wary again.

"Hi, Lisa, just talking to Michael here. Did you get things booked for tomorrow?"

She answered Patrick but looked at Michael. "It's all done. You know Patrick?"

Michael ignored her stare and looked at Patrick. "Well, we both know each other through General Dragan."

Patrick laughed at their private joke, and Michael felt a twinge of contempt for him.

Lisa addressed both of them, first Patrick, then Michael. "Michael's from Dumfries. We're going to hand out leaflets in George Square tomorrow. We should really have a licence, but we probably won't bother getting one."

It was a challenge, but Michael and Murray were up to it. "Yes, we did that at the harbour at Stranraer. We used the money we collected to buy war bonds."

It was towards the upper end of Murray's list of outrageous lies. Instead of questioning him, Patrick and Lisa looked at each other. "We thought of doing that, didn't we, Lisa? But we weren't sure if we wouldn't be better keeping the money for leaflets."

Both of them looked uncomfortable. Michael decided to be sympathetic. "Afterwards, we wished we'd kept some of it. Things are difficult when you don't have a lot of members." They nodded, but Michael wasn't finished. "Where do you meet? Dumfries isn't that far away. Maybe I could come up sometime."

Lisa sat down next to him, suddenly animated, forgetting she didn't know him. "It depends. We usually meet in a room above a bar in the city centre. I can give you the address later if you want?"

"Yes, maybe I can get it from you before I leave."

More people came in. Michael didn't recognise any of them. Probably the important people arrived first. Patrick shook Michael's hand and told him how great it was to meet him before he went off to speak to some of the new arrivals. Lisa stayed, continuing to talk to Michael as if she knew him well. "The speaker was in Agadez for a long time."

"What did they do there?"

"Driving, I think."

Michael went into shock. Kenny. Kenny hadn't gone back to the war. He had taken a job giving talks. The shock quickly turned to disappointment as he realised he would have heard all the stories. Disappointment became horror as he remembered how boring they all were. He dismissed the thought before he had the chance to feel guilty about it.

"What's his name?"

Lisa looked surprised. "Laura Miller."

"Oh." A woman. Not Kenny. Michael was relieved and disappointed at the same time.

"She was the only survivor when her unit was attacked. She made it back to our lines a few weeks later."

Michael thought of his father. He wasn't supposed to think about him until he got home. What would his father think if he could see him now? Michael tried not to think about it but found he had already spoken. "My father didn't survive."

He expected it either to ruin the atmosphere or to result in an outpouring of sympathy from the girl. Instead, Lisa became animated again. "My father was at Sokode. My brothers were at Kaolack, both on the same day. After that, my mother sent me to live with my auntie so she could volunteer. She was the head of her local committee. She was at Kiffa. I'm going to join up as soon as they'll let me go. My auntie wants me to be an officer, but that can delay you for ages. When I get old enough, on my birthday, I'm going north to join the 7th Highlanders. Do you know they don't have their own support sections like supply or engineers or anything? Just pure infantry. I've already signed a PRC, so they'll have to take me. Sometimes they don't like taking girls, but they'll have to take me because I've got a PRC."

She sang the second half of the last sentence. It was obviously a slogan, maybe from an advert or one she had made up. Michael tried to look and feel inspired. Instead, he felt sorry for her. Everything was being taken away, and she was just grateful she was part of it all.

"Did you get letters?"

"Yes, my dad got a medal and a letter from his officer saying that even after he was hit, he managed to drag two other soldiers out of danger before he fell. Because both my brothers fell, my mum got a letter signed by a colonel and a special medal. They don't know what happened to my mum, but she would have probably got a medal if they did."

She didn't even seem upset. The ghosts called medals wooden spoons, but Michael didn't know why. He forgot the girl for a few seconds. Letters? They always sent letters. Where was his father's? It should have been sent by now. It might tell him all about what happened. How could he have forgotten? He had taken so much interest in other people, but he had forgotten about his own father. He would have to check when he got back.

It wasn't fun anymore. A few minutes ago, he had felt comfortable and… vindicated, like everything he had always believed was true because he was in a room with people who all believed the same things. Now it was all wrong. They were all wrong. He was wrong. He felt dirty and childish at the same time. Lisa's whole family was dead, and she was pleased. Had people always been like that? He imagined men in a black and white world building the war memorial in George Square. Had they been pleased? Had they even been proud? Now people couldn't look at it without seeing General Chen. His shadow fell on it. Was that right? You weren't allowed to climb on memorials, so why was it okay for General Chen to cast his shadow over it?

He felt guilty because, unlike Lisa, he grudged the sacrifice his father had made. Was that like betraying him? At the same time, he felt sure his father wouldn't have wanted him to be at this meeting. There was hardly anybody here. Was he really in the right place? How could these people have the right answer if there was nobody here? But then, what was the right answer? He spoke again by accident. "I miss my dad."

Lisa didn't pause. "You will meet again."

"Do you miss your mum?"

"I know I'll meet her again. I'll meet her soon."

Michael thought he understood. Lisa had to kill herself. She had to kill herself in a special way to earn the right to see her mother again. Michael was sure his father didn't need him to do that. He was sure his father would want to see him, anyway. If he had had the choice, he would even have stayed. Lisa's mum hadn't. She had left to earn her place with her husband and sons, leaving Lisa to do the same as soon as she was able.

Michael thought about his mother. He hadn't really thought about how she felt before. No, that wasn't true. He had thought about it, but… he had dismissed it. He had contempt for her and how she felt. And for Uncle Joe. And for Cathy. He tried hard but couldn't think of anyone who had contempt for how he felt. All he had thought about was his father not being there. He had never thought about his mum losing her husband or Uncle Joe being left to take care of everything, as usual. How hard was Uncle Joe's life? Michael thought about how he had manipulated everyone to get what he wanted. For the first time, he questioned whether it had all been worth it.

As the war hero walked in, a boy stood up to leave. Everyone was looking at him. Nobody understood what he was doing. He was doing exactly the wrong thing. He knew everybody in the room thought he was doing the wrong thing. A girl with badly cut hair sat open-mouthed as he wished her good luck with everything and walked out. The boy missed the speech and the chance to make lots of new, interesting friends. He didn't explain anything, which was just as well because nobody would have understood.

He didn't sign a form, and he didn't agree to anything. Later, a recruiter would collect all the signed forms for processing.

He would look through them twice for a form signed by a boy called Michael. If he had found it, then it wouldn't have been sent for processing. A relative of the boy, a man who had served with the Thirty-Second, had caught him outside and shown him a doctor's letter, explaining that the boy was dying. The man wanted the signed form for the boy's father to put on his wall. No need to tell the boy there was no point in him signing. The recruiter was going to give the form to the man afterwards, except there wasn't a form. As far as the recruiter could remember, there hadn't even been a boy. He never saw the man again. He hoped that whatever had happened, it had turned out all right in the end.

40

There were five of them at the circular table, which was covered in empty and half-empty glasses. Jack sat beside George. Murray sat across from Jack, between the other two. Jack faced the window, which may just have been the way things had worked out. Except for the five, the hotel bar was empty. There was no need for them to be sitting so far away from where the drinks were poured, emphasising the empty cavernous nature of the bar. Nobody discussed anything important, and the conversation was never interesting enough to stop people from going to get more drinks. There were too many people there for anybody to discuss anything important.

Jack stood up. "I should go and get Michael."

It wasn't a question, and so nobody answered. Nobody noticed that it was too early.

He met Michael at the door of the hotel. He had known something was wrong when he saw the boy walking along the street outside. Now he could see Michael was upset, so he didn't ask why he had left the hall when he had been told not to.

"How did it go?"

Silence. Jack glanced at the wall as if he expected to see the other journalists through it. He put his hand on Michael's shoulder and mouthed something at the receptionist, who nodded sympathetically.

"Let's go downstairs where we can talk."

They sat alone in a large function room. It reminded Michael of the room he had just left, except this one contained tables as well as chairs, and the bar was closed off by a large metal grille which made it obvious that the room had no interest in their lives or conversation.

"It didn't go well then?"

Michael told him everything. He told him how well Murray's list had worked and how he had made friends. Then he told him about Lisa. Jack didn't react to any of it. He didn't look surprised or sympathetic or even particularly interested. He just listened.

"I don't know what I should think about my father. Is it really glorious when they die? Is it like General Chen says? Is it all okay?"

There was a pause as the journalist tapped his fingers on the table. "What do you want me to say?"

"I want you to tell me the truth. Nobody ever tells me the truth. You've seen it. You know what it's like."

"Do I?"

"Yes, so why won't you tell me? Why won't anyone tell me?"

"Maybe because it's not that simple. Maybe there isn't one truth."

"Just tell me. Is the general wrong?"

"I can't. It's not that simple. Chen, Neckerman, it's not a choice. Glory, waste, it's not black and white."

"Just tell me what it's like!"

Jack sighed and leaned back in his chair. He looked around the room as if he might see the answer there. "Sometimes it's glorious, I suppose. People quite enjoy it, in some ways, sometimes. That's... that's something you don't really hear very much, but it's true sometimes. I don't mean they enjoy the nobility or the glory of it all. More like doing things, the activity, the act. It's hard to explain. Mostly it's bad, sometimes just because it's boring. Mostly because it's terrifying and blah, blah, blah. But I don't think that's what you're asking. You want to know if it's worth it at the end, at the very end."

"Yes, is it worth it? Do they think it's worth it?"

Jack leaned forward across the table, whispering and hesitating, even though there was nobody else around. "They don't want to go. No matter what they say, no matter what they do to bring it about, no matter who they save. At the end, they don't want to go. They scream and beg, and they want to stay here with us. I don't know if that means anything. I don't know if it means Chen is wrong or… what. I don't think Lisa is lying, and there's every chance she'll do all the things she thinks she will, but… at the end, if she has the chance, she'll beg not to join her mother. That is the truth. That's what I have seen."

There was a pause as Michael absorbed the information. Eventually, he said, "My dad is dead."

"Mine too."

"Yours was old."

"It doesn't make any difference. I imagine it's still the same. The only thing that might make it easier is not being there when it happens, and that's only because it seems less real. Maybe that's why people leave home."

"When your dad died, were you expecting it?"

"I don't know if you ever do, not really. He had been ill for years, but that doesn't really prepare you, maybe the opposite. Once, a doctor at the hospital took me aside and told me that my father wouldn't last six months. A year later, he was still alive, and when he went back, it turned out the doctor we had spoken to was dead. When things like that happen, I suppose you get a false sense of security.

"Why do you think you're still alive?"

"Well, that's an interesting one. I am what you call a statistical anomaly, or maybe a statistical inevitability. Someone has to survive. Someone has to be the one in a million. Unlikely to be me in particular, but certain to be someone somewhere. Just like someone somewhere has to win the lottery each week. It has to happen to someone."

"But is this what it is all for? To make jokes with George and Murray while the world ends? To sit and drink?"

"What else would you have us do?"

"But they don't care that everyone else is dying!"

"Maybe, maybe not. What can they do? Did you know George had three children? All gone within the same month. They were at Gondar. They say that was what killed his wife,

Margaret. Murray's brother is somewhere in Africa. Do you think he'll come back? Do you think Murray does? He doesn't have any other family. There are people who have it worse than you. Someone wants to open your eyes."

The tone of the last sentence made Michael feel very small. "I'm sorry."

"What else would you have us do but make jokes? I had a life once. This isn't how I pictured it turning out. You do what you can. You grab onto anything that keeps you going. You make jokes or drink or get obsessed with things, attend silly meetings, collect things, whatever. I collect diaries."

"Diaries?"

"Yes, from dead soldiers, mostly. I'm like a vulture. Way I see it, they would rather have someone read what they've written than have it die with them. Some are good, some… aren't quite as good. It doesn't matter. It turned into a kind of game, trying to get as close to the end as possible. Maybe I imagined one day I would find one where someone had written *aaaargh* on the final page just as they died. Does that make me a monster?"

Michael suddenly recalled a bookcase with a few books missing.

"Your father's diaries. Those were the only books you took."

"You are very perceptive, Michael. I wonder how you have stopped that sending you mad."

"I want to be like you. I want to understand everything."

"Really? Well, first of all, I don't really understand any of this. I don't think anyone does. If you spend your life searching for a final answer, you will go mad. Or you'll get so desperate you'll oversimplify things, like Chen, then obsess, then go mad. Secondly, there's a lot to be said for missing things. Do you really want to see the sadness in everyone's eyes? See through every lie? See what's behind everything? Every place you go, do you want to see how the skirting boards aren't finished exactly right, then see the hand that made them? The next time you see a girl on a train with her arms folded and shoulders hunched, do you want to feel how much she hates the way she looks, see the signs of how unhappy she is, fill in her life story in a few seconds?"

"I already do that. Apart from the important things."

"Like what?"

"Like the war and… and Uncle Joe."

"Joe?"

"Yes. Why is he… like he is?"

"You know why, just like you knew that I had told security you were dying. You just aren't thinking clearly, but you should be able to work it out. As for the war… there isn't an answer. Maybe war is just the natural state of things. Do you think all the people the Romans conquered understood what was happening?"

"Probably not. But this is different."

"Why? Because The Enemy are evil?"

"Don't you think They are evil?"

"Yes, by any definition. So what?"

"But They kill and torture and don't care about us at all."

"I know, it's terrible. By the way, did you enjoy that chicken you had for lunch?"

"That's different."

"Probably, but the chicken might not have seen it that way. You have to find some way of accepting all of this."

"How?"

"That's up to you. Lisa collects medals and goes to meetings. Daniel MacBryden killed people, though I'm not sure how much of that was to do with the war. I collect diaries. I even wrote a book once, but then I lost it."

Michael felt a surprisingly small twinge of guilt. "Can't you rewrite it?"

"No, doesn't work like that. I probably wouldn't have ever finished it, anyway. I kept worrying that I'd finish it, and then I'd have something else to say and have to write a whole new book."

"Will you ever go back?"

"Maybe. Can't decide. Problem with me is I love adventure, but I hate excitement. Besides, I've survived so long now that I feel like I'm pushing my luck."

Michael looked at him, unsure if he was serious. "Really?"

"Really. Honestly, I should have been dead long before now. It's getting embarrassing. You get to feel like you're always meant to survive. Worse than that, you start to think The Enemy might only be coming because you're there. You also lose your fear of them, and when you don't fear something anymore, you start to feel like it's a friend. It makes you feel very guilty."

"Maybe you should stay here."

"And do what?"

"Write a book? Tell people what you know. They would want to know what the war is really like."

Jack thought for a moment. "You know what this war is really like? Have you ever played Monopoly?"

"Yes."

"And it always ends in an argument?"

"Yes."

"You know why? It's not because someone loses. It's because of the way they lose. At some point, you realise you can't win, but you can't stop playing because you haven't actually lost. It takes hours for the game to finish. In the meantime, you get increasingly frustrated and angry as everything falls apart and the winner enjoys slowly crushing you. Not only that, but the other players bend over backwards to keep you in the game because they're having such a good time. That's the war."

"So we've lost."

"Of course, unless they decide they want us to win for some reason. There is no prospect of victory. We just get to watch it all fall to pieces. Demographic Collapse, people turning on each other, that's what's happening. Chen is trying to kick the board over."

"Then what's the point?"

"Maybe this is the point. Days out, talking to people, doing things, enjoying yourself for a few hours. Maybe that's what your father died for, to give you these few hours. Victories are an illusion, a bonus."

"You said we couldn't win."

"We can't, but we can still have victories. Okay, here's an example. What do you know about the Battle of Agincourt?"

"Henry the Fifth defeated the French."

"Glorious victory, a total slaughter. What then?"

"What do you mean?"

"I mean, what happened afterwards?"

"I don't know."

"Of course, you don't, and nobody cares. It doesn't matter who won in the long run or if the battle made any difference at all. It's not important. We can still have those victories. I've seen them. Those moments when The Enemy was slaughtered like cattle, driven back, totally defeated. They came back again the next day, but so what?"

"So, what do we do now?"

"We just get on with it. Come upstairs with me, and we'll have a drink with them. They've been drinking pain-in-the-arse juice for ages, but they're still bearable. You'll enjoy it well enough."

Michael looked unconvinced. Jack tried again. "Look, someone once said a very wise thing to me. Would you like to hear it?"

"Okay."

"He said, 'Jack, you may be depressed, you may want to die, to kill yourself or whatever, but you know what? However bad it is, you've probably only got another forty or fifty years anyway, so what does it matter?'"

Michael wasn't sure it made sense, but Jack kept talking. "And you know what? Frankly, you'll be lucky if you get that long. The situation has improved immeasurably since your Uncle Joe said that to me many years ago. Come upstairs. There's no war there. You can worry about the rest of the world in the morning." Jack stood up, and Michael found himself doing the same.

Upstairs, four journalists hardly noticed a fifth and a boy approaching their table. There was music from somewhere. A country singer was gleefully telling his wife he was leaving.

Murray seemed pleased to see Jack. "Jack! We were just discussing why you're not dead yet."

"I said it was because the speed you run at and the direction away makes you hard to hit," George said.

"Whereas I said it was because of the enormous distance you always keep between you and danger."

"However, both of us now realise that both theories fall down due to the enormous size of your arse, which would make you a well-nigh unmissable target at any speed or distance."

As the two laughed far harder than was justified, Jack ignored them. "Michael, you know George and Murray. These are some new friends of ours, Wilson and Robert. Everybody, this is Michael, a friend of mine who isn't terminally ill."

Murray leaned across to Michael as he sat down. "Michael, ignore Jack. He's depressed because he's not drinking."

"No, I'm depressed because you keep putting Johnny Cash on the jukebox."

Johnny Cash. That was Johnny Cash. The voice had now started singing about why he always wore black. Michael wondered if he would get to hear the song from The Book.

One of the others spoke, and Michael realised he had immediately forgotten which name went with which person. He decided provisionally that the man would be called Wilson. "I meant to ask you, Jack, don't you work with Emma? How is she doing?"

Jack's mood darkened, and there was a pause before he answered. "Emma was at Melbourne."

The conversation died, and there was another long pause as Wilson thought of something to say.

"I didn't know."

There was another long silence. There was probably more to be said. Eventually, the one that was probably Robert said, "Max killed himself. Shot himself. Found him in a hotel room somewhere."

Yet another long silence. It didn't seem likely to Michael that the fun he had been promised would materialise anytime soon. Nobody was looking at anyone except Michael, who was looking at everyone.

George must have felt it was his turn to speak. "Seems a bit impatient."

The silence pressed down on all of them. Murray reached for his drink. "Well, you know what they say, do not stop to mourn. Better men will die tomorrow."

George seized the chance to reignite the conversation. "Like Jack, you mean?"

"Well, he is overdue."

Jack got into the spirit of things again. "I'll have you know I've already died once. Unfortunately, the world appears to consider me indispensable."

Murray pointed his drink at Jack. "The cemeteries of the world are full of indispensable men."

Wilson moved forward. "Charles de Gaulle!"

George leaned towards Jack in mock confidence. "He said it in French, of course, Jack. It's a different language."

Murray laughed. "I keep meaning to ask you, Jack. How come you travel all over the world, but you can't speak any foreign languages?"

Jack sat up straight in his chair. "Learning languages is a pointless quest to meet interesting people. I prefer not to kid myself that people are any better company just because they're talking gibberish."

Michael had noticed that the jokes were usually aimed at Jack, but it never seemed to make him angry. It didn't seem to be that they disliked him, maybe the opposite.

As Murray got up to go to the toilet, Michael noticed everyone ignoring him leaving. Would they notice if he didn't come back? What was this gathering? Did the journalists really care about each other? Were they just fulfilling roles, playing a game?

George continued to provide more evidence for Michael's observations regarding his attitude towards Jack. "Speaking of gibberish, Jack, did you ever finish your book?"

"No, I lost it when I was dead. Emma never finished her last one either." Suddenly he became serious, as if he had remembered something. "George, how did they catch Daniel MacBryden?"

"That was near here. I think it was the postman. He saw something in the hall. Was it a backpack or something? Emma could have told you. It is strange her being gone."

The conversation threatened to die again, but Jack spoke quickly, preventing the silence from taking hold. He looked up at the ceiling and spread his hands as if waiting for a sign from above. "Yes. I suppose she's up there now. She'll be looking down on all of us. Just like she used to when she was alive."

There was a sharp intake of breath, which Jack waved away. "Oh, come on, you know what I'm talking about."

The atmosphere cleared again, and there was no threat of the silence coming back. Now it was George's turn to be serious. "You know, Jack, I always thought you two might have ended up together."

Jack stretched, rubbing the back of his head and yawning. "No. You know what she was like politically. We weren't suited." Another short pause, but there was more coming. "Besides, she looked like a horse."

Jack smiled, and everyone else laughed. Michael found himself disapproving. It didn't seem right. Despite what Jack had told him earlier, none of it seemed right. You shouldn't make fun of the dead. Lisa and the others might have cared about the wrong things, but it seemed like the journalists didn't really care about anything.

Jack hadn't noticed Michael's disapproval, and he leaned over to speak to him as Murray returned to the table. "Murray wrote a book once. You should try to get a copy. You never know when you might need something to wedge a door open."

"Hey, Jack, that book is my legacy."

George threw his hands up. "All this book writing, chasing fame and fortune, whatever happened to journalistic integrity?"

Murray answered, "There was no money in it."

George pointed at Murray. "Well, once the war is over, I plan to write the definitive book of the entire thing. It will be a book with an important message."

Murray looked at Jack. "Who for?"

Jack smiled. "Depends which side wins."

Murray sat up straight and saluted slowly, wiping an imaginary tear from his eye. "It'll be us. Chen will get us back on track."

The one who was probably Wilson smiled. "Well, my only criticism of General Chen is he doesn't go far enough."

George looked genuinely unhappy. "He's a bloody warmonger."

Murray was off-duty and apparently unwilling to take anything seriously. "Why can you only mong war? Or fish? Or iron? Actually, that reminds me, where's the drinkmonger?"

The one that might have been Robert put his hand up before standing up and walking off in search of the bar.

George finished what was left of his drink now that there was the promise of more. "This whole war is pointless."

Jack shook his head. "I disagree. I think it's exactly the opposite, as wars go."

Murray sighed. "The opposite? Point-ful? Come along, Jack, that's not even a word."

"No, I mean it. Even though we can't win, or maybe because we can't win, it has meaning Think about it. Pointless is starting a war because it's too difficult to find a peaceful solution. Then you find the war is too much hassle, and after a few years, you come to an agreement and stop it. Then you have the peaceful solution you could have had at the beginning. That's pointless. This is the opposite. It's about the only real, unavoidable war I've ever heard of."

Murray thought for a moment. "No, I think it's pointless. I heard The Enemy are all left-handed…"

Michael looked in surprise at Jack, who shook his head to show it wasn't true. He rolled his eyes to indicate there was a punchline coming. Murray continued, "What's the point of them winning? Even if they conquer our planet, they won't be able to use any of our scissors."

There were more smiles than groans, and really that was all Murray was looking for.

Jack refused to let the conversation slip. "You know what the Chen-friends are chanting since those new contracts came in?" Blank looks invited him to continue. "They'll have to take me. I've got a PRC!"

Murray dropped back into his seat and rolled his eyes. George looked angry. "Call me traditional, but I prefer 'Hell no, we won't go!'"

At that moment, the one who was probably Robert came back with the drinks. Michael noticed there was nothing for him, confirming that he was invisible. "I didn't get anything for you, Jack. I didn't think you were drinking."

Murray leaned forward to Jack, suddenly serious. "If there's anything else you want, Jack, I can arrange it."

"No, I definitely don't. I'm trying to convince the authorities I'm still alive. I don't think being shot by the SCD would help my case."

Murray shrugged. "It's an SCD man I would have been dealing with."

Again, Michael was shocked. He had heard about drugs if that was what Murray was talking about. Some people used to take them, but that had been sorted out in the Renewal, and there weren't any drug addicts—the modern term was drug slaves—anymore. Given a choice between Murray and Lisa, Michael wasn't sure who he would choose. He was even having second thoughts about having left the meeting.

The journalists talked on and on, but nobody provided any of the answers he had been told didn't exist. He was relieved when the journalists became drunker and drunker, and their conversation became more and more disjointed and clumsy. As the conversation creaked and groaned under the weight of the alcohol, he knew he wouldn't have to wait much longer. Eventually, the conversation became too sloppy for sober people to enjoy. Metaphors began to stretch. Negatives began to double, tenses began to shift, and modifiers were left dangling until Jack eventually decided the night was over. By the time they left, it made no difference to anyone, although they all thought it did.

As Jack left Michael unlocking the door to his room, he heard the boy say, "Thanks."

"For that?" Jack screwed up his face and pointed downstairs.

"No. For everything else."

"No problem. It's very noisy."

"What is?"

"Riding in a tank. Very noisy and uncomfortable. You're not missing anything."

"That's easy for you to say. You've done it."

Jack shrugged. "I suppose. See you tomorrow."

The boy opened the door to his room and got ready for bed. It wasn't long before he was asleep. He wanted to make sure he wasn't tired for the next day. He had important conversations to have with the journalist.

41

It had just been the two of them at breakfast. Murray and George weren't there, but Jack didn't seem surprised. Michael had said they might not see George or Murray before the journey back to Dumfries, but Jack didn't seem to care, despite them apparently being such good friends. He didn't seem to think that they would care, either.

Chen got away. Something else that didn't surprise Jack. Michael hadn't wanted General Chen arrested, but it still didn't seem right. If the government wanted to arrest him, they could have. Why didn't people just do what they were supposed to do?

The hotel had looked different in the morning. Even the receptionist was different. It was like the previous day hadn't happened. Michael hadn't gone to George Square, although he had thought about it. He wasn't even sure if Lisa and the others would be there, anyway.

The train pulled out of the station. They would be home by late afternoon. Uncle Joe would pick them up in Dumfries. It struck Michael that everything was happening in reverse. Maybe when they got back, everything would be like it was before. He couldn't decide if that would be such a bad thing.

He noticed adverts more now than he had before, all over the station, all over the train. Everybody was smiling. Everybody was always young. The real world was very different. Michael hadn't really noticed before. He knew it wasn't like that back at the hotel. He had always known that. Now he realised he had always assumed the hotel was the exception. He had always assumed that there was somewhere else where people were smiling. The hotel, Portpatrick, Stranraer, he had assumed that everywhere he had ever been was an exception. Now he knew they weren't. They were the reality. It was the world shown in the adverts that didn't exist.

The train passed through towns and the countryside, rewinding the previous day's journey. Sometimes it was carried high in the air, sometimes almost through people's back gardens. Trees clawed at it as it slipped backwards in time, recoiling towards Dumfries. The journalist kept counting them. Michael knew he could speak to him now, but it was risky. Michael might accidentally mention something that was in The Book and give himself away. He might push the journalist too far. Jack hadn't refused to answer any of Michael's questions yet, but maybe the next one would be the one he refused. What would happen then? He needed something simple to start with. He tried to think of something to say to the journalist.

It might have been a statement of fact, but the inflection suggested it was a correction. "You know, General Chen isn't Vietnamese."

The journalist replied with a puzzled look, unclear why this was an issue. Michael continued undeterred, convinced it would all soon make sense. "You said he was Vietnamese when you were speaking to George."

Jack still didn't respond. The trees danced past the window, heading back to Glasgow.

"He's really Chinese. Both his parents are from China."

There was still no response. Outside, Dumfries hurtled towards them. Somewhere Uncle Joe had already set out. He would catch up with Dumfries just before it screeched to a halt around a silent carriage.

In the absence of a response, Michael began thinking out loud. "There was a war in Vietnam a while ago, before the Unified Command. I think maybe even before the United Nations."

He decided to ask a question. Jack would have to answer a question. "What did Murray mean last night?"

The question wasn't even clear, so Michael knew Jack would have to ask him a question back to find out what he meant.

Then he would feel like he had to answer. It would be like he was responsible for the question.

The trees became less interesting. Jack woke up and turned to him. He wasn't really gone. He just hadn't been concentrating. Now he noticed the boy next to him. "When?"

"When he said about something else apart from alcohol?"

"He was probably joking. You know what he's like."

"Joking about what?"

Michael realised Jack wasn't going to answer a naïve child. Maybe he would answer if Michael wasn't so unrealistically stupid. "I thought it was drugs. Was it drugs? I thought there weren't any drugs anymore. Do some people still take drugs?"

Now Jack answered, almost. "There are always drugs. Alcohol is a drug. The question you are asking is, do people still take illegal drugs?"

"Okay, do people still take illegal drugs?"

"Maybe I'm the wrong person to ask. I never did anyway. It would certainly be very risky for anyone to do it now."

"But it might still happen?"

"It's possible."

The Renewal was supposed to have stopped things like that. Maybe it hadn't. "But the police, the SCD... why would anyone risk it?"

Jack smiled. "You know, it's very lazy. The way you won't think about things. You know the answer to that. Work it out. Come on."

A test. A good-natured test, but still a test. There was still room to fail, still the chance to go down in Jack's estimation. Michael tried to answer his own question. "Murray said it was someone in the SCD."

Jack waited, watching Michael's thoughts as if he was amused by their lack of speed.

"But the SCD are the ones who stop people taking drugs. That must be true because if they didn't, everybody would be doing it, like before the Renewal."

Jack winced at the imperfect assessment but let Michael continue.

"So some people still do drugs, even though they might get shot. But they wouldn't, not if they really thought they would get shot."

Jack smiled again.

"So they must think they won't get shot. But they will."

Michael paused as he thought the unthinkable. "Unless... unless they're the ones who do the shooting."

It was ridiculous, but Murray did say it was someone in the SCD.

"The SCD are the ones who do drugs?"

Jack winced again. "All of them?"

Michael corrected himself. "The SCD are the only ones who could do drugs? Or sell drugs?"

Jack looked happier.

Michael's thoughts were so ridiculous he couldn't stop them from coming out as questions. "The only ones who feel safe enough to do drugs, or sell drugs, are the ones who are in charge of enforcing the rules?"

Jack was expressionless, looking at Michael as the boy summed up all of his thoughts.

"That's ridiculous."

"No. That's inevitable."

"But they could still get caught."

"Yes, but they might have more chance of getting away with it."

"That's crazy."

"That's logic. That's why the centre always rots first. There's no danger of losing control in some faraway place on the fringes of things. If there's any trouble, they threaten the people in charge there and have a crackdown. It's different at the centre... you don't want to have to do all that on your own doorstep, to threaten your own people, your own existence. The centre rots first, and the tighter you screw things down, the more power you take, the safer those with it feel. It is the old problem of who guards the guards?"

Michael thought about it. It couldn't be true. Surely, things were more chaotic. The further down the chain you got, the more out of sight people were.

Jack read his thoughts. "You expected Glasgow to be cleaner, brighter, more… orthodox than Dumfries. But it wasn't. The people at the centre don't take the orders as seriously. How could they? They wrote them. Isn't Chen somehow less impressive now you've seen him? It is the same thing. Harder to truly believe when you're at the top."

Michael felt like he was being taught things, which was different to learning things. He wanted to ask questions, not to be told things. "Why do you hate the SCD?"

"You know I don't. I'll answer the question you should have asked, the one you would have asked if you weren't trying to annoy me. I am uncomfortable around the SCD because I understand what happens to someone when you give them that much power."

"But they only hurt bad people."

"So you say. But, you have to understand people. Do you know what a stereotype is?"

"Yes, it's when you assume people will be a certain way because of how they look."

"Think of it more like an easy way of understanding how people are likely to behave, how they think they're meant to behave. The thing to understand is that people love stereotypes."

"Because they're lazy?"

"No, because it's comfortable. You think it's just a way of judging people, but it's not just that. It's a way of them knowing how they should behave. It means they don't have to work it out for themselves, means they have a set of guidelines to follow and reassures them they're doing the right thing. People like stereotypes. I read somewhere that the mafia didn't call each other *Godfather* until they saw the film. Do you see what I'm getting at?"

Michael had read that somewhere as well. "I suppose. The SCD behave like they're meant to."

"More like they behave like they think they're meant to. More than that, the stereotype possesses them, makes it hard for them to do anything else. You can reason with a person. Harder to reason with a stereotype."

"But they can still think. They're still people."

"Yes, but they're... buried beneath that uniform. It tells them what's acceptable. That's all people really want. They want to be reassured that their behaviour is acceptable. I sometimes think that's why, when people are uncomfortable doing something, if you can just get them to do it a few times, they get used to it. Maybe it convinces them it's normal."

"Lots of people wear uniforms."

Jack leaned across the table. "Yes, and maybe you should think about that. But, ignoring that for a moment, not everyone who wears a uniform carries a gun and is expected to use it on people on a daily basis."

Jack sat back in his chair. "Here's a question. Where do you feel you are now?"

"Here, on a train."

Maybe Jack was still mad.

"No, I mean in yourself. If I cut off your arm, you wouldn't fall on the ground with it, would you?"

Michael looked at his arm while trying to make it look like he wasn't.

Jack continued. "Most people feel like they're somewhere behind their eyes. Interestingly, blind people apparently report that they're in their fingers, their dominant sense being touch. Playing a computer game, you probably feel like you're on the screen somewhere. Do you understand what I mean?"

"I think so."

"Now, when someone draws their gun and is just about to use it... where do you think they are? I'd guess they're in the gun, and I don't like talking to guns who have a very narrow, fixed idea of the types of things they should be doing."

"But if they have so much power, why do anything they're supposed to? Why not just do anything they like?"

"Because they have orders and their stereotype obeys orders. More than that, their stereotype *likes* orders."

Michael thought about the journalists behaving just like journalists, soldiers behaving just like soldiers, drinking just like soldiers. They were always in big groups, always watching each other. Everybody was doing what they thought they were meant to. Well, maybe not everyone. What was Uncle Joe meant to do? What was Michael's mother meant to do? Maybe they were unhappy because they didn't know what they were meant to be doing.

Michael felt he had to say something to end the conversation. It was moving faster than he could think. "Maybe Murray was just joking, anyway." Michael wasn't sure that was the point, but it gave him a chance to change the subject. "He was joking a lot. It was probably because he was drinking. People always behave differently when they are drinking. It's the alcohol. The alcohol makes them do it."

Michael thought Jack would approve, as he didn't drink. Instead, he stayed just as serious and was slightly annoyed. "You do realise, of course, that alcohol is an inanimate object? It isn't capable of doing things on its own. It isn't capable of *making* people do anything."

"I know. But—"

"But what? Alcohol didn't do anything to Murray. People can't blame everything on alcohol, not when they know what it does."

There was silence again as Jack went back to counting trees. He was thinking about something. The previous conversation wasn't dead yet and was trying to reignite. Michael could see Jack struggling against it. Eventually, the ashes burst into flames once more. "I had a diary once. It was by… I don't remember whose it was. I could make it up to make myself sound more sensitive than I am, but I don't remember who he was, not really. He wrote about being a shell, a bullet. I wonder if he ever felt like he was leaving the gun after it fired. I wonder if he felt like he was in the bullet, inside the thing he was killing."

Jack was thinking out loud. Michael couldn't think of anything to say. Luckily, after a few seconds, Jack started talking again. "I used to have a few things like that, diaries. It's strange when you read something that someone has noticed, and you realise you agree with them or that you thought the same thing and thought it was just you. You are pleased. You think about how well you would get on with the writer. Then you remember they're dead."

Jack was still counting the trees, but they seemed to be irritating him now. Michael had thought of something to say. "You said some were better than others."

"Yes, some of them were very good. I generally only kept the good ones. I used to have one from a sniper. The last entry was all about him describing the process of killing. Well, not really the process of killing because, after all, that's fairly mundane but… talking about how he carried it out, shifting back and forth, deciding what he was going to do. I wish I still had it."

"You might get it back one day."

Jack sat back and sighed, bored with the trees. "No, not now. Sometimes you just have to accept these things. Didn't I tell you that? Otherwise, you go mad."

Michael looked at Jack with a blank expression that took a great deal of effort to manufacture and present. He made the pause last too long, and the silence deafened Jack until he had to speak to drown it out. "Like me."

"Murray and George said…" Michael let the sentence trail off, assuming Jack would start speaking again. Instead, it gave way to silence. Eventually, Jack said, "I became ill some time ago. It's… not unusual. I was away for a long time. I didn't notice it happening. Then it was too late. I'm fine now. I saw… people. They have people, counsellors, and padres, not many, not now."

Michael accidentally changed the subject. "My dad is a padre… was a padre. In the army."

Jack's response was automatic. "Praise God and pass the ammunition." But as soon as he realised he was speaking, he was more thoughtful. "A strange job. Bit like mine, except they don't write it all down, and they're there to help."

Michael wasn't sure if he was telling Jack things he already knew. How much did the journalist know about him, about the hotel? It was impossible to know. He had to assume Jack didn't know anything.

"Do you know what happened when my dad was back?"

A practised blank look from Jack. Michael had to continue on his own.

"Uncle Joe made him leave."

The same blank look.

The atmosphere had changed. Jack was quiet. He wasn't telling anyone to stop talking because he would have to have a reason to do that. Jack wasn't showing any interest, either. He had no reason to. He just sat there while Michael talked. It was as if he wasn't even there. He counted trees for a while. He would always be able to claim that he hadn't really been listening. Not listening to the story about the boy and the padre. The night the padre had too much to drink, and the day after when he had to go, all the details. Not listening to the boy telling him about beds and vodka bottles and Uncle Joe. Not listening to the smallest details, the details the person telling the story didn't notice. The details that passed unnoticed, and only some people heard, even if you didn't think they were listening.

Jack stayed, not listening until Michael had finished. After Michael thought he had finished, Jack still hadn't said anything, and the silence persuaded Michael that he had more to say. He had more details, more things that didn't matter.

It seemed like a long time before Jack spoke. The silence eventually dragged him away from the trees. "I bet you cried. I bet you were upset."

For a split second, until he looked at Jack, Michael thought he was being horrible. He let Jack speak.

"I didn't. I didn't feel anything. No response. I had been upset over other people before but... you get used to it. No, you get numb. It just becomes normal."

It was the first time he had seen Jack like this since he had met him in the house in Dumfries. "Was your dad… didn't you like him?"

"Of course. It wasn't because of that. When I was ill… you don't feel things anymore. You just don't feel anything, not happy, not sad, nothing. You just exist. He died, and it didn't make any difference. Now… I feel it now, but… it's not the same. You still have your mother, Uncle Joe. When you have nobody left, it's like you have a bad dream, and nobody comes to see what's wrong."

"I came."

"Yes, you did. One day, I'll have to think about that."

The subject needed to be changed quickly. "The soldiers have bad dreams a lot. The ghosts, not the infantry."

Jack seemed to know what both the names meant. Maybe Uncle Joe had explained it.

"And nobody ever comes."

"Sometimes Uncle Joe does if he hears. He's always on duty, even during the night. Maybe that's why he doesn't drink very much. Maybe it's because he always has to be on duty for the soldiers."

"Maybe the soldiers have put him off alcohol."

Jack looked sad. Michael had already decided that he would give him The Book back. As soon as he was finished with it, he would make sure Jack got it back. Maybe that would make him happier.

Dumfries was getting closer, giving Michael something to say. "We're nearly there." It wasn't as interesting as the trees, so Michael had to keep talking to himself. "The journey back seemed a lot faster. I don't know why."

"When you're going back, you start to see things you recognise towards the end of the journey, and you associate it with being home. On journeys away, you don't get that, and you don't feel like you're there until you get out of the train. That's why."

Michael hadn't really expected an answer. Jack had probably done a lot of travelling. He was right. They weren't really back yet. Even so, Uncle Joe was probably at the station waiting for them, ready to take them back to the hotel.

"How long are you going to be at the hotel?"

The question caught Jack off guard. "I don't know, maybe a while."

"That should be okay. The hotel hasn't been full for ages. Sometimes it is when they send a lot of the infantry. It can get pretty busy. I suppose Uncle Joe would let you stay, anyway."

Something was irritating Jack. "Don't you ever wonder why the infantry are there? Why there are so many young soldiers?"

"The colonel sends them. If there isn't room at the base."

Michael couldn't understand what was wrong with Jack. "Yes, but don't you ever wonder why there is no room at that base? Why do they need to use rooms in the hotel? Don't you ever question it?"

"The colonel must need the space. Maybe he sends them there for a sort of holiday. They usually come for a few days between training and things."

"And there's never any trouble?"

"If there is, the colonel sorts it out."

"How much do you know about the colonel? How much do you know about what goes on up there?"

"The colonel has known all of us for years. We could probably get you a visit to the base if you wanted. We would probably just have to speak to Uncle Joe."

"Uncle Joe knows him well, doesn't he?"

"Yes, for a long time, since even before The Renewal."

"Yes. Was there much of a Renewal down where you are?"

"Well, I was too young to remember, but yes, there used to be criminals and bad people where we live as well. They were all taken away."

"That's lucky. Were they all poor people?"

"No, some of them had businesses and everything. They had to find people to run them after The Renewal."

"I see. Well, at least some of the good people did well."

Michael sensed Jack was up to something, but he couldn't see what. The colonel, it must be the colonel. Jack wanted to know about the colonel and the base. What happened there? Maybe he wanted to write a story about it. He was probably trying to get information. That was probably why he was staying at the hotel for a while.

"The colonel is in charge of everything at the base. He can do anything."

"Anything? Well, he must have to check some things with Glasgow. If there is anyone to be punished, or if it's something to do with the law."

"No, it all happens at the base."

"Well, he sounds like a very important man."

"Yes, we're very lucky Uncle Joe knows him so well."

The boy couldn't see it. He was too young. He was too close to it. The journalist knew it didn't matter, anyway. None of it mattered.

Soon afterwards, Dumfries appeared at the windows. Joe would be there somewhere, always reliable. The boy and the journalist stepped off the train. On the way back, the journalist would be left in peace, even if he wasn't really able to experience any. The boy would spend the whole journey back telling stories. The journalist had done as he was asked. It remained to be seen what else there was to be done.

42

Michael slept on the way home as Uncle Joe used the car to push Dumfries into the distance. His dreams were confused. A man on a train was looking for something. Someone was chasing him. Bumps in the road kept jerking him back to reality, but his brain told him to ignore them and kept him searching and running.

When they arrived back at the hotel, Michael was first surprised to see that everything was still the same, then was surprised that he had thought it might not be. He thought he had lots to tell people, but the more he told it, the more it seemed like it was just the same two or three things over and over again. It seemed so easy to tell the story, and it was over so quickly it didn't seem to be as important and impressive as it had seemed at the time. He didn't tell anybody about Lisa and the meeting, and Jack didn't mention it either. Everything was still the same. Back in the hotel, the journalist still sat in the bar, and the ghosts still drank. Michael's mother was still silent and distant, and Uncle Joe was still Uncle Joe.

That night, Cathy talked to Jack while he sat at the bar. This time she spoke first, telling him that there was a third country called Guinea in Africa. Michael couldn't work up enough interest to listen to them and headed back to his room.

It wasn't difficult to find the diary. There weren't very many in the box, about half a dozen, not counting Jack's. He did say he had only kept the best ones. It wasn't very big and looked a lot older than it probably was. The writing was very small, two lines crammed into each line on the page.

I knew there were five of them. I saw two standing outside. I would have said They were talking, but I was too far away to hear. Anyway, I'm not sure They talk. I know if you hit Them right, They scream for a long time. That's the trick. It brings the others running.

They stood there for a while. I watched Them looking around at our world. You could almost imagine They were on holiday. Maybe They were just doing Their job, just like me. Maybe They didn't have any choice. I imagined families waiting for them to come home. Wives, children. For a moment, I thought maybe we were all the same. Not the same, though. I don't kill women and children, at least not as far as I know. I don't kill and burn and torture for no reason.

I target the larger of the two murderers. I place the crosshairs over his right eye. Not like me. Not like us. He is a demon. He looks at me, but I am invisible. Not just me, but everyone behind me. My family, Alice, Jonathan, and Amanda. All one step behind me. He will kill them all. He will kill me first, then torture them. He will do it to make others keep fighting. He will turn my family into a warning. Not this one. I will stop him. I breathe with him and stand beside him. I see what he sees. I feel the weight of his gun in my hand. I am an unimaginable distance from home, on an alien rock, waiting for orders. I do not know I am about to die. I do not know my wife is about to become a widow. I look at the trees far away and see only trees.

The smaller of the two walks away. I switch my attention to him. The crosshairs follow the back of his head. He is bored. He is tired. I feel it. Tired of being here. Tired of orders. He wishes he was at home with his family. He wishes the war was over. He does not want to kill. He will kill. If I do not.

I have waited for a day, not moving, lying in my own filth. I will wait another if necessary. Maybe one more after that. They arrived in a small vehicle twelve hours ago. Tired, glad to be somewhere away from the killing. Family men. We could learn so much from each other. They have taught me so much already in this short time. Two hours ago, they set their souvenirs out in front of them, on the back of their little car. A small jar of teeth, a hand, and some other pieces. I did not kill them then, but only because I knew I would later. Someone's children's teeth. Someone's mother's hand. The blood all over it told me it had been removed while the owner was still alive. They are not like me. They are nothing like me.

They will kill everything. I am all that stands in their way. Dead strangers beg to be avenged. I grip my rifle tightly and decide. No indication of rank. Good. The decision will be frivolous. Let the tall one go first. The short one walking back to sit down on the back of the vehicle. Both are dead. They were dead twelve hours ago.

How long have they been alive? How many mornings? How many nights? How many wasted hours? All for this moment.

They understand our language. We do not understand theirs, if they have one. We must have taught them. They sat above us, eavesdropping on Sesame Street. We taught them.

Let me teach you more, tall murderer. The crosshairs drift down from his head. I will not kill it. I will learn from it. A shot in the abdomen would leave it alive, but it's not enough. I aim lower. I want to imagine it is embarrassed as it calls for help.

The others are inside the building. Knock knock. I keep both of my eyes open. One sees the tall thing's uniform suddenly burst open. Red. The other eye sees everything. Tall thing falls. I am too far away to hear them talking but close enough to hear it screaming. Faint from this distance. Irrelevant to me.

Short thing sits upright. I wait for it to think. It takes less than a fraction of a second. It looks at me. I do not move. It looks at where I am, then where I am not. It does not know the difference. I hear Alice calling. Someone in the house.

Downstairs. Danger. I will defend her. I will defend our property. As it looks across at tall thing, short thing's chest bursts open, and it is nailed back into its seat. You should not be here. None of you should be here.

They scream as the crosshairs settle over the doorway. I hear one of them firing pointlessly into the trees. Irrelevant to me. A third. Standing there, the crosshairs on his head. I wait. He has no interest in the others, only in the situation. Two shots already. The sniper may have moved on. He should have moved on. Instead, I wait.

What if he had done something differently? Got up later this morning, sat in a different chair. Would it have made a difference? Is it destiny? Does he understand in this moment it might all end now? Do his colleagues realise it is ending? I hope so.

I do not fire. I will him to make the mistake. He takes one step forward. He waits. I do not fire. I am probably gone. I smile. Amanda asks me if there are monsters under the bed. His leg betrays him, exploding, sending him to the ground. I fire a second shot quickly, aiming carefully, hitting the doorframe to his left, sending a shower of splinters up into the air. I fire again, making the ground by the doorframe erupt.

He looks at the vehicle on his right and the exploding doorframe behind him. He makes two bad decisions, one leading to the other. He decides I am not a good shot. He decides he might make it behind the vehicle, that it is safer than crawling back inside. An illogical decision. He could be forgiven. Not by me. I let him crawl to within a foot of safety. Others are still in the building. Knock knock. I take both of his arms, and he howls for an encore. Jonathan asks me if I think he will ever be an astronaut. Of course. Crawling thing's side blows open, leaving a messy, gushing gap. I laugh silently, and the crosshairs return to the door.

Nobody home. I wait. They continue screaming. I see short thing panting silently, holding his chest closed.

Three soldiers dying. Thinking of their families. Cursing war. Praying to me for salvation. They just want a chance. Another chance. Thinking of all the things they have done, all the things they will never do. Unfortunately for them, I am also thinking about all of those things.

Amanda asks me why I have to go away. I think about the answer while a fourth thing cautiously edges into the doorway. Its head appears beside the doorframe, and I instantly remove it at the neck. What remains of it falls into the doorway. I notice, with interest, that the head is still loosely attached.

Everything is screaming, except headless thing, who doesn't have a head, and short thing, who is silently panting. The crosshairs leave the doorway, giving anything in the building time to make a bad decision.

The crosshairs return to tall thing. He screams and screams, pounding his hands against the ground. I will teach you something today, tall thing. Something they do not cover on Sesame Street. The crosshairs stroke his hand. Somewhere Alice is crying. The title of this lesson, tall thing, is irony. His hand detonates, showering him with souvenirs. He screams unoriginally at the raggedy mess. Irony.

In my head, I am surrounded by the bodies of children in a village They have abandoned for us to find. I imagine the bodies lying amongst the screaming things, and I recall the rage. I release it into my bloodstream. Short thing is still panting, praying for a miracle, praying for another chance. He gets the same chance he would have given my family. No chance. I wait for his head to turn so I see him in profile. Amanda hugs me as his lower jaw explodes, removing most of his face. And all of his teeth.

I survey the scene of hopelessness and agony. It evokes no emotional response within me. I reload and think about how I should have relocated by now. I think about how I am too close. I think about how I should not be working alone.

If I had been born on their world, would I be like them? I think about it as I reload but produce the same answers as always. I was not, and I am not.

I wait two full minutes. For anything out there, it will be a long time. The fifth appears, crouching behind the doorframe. I must be gone by now. It should wait until it is sure, but there is another time pressure. Its colleagues are dying. It won't care, but they may know where I am. He must get the information from them.

Short thing looks dead, and it seems what is left of crawling thing has passed out. Tall thing is too busy screaming to help. The fifth thing crouches behind the doorframe, near what is left of its four colleagues, and waits.

I watch as tall thing composes itself and struggles towards the doorway. It shows incredible determination, clearly mindful of some higher purpose. With its remaining hand, it points over towards my right, then my left, not really sure.

I know my enemy. They will have called for help. I have to go. I also know my weapon. Powerful, accurate, and loaded with ammunition that was probably illegal before this war started. I also know what the building is made of. I can see enough of thing five to fill in the rest. I imagine an outline drawn on the wall.

I switch my rifle to semi-automatic and wonder what Elizabeth is doing. As I empty my weapon, a section of the wall shreds, a bloodless shadow of what happens behind it. A fifth thing is slumped on the floor as I reload for the second time.

Tall thing doesn't start screaming again. Silently, he points straight at me. I would like to say there was something between us, but there wasn't. Not like me at all. I ignore him and remove the heads of his two colleagues, who may have been dead, anyway. Just making sure the information in their heads is deleted. Finally, I think about tall thing's family, missing him, maybe crying when they get the news. Good. I think of Jonathan's first day at school as I cut tall thing to pieces. Erasing him piece by piece. Taking his head last. Then I leave to wait for the next time.

As I leave, a tune pops into my head. I can't remember what the song is. A children's song. Maybe Jonathan would know.

Michael put the diary down, closing it carefully. It was just another story from the war. He had read lots of them. Before, they had been exciting and interesting, but now he didn't know how he felt. Something was wrong with the story. The same thing that was wrong about everything. A sniper with a family, the spiteful good guy. Nothing seemed as it should be. Everything was twisted and complicated. Only The Enemy were not. Maybe that was just because nobody knew enough about them.

He thought about Lisa, determined and lost. His father, tired and sad. Jack, indifferent and expert. His mother, important and absent. Uncle Joe, all-powerful and responsible. Cathy, cheerful and heartbroken. Kenny, heroic and weak. Everybody was changed. Everybody was serious.

Michael would give Jack his book back, along with all the diaries. He wasn't sure how yet, but he was definitely going to give them back. He didn't need them anymore and found it hard to think of anything he did want. There were plenty of things he should want. His mother? His father? He wasn't sure. Should he still want to be a soldier? A journalist? Should he want to stay alive?

Tomorrow, he would have dinner with Jack. Jack hadn't told him. He had heard him talking about it with Cathy. Jack, Uncle Joe, Michael, and his mother. It was strange that they hadn't eaten together before. Maybe it suited everyone not to. Even so, it didn't really look right. Eating together was probably something they had to do at least once.

As he tidied away the diaries and closed the door on the smiling faces, Michael thought about taking The Book and handing it back to Jack at the table. It was probably not a good idea. Everybody would probably get angry. It was hard to do the right thing, complicated.

Lying back in bed, he thought about what it would be like to be dead. Would there just be nothing? Forever? Would it seem like forever? Probably not if you were dead. He tried to imagine nothing at all. He tried to imagine not even existing, not just waiting in the darkness, observing, but not being there at all. He wasn't sure he could. He couldn't imagine everything going on without him. The world wouldn't even pause. It would just keep ongoing, just like after his father died. A couple of months afterwards, there would be a memorial service. His father. He believed in something. He believed everybody would meet again, just like General Chen. Was General Chen's heaven the same place as his father's? How could everybody have the same heaven if everyone liked different things? Maybe heaven was everybody liking the same things. But then, would they still be the same people?

He imagined The Enemy's heaven next door, noisy and secure. Maybe They didn't have one. Maybe They had a hell. Maybe They wouldn't know the difference.

The ideas crowded into his head until he couldn't think anymore. Everything was so complicated, and nothing could be fixed. The thoughts chased each other until he fell asleep.

43

The next day passed slowly. His father's letter didn't arrive. Nothing arrived. The ghosts drank, and outside, the waves washed against the rocks as the empty hours passed on their way to somewhere else. They had already passed over other places, other countries. The hotel was one of their last stops before they set out across the Atlantic, bringing morning to the Americans. Perhaps they would make better use of it.

Michael struggled to fill the hours. Guilt spoiled his idleness, preventing him from relaxing. So many things he could have been doing, schoolwork, helping Cathy. Tomorrow, there was always tomorrow. Probably.

He thought about The Book. Maybe he could copy it before he gave it back. A few hundred pages, maybe four or five pages an hour. Weeks of work. His grasp of the mathematics robbed him of motivation.

Michael could talk to his mother. He could knock on her door, but he didn't want to. He wouldn't want to tomorrow either. Michael was at the age when he was starting to understand that things didn't happen any more easily tomorrow than they did today. If you didn't do something today, it wasn't any more likely that you would do it tomorrow. Not doing something today was much the same as not doing something for a year. He should knock on her door. Why was nobody else doing it? They were probably planning to do it tomorrow.

He thought about how he would feel one day if his mother wasn't there anymore. He would wish he had this chance again. Michael would wish he had done something now, today. It didn't help his motivation. The foresight he had would only increase his guilt when the time came. It would only affect the future. It wouldn't affect what he did in the present, although it would taint it further.

He would see his mother at dinner, anyway. He found it a good enough excuse not to do anything. The present owed more to the past than to the future. Things looked as they always had. Even the new things were beginning to become tarnished. Jack was spending more time at the bar. Although Jack didn't seem to drink very much, Michael felt like the hotel was affecting him. He had hoped it would be the other way round.

Michael hung around in the bar and thought, not for the first time, how fortunate it was that he wasn't old enough to drink. He couldn't think of anything to do. None of the older people had that problem. There was always one thing they could think of doing. The easy thing. Michael was still young enough to be amazed at the way adults worshipped alcohol, but he was not young enough to believe that he wouldn't do the same one day.

As the hours shuffled past, they carried Michael back and forth, eventually washing him out of the hotel. He found himself on the beach, watching the waves roll in. Next, they pushed him through the town, past boarded-up houses and boarded-up old people. By the time they brought him back, it was time for dinner.

Things were slightly different at dinner but only as different as they had to be for things to make sense. It wouldn't have made sense for his mother and Uncle Joe to sit in silence, so they didn't. Nothing had really changed.

His mother asked him where he thought Jack should sit. Michael pointed to the seat where his father used to sit, and his mother nodded and set the place for dinner. Uncle Joe read from the newspaper, making observational comments about the least interesting and least controversial stories, seeing if he could get a small conversation going before Jack arrived. Just a small one that wouldn't flare up and burn out before their visitor arrived.

Jack was late, but nobody else was worried as far as Michael could see. His mother busied herself cooking, and Uncle Joe continued reading the paper aloud at random intervals, producing tuts and sighs from those present that reassured him he was still a sane man among sane people.

Michael worried Jack wouldn't arrive. He ran through the unpleasant scenario in his head over and over again. They would have to eat in silence, and then everyone would have to avoid each other. Michael had already experienced the whole situation twice before he even realised he had been thinking about it.

There was a chance that one day Michael would realise worrying so much was pointless. It meant that even when things didn't go wrong, they may as well have because he would have experienced the worst case scenario half a dozen times. Unfortunately, that day would not be today. Just after Jack hadn't arrived for the fifth time, Jack arrived.

If anybody except Michael was relieved he had arrived, they didn't show it. Michael found it hard to be so casual and got up to show Jack where to sit. Nobody spoke, relying instead on friendly grunts and nods. By the time Michael sat back down, Uncle Joe didn't have a newspaper anymore, and his mother was putting food on the plates.

Somebody would have to speak soon. Uncle Joe breathed in and out with stoic determination while he watched the potatoes being served. Jack stared into space, impassive and oblivious to the unbearable pressure. Michael switched his attention back and forth between the two, ready for the first words to be spoken.

The food arrived at the table, and still, nobody spoke. Nobody wanted to be the first to speak. Nobody wanted to make a mistake and talk about the wrong thing. There were too many things to say, dead fathers, arguing generals, and uncertain futures. They were all problems that people didn't discuss, and it was hard to think of something to say. Surely they wouldn't eat in silence? Michael started worrying again.

He kept glancing back and forth between Jack and Uncle Joe, willing them to speak. The pressure of the silence pushed down on him, and he had to concentrate to stop from grimacing.

Eventually, it was his mother who spoke as she sat down. "Michael, would you like to say grace?"

Say grace? She wanted him to say grace, just like when his father was home. His mind went blank. His mother had already clasped her hands. Uncle Joe had managed to force his palms together by rocking from side to side and repositioning himself in his chair. He scowled at the food from above with what was now grim, stoic determination. Jack smiled expectantly at Michael.

Michael had said grace many times but struggled to remember how it was done. It was too much pressure this time. If he said the wrong things, it might mean sitting in silence all night. He squeezed his eyes shut. In preparation, he went through the most disastrous outcome in his head five times before he began to speak.

He thanked the Lord for the food they were about to eat and all the many ways they were blessed. He didn't feel he had to name them, and it was safer not to. He was sure God would know what he was talking about. At the end of the sentence, he panicked, thinking he hadn't said enough, and searched for something else to say. The whole process took place in a fraction of a second, a space of time so short that it would scarcely have seemed adequate for the purpose.

Michael hoped the Lord would bless their guest, just in case He was caught out by the slightly changed table arrangements. That seemed adequate. It would have been enough, and the tone was right. It was reasonably short but slightly personal and unique. Except he started to panic again. It was too bland, not meaningful enough. He needed to say something that would wake people up, or everyone would sit in silence again. For the sixth time, this time for real.

He hoped the Lord would look after all the soldiers in the hotel. He also hoped he would look after all the soldiers on the front. That would have been enough, but the panic grew. He had said too much, and now it seemed strange. He had to finish it properly and say something. He pointed out that the war had been long, but they were all confident of final victory with the Lord's help. Then he paused as panic ripped through him. He felt a wave of sweat pulsing over him as he realised he had talked even more and still didn't have a good way to finish. The pause stretched into half a second, then a full second. Was he finished? His mind raced. Uncle Joe, blind, rocked from side to side again. Unseen to the others. Jack opened one eye for a moment to check everybody was still praying.

Then it happened. He didn't mean it. He wouldn't have done it if he hadn't been so panicked. If the silence and the darkness hadn't forced it out of him, he would have had something else to say. As it was, he had to say something that meant something. He had come this far. There had to be a point, some point, any point. He must have been building up to something.

Michael's body screamed for him to say something as his heart hammered in his chest. In the silence, a part of his mind that wasn't usually allowed to take important decisions presented a solution. It was literally the only thing he could think of. He had read it several times. He had memorised it—a prayer he now had to say. As he spoke, he was blind to where he had read it. "Lord have mercy on us. Have you mercy too. We never did offend you in our lives. O, banish us my Lord but kill us not. Kill us tomorrow, let us live tonight. But half an hour. But while we say one prayer."

He said *Amen* quickly, as if that would make up for having talked for such a long time. The three echoed him, some more quizzically than others, and they all opened their eyes. Uncle Joe scowled at one of his potatoes as Jack looked like he was trying to remember something. Michael's mother started eating. Uncle Joe was the first to speak, turning to Jack. "Amazing what they teach them at school these days."

Jack stopped thinking about whatever it was he was thinking about. "Yes. Very interesting."

"I thought it was all Burns these days."

"Yes, I think I heard that."

"I think they get a better education these days. More... detail. More focus."

"Well, I never really liked Burns."

"I remember. "

Michael couldn't see any connection between the prayer and whatever Uncle Joe was talking about. They did still do Robert Burns at school. Michael didn't feel much about it either way. It was just something else to learn.

Now that the panic was over, all the parts of Michael's brain that had failed to provide a solution began to disapprove of the one he had found. It was from The Book. The prayer was from The Book. What if Jack recognised it? Why should he? It was probably just a prayer that lots of people used. He didn't seem to have worked anything out. Michael looked at Jack as he talked to Uncle Joe. Now they were talking about nineteen eighty-four. Michael wasn't sure that made sense. Surely that was too long ago. Did Uncle Joe teach Jack that far back? It didn't matter. At least they were talking. Michael's panic gradually subsided.

As the evening wore on, everyone kept talking. Nobody talked about generals or colonels or dead fathers or even the future. Mostly, they talked about the past, about Uncle Joe, teaching, and what Jack had been like at school. Jack lied a bit more about his job, but not any more than he had to. They talked a little about how long Jack would be able to stay, and even Michael's mother spoke a little, mostly about the hotel and how busy it was.

Later, they talked about books and writers. They talked about Robert Burns again, and Michael's mother said she hadn't read Burns since school. At some point after that, she said she liked someone called Lewis Carroll. Michael didn't know what she was talking about, but soon the three adults started saying things to each other that didn't make any sense, and he realised they were quoting something from whatever he had written.

He eventually worked out that they were talking about *Alice in Wonderland*, a cartoon he had once seen. When he worked that out, he quickly realised that it couldn't just be a cartoon. Otherwise, they wouldn't all be talking about it. There must have been a book which the cartoon was probably based on. He wasn't sure why everyone was so interested in it. Probably it was more famous than he had realised.

Although they talked about the trip to Glasgow, they didn't talk about General Chen. Michael tried not to say very much. The adults were happy talking to each other. Uncle Joe suggested that the next day Michael should show Jack around the town. Michael was surprised that Jack agreed, as he must have seen it all already, but was pleased he would have another chance to talk to him properly.

After dinner, everybody stayed much longer than Michael had expected. They talked around the same subjects over and over again, but nobody really said anything. At eight o'clock, Jack finally left. Michael guessed he was going down to the bar but didn't ask him. As soon as he left, Michael headed back to his room. He wanted to have another look at The Book. After all, he would be giving it back as soon as he worked out how to do it.

44

Jack had been late. He had told Michael he would meet him on the beach as he had some letters to write. He had been almost twenty minutes late, but it didn't matter. They had walked the length of the beach and now stood watching the waves. Jack didn't seem as cheerful as he had been the previous night. On the beach, he didn't talk much at first, instead staring off into the distance. "That's the thing about beaches. They're always windy. It's because of the sea. I would like beaches if they weren't near the sea."

"We could go into the town."

"Will it be windy?"

"Maybe."

There was a long pause as Jack turned and looked back at the town.

"What do you find to do here all day?"

Michael thought it was a strange question. What did that mean? What did anybody find to do? Michael looked across to the town as well, as if the answer might lie there.

"I help at the hotel and stuff. When I was younger, I used to collect shells."

It didn't sound enough when he said it out loud. However, it was enough for Jack to move on to something else.

"Time passes slowly here. It's not natural."

"That's good, isn't it?"

No reply. Michael tried again. "Do you want time to pass quickly?"

"It doesn't matter what I want. It's the way things are. You're young, but you must have already noticed it. Years don't last as long as they used to. It gets much worse at my age. The years go past faster and faster. That's the way it's meant to be. This place changes all of that. Everything slows down again. Not the way it should be."

Michael watched as Jack examined a stone he had picked up. He hadn't heard Jack talk like this before, at least not out loud. He seemed more agitated than usual. In The Book he often sounded like this, especially towards the end when everything was handwritten.

Jack turned the pebble over in his hand. "When you look at these from far away, they just look grey, simple. If you take the time to look at them close up, they are much more complicated. Different colours, different types of rock..."

Jack had been like this all morning. Michael hadn't really been able to talk to him. He was too far away. Something was wrong, but Michael wasn't sure what. There hadn't been any letters, and as far as Michael knew, there hadn't been any phone calls. Jack hadn't actually said anything. Still, something was wrong.

For the first time in ages, Michael was aware that Jack was an adult, and he was a child. He was standing here on the beach with an adult who had adult problems. There was a large distance between them.

Above them, birds circled and called to each other, reminding Michael that his current problem was of no concern to the wider world. Out at sea, a boat caught Jack's attention.

"My uncle had a boat once."

Jack had never mentioned having an uncle before, but Michael quickly realised that most people probably had uncles, at least to begin with.

"He used to take me out in it sometimes."

The sentences were being left unfinished, which made them sound important. It also made it harder to say anything in reply. Michael decided to let him talk.

"He loved that boat. He picked the name himself. It seemed to mean a lot to him. Don't know why. Never meant much to me."

That sentence was definitely finished. Michael looked out at the boat and felt he had to say something. He chose to ask a question, the most obvious question.

"What was it called?"

Jack stared at the back of Michael's head with eyes that were almost empty.

"Desdemona."

The name didn't mean anything to Michael. It sounded like a girl's name, but boats were usually named after girls. He thought about telling Jack that but decided Jack probably already knew. Michael watched some birds diving into the waves as Jack stared unblinking at the back of his head.

"You haven't heard it before?"

"No."

"My uncle's gone now. I suppose we'll never know."

Michael didn't even bother nodding in agreement. The journalist had probably had too much to drink the night before. It was probably making him sad. Michael thought again about giving him The Book back. It didn't seem like the right time to talk about it, not while he was obsessed with boats and things.

"Is Uncle Joe the only family you have left apart from your mother?"

"Yes. Now my dad's gone. I remember my Auntie Anne a little, but she died when I was young."

"I remember."

"She had a funeral." Jack was silent, but Michael felt the need to keep talking. "Uncle Joe looks after us now."

Michael was relaxed. To someone else on the beach, it might have looked like he didn't have a care in the world. Another person on the beach might have resented that, and Michael might have noticed their resentment if he hadn't been so busy watching the waves.

"What did your dad think of Uncle Joe?"

Michael had to think for a moment. "They didn't get on all the time. They didn't really argue, not properly. I'm not sure why they didn't get on."

"Is that why Joe sent him away? Did they argue that day?"

"No. It must have been because Dad got drunk. That was just a mistake, but Uncle Joe didn't give him another chance."

The journalist sat on a rock beside Michael and stared out to sea.

"Maybe he did something else. Maybe there was another misunderstanding. Maybe… maybe Joe felt guilty for selling him the alcohol."

"No, I don't think so."

Jack didn't sound like he was trying to work out what had happened. He sounded like he was trying to make Michael work out what had happened. As the waves continued appearing from nowhere and exhausting themselves on the beach, Michael found himself thinking about that night again. He had missed something, but he couldn't work out what it was. What Jack said could be true, but Michael knew it wasn't. But why? Another question interrupted his train of thought.

"What was he drinking, anyway?"

"Vodka."

Vodka. He could still see the bottle under the bed. There had been something strange about it, something important. The journalist waited, letting the boy think for a moment before he asked the next question.

"I suppose Cathy kept selling him it."

"She didn't sell him it." She hadn't sold him it. How did he know that? Foreign vodka, it was foreign. "She didn't. He brought it with him."

What? That meant… something. Before he could think what it meant, he was interrupted. After that, the questions came so fast that he didn't have a chance to think.

"How do you know?"

"It was foreign vodka."

"How do you know?"

"I saw the bottle."

"Where?"

"In his room. After he was gone."

"So you searched his room?"

"No, not really. I didn't have to."

"Why?"

"There was hardly anything in the room."

"So he took everything?"

"Yes. No. Yes, but someone cleared the room after he was gone."

"How soon after?"

"Just after he left."

"Why?"

"So I wouldn't see it."

"So you wouldn't see what? What was there to see?"

"The vodka bottle."

"Why did they want to get rid of that?"

"Because… because they didn't want me to know about it."

"But you did see it. Why?"

"It was under the bed."

"So they missed it?"

"They must have."

"But if they didn't see it, why would they clear the room? Why would they leave the one thing they were trying to remove?"

It was obvious. It had always been obvious. He had just been too close.

"Because there was more than one. He brought more than one."

He brought more than one. His father had come home to see him, but he had brought alcohol, lots of alcohol. That was why he had been sent away. That was why Uncle Joe had sent him away. It meant something bigger, something too horrible for Michael to think about at the moment. He turned to Jack to share his revelation but was surprised to see that the journalist looked unsympathetic. He was already staring at Michael, and his eyes looked empty.

When Michael spoke, his words came out weakly. "I didn't think. I didn't realise."

There was no sympathy. "Of course, you didn't. You were too wrapped up in yourself. Everyone always is. They don't see anything. They just blunder through life, grabbing anything that catches their eye, never thinking about consequences. When it all goes wrong, they don't apologise. They just cry and say *I didn't think*, looking for sympathy, like that's the way it had to be! Like they're the only one that's important!"

Michael hadn't expected this. The man next to him was angry, but it wasn't clear why. An adult was angry at him, and he didn't know what to do. Why was he so angry? Had he gone mad again?

"I suppose I was just glad to have my dad back."

"Of course, you were. That's all you people care about. No matter what's happened, as long as you get to take what you want from the wreckage and walk away, you don't care. I see it all the time. All you want is a few pieces of information so that you can feel like you know what's going on. You want a gory story, a piece of excitement. You want to read all about it, and you don't care what everyone else is going through, what they see, what they have to do. You want to get what you want and walk away."

The man was getting louder. Michael was trying not to cry. The man was very angry, but Michael wasn't sure if it was at him in particular.

"You don't really care! You just want to wallow in all the misery and pain and then move on. Do you have any idea what I've seen? Do you have any idea what I've done?"

Michael thought he did and wanted to say so but thought he couldn't.

"You want to hear the best bits? I wish I could put you there for a few hours. I can tell you, but it'll never be the same. It won't make you afraid. It won't stop you sleeping. It's just pornography to all of you. You all make me sick. Sometimes I think The Enemy are more honest than we are. At least They don't pretend to be disgusted when They watch people being butchered. Just remember, it works both ways. One day it will be you. One day, someone like me will look at your body and try to think of a story."

The man kept shouting at the crying boy. "You know we limit what we show? Not because of censorship. We just don't ever show you the worst things. All the pictures and videos you never see. They are too disgusting, too distressing. Everyone likes to think they're protecting you, but I know better. I know we're scared of how much you'd all love it. How much you'd cry into your hankies and ask for more. It would never be enough. You'd still want to see something worse, something you could be more horrified by. You can't help yourselves. Given the choice, you wouldn't leave us with anything."

Michael knew the man knew about The Book and the diaries. He wasn't sure how, but it probably had something to do with the prayer. It probably wasn't as famous as Michael had hoped.

After the man had finished shouting, he shook his head and walked away. Michael knew he wasn't coming back. He should have given him The Book back. He shouldn't have kept it in the first place. Michael knew the journalist wouldn't look back. He had just been a favour Jack had to do. Now the favour was done, and he didn't matter anymore. The deal was off. Jack wouldn't get to write about the colonel, but he probably didn't care anymore.

Michael knew he should let him go. That would be the right thing to do. It would also be the difficult thing to do.

The boy ran after the man, but Jack ignored him. The boy asked where he was going, but he didn't get a reply. He knew what he should say. He should say that the man could have his books and diaries back, but he couldn't. Even though he'd planned to give them back, he just couldn't say it. Even though he knew he didn't have them anymore, he still couldn't make himself say it.

Michael knew Jack had The Book. He didn't know when or how he had taken it, but he knew he had. Probably that was why he had been late.

Offering to give everything back wouldn't risk anything, but still, he couldn't say it. If he said it, he would have to admit to taking The Book. Even though Jack knew anyway, he still didn't want to admit to it.

Suddenly, the man stopped. "You should have done something. Why won't you do anything? Why haven't any of you done anything? Why don't any of us do anything? We are just consumers, vultures. None of us do anything. We just endure, ignoring each other. You need to stop ignoring it."

He knew what Jack was talking about. There wasn't an answer. At least there wasn't one either of them would believe. Because he didn't realise? Because there was always tomorrow? Because it wasn't important enough? Could he have done something? A few hours in Stranraer wasn't really enough. Anyway, that had been for him, not for her.

"I don't know… I don't know what to do. I don't know what's going on."

"Then find out."

"How? Nobody will tell me."

Everything he said to the man seemed to frustrate him more. "You're pathetic. Ask again. If you don't know how to ask, think. I know you know how to do that. What do people do when they're alone in a room for hours and hours on end? Stare at the wall?"

"Read? She doesn't have a lot of books."

"So what else?"

"Write."

It was obvious. Why was it always obvious afterwards? He had to get back to the hotel. The Book didn't matter anymore. Jack could have it back. As the journalist walked away, the boy ran back to the hotel. He had been looking for answers in the wrong place all along. Now he had to put something right. Jack was right. He was right about everything. Michael had missed something important, something obvious. He had to do something.

45

His mother's room didn't have any pictures of his father. He hadn't noticed that before. It was all very wrong. Him being in her room was wrong. He shouldn't be here if she wasn't. She was out for the day. Gone to Stranraer to get… something. Michael felt bad for not paying attention. Her going on her trips to Stranraer occasionally helped them believe everything was fine, but everything wasn't fine. Things hadn't been fine for a long time.

For a second, Michael wondered if she ever went into his room while he wasn't there, but he had more important things to think about at the moment. Maybe he just didn't want to think about it. He slid his hand under the mattress. It occurred to him he might not be able to put everything back the way it had been before, but that also wasn't important enough to worry about.

There was nothing. Nothing under the mattress. Nothing at the bottom of the wardrobe. He felt stupid. Worse, he felt other people would think he was stupid. Jack would have told him to think, but maybe Jack was wrong. Maybe she hadn't been writing. But Jack was always right. Michael had to think. He was thinking like a child. Children needed to hide things to stop adults from finding them. Adults didn't have to worry about that. It would be somewhere convenient, obvious. The drawer in her bedside cabinet.

In the drawer, there were three books. The first two had nothing printed on the outside. They were notebooks. The third was blue with the title and author's name written in gold. A children's book? He had heard the author's name before.

Lewis Carroll, it was the name from the previous night. The book was Alice in Wonderland. This was the book his mother had been talking about. He opened it at the first page to find that somebody had written a message inside it in black fountain pen. The kind Michael knew his father always used. "To Alice, from the Mad Hatter." It was dated his mother's birthday, the year before he was born.

Michael casually flipped the book open and froze in horror as dozens of tiny paper fragments fell out. Most fell dead to the ground in a clump. Others fluttered lazily after them, oblivious to their meaning.

The pages of the book, or what was left of them, were covered in notes and drawings. Lines drawn in blue pen picked out words and sentences. Arrows pointed to shapes drawn over the text. Squares took a circled word at each of their corners and were filled with scrawled notes. Hexagons and triangles intersected, picking out still more circled words. Pages had pieces missing, lots of pages. Sometimes just a few words, carefully cut out so words on a following page would show through the gap and replace those that were missing. Sometimes whole paragraphs, whole pages, were missing. Michael didn't take the time to read the story, but it didn't seem to make much sense, anyway.

Wrong, everything was wrong. This was too much. What should he do? He set the book down without attempting to pick the pieces up off the floor. He still had to look at the two notebooks. Part of him clung to the hope that somehow, whatever was in the other two books would cancel out what he had found in the first. He was aware of his hands shaking. He opened one of them, found it was a diary, and closed it immediately. It was what he had come looking for. It had more answers in it than something written by a stranger. Michael couldn't read it. He shouldn't read it. He would have to read it.

First, he would look at the other book. It was something different. Michael opened it somewhere in the middle to find it had words taped to each page. Words from the blue book.

Words from Alice in Wonderland. Words that had been cut out. Underneath them, there were more notes and long rambling discussions. Like the first book, it was terrifying, but he wasn't sure exactly why.

He stopped to read a page. At the top of the page he had chosen, there were two fragments taped together:

"'You won't make yourself a bit realler by crying', Tweedledee remarked: 'there's nothing to cry about.'; 'If I wasn't real,' Alice said–half laughing through her tears, it all seemed so ridiculous–'I shouldn't be able to cry.'"

Beneath it, neat writing wandered over the page, oblivious to the lines that it was meant to be guided by.

I am real. If I cry, it doesn't make me more or less real. If I cry, I am still real, even if I don't feel like me anymore. Even if I am someone else, I am still real. Other people are real too. Even the ones who don't cry are real. Even the ones who don't cry real tears are real. Everything is real. Even if nobody believes it and nobody cries, it is still real. Even in the future, when people don't believe any of this, as we do not, they will still be real. Real tears. Real crying. Real me real tomorrow real yesterday real REAL Real REAL. All real.

Each page Michael checked was similar. It was nonsense, printed nonsense and handwritten nonsense, page after page. The notebook contained a huge amount of time. Someone had spent a lot of time writing in it, taping the fragments in and writing about them. Someone hadn't realised it was… someone hadn't realised it wasn't normal. But it wasn't someone. It was his mother. No, she couldn't have. Because that would mean… She couldn't have. Nothing made sense. At least, nothing made the kind of sense he wanted it to. It was too difficult, too grown-up. He shouldn't have to know, but he could know. He stared at the unopened diary. It contained frozen thoughts and secret answers. He could know everything. Not about some war that didn't involve him, but about everything, about everyone. He put down the notebook and placed one hand on the diary. As he tightened his grip on it, he heard the voice from behind him. A sad, tired voice. A man's voice.

"I don't think you should read that one." There was a pause before the voice sighed an explanation. "Even I don't read that one."

Uncle Joe didn't sound angry. How long had he been standing at the door? Michael took his hand away from the diary. They didn't look at each other as Uncle Joe slowly crossed the room. The old man opened the drawer again and swept the diary and the notebook into it. "We are all entitled to some secrets. Nobody should have to give everything away. Even if they don't know, they're giving it away". Michael thought about what Jack had said earlier. *Given the choice, you wouldn't leave us with anything.* Uncle Joe was right. As the old man closed the drawer, he picked up the blue book with the gold writing and turned it over in his hands. He spoke quietly, again sighing out the words, "As far as I can tell, she thinks it is some kind of code."

Michael still couldn't think of anything to say.

Uncle Joe put the book down again. "It's been worse lately. Still, it might settle down again."

Michael had to ask. He was too stunned to think of something clever to say. "Is Mum ill?"

He waited for the old man's opinion. His medical opinion as an ex-teacher.

"Why don't you pick up these pages and we can put the book back?"

"Tell me."

They both looked at the book. "What is there to tell? Your mother… did this. We should put it back. All else is opinion, and why should mine be worth more than yours?"

"Tell me what's going on."

When Uncle Joe spoke, it was very quiet, as if he was saying it to someone else or remembering something. "Demand me nothing. What you know, you know. From this time forth I never will speak word."

It didn't make any sense to Michael. It sounded like someone else's words.

"You know Shakespeare, don't you? You knew Othello well enough to quote it last night."

Shakespeare. It wasn't a prayer. It was from something else. Jack must have recognised it. It would have been obvious to him. Just like everything always was to Jack. Michael had never read any Shakespeare. He couldn't tell Uncle Joe that. When he spoke, it was half explanation, half excuse. "I haven't really read all of it."

Uncle Joe just nodded slowly. They couldn't look at each other.

Michael wondered what Othello was about. "Does it have a happy ending?"

"Not for Desdemona. Not for anyone, really."

Desdemona. Jack had been checking. It was obvious.

"Is it just since Dad… went away?"

Since he died, that was what he meant. Why couldn't he say it?

"No, longer, but it's been worse since then. It will get better again."

There was a long pause. Michael looked at the pieces of paper on the floor. He remembered about Jack. It didn't seem important at the moment, but part of him knew it would be later. "I think Jack's going to leave."

"Yes."

"I think he took something."

"Yes. He was seen. He won't get far."

He won't get far. Who was looking for him? Michael thought about whether he wanted Jack to be brought back. Did he have anything left to say to him?

"Will they bring him back here?"

"No need. He's done enough to not be seen again."

What did Uncle Joe mean? He had fulfilled his purpose? Or something else? Michael was sure he knew what Uncle Joe meant. "They'll hang him, won't they?"

"Not for me to say."

It would be the perfect ending for Uncle Joe. He wouldn't have to deliver on his side of the deal. He'd have gained a favour for free. Michael had already realised what the deal had been. Jack's payment for taking Michael to Glasgow would be the colonel. Michael had worked it out after the train journey. All the things the colonel shouldn't be doing, all the corners that were cut, all the deals that were done. Jack had been going to write about it all. Now he wouldn't. They would never see him again. No, Michael realised he had to see him again. He had to apologise. He had to explain things.

"Bring him back here."

"Why?"

"I need to speak to him."

"No, you don't."

"I want to speak to him."

"Why?"

How much should he tell Uncle Joe? It was over now, anyway. Everything had changed. Jack had The Book. Michael knew his father had... done something he hadn't expected. Maybe worse than that, his mother... He had to think about what had happened with his mother. Was there any point in covering things up anymore? He wasn't sure. In any case, he couldn't be clever. There was too much to think about. He couldn't think of a suitable lie. He would have to settle for the truth, almost. "He gave me something. Then he needed it back. I want to talk to him."

Uncle Joe thought so hard Michael could hear him breathing. He looked like he wouldn't be able to help. He looked like he wouldn't be able to think of a good enough reason. Michael gave him one, almost. "Please, Uncle Joe?"

It was enough. Uncle Joe motioned at the pieces of paper on the floor. "Can you pick these things up, put the book back, and meet me downstairs in twenty minutes?"

"Yes."

Uncle Joe didn't pat him on the back. He didn't give him a reassuring smile. He just left. As Michael had answered his uncle, he had hoped he wasn't lying. He hoped he could pick the pieces up.

As he gathered up the pieces, he shuddered, thinking about how difficult it would be to put the book back together again. He reassured himself that he wouldn't have to, but the idea that there was an impossible job to do stayed with him. Eventually, he was finished. He piled the pieces back into the book, closed it, and put it back in the drawer with the others. He decided to leave his mother's room, but he knew he couldn't go downstairs yet. Uncle Joe meant what he said, and he never said anything by accident. He didn't just want Michael to wait for a while. He meant him to wait for twenty minutes. Michael would go back to his room to wait for the twenty minutes to be up.

When he opened the door, the wardrobe wasn't open, and his clothes weren't strewn all over the room. The lock on the door wasn't forced, and the room hadn't been turned upside down. Even so, he knew The Book was gone, along with the diaries. He checked anyway. It was gone. They were gone. Everything else was still there, even his favourite thing. He knew he shouldn't be upset about The Book and the diaries, and he wasn't sure how he felt about it. They weren't his. The Book was a visitor that had gone home. He felt he had outgrown it, anyway.

He knew he should be pleased that everything else was still there. Instead, the lack of mess and the fact that Jack hadn't taken anything else made him feel… offended. He was insulted that nothing else was worth stealing. His Norwegian knife, his letters, all of it was of no interest. Maybe Jack was tired of all that. He was also offended that his hiding place had apparently been so obvious. Maybe Jack had overturned the bed, pulled out all the drawers, and then tidied up afterwards. Probably not, but maybe Michael would have the chance to ask him later.

46

The bar was empty. There were no ghosts, no infantry, and no Cathy. Uncle Joe sat in the corner, a drink in front of him. Everything had stopped. Uncle Joe had stopped time. He had banished the ghosts from the bar along with the living. Only the seagulls outside had ignored him, circling and calling to each other, mocking the drama inside the hotel.

Michael sat down across from the old man. Uncle Joe spoke first, making clear that there wasn't any tension. "Would you like a drink?"

"No, thank you."

The world was paused. Uncle Joe had taken them outside the game, but it wasn't clear what would happen next. Maybe Uncle Joe knew.

"What now?"

"Now we wait."

"For how long?"

"As long as it takes."

Michael looked around at the door. It showed no sign yet that it was ready to play its part in the proceedings. Uncle Joe produced a newspaper from somewhere and began doing the crossword. He didn't look up.

"Didn't you bring anything to read?"

What did he know? What did the old man know?

"No. I finished the book I was reading."

"Shame. Maybe you should go and get something. We could be here a long time."

"What if they don't find him?"

"Then we'll be here a very long time."

Uncle Joe probably didn't mind waiting. Michael decided he would do the same. He didn't want to go back and get something to read. Instead, he would wait and listen to the silence. It was on Uncle Joe's side, as always, waiting with him.

Michael waited a long time. As the minutes passed, he thought again about Uncle Joe. Who was he? Who was this old man sitting doing the crossword? He must be a bad person. He had killed Michael's father, maybe other people, too. Then again, he had also made sure that Michael got to see General Chen. Maybe he had looked after his mother as well, but Michael hadn't thought about that properly yet. Would Jack have helped him understand Uncle Joe? Maybe even Jack and his questions wouldn't help with Uncle Joe. Things always became obvious when Jack asked questions. Maybe questions were the key.

What did he know about Uncle Joe? Jack would have told him he knew the answer already. He just had to think about it properly. He tried to concentrate on the old man. What important things did he know about him? He was married to Auntie Anne, then she died. Was he different before that? His mother might know. How long ago was it? A long time ago, when Michael was young. Was it before the war started or after? It was after, he remembered. What did he remember? He remembered them coming back from the memorial. No, the funeral, it was a funeral. He knew it was soon after everything started. Why? Everyone was talking about it. It was new. At the funeral, it must have been new. So? She must have died at almost the same time as the war started. He hadn't noticed before. Why? Because there was never any remembrance service, no visit to a grave. Why? He didn't know. Why? Why not? Why might that not happen? Why might it be strange? It was the same date as the start of the war. At the funeral, everyone would have talked about that. Even if they had remembered it, they would have ended up remembering the wrong thing.

Was that the answer? Was that why Uncle Joe was Uncle Joe? He wasn't sure. Maybe it took more than that to turn someone into Uncle Joe. Michael watched the old man doing the crossword. Nobody had cared. The world had been ending, and they were all thinking about themselves, just like Jack said. They were too wrapped up in themselves. Everyone always was. They didn't see anything.

Everyone had been distracted. Uncle Joe must have had to deal with everything by himself. Michael felt suddenly pleased with himself for working it all out, and then felt guilty for becoming distracted. He looked at Uncle Joe again. Life was hard. The old man picked at the crossword, solving problems other people had created.

Michael waited for another eternity before speaking. It couldn't have been that long because Uncle Joe wasn't finished with the crossword. Michael still had too many things in his head to think of anything clever to say. He decided just to ask the question and see what happened.

"Was it difficult when Auntie Anne died?"

Uncle Joe didn't look up. He finished another clue in the crossword before he spoke. "That was a long time ago."

"It was the same time the war started, wasn't it?"

Uncle Joe looked up. He looked straight at Michael, trying to see into his thoughts. Michael looked right back at him, trying to do the same. He wasn't afraid. Uncle Joe couldn't get angry because Michael hadn't done anything wrong. He couldn't say he didn't want to talk about it because Uncle Joe didn't say things like that. Uncle Joe didn't want things or not want things. He just worked with what he was given. Finally, he inhaled noisily, like an annoyed version of a sigh, and looked back down at the crossword. Michael knew he couldn't even say he didn't remember because he had to remember either way.

"I don't remember."

It was a ridiculous thing to say.

"You do. And it was."

Uncle Joe's eyes narrowed, and he looked at Michael, ready for anything. Michael spoke very slowly and quietly so he couldn't be misunderstood. "It must have been very difficult. I'm sorry if people weren't…"

Michael had trouble finishing the sentence. Uncle Joe unexpectedly finished it for him.

"Interested? You're sorry if they weren't interested? Not their fault. Other things to worry about. We all have other things to worry about now. What does it matter anyway? Interested, not interested, all the same. The sun comes up the next day just the same. You know that."

All the same. Michael was sure it wasn't all the same. Did Uncle Joe really think it was all the same? Nobody could really think that, could they? Maybe Uncle Joe wasn't a real person. Maybe he just… existed. Maybe he was just a thing that got up in the mornings and dealt with things. Maybe one day long ago, the real person he was had just drifted away, and nobody thought to call him back.

Michael wasn't sure if he should feel sorry for Uncle Joe or not. Maybe he should envy him. No, he definitely didn't envy him, but at least the old man had spoken to him. Maybe Uncle Joe would tell him about his dad and the night with the vodka. He probably wouldn't. He probably had reasons for not talking about it. Uncle Joe had reasons for everything. He was about to ask him when the door opened, and he had to turn his head to see what was going on.

Soldiers, older than the infantry and more alive than the ghosts. Two of them entered first, then stood aside to reveal Jack, set against a background of two more. None of them were holding him or even seemed to have noticed him, although they noticed everything else in the room. Jack seemed to be in some discomfort and was clutching his side. He stood there as one of the soldiers stepped forward and put a bag down beside Uncle Joe before retreating into the background again. The bag was heavy. Michael knew what was in it.

Jack's voice sounded more serious than the words he spoke. "Good afternoon, Joe. I was just heading home when these gentlemen suggested you might want to speak to me."

Uncle Joe tapped his index finger on the table in time to something nobody else could hear.

Michael was again aware that he could hear the old man breathing in and out. It was amazing how quickly things could change. Things had been calm a moment ago. Now it felt like anything might happen.

"Your writing was always predictable, Jack, especially the endings."

Jack ignored the comment as he ignored the soldiers around him. He seemed impatient.

"I didn't think you'd have any reason to drag me back here. Did you get my message?"

"I got your message. Taking yourself home. It appears you took something else. You were seen."

"Ah. I see." Jack's face hardened, and he stood up straighter or tried to.

"They hang people for stealing, Jack."

"Well, I don't know if it's stealing if you are taking something that belongs to you."

"Perhaps. But then, if you break in while you're doing it, they'll hang you for that instead."

"Hanged for breaking in somewhere and taking back what's yours? Hardly seems fair, but then, what is these days?"

"Well, exactly. Less well-educated people than us might describe it as ironic. I consider it merely curious. Ironic would be your actions and resultant death were the only thing which prevented you from regaining the item. That and you being dead already. That might do it. *Journalist hanged for stealing own possessions, just as he came back to life. Tragic irony not lost upon him*. That might be what the headline would say, not that there will be any headlines, you understand."

"Just as well, really. I think it's a bit too wordy."

Uncle Joe stood up, picking up the bag. Michael held his breath, hoping the old man wouldn't look inside it. Uncle Joe's voice became quiet and serious. "After everything we talked about and everything we agreed. You should have come to me, Jack. You should have come to me."

"Maybe."

"Unless there was something you thought I was better off not knowing."

"Trust me, Joe. I know dozens of things you are all better off not knowing. I only wish I didn't know them."

Someone was going to look in the bag. Someone was going to say something. Then both of them would be angry at Michael. He couldn't wait any longer. "It was my fault! I took it!"

Nobody looked at him. Uncle Joe kept looking at Jack. "Of course, it's not your fault, Michael. You didn't take anything."

Uncle Joe didn't understand. That would make it worse. When Uncle Joe found out he had been keeping secrets, it would be terrible. He suddenly remembered his father's warning never to betray Uncle Joe. It was too late. "You don't know what's in the bag!"

"Of course, I know what's in the bag. Who do you think gives the postman his Christmas bonus?"

It was impossible. Michael's surprise was reflected in Jack's face, but Jack's disbelief quickly turned to anger, suddenly animating him. "You stupid old man!"

Uncle Joe remained unconcerned. "No harm in it. Everyone needs something to occupy their time, something to escape into. Sometimes I wonder if that wasn't your problem, Jack."

The journalist pointed at Michael but continued to address the old man. "You have no idea. You have no idea what he's been doing. You have no idea what he's got."

"The letters? They are harmless enough. Souvenirs? He can collect them if he wants. There is no harm in him having an interest, not if it's contained, not if it's safe. Just like him going to Glasgow. It was safe enough as long as he was with you."

Jack's anger faded back into disbelief. He shook his head. "You stupid, arrogant old fool. What have you done?"

"I have done what needed to be done."

"I would never have agreed to this if I had known."

"You agreed to what was offered. The rest wasn't your concern."

"You old fool. You have no idea."

Michael couldn't stop himself from speaking again. "It was a deal, wasn't it?"

The two looked at Michael, then went back to staring at each other.

"You taking me to Glasgow was part of a deal. I know all about it."

Jack looked at Uncle Joe, asking the old man questions he was really asking himself. "You told him, Joe? No, even you would have done that."

The old man stayed silent. Michael filled the silence. "You took me to Glasgow so Uncle Joe would let you write all about the colonel. So you could get famous."

Jack looked puzzled, then laughed. "That's what you told him, Joe? Oh dear, oh dear, he has it all confused, doesn't he, Joe?"

For the first time, Uncle Joe looked as if things weren't going how he expected. "I didn't tell him anything. I—"

"You see, Michael, you're right. My half of the bargain was taking you to Glasgow. But your uncle's half… that had nothing to do with the colonel."

"But on the train, you were asking about him?"

"I was just trying to get you to open your eyes to the kind of place you are living in. Don't think for a second that anyone cares what the colonel does out here as long as there's no trouble. Hanging me wouldn't cause any trouble at all. In fact, I could get shot right here, and nobody would care. Isn't that right, Joe?"

Michael wasn't sure if Uncle Joe would really kill Jack. Maybe he had left it too long. In The Book, Jack said if people didn't kill quickly, in the heat of the moment, then they found it much harder. But then again, he also said that people who kept threatening to do something were less likely to do it, and Uncle Joe hadn't really threatened him very much. Michael had noticed that Jack hadn't said that Uncle Joe would never get away with it, that he would stop him. He thought people were meant to say things like that.

Uncle Joe stayed silent, but his grip on the bag had tightened. The soldiers in the background looked unsure of what to do. Their hands rested on their pistols, which Michael knew was what soldiers did when they were nervous. Everyone was ready for Michael's inevitable question. "But then, what did you get?"

The bag hit Jack in the chest as Uncle Joe exploded. "Take your damn bag and go! Leave us! Before I show you how much it wouldn't matter!"

As Jack stumbled backwards, he glanced at the bar. He had spent all of his time there, even though he didn't drink very much. Michael instinctively followed his gaze to where Cathy usually stood. Suddenly, it was obvious. The other half of the bargain. It wasn't anything complicated at all.

No, not even Uncle Joe would do that. Michael couldn't even think about it. He looked at Uncle Joe, shaking with… with rage? Something else?

"Uncle Joe? You didn't…"

The old man ignored him and shouted, "Take the damn book and go!"

Jack smiled. "Say it ain't so, Joe. Tell him people aren't for sale. Tell him that isn't how it works."

"You smug bastard! How many lives have you watched fall to pieces? How many people did you ever help? What responsibility did you ever take? Sitting in an office, writing about other people. What gives you the right? Take your book and go!"

It all bounced off Jack. "Don't you want to know what's in it? The book you let Michael take? The book you gave him?"

"Stories of your little life. What more is there to know? You think he shouldn't know about the real world? Some light relief to assuage his curiosity. I shouldn't imagine it's that well written, but I'm sure he didn't notice."

"You didn't even read it, did you, you arrogant old fool?"

"I knew what it was, and I knew when it was coming. I had no need to check it. You think I'm worried about what he might read? A few tales about drinking and messing around with a few silly girls. Some story about you with some little tart behind a photocopier? He's a big boy now. I'm sure he's already heard all about such things. "

Jack paused, nodding. It all made sense to Michael now. From somewhere, memories began to volunteer themselves—Jack spending time in the bar, maybe too much time. All those times when Michael couldn't find Cathy where he expected her to be, and nobody else seeming to find it unusual. The way Uncle Joe never found out about The Book or the letters, and the journalist being so helpful. He should have known that people didn't do anything without a good reason. The Book was very clear about things like that.

Jack took his time before he said anything. When he did, he spoke very quietly. "I didn't work in an office, Joe."

"Of course, you did. Your father told me all about it. He was so proud of you, stuck pushing paper around in some little cupboard."

"Not me, Joe. He told you what I told him. He would only have worried."

"What?" Uncle Joe snorted derisively, but he didn't sound as confident as before.

"I was there, Joe. I was there at Porto Novo, Kano, and even Adelaide. Plus dozens of little places you won't have heard of before and certainly won't hear of again. I was there. I've seen Them. I've seen it."

"You're lying."

"You know I'm not. I saw it all. I saw it all and more, and now, thanks to you, so has he."

"No…"

"Oh, yes. And those letters? He didn't just read them. He replied to them, and they sent him more. Not just letters either, but photos, souvenirs, and trophies. He collected enough for a little shrine. You should see what else he has. You should see his favourite thing, all wrapped up in a little box."

Michael felt his face turning red. Jack was enjoying this. Uncle Joe looked at Michael, wanting him to deny it, any of it.

"Michael? Oh, God."

The old man's eyes closed, and his head disappeared into his hands. When they fell from his face again, his right hand pointed at Jack. "I should kill you."

"Why? I didn't do anything. You're the one who insists on playing God all the time. Actually, I don't think you're that good at it. I think God probably knows better than to try so hard."

Uncle Joe looked at Jack with hate in his eyes and stepped closer until his hand and finger were only a few inches away from the journalist's chest, punctuating his words. "You can ask him when you meet him later. If that's where you're going."

"So you're still planning to have me hanged by your friend up at the camp?"

"Yes, I am."

"That sounds about right. I suppose you'll be glad to be rid of me. That makes things so much simpler, doesn't it? But before I go, tell me, does everyone know who finally rid you of that troublesome priest?"

Michael had never seen anyone speak to Uncle Joe this way. He had always assumed it would make Uncle Joe do something terrible, but still, the soldiers stood, watching, uncommanded.

"You want me to kill you right here, right now? Is that what this is about?"

"I'm trying to help you. Michael thinks you killed him."

"I know what he thinks."

"He'll work out the truth, eventually. He's clever. Then what'll you tell him?"

"Leave him alone."

"Tell him, Michael. You think he made your father leave because of that night, and that was why your father died, don't you?"

It was. He knew it was. Nobody could get angry at him for telling the truth, especially if they had asked him to. "He did."

"Did he?"

"You know he did."

"Okay. Then answer me this. Have you noticed that you aren't very angry at him?"

"What do you mean?"

"I mean, you live in the same house as the man you say killed your father and seem to manage to survive day to day without stabbing him in his sleep. Doesn't make much sense."

Michael shrugged and looked at the table. Uncle Joe waved his hand at Jack, trying to sweep the conversation away. "Michael knows what I did was for the best."

"No, he doesn't. Tell me, Michael, what did you work out earlier?"

"My dad… might have brought the alcohol with him."

"Yes, which means?"

"Maybe he did it more than once."

"You see, Joe? For God's sake, talk to him!"

The old man turned and walked back to the table, still trying to wave away the conversation. "I don't know what you two are talking about."

He sat down, slumped in the chair, one hand over his mouth in case he spoke by accident. Jack instead turned to Michael. "Was Joe angry? When he threw him out. Was your Uncle Joe angry?"

"Not really… I don't think so."

"Then why did he throw him out?"

"Because of what happened."

"Did he tell you that?"

"Yes, he said… no. No. No, he didn't. And he wasn't angry. He was scared."

"Why? Why would he be scared? Why would your Uncle Joe be scared?"

Why would Uncle Joe be scared? Nothing scared Uncle Joe. He didn't care about anything enough to be scared. He didn't even care about the war, about what might happen to him. The only thing he cared about was Michael and his mum.

"There was a phone call. He said there was a phone call. He must have been scared by the phone call."

"Why would that make him throw your dad out?"

Why? He wasn't scared by Michael's dad, was he? It was obvious. Why was it always obvious afterwards?

"He was protecting him."

"From what?"

"Someone on the phone."

"Then why not phone the colonel and ask him to sort it out?"

Why not? The colonel sorted everything. Everyone was afraid of the colonel. It was obvious.

"It was the colonel on the phone. It must have been the colonel who phoned."

"Why?"

"The colonel was after Dad."

Michael looked at Uncle Joe. He was slumped in his chair, his finger tapping the table again. Uncle Joe looked right at him with empty eyes.

"Tell him, Joe. He'll understand. He knows enough already."

A wave of Uncle Joe's hand sent the soldiers away. The silence returned to the room again. Uncle Joe looked tired, too tired to fight. He was thinking about what to say. He was too tired to cope with the silence, and eventually, it forced the words out of him. Uncle Joe sat up straight and looked at Michael. The sentences came out one at a time, with long pauses between them. The kind of long pauses someone can only leave when they're confident they will not be interrupted. "Fine. If you really want to know. If you really have to know. Your father drank, Michael. Often."

The old man waited for a response. Michael felt himself getting ready to defend his father. It wasn't fair of Uncle Joe to turn everything round now. "So? You drink. There's nothing wrong with that."

"No, there isn't. That's because I'm not an alcoholic."

"He wasn't an alcoholic."

There was a long pause, and Uncle Joe leaned forward, looking down at the newspaper on the table. "It wasn't easy when he was here, not for any of us."

"I don't remember anything like that."

"Good. But sometimes, it's not about what you remember or about what happened. It's about what didn't happen. The nights he wasn't home, and the days you didn't see him. Life's like that sometimes. It's not about what happens. It's about what doesn't happen."

Michael looked across at Jack, who had sat at a table on the other side of the bar. He didn't look at them. He would be no help. It was up to Michael.

"He was busy."

"He was drunk, Michael. All those times, he was drunk."

Michael wanted to scream that it wasn't true, but something stopped him. He wasn't sure why, but he couldn't make himself do it. Instead, he said something else. "Dad could have stopped. He didn't have to go away."

"Yes, he did."

"Why?"

Uncle Joe glanced over Michael's shoulder at Jack. Then he looked around the bar as if there might be an alternative to the conversation. There wasn't.

"Fine. I'll make this short. A long time ago, your father got drunk with some soldiers. Nothing unusual there. It seems he insisted on giving one of them a lift back to the base. The car crashed. It was your father's fault. He ran it off the road. He was fine, walked home, and went to bed. The soldier died, Michael. He bled to death by the road, and your father didn't get any help for him. He died because of your father."

"He wouldn't have done that."

Uncle Joe raised his voice. "How would you know? How would you know what James would have done?" As he regained control of himself, his voice dropped again. "He was drunk. He was so drunk he probably forgot there was anyone else there."

Uncle Joe stopped and lowered his head to try to see Michael's face and gauge his response. "Do you want to hear the rest?"

Michael shrugged. The old man took a deep breath and continued. "The colonel knew the soldier. He... you have to realise what it's like for two people who have fought together. They were like brothers. He was furious. The grief, you see. He turned up here with some others, out of his mind with rage. The colonel said they were going to…" The sentence trailed off. Uncle Joe was looking at the door. He caught himself and continued. "Luckily, James wasn't here. I begged them. It was no good. I showed the colonel your picture while your mother pleaded with him. I told him… he couldn't, for your sake, your mother's."

Michael found himself looking at the bar. "Cathy was here. Cathy knows…"

"Yes, she was here. She knows. You can ask her what happened later if you don't believe me. I calmed them down, Michael, enough to talk for a few seconds. We made a deal. No, we came to an arrangement, something everybody could just about live with. Your father would go. He would leave and never come back. He left the next morning and went to serve. They were glad to have him."

"But… what about Mum and me?"

Uncle Joe took his hand. Michael didn't know Uncle Joe could do things like that.

"They would have killed him that night, Michael. He either left the next day, or we buried him. It was that simple. Sometimes that's the way it is. Sometimes you have to choose between two bad choices. And when the choice is easy… sometimes that's worse, sometimes that makes you feel even more guilty."

"Why did he have to leave the second time?"

Uncle Joe sat back again. "You're asking the wrong question. The right question is, why did he come back?"

"Why did he come back?"

Uncle Joe shook his head. "I don't know. Maybe he missed you, missed Mary. I don't know. I tried, Michael. They knew he was back. I couldn't stop them."

"Did you really try?"

"I really tried. I swear."

"Why didn't you tell me?"

The old man shrugged. "You would have hated me for telling you."

"But I hated you for what I thought you'd done."

"Maybe. But you didn't hate him. I thought that was more important. I thought you had the right not to hate him. You don't hate him, do you?"

"No."

"Good."

Everything was changing. Everything was different. Michael had seen what Uncle Joe could do. He looked at the spot in the bar where the ghost had been attacked. He looked across at Jack. Would Uncle Joe have let them hang him? Another image came into his mind, something that might have happened earlier. An old man talking to Cathy, asking her where her friend was, threatening things, terrible things. He shook the image out of his head. Uncle Joe hadn't killed his father. He had just let Michael think he had. It must be difficult to make someone you love hate you just because it's the right thing to do, the only thing to do. Michael wondered if he would have done the same thing for his mother, his father. A new thought occurred to him. Who had killed his father?

"Did the colonel kill him?"

"No. Once he was gone, the colonel let it go, more or less. Things went back to the way they were. The colonel is very fond of you, Michael."

Something was missing. Something didn't add up. Why would the colonel have helped them so much? There was something else. Something Uncle Joe wasn't telling him.

"The arrangement. That wasn't all there was to the arrangement, was it?"

"No. No, there was more." The old man had given up on keeping secrets. He shrugged. "I agreed to stay here as long as I could be of use to the colonel. It's worked out well enough."

"We're all prisoners? We can't leave?"

"No, you can leave. It's just me. I have a promise to keep."

"But Dad's gone now."

"I know, but it doesn't work that way. You mustn't hate the colonel. You mustn't hate anyone. Things just fall a particular way."

Michael didn't look round at Jack this time. He just raised his voice. "Did you know?"

A tired voice answered from somewhere behind him. "Not everything."

Now everybody knew everything. How would they go on? He asked the question Uncle Joe was waiting for. "What do we do now?"

Uncle Joe looked at him, suddenly interested. "What do you want to do?"

"I don't know. Everything's a mess."

The old man shrugged. "It's always like that. You just do what you can."

From the back of the empty bar, a tired voice spoke again. "I should go. Unless you still want to hang me."

Uncle Joe didn't seem angry anymore but wasn't friendly either. "I do, but I suppose it would be better if you left."

Michael wondered if there was any reason for Jack to go now. Everybody knew about The Book. Everybody knew about everything. "Couldn't he stay?"

Uncle Joe smiled. "You mean stay here for a while, teach you to be a journalist, help your Mum get better, maybe write that article on the colonel?"

"Why not?"

"I don't think it's really, Jack. Do you, Jack?"

Jack was standing up and already had the bag in his hand. "No. No, I don't think it is. All a bit Shakespearean for me, I think. All those loose ends tied up, everyone living happily ever after. I don't think it would work, Michael."

Michael knew he would leave. He had always known. "We could try."

"I don't think so, sorry. If it's any consolation, the first time I am in mortal danger again, I'll regret not staying here. I'm free to go, Joe?"

"I have no further interest in you."

"Thanks. Thanks for everything. Well, almost everything. It's been… interesting."

Part of Michael hoped that the soldiers outside wouldn't let the journalist go. He hoped they would grab him, take him to the colonel, and keep him somewhere. The soldiers didn't care anymore. They only cared when they were told to. Michael knew it didn't really matter. Even if Jack had stayed, nothing would have been the same.

Michael watched from the window as the journalist walked into town. He wondered if he had shared anything with Jack at all or if he had really just been a favour. Maybe it didn't matter. Jack was gone. He hadn't wanted to be part of their world anymore. Michael knew he hadn't even been important enough not to be left as a loose end. He didn't get a smile as the journalist left, just as Uncle Joe hadn't got a handshake. The man didn't care. It had been silly to think he ever might have. Uncle Joe knew that. He knew everything.

Uncle Joe didn't watch, and he didn't speak. He just sat there until the silence forced the crossword back into his hands. He didn't speak, not even when the soldiers had been waved back into town, dismissed from the old man's world. Michael was left to speak whenever he was ready. Once they were alone, the old man only had to wait a few minutes. Michael knew he would have waited longer if he had to. An hour, a day, a thousand years, it was all the same to the old man.

Michael sat down across from him. "So, things just go back to the way they were?"

Uncle Joe thought about it. "No, they don't have to. Maybe we can do things a little differently. Maybe you can help me out some more."

"Maybe."

"Your mother will be back soon. Maybe we could both go and see her."

"Maybe. I don't think I'd know what to say."

"That depends on what you want to talk about."

"I don't mind."

"Then it doesn't matter as long as you say something, and you're sure to do that if you only talk long enough."

It sounded like someone else's words again, but Michael was too tired to think about it. He would help. There was nothing else left to do. Maybe there was nothing else that really mattered, anyway. It didn't matter if there was a war, and if there was, it didn't matter who was in charge. All that really mattered was what was around them, the hotel, the people. Uncle Joe understood that.

"I never thanked you, Uncle Joe."

"What for?"

"For being interested."

"You're welcome." Uncle Joe nodded. He thought for a moment, then looked at Michael. "You saved your father's life, you know. Twice."

Michael shrugged. "I didn't do it on purpose."

Uncle Joe returned the shrug with a sigh. "Well, maybe that's why it worked so well."

They talked for a while. Michael knew that soon the world would have to start up again. He knew it wouldn't be like this all the time from now on. It couldn't be. You were only able to talk properly sometimes. He had talked to his mother in Stranraer once. Uncle Joe had suggested they go there. Maybe that had been a coincidence, maybe not.

Later, when she returned, they went upstairs together to see her. Things weren't perfect. In fact, Michael wasn't sure if they were worse or better than the day before. Maybe they were clearer, and that was a start. As they sat together in his mother's room, they talked about nothing important. In her room, there was no war, and nobody was dead. Michael made sure he opened the windows a little before they talked. Just in case anything needed to get out. If it had, he imagined it would have drifted up into the air, joining other things seeping out of cracks in the window frames and open doors, swirling up into the sky to join all the others, good and bad. Countless billions of them hanging like smoke over all the people and seagulls below, more joining all the time for years and years into the future as they had for years and years into the past. A hotel missing a young boy who used to live there, growing older all the time. An old man reading out a letter from someone. A young man in uniform sitting beside his mother's bed. Sometimes it was hard to tell the good from the bad and the old from the new, but it didn't matter as long as you remembered what was important and let go of what wasn't.

The boy in the hotel didn't have The Book anymore, but he had decided to read something else. He would read *Alice in Wonderland.* He was fairly sure it wasn't a code, but that wasn't important. Uncle Joe told him not to be disappointed. The book didn't make any sense at all, but that wasn't important either. Most things didn't make sense these days. You just did what you could.

BOOK TWO OF THE HEADLANDS SERIES

HUMAN INTEREST

Iain Houston

Sarah laughed, "I'm sorry for upsetting your important friend. I'll be more tolerant next time."

He knew she wouldn't be. Maybe she was right though. An important friend. Maybe Murray could be useful. Michael knew there were important people, famous people, even rich people. Even in times like these. Was it possible to become one of them?

Escaping basic training and life at the front to work as a journalist seems like a lucky break. But things aren't easy when everyone else is more capable than you are. Especially the young female journalist who also managed to avoid military service, for reasons that aren't entirely clear.

When a face from the past offers Michael an opportunity to better his position he is drawn into a world of favours and intrigue. But why does Murray want him to investigate the story of a long dead murderer? And is anyone what they really seem?

AUTUMN 2023

Printed in Great Britain
by Amazon

26788716R00240